LOVING SPIRITS AT THE VINTAGE TEASHOP

GHOSTS OF ROWAN VALE BOOK 2

SHARON BOOTH

Boldwood

First published in Great Britain in 2025 by Boldwood Books Ltd.

Copyright © Sharon Booth, 2025

Cover Design by Rachel Lawston

Cover Images: Rachel Lawston

A CIP catalogue record for this book is available from the British Library.

Paperback ISBN 978-1-83656-758-5

Large Print ISBN 978-1-83656-757-8

Hardback ISBN 978-1-83656-756-1

Ebook ISBN 978-1-83656-759-2

Kindle ISBN 978-1-83656-760-8

Audio CD ISBN 978-1-83656-751-6

MP3 CD ISBN 978-1-83656-752-3

Digital audio download ISBN 978-1-83656-755-4

This book is printed on certified sustainable paper. Boldwood Books is dedicated to putting sustainability at the heart of our business. For more information please visit https://www.boldwoodbooks.com/about-us/sustainability/

Boldwood Books Ltd, 23 Bowerdean Street, London, SW6 3TN

www.boldwoodbooks.com

For Herbert Kean, with love. I wish I'd known you better.

1

'Listen up, everyone. Sorry for the short notice but I wanted to get you all together to put something to you.'

Callie Chase – new owner of our village, Rowan Vale, and by extension, my landlady – smiled nervously round at us all from her position on the stage.

'It's just... Well, I've had this great idea.'

There was some shuffling and exchanging of glances. A few of the older members of our community weren't yet entirely convinced that Callie was old enough or experienced enough to run the Harling Estate, which included Rowan Vale, and there had been some mutterings in certain quarters that the previous owner, Sir Lawrence Davenport, or Lawrie as we knew him, should be consulted on all matters. The fact that Callie had said this was *her* idea clearly didn't fill them with optimism.

Call me a cynic, but I couldn't help wondering if part of the problem was that she was a woman. As far as I was aware, there'd never been a female owner of Rowan Vale before. What would the oldies' reaction be if it had been Lawrie's grandson, Brodie, who'd had the idea, I wondered. Maybe that was why Callie had brought him with her to this impromptu meeting at The Magic Lantern, the village's vintage cinema.

'Here we go,' said a familiar, cheerful voice in my ear. 'All them old codgers will pour cold water on this before they've even heard what she has to say. You mark my words.'

'Aunt Polly,' I said, beaming at the attractive, dark-haired woman who'd slipped into the empty seat behind me. 'You came!'

'Course I came! You know me, lovey. I like to know what's going on round here.' She gave me a cheeky wink. 'How are you, Shona? How's them grandkiddies of yours? Our Jimmy not with you?'

'They're fine, thanks. Dad's having a lazy day in the garden,' I told her. 'Making the most of the sunshine, not to mention the peace and quiet.'

'Ooh, I don't blame him.' She closed her eyes

briefly and sighed. 'How I'd love to feel the sun on my skin again.' Then her eyes flew open and she grinned. 'Ah well, can't have everything in life, can we? Or afterlife, as the case may be.' She giggled and I felt the familiar tug of love for my great-aunt, and thought, once again, how much fun she must have been when she was alive.

'Go on then,' someone at the front said, rather grouchily. 'We haven't got all day. What's this so-called big idea?'

'Have you ever heard the like?' Aunt Polly said, shocked. 'Fancy talking to young Callie like that! They wouldn't talk to Lawrie that way, would they? Brodie ought to say something.'

Brodie certainly looked as if he wanted to. Sitting on a chair next to Callie's on the stage, he was glaring at the heckler, his brows knitted together quite alarmingly.

'There's no need to be rude, Mr Thwaite,' Callie said firmly. 'If you'd all stop muttering and fidgeting, I'd be able to tell you, wouldn't I?'

'Ha!' Aunt Polly nodded in satisfaction. 'Quite right, too. Who needs Brodie? You go, girl.'

'I don't think Callie needs Brodie to stand up for her,' I said. 'But it's nice he's here to support her.'

Brodie was Callie's boyfriend, and by rights, he

and his father should have been in line to own Rowan Vale: a beautiful little village nestling on the Harling Estate in the Cotswolds countryside. Instead, however, the whole shebang had been sold to Callie Chase back in May, even though she was a complete outsider.

Of course, we'd all known a sale was inevitable. This wasn't just any old village in any old estate. Rowan Vale was run as a living history museum, and we had beautiful woodland and parkland surrounding us, as well as some historic standing stones and a stone-age barrow. All these things made our home special. But what set it apart from most other places was that, for some inexplicable reason, we had an abundance of ghosts sharing the estate with us.

There was an unwritten rule that the owner of the Harling Estate must have the ability to see and communicate with them all. Sir Lawrence could. Unfortunately, neither his son nor his grandson had inherited his ability, hence the sale of the estate to Callie, who, although not from around this area, had somehow been born with the gift, as had her eleven-year-old daughter, Imogen.

Some of the residents of the village came from families who'd lived here for generations and had their very own ancestral ghost. My family had Aunt

Polly. I could see her all right, but I couldn't see the other ghosts.

That was the way it had always worked in Rowan Vale. Gifted ones like Callie were few and far between. The rest of us could only see our own dearly departed blood relatives, and not everyone could even do that. And, of course, some of the ghosts had no relatives left here at all and no way of communicating with the living. That was why it was so important that the owner of the estate could see them all and give them a voice.

Callie had been a godsend, whatever some of the oldies thought of her. Brodie obviously thought so, too, I mused with a wry smile. She'd only moved here less than two months ago, and they were already a couple. Fast work!

As Callie got to her feet, Brodie shuffled uncomfortably in his chair, and I could tell he was dying to intervene but was wisely allowing her to deal with things in her own way. Not only a fast worker but a fast learner then!

'Right,' Callie said, holding up her hands. 'I want you to know that I really appreciate you coming to this meeting at such short notice, and I'd like to thank Robyn and Curtis for allowing us to use the cinema in between today's showings of *Passport to Pimlico*.'

She cleared her throat.

'Okay, so what I wanted to put to you is this: I want to host a 1940s weekend in the village.'

She waited for our response, and I saw some puzzled looks, some shrugs, some excited nods, and a lot of widened eyes. I remembered Aunt Polly sitting behind me and held my breath. What would she think to this? After all, she'd died in 1948. Would it bring back painful memories? Or would she be delighted to be taken back to her final decade, when she'd been young, vibrant, and gloriously alive?

'Well,' she said softly. 'I wasn't expecting that.'

Before I could work out whether she thought it a good or a bad thing, Callie continued.

'I know we already get lots of visitors to Rowan Vale, but I've been thinking that we could attract even more of them by staging a series of events throughout the year, and this could be the first of them. We have this wonderful vintage cinema here,' she said enthusiastically, 'and there's the farm, of course, with the land girls and the prisoners of war. And we have Blighty's Bakery and Mrs Herron's Teashop. I thought it would be nice to celebrate the forties properly by holding a weekend event, where visitors could also dress up in vintage clothes. It could be an awful lot of fun...'

Her voice trailed off as she looked around us. There was momentary silence.

'We have the Swinging Sixties street,' someone called, 'and a Victorian area. Why the forties? Surely,' she added, standing up to appeal to the audience, 'the sixties would be more fun?'

Aunt Polly tutted. 'That's Sheila Wood. Her daughter works in the hairdressing salon. No wonder she's pushing the sixties.'

'As I said, the forties weekend would simply be one event of the year,' Callie replied. 'I'm sure we could hold other events in due course, where we focus on other eras.'

Brodie had clearly had enough. He got to his feet and, miraculously, Sheila Wood immediately sat down.

'From what Callie's told me of her plans, I think the 1940s event would be a lot of fun,' he said firmly.

'You should have been there. You wouldn't have thought it much fun then,' said old Mr Baldwin, nodding furiously.

'Blooming cheek!' Aunt Polly gasped. 'Ernie Baldwin was only born in 1945! Like he remembers any of it anyway!'

'But you do,' I said gently. 'Are you okay with this?'

She smiled at me. 'Me, love? Don't you worry about me. I'm long past the wallowing stage, believe me. Besides, I'm always up for a party, and I reckon with a bit of help, Callie could give this village a proper good do. I'm all for it.'

'Right,' I said, relieved. I stood up. 'Sounds great, Callie,' I called. 'What do you want us to do?'

I was rewarded with huge smiles from Callie and Brodie.

'Well, Mrs Herron's Teashop is always busy, and I've no doubt you'll get extra traffic coming your way over the weekend. Just keep being your usual wonderful selves,' she said.

'*That* we can do,' I assured her and sat back down to some laughter.

'That's all very well,' said Kerry Chesterton, who ran the Victorian sweet shop with her husband, Derek. 'But where does that leave the rest of us? If the event's going to be focused on the forties, what happens to the Victorian shops on the green? And the Swinging Sixties street?'

Behind me, I heard Aunt Polly tut. 'You're not kidding, Walter,' she muttered. 'I don't know how you can stand living with her.'

I gathered she was talking to Walter Tasker, a ghost who shared the Chestertons' flat above the sweet shop. I wondered how many more of the ghosts were present at the meeting. Were they heckling poor Callie, too?

'Are we expected to close up that weekend?' asked Jasper Edgecumbe, the 'Victorian' photographer. 'I shall want compensation if that's the case.'

'Good grief, give her a chance!' Clara Milsom, a local who was already good friends with Callie, glared fiercely at him. She saw me looking at her and rolled her eyes. I grinned back. We were definitely of one mind about all this.

'Is there going to be a guided route around the village, bypassing our street?' demanded one of the women who worked in the 1960s fish and chip shop. 'Because I don't think that's at all fair, and if that's the case, we ought to be entitled to a deduction in rent that week. A *big* deduction,' she added darkly.

Brodie opened his mouth to speak but Callie beat him to it.

'Look, I haven't worked out all the details yet,' she admitted, '*but,*' she added quickly, 'none of you will lose out. If anything, I'd expect an increase in profits. If we do this right, we'll have an influx of new visitors to the village, and, more than anything, it will be *fun!*'

She turned her head to the left as if someone was standing beside her and nodded. 'Absolutely, Isaac. The pub will no doubt be overflowing, so that should please Penny.'

'It sounds as if one ghost at least is happy enough about it all,' I murmured.

Aunt Polly nodded. 'Not just one. There's not a single dissenting voice among us but wait till the Reverend Silas Alexander gets wind of it. He hates anything that brings more tourists in. That fist of his that he's always shaking in protest will likely drop off.'

I'd heard about the angry ghost from her before. Apparently, Silas had been vicar of our local church, All Souls, until he'd died in 1927. He couldn't get over the way Rowan Vale had blossomed into a tourist village, and even worse, that we now had a female vicar, Amelia, in his place. Not for the first time, I wished I had Callie's gift. I'd love to have seen his face when he heard the news.

'When's the weekend going to happen, Callie?' called Erin, who worked as a 'land girl' at Rowan Farm, which was run as it would have been back in the forties.

Callie glanced at Brodie, who put his arm around her protectively.

'Well,' she said nervously, 'that's the thing. I know it doesn't leave us much time, but I was thinking September.'

'September?' There were lots of groans and incredulous gasps.

Even I had to admit it didn't give us much time. It was already July, after all.

'*Mid*-September,' she said, as if that made it better. 'I know it's asking a lot, but—'

'You're not wrong there,' someone called.

'We're more than up to the job,' Brodie said firmly. 'We've got so much already in place, after all. It's not like we're starting from scratch. Look, Callie and I are going to work out the details this week and we'll be sending all the information out to you via the new estate newsletter. You *have* all signed up to it, I presume?'

'I don't have the internet,' said Mr Thwaite. 'And I can't say as I want it, neither.'

'Any household not registered for the email will get a printed version put through their letterbox,' Brodie assured him. 'In the meantime, if you do have the internet and you haven't yet registered for the newsletter, it will really help us if you'd do that.'

'Sometimes,' Aunt Polly said, 'it's like I'm in a foreign country, the things people say. Internet! Newsletters! What the bloody hell are they when they're at home?'

'Don't worry,' I said. 'All sorted. I signed up for it last week.'

'Aw, you're a genius, that's what you are, Shona Deakin,' she told me proudly.

'Bannerman,' I reminded her. 'I'm Shona Bannerman.'

'Hmm. What do you want to keep *his* name for? I heard tell that you can go back to your maiden name if you like, once you're divorced, and you've been divorced a good while now.'

'But my daughters are Bannermans,' I reminded her.

'Not your Christie,' she pointed out. 'She's a married woman now and—'

'Shh,' I whispered. 'I'm trying to listen.'

'As soon as we've ironed out more of the details, we'll let you know,' Callie promised us. 'I just wanted to give you the heads up as soon as I could, given how short of time we are. What I really want to know for now is, in principle at least, how many of you are in favour of the 1940s weekend? Can we have a show of hands, please?'

'Those in favour,' Brodie called.

A sea of hands shot up.

'Those against?'

There were half a dozen or so hands that wobbled in the air as if not entirely sure if they should be there or not.

'Great,' Callie said happily. 'That's carried then. You'll be hearing from us in the next few days with more details. Thanks so much, all of you, for coming.'

'Well, would you believe that?' Aunt Polly said as I got to my feet and grabbed my jacket from the back of the seat. 'All that fuss and moaning, and when push comes to shove, they nearly all bloody want it!'

'Of course they do,' I said, laughing. 'You should know this village by now, Aunt Polly.'

'You off to the teashop, love?' she asked.

I shook my head. 'Day off. I'm going home to check on Dad and then I've got Christie and the kids coming round for dinner, so I'll be sorting that out. Come back with me if you like?'

She beamed at me. 'Ooh, I might just do that. I'd like to see the little ones again. You know, I'm almost sure our Maddie could see me. Last time I was at yours, she smiled at me. *Directly* at me. Least, I think she did. Might have been wind.'

'Might well have been, but we'll see, eh? Come on. Let's go home, and you can keep Dad company in the garden while I peel the potatoes.'

2

Dad was dozing in his favourite garden chair when I opened the back door of our cottage and stepped outside. Having just turned seventy-four, he was adamant that he'd earned his rest, and that he wasn't going to let anyone make him feel guilty for spending a good portion of his day doing, as he put it, 'sod all'.

I don't know who he was trying to convince. We'd been telling him to take it easier ever since he'd finally retired from his job at the garage just four years ago, so he was preaching to the converted.

'I wasn't asleep,' were his first words to me as he jolted upright so fast, he nearly knocked the half-full glass of beer off the table next to him.

Before I could reply, his face lit up at the sight of

his beloved aunt, and he cried, 'Polly! How smashing to see you. Come and sit down next to me.'

'Don't mind if I do, Jimmy,' she said warmly. 'Always happy to spend time with my favourite nephew.'

'Your only nephew,' he pointed out. 'Not much of a compliment really.'

'Go on with you!' She gave him a playful nudge which, naturally, he couldn't feel but made him chuckle anyway. I gave them both a fond look and said, 'I'll put the kettle on. Tea or coffee, Dad?'

'Now what do you think?' he said, pushing away his beer as if it was no longer any use to him. 'Deakins are tea drinkers, as well you know. Did we open a coffee shop in the village? Did we heck. A teashop's what we run and tea's what we drink.'

'I quite like a coffee,' I admitted, trying not to grin.

As expected, he gave an exasperated 'Pah!' and waved me away.

'Forgets she's a Deakin sometimes,' he confided in Aunt Polly. 'Been a Bannerman too long.'

'I was just saying to her, Jimmy, that she's been divorced for years. Ought to change her name back if you ask me.'

'I can still hear you, you know!' I called from the kitchen, where I was rooting in the cupboard for two mugs.

'Nothing we haven't said to your face,' called back Aunt Polly.

I shook my head, but the smile had faded. As I vaguely heard them chatting to each other in the garden, my mind strayed to the issue of my name, and whether I should change it back to Deakin. After all, Dad and Aunt Polly were right. I'd been divorced for years – ever since my husband, Luke, had decided he was done playing happy families and wanted his freedom.

'I just need to clear my head,' he'd told me. 'I need to live alone for a while. Just till I figure things out. I need some space.'

Needing *some space* had turned into a year, and before I knew it, the divorce papers had landed on my doormat, and I was suddenly the ex-Mrs Bannerman. I could have refused to sign them, just to be awkward, but what would have been the point?

'Have you gone to India for that tea?' Dad called and I laughed.

'Coming right up!'

I still felt a pang of guilt as I carried the two mugs of tea into the garden. I knew Aunt Polly couldn't drink but it didn't stop me from feeling I should have offered her one, as stupid as that sounds.

'I was just telling your dad about the meeting,' she said, as I settled myself in the chair next to hers.

I pushed a mug towards Dad and nodded. 'It sounds like fun, doesn't it?'

He glanced at his aunt. 'Well, the forties weren't all fun, I'm sure. I hope young Callie remembers that and treats the occasion with some respect.'

Aunt Polly giggled. 'Respect? Give over, Jimmy! We want to give people a good time, not have them crying into their beer. I might have a word with young Callie. Give her some advice, like. I'm sure she'd appreciate it.'

'Are – are you sure, Polly?' he asked.

There was real concern in his eyes, and I knew why.

Because Aunt Polly hadn't just died in the 1940s.

She'd been murdered.

3

POLLY

Polly was having a good time, sharing this beautiful afternoon with her family in the garden of the place she'd once called home, especially now Christie had arrived with her little girls, Autumn and Maddie. She was glad a whole new generation was enjoying Starling Cottage.

She'd grown up here. Her schoolfriends had come to tea here on her birthday. Her dad had grown carrots, cabbages, and potatoes in the very beds where flowers now bloomed. In the kitchen, Polly's mum had taught her to cook and bake, how to iron Dad's shirts properly, and how to clean the oven until it gleamed.

She'd never minded helping her mum, though when her two brothers came along and they weren't required to do their fair share of the housework, she did wonder to herself why that should be the case, and vowed there and then that if she ever had a son, he'd roll up his sleeves in the kitchen and no arguments.

Ray and Norman had been real surprises. Mum and Dad had thought they couldn't have any more children, but Ray arrived when Polly was thirteen, and then four years later, in 1927, what Mum took to be the change of life turned out to be Polly's youngest sibling, Norman.

Polly hadn't lived at Starling Cottage for long with her brothers. At eighteen, she married Charlie Herron, the boy next door, and the two of them moved in with Charlie's mum and dad until a cottage became available in the village, and they'd relocated to their first – and, as it turned out, only – marital home. The Brambles. She'd loved it there, and had polished and cleaned and cooked so Charlie would have a beautiful home he could be proud of.

'There's a clever girl! Look at her go now. There'll be no stopping her, now she's off.'

Shona's excited exclamation drew Polly's attention back to the present, and she stared down at little Maddie, who had tottered away from her mum and gran and was standing just a foot or so in front of Polly.

There was no doubt in Polly's mind; Maddie could see her. The last time the two had met, Maddie had only been around nine months old, and it had been difficult to be certain. Now, though, she was fourteen months and it was a different story. She stood alone, her chubby legs slightly bowed, her toes curling a little into the grass, brow furrowed as she stared long and hard at Polly, as if trying to work out who or what she was. Then she waved her arms excitedly, causing her to lose her balance and land on the ground, where she emitted a giggle that quite melted Polly's long-redundant heart.

'I knew it!' she exclaimed, as Maddie happily gurgled at her. 'Didn't I tell you, Shona?'

'You're right,' Shona said, clearly delighted as she scooped her youngest granddaughter onto her knee and rewarded her with a kiss. 'She can see you!'

'How unfair is that?' Christie groaned in exasperation. 'My own daughter can do what I can't.' She cuddled three-year-old Autumn to her and said, 'At least you're like me, sweetheart. Though I wish you weren't. You're going to be as jealous of Maddie as I always was of Pippa.'

Bless her. Polly was very fond of her eldest greatniece, and often wished they could chat properly, like she could with Christie's sister, Pippa. Christie was a lot like her mum: a kind, nurturing soul. She'd married her childhood sweetheart, Scott, five years ago, when she was just twenty-one.

Shona had worried that they were too young, but Christie had insisted that she knew he was right for her, and Jimmy had pointed out that her mum had only been nineteen when he'd married *her* and look how happy they'd been.

As it turned out, Shona had nothing to worry about. Scott was a good man. Like Jimmy, he was a mechanic, living and working in nearby Kingsford Wold. The whole family liked him, and he took good care of Christie and the two daughters they shared.

'I know, love,' Shona said with a sigh. 'It's funny, isn't it? Who can see her and who can't. You'd think with us all being related to her, we'd all be able to see her.'

'It doesn't work that way, though,' Polly said. 'There are a couple of ghosts in this village who have a few blood descendants who can't see them at all, so there's only Callie and Lawrie they can talk to. I'm one of the lucky ones, having you and Jimmy, and Pippa, and now little Maddie. I wish Autumn and Christie could see me, but at least I still feel like part of the family.'

'You'll always be part of the family, Polly,' Jimmy

said firmly. 'My dad thought the world of you. You know that.'

'Aw, our Norman.' Polly sighed. Sometimes, it all seemed such a long time ago. Well, she supposed it had been. Hard to believe but it had been over twenty years since she'd last seen her youngest brother. When he'd died, he'd passed over. Part of her had hoped he'd linger in Rowan Vale, as she had, but deep down, she was glad he'd got the peace he so deserved. He'd always been a good lad, just like his son, Jimmy.

She closed her eyes for a moment, remembering those far-off days when she was young and carefree – and alive. Before the war, when everything seemed bathed in golden sunshine, and there were long days of working on the farm, cosy evenings in the bar at The Quicken Tree or by the fire at home, and so much love and laughter.

That was before 1938, when she and her mum took on the new village teashop that had opened in a formerly derelict building attached to the mill, and it became Deakin's. Polly had left the farm, where she'd worked in the dairy, and was made manageress in their new venture. Mum was quite happy to use her cooking and baking skills, but she wanted no truck with the business side of things, whereas Polly was eager to learn.

Dad, meanwhile, had stayed working alongside Charlie on the farm, and when they were old enough, her younger brothers Ray and Norman had joined them.

She pushed away the familiar, hollow feeling that always swamped her when she allowed her mind to dwell on the past for too long. It made no sense to do so. It was gone. *They* were gone. There was no one in her family left alive from those times, but at least she had Norman's son, Jimmy, as consolation. And Shona. Thank God for Shona.

She smiled over at her great-niece, who was currently smothering a chuckling Maddie in kisses. Short and curvy, with shoulder-length, dark-brown hair and sparkling blue eyes, Shona was a lovely person. She certainly hadn't deserved the treatment she'd received from that lousy husband of hers.

Polly had to admit she'd never taken to Luke Bannerman and had been disappointed when Shona married him and moved to Birmingham. She'd always been far too good for him in Polly's opinion, and she'd been proved right, although she genuinely wished she hadn't been, because knowing Shona's heart had been broken had almost broken hers.

It had been wonderful when she'd come home where she belonged, and even better when she became manageress of the teashop, just as Polly had once been. She kept the place immaculate, and apart from a few (well, a lot) of changes to the menu, and a far more modern kitchen, it was almost exactly like it had been back in the day. The staff even wore vintage dresses and aprons to work, and sometimes, Polly could almost believe she was one of them, going about her business and being part of a happy team, as she'd been in life.

Shona had repainted the walls a warm cream colour, and even sourced similar green and white gingham tablecloths to the ones Polly had once bought for Deakin's, although they now had wipe-down covers on the tabletops to make them easier to keep clean.

And all that pretty, mismatched china! Such lovely little tea sets that Shona had sourced from second-hand shops and antique markets all over the Cotswolds. Nothing had been too much trouble for her. She'd wanted Polly to feel right at home. Such a good girl.

Yes, these past twelve years had been good ones for the family. It was a shame Christie couldn't see her, but she'd bonded well with Shona's youngest, Pippa, and Jimmy and Shona made sure that Polly was included in family occasions, bless them. She couldn't complain. She really couldn't.

And now there was something else to look forward to... A 1940s weekend.

Polly leaned back in her chair and lifted her gaze to the heavens. It was a beautiful day with no clouds in the cornflower-blue sky.

July.

It had been July 1941 when she'd got the confirmation that her beloved Charlie had been killed during the Battle of Crete.

She remembered the last letter she'd ever received from him. It was full of love, optimism, and determination. He was coming home soon, he'd said, more with hope and longing than certainty. And when he did, maybe they'd start that family after all, even though she was getting on a bit, having reached the grand old age of thirty.

'Bloody cheek!' she'd exclaimed before mopping away her tears and running her little finger down the image of his face, looking so serious in the photograph he'd enclosed with his letter.

She and Charlie had been boyfriend and girlfriend since they were thirteen years old. She'd never loved anyone else. The whole family adored Charlie, and when the news came that he wouldn't be coming home, it had broken her mum and dad almost as much as it had broken her. Norman, too. Still too young to sign up, he'd been devastated. He and Ray had idolised Charlie.

Ray could have stayed home when war broke out, being a farm labourer, but he wanted to follow his hero brother-in-law into battle and had lied about his age, enlisting in late 1940 when he was just seventeen.

The whole family had hoped and prayed that both Charlie and Ray would come home safe, but it wasn't to be. Charlie never came home. And Ray – well, Ray had been damaged during the Normandy Campaign in June 1944. Badly damaged. He was never the same again.

War, she thought bitterly, had taken so much from the Deakins. Maybe celebrating the 1940s wasn't such a good idea after all.

And yet...

Her shoulders dropped and she thought wistfully that it hadn't been all bad. There had been good times when the boys came home on leave and the family was reunited. There had been strong bonds formed in the village as everyone pulled together and dealt with the hardships and grief that came their way. There had been new friendships forged as the women of Rowan Vale picked her up after her devastating loss and kept her going with their compassion and warm humour. There had been – as hard as it was to imagine – laughter. And there had been so much love...

'You know what I think? I think our Pippa ought to write about this 1940s weekend for *The Cotswolds Courier*. What do you think, Mum?'

Polly's attention was caught by Christie's question, and she mentally shook her head. She was done brooding, remember? Fancy letting her mind go wandering back to that time and getting all maudlin like that! If there was going to be a 1940s weekend in the village, she wanted to enjoy it. She'd remember all the good times and put the darkness aside. It belonged in the past. Her mum always used to say that no good ever came from wallowing, and she was right.

Shona carefully put Maddie on the grass, not letting go of her hands until the toddler had got her balance, then beamed proudly as Maddie took a few tentative steps towards her great-grandad.

'That's a good idea, actually,' she said at last, turning to her eldest daughter. 'Callie did say she wanted to attract more people to Rowan Vale, and a feature in the newspaper might be just the job.'

While Christie was happy as a wife and mum, working part-time in a gift shop, her sister, Pippa, had taken a different path. She'd gone to university, studied journalism, and three years after graduating, was now living and working in Much Melton, reporting on local news for *The Cotswolds Courier*. Christie's idea made a lot of sense.

'More tourists, eh?' Jimmy chuckled as he held out his arms to Maddie. 'Reverend Silas is going to love that, eh, Polly?'

She grinned. 'That's what I said!'

'Wish I could meet him,' Jimmy said wistfully. 'I've heard such a lot about him from Dad and you; he sounds like a real character.'

'A real character's one way of putting it. A right miserable old sod is another,' Polly told him. 'Amelia's very lucky she can't see or hear him, sharing that vicarage with him. That's all I can say.'

'I might give Pippa a ring,' Shona said thoughtfully. 'See if she'd be up for covering the story.'

'Maybe wait until you get that newsletter, love,' Jimmy advised her. 'Find out if it's definitely going ahead and what it's going to be exactly, then I'd speak to Callie. Check she's okay with Pippa covering it. Then put it to Pippa.'

'I'd put it to Pippa before mentioning it to Callie,' Christie said, smoothing Autumn's hair. 'She might not think it worth covering and you don't want to get Callie's hopes up for nothing.'

'Of course she'll think it's worth covering,' Polly said indignantly, forgetting for a moment that Christie couldn't hear her. 'It's going to be brilliant. I can't wait.'

She was going to enjoy every moment. She'd quite made her mind up on that. And she wasn't going to let any dark shadows from the past spoil it for her.

4

'This is brilliant, Shona! When Pippa agreed to give us a write-up, I never expected her to be so thorough!'

We were sitting at a table in the teashop, and I'd been anxiously waiting for Callie's verdict on Pippa's feature. I needn't have worried. I beamed with maternal pride as Callie lowered the copy of last night's *Cotswolds Courier,* looking deeply impressed by what she'd just read.

'She's always been very thorough in whatever she does. No half-measures with our Pippa,' I told her.

My youngest had certainly done Rowan Vale proud. Not only had she interviewed Callie and Brodie, but she'd also talked to Betty and Nick from the farm, the staff at the cinema, the mill museum, the bakery – and me, of course. She'd made the event sound amazing, and I wasn't surprised that Callie was so pleased.

'Will you thank her for me when you see her? I hope she's going to be attending – just as a guest, I mean. I'm not expecting her to write another piece.'

'As a matter of fact,' I said, 'she's already confirmed she's going to be here to cover it. It's local news, after all. *The Courier* are going to promote it over the next few weeks so we should have a nice crowd at the event.'

Callie visibly swallowed. 'Blimey. Whose bright idea was this again?'

'Yours,' I said firmly, 'and a very good one it is, too.'

'You think? This all started, you know, because Lawrie got a phone call from an old friend of his, asking if it would be possible to hold a vintage car rally in the village. The field they usually use has been snapped up for development and, even though work won't start until next year, the new owner just dropped the bombshell on them that they can't use it any more. Lawrie asked me if it would be okay.

'Of course, I said yes. Then I thought about all those old cars rolling into the village and it stirred something in my mind. Many of them are from the thirties and forties, apparently, and someone's even got an old wartime American army jeep! They said they'd be very happy to be part of the event if it went ahead so...' She gazed down at the paper. 'Maybe I got a bit carried away.'

'Why are you doubting yourself?' Aunt Polly demanded. 'If you hadn't thought it would work, you wouldn't have suggested it in the first place, would you? This is just nerves, love. It sounds like smashing fun to me.'

'Not everyone in this village seems so keen,' Callie murmured. Her gaze slid over to the corner table where Erin and Rissa, the two young women employed to act as land girls on Rowan Farm, were chatting over cups of tea and slices of Victoria sponge.

'Hmm. Well, we all know Rissa's problem,' I said softly. I felt a bit sorry for the girl. Everyone in the village knew she'd had a massive crush on Brodie. They'd even dated for a while until she got too intense. It seemed Rissa was still carrying a torch for him because she'd made it very clear she didn't like Callie and she wanted no truck with the 1940s weekend, whatever her employers said.

'You don't want to worry about the odd few naysayers,' Aunt Polly told her. 'Most people are all for it. I hear things, you know. Accidentally, like.'

I tried not to laugh, knowing how much she loved to eavesdrop on the locals and pick up any gossip.

'And what I hear,' she continued, ignoring the smirk I knew I'd failed to hide, 'is that most people are excited about this weekend you're organising. Even that moaning old Mr Thwaite's said a few grudging positive things about it.'

'Thank you, Mrs Herron,' Callie said gratefully. 'That's a relief to hear.'

'My name's Polly, love. I've told you before. Mrs Herron was my mother-in-law and bless her, I loved her to bits but I'm not that old! I'm only thirty-seven, you know.'

Callie and I tactfully didn't point out that, strictly speaking, she was well over a hundred years old if you counted all her birthdays since she'd died.

'Thank you, Polly.' Callie corrected herself with a smile. 'I know it's a good idea but it's a tight deadline. It's just, the car rally's always held then, apparently, and I thought, with September being when war was declared, it all fitted. And besides, any later in the year and we'd be more likely to have bad weather.'

'Not that you can guarantee good weather at any time in this country,' I pointed out, nodding at the teashop windows, through which we could see grey skies. The mid-July sunshine hadn't lasted long.

Callie nibbled on the cheese scone I'd given her and scanned the article that Pippa had written for *The Courier* once again.

'She's made it sound really good,' she said, clearly feeling a bit happier. Though that could have been down to the scone, which was delicious, if I do say so myself.

'That's because it will be,' Aunt Polly promised. 'All the ghosts are on board, you know. Well – nearly all of them.'

'Let me guess who isn't,' Callie said, wrinkling her nose. 'Silas Alexander?'

Aunt Polly laughed. 'What are you? A clairvoyant?' She folded her arms and leaned towards Callie. 'What about them two up at the Hall? Are they up for it?'

Callie squirmed slightly in her chair. 'Er...'

'Gotcha.' Aunt Polly nodded knowingly. 'I was chatting to Isaac the other day,' she said, referring to the ghost of a seventeenth century former landlord of The Quicken Tree, 'and he was saying he doubted very much that we'd see the old – I mean, Agnes Ashcroft. She's far too grand to honour us with her presence. And sadly, Aubrey Wyndham's as bad these days. He used to be a lovely chap, you know, but now he's gone the same way as his so-called lady wife.'

Agnes and Aubrey were two ghosts who lived at

Callie's home, Howling Hall. Oops, I mean *Harling* Hall! Built by the original owners of the Harling Estate (they'd even been mentioned in the Domesday Book) it was a beautiful, sixteenth-century manor house, until recently owned by Sir Lawrence Davenport (or Lawrie as we all called him) and before that, by every previous owner of the estate since it was built.

Aubrey had once been one of those owners. According to Aunt Polly, he was a Victorian gentleman who'd somehow, *postmortem*, saddled himself with the imperious Agnes Ashcroft, who'd been the wife of a previous owner during the Georgian and Regency period.

It amused the ghosts that *Lady Muck,* as some of them called her, was living in sin with Aubrey. Apparently, Silas Alexander didn't find it so funny, but then, he didn't find anything funny by the sound of it.

Agnes and Aubrey never visited the village these days. Aunt Polly said they hadn't been near for donkey's years.

Callie also leaned forward and whispered to Aunt Polly, 'Do you know why they don't leave the grounds of the Hall? I thought it might be because of Silas. From what I've seen and heard, he's always having a go about them and their sinful ways. He calls the Hall a den of iniquity.' She reddened. 'I wonder what he thinks about me and Brodie sharing the place now we're together? Not,' she added quickly, 'that we share a suite. Brodie and Lawrie have their own suite in the east wing, and Immi and I are in the west wing. Even so...'

'I've wondered myself,' Aunt Polly confessed. 'Not about you and Brodie! I mean, about why they won't come to the village. They used to, after all, even when I joined the ranks of ghosts. I know it upset Agnes when Silas ranted at her, but she'd just turn up her nose and ignore him. Or I *thought* she was ignoring him. Maybe it went deeper than we realised. But Aubrey just used to shake his head and tell Silas he was a sad little man. He insisted that he and Agnes had done nothing to be ashamed of, and that Silas ought to be the one who was ashamed, haranguing a lady like Agnes who'd done nothing to deserve it, and him a man of the cloth.'

'So you don't think it *is* because of Silas then?' I asked, curious even though I'd never seen or heard any of the ghosts they were discussing.

'Well...' Aunt Polly tilted her head, considering. 'When I think about it, Agnes's visits got further and further apart, but Aubrey still liked a daily wander. But they both completely stopped coming here about

– what? Ten, fifteen years ago? Not entirely sure when it was exactly, but somewhere around then. Maybe Silas said something particularly brutal that upset them.' She shook her head. 'I wouldn't put it past him. Man of the cloth indeed. Huh!'

I glanced round, noting a few more tables had filled up with customers.

'I'd better give Paige a hand,' I said, getting to my feet.

'And I'd better get back home,' Callie said, before popping the last of the scone into her mouth.

At that moment, Rissa and Erin got up to leave, throwing jackets over their working uniforms of breeches and green jumpers. Erin nodded and gave us a rather sheepish smile as she passed our table, mumbling something about going next door to buy pasties for Bram and Lars, their co-workers on the farm. Rissa pointedly ignored us, and we watched as they both left the teashop and passed by the window, heading to Blighty's.

'Little madam,' Aunt Polly said with a sigh.

'It's all a bit awkward,' Callie admitted. 'I do feel quite bad about her.'

'No need,' I assured her. 'Rissa and Brodie broke up long before you arrived on the scene. She's just going to have to learn to accept that. If someone doesn't love you, wishing it was different won't make it so.'

Didn't I know it! How long had I wished I could make Luke love me again? Far too long.

For six months after he'd left home, I'd tried to persuade him to come back, and he'd always given me hope. He'd said he was working on himself and that it would make him a better husband and father in the long run. I needed to be patient. Stop hassling him.

So, for the next three months, I said nothing and left him to it, all the time hoping things would work out and he'd *find himself* and come home.

Well, he didn't find himself, but he did find someone else. It turned out he'd found her a few months before he'd even *lost himself*. She was someone he clearly didn't mind sharing his precious space with. Eight years younger than me, at least six inches taller, and with legs I'd have killed for.

At the time, I'd thought it was the end of the world, yet I was so much happier now than I'd ever been with him. I just wished I'd known all the happiness my future had in store for me. I'd have stopped sobbing into endless mugs of hot chocolate and binge eating flapjacks a lot sooner. I was still carrying the weight I'd put on during that time all these years later.

Mind you, I still loved a flapjack or three, so it wasn't surprising.

'Not always easy, though,' Aunt Polly said, sounding suddenly wistful. 'Love's a funny thing, and you can't just turn it off like a tap, even when the other person's gone from you. The ache remains.'

I wished I could hug her. She must still miss Uncle Charlie a lot, bless her. They'd been teenage sweethearts, and she'd lost him far too young.

As if sensing my surge of sympathy, she blinked and sat up straight. 'Hark at me, getting all sentimental! Shona's right, Callie. Rissa's just going to have to get over it and that's a fact. It's for her own sake as much as yours or Brodie's. It won't do her no favours to wallow.'

'I must get back to work,' I said, patting Callie on the shoulder. 'You can keep that newspaper, if you like. I've got another copy at home.'

Six, actually. I was a *very* proud mother.

'Oh, thanks. I'll take it to show everyone at the Hall,' she said with a smile.

I hurried over to where a young couple were waiting to place their order. Callie waved and left the shop, and out of the corner of my eye, I saw Aunt Polly shift over to another table, where she sat opposite two oblivious old ladies who were having a jolly good natter over tea and ginger cake. I had no doubt that my great-aunt would relish every moment of their conversation and enjoy relating it word for word to me afterwards even more. Not that I'd let her, of course. I did have some morals.

For the next few minutes, I was kept busy as Paige took orders from customers and I saw to the payments at the counter. I was just about to head into the kitchen to start preparing food when the door was pushed open and a man walked in.

What popped into my head immediately was, *Ooh! He's nice!* I blushed furiously as if I'd said that out loud. Paige was collecting dirty dishes from the tables, so I hovered by the counter, as he didn't take a seat but, after looking around, came straight over.

I guessed he was around my age. Maybe a bit older. It was hard to be sure because everyone said I looked young for my age, which was fifty. Ish. Okay, fifty-two, but I hardly had a line on my face. Whenever anyone complimented me on my youthful appearance, I'd half-joke that it was the fat plumping up my skin and keeping the lines at bay, but Dad and the kids always shook their heads and said I was beautiful, and the girls told me they hoped they'd inherited my genes.

So, yes, maybe he was in his mid-fifties. He

seemed very tall, but then I'm only five foot two, so everyone seems pretty tall to me. Even so, I'd guess he was around six foot. He had light-brown hair with a distinct wave in it, a neatly trimmed beard, and hazel eyes. He was wearing a grey sweater with a pale-blue shirt underneath, dark trousers, and a charcoal over-coat, despite it being quite warm outside – even with the overcast skies.

'Can I help you?'

Huh? What happened to my voice? It came out all breathy and girly like a poor man's Marilyn Monroe. Luckily, he didn't seem to notice.

'Excuse me please, could you tell me if you have seen my daughter recently? Her name is Larissa. Larissa Meyer. I have been to her place of work and was told she was coming here for lunch.'

First of all, it struck me that he had a lovely voice. Really... sexy. Secondly, I registered that he had the trace of an accent of some sort. Thirdly, I couldn't for the life of me think who Larissa Meyer was. And fourthly, and most surprisingly, Aunt Polly was staring at him like... well, like she'd seen a ghost, which was ironic, if you like. She half-rose from her chair before dropping back down into it and gazing at him, open-mouthed.

Maybe *she* thought he was sexy, too. Well, he was

too old for her, which seemed such a silly thought given she'd been born in 1910. I blinked, realising he was still waiting for an answer.

'I'm sorry. Larissa Meyer? I don't think I know her.'

He gave me a puzzled look. 'It says in the paper she works at Rowan Farm. The lady in the farmyard told me Rissa has come here.'

'Oh!' The fog lifted. 'Rissa! Yes, she was here but she's left now. Actually,' I said, remembering, 'she was going next door to the bakery. If you hurry, you might catch her. It depends if they have a queue.'

In July, it was highly likely there'd be a queue, so I thought he had a pretty good chance of finding her there.

'Thank you.' He nodded and hurried out of the teashop, leaving me to give a big sigh.

Well, that had been a nice interlude. Back to work. Fancy Rissa having a dad who looked like that! And I'd had no idea her surname was Meyer. Or that her full name was Larissa, come to that.

My thoughts were derailed as Aunt Polly jumped up and ran out through the door. Literally. I mean, it wasn't open, and it still shook me when I saw her do things like that, even though I'd grown up with her walking into rooms through closed doors and brick walls.

She didn't even say goodbye or look in my direction and I frowned. What was her hurry?

Then I realised she was probably going to do what Aunt Polly loved to do: eavesdrop. A handsome stranger had just turned up in the village and he was Rissa's father. Rissa, of all people! And he'd sounded quite desperate to see her, so maybe he was on an urgent mission. Aunt Polly wouldn't be able to resist that. She'd no doubt report back to me when she'd found out what he wanted.

Yes, I did have morals. But maybe, just this once, I'd let her talk.

5

POLLY

The man was sitting on the bench that faced the old mill and the river. He wasn't looking in that direction, though. He sat at an angle, gazing intently at the bakery, clearly watching for Rissa.

Polly hesitated, then slowly sat next to him, almost afraid that he would turn and stare at her. Ask her why she had followed him. What it was she wanted.

She shook her head impatiently. She was being daft, and she knew it. If her heart could beat, she imagined it would be drumming furiously right now, and she wasn't even sure why.

Well, that wasn't strictly true. If she was being honest with herself, she knew why. It was that voice. That refined, polite voice with the accent. Not as noticeable as *his* had been. Much fainter, as if this man had lived in England a long time.

It had given her such a turn, coming out of the blue like that. She'd just been sitting there at the table in the teashop, idly listening to two old ladies nattering on about the mundane, ordinary things in their lives.

One's hip was giving her trouble. The other had rheumatism in her hands. They couldn't believe how much the price of their groceries had gone up over the last few years.

Both agreed that this country was going to the dogs and it had all started with those terrible hippies and the concept of free love back in the 1960s.

Polly's mind had started to wander at that point, moving from memories of the 1960s back to the 1940s. She'd thought about Pippa's article in *The Courier* and smiled to herself as she imagined the village transported back in time, with vintage cars lined up along the street, and all the other things Callie and Brodie had planned for the weekend event.

She hadn't taken any notice when the man walked in, barely glancing up at him when the bell above the teashop door jangled. But then he'd spoken to Shona, and she'd jerked up in shock, her head whipping round to get a better look at him, because surely, *surely* he couldn't be who...

Of course he wasn't. How could he be, after all this time? But she hadn't been able to stop herself from following him out of the teashop, curious to get a better look at him.

Now, as she sat so close to him on the bench, she could see that he was nothing like him. This man wasn't blond for a start. He didn't have blue eyes. He was broader, and older. And he didn't have that look about him. That look Polly would never forget.

'Larissa!'

She jumped as he leapt to his feet and darted towards the bakery. Rissa and Erin had just come out of Blighty's, bulging carrier bags swinging from each of their hands, as if they'd bought up half the shop.

Rissa paled. 'Dad!'

Erin raised an eyebrow. 'That's your dad?'

'Larissa, what are you doing here?' He sounded odd, Polly thought. Sort of angry and sort of shaky at the same time. 'Here, of all places!'

'What are *you* doing here?' she demanded, a crimson flush flooding the face that just moments ago had been white.

'I saw the article,' he said heavily. 'I couldn't believe it. You lied to me, Rissa. All this time, you lied to me.'

Erin cleared her throat. 'Er, I'll meet you back at the farm,' she said. 'Shall I take your bag?'

Rissa nodded dumbly and handed her friend the carrier bag. Erin gave the man a curious look then headed towards the mill, rounding the corner and disappearing from view.

Polly realised she'd twisted a strand of her hair tightly around her forefinger and unravelled it immediately. She was intrigued. What did he mean, *Here, of all places*?

'London,' the man growled. 'You said you were living in London. How long has this deception been going on? Please, no more lies. At least do me the courtesy of some honesty at last.'

'Do we really have to do this, Dad?'

'We do. And if you don't give me some answers, maybe I will ask other people. The person in the bakery, perhaps? Or that lady in the teashop. Maybe I will go back to Rowan Farm and discuss the situation with your employers over tea and cake?'

Rissa glanced around warily then slumped. 'Okay, you win. Let's sit on that bench, but please, please keep your voice down, okay?'

Polly hastily shuffled over as the two of them

headed back towards her. Rissa and her father sat in silence for a few moments. Polly was almost sure she could hear Rissa's heart thudding, and she could certainly see the man's jaw pulsing as if he was trying very hard to stay calm.

She wondered who would break the silence first.

'How could you do this thing, Rissa?'

He turned to face his daughter, and Polly's eyes softened as she saw his own eyes were gleaming with unshed tears. Even as she felt a pang of sympathy for him, she felt something else too. Her stomach rolled and she stood up, pacing up and down as she tried to calm herself. What on earth was wrong with her? This man wasn't him. She had no reason to connect them, apart from the fact that they had a similar accent. She needed to get a grip.

'Focus, woman,' she muttered to herself. 'This is just a bit of gossip, that's all. Something for me to take back to Shona later on.'

'You wouldn't understand,' Rissa said, folding her arms.

'Try me. I want to understand. I want to understand how you could tell your own father that you were living and working in London when, according to the interview *those people* gave, you have been working as a land girl on their farm and are a – what did they call you now – "much-valued member of the team".'

Rissa closed her eyes. 'Bloody Betty and her big mouth.'

The man gasped. 'That's all you have to say? You blame your employer for letting the cats out of the bag?'

'Cat,' Rissa said sullenly. 'And don't get indignant on her behalf. I heard the scornful way you said, "*those people*". I can imagine all too well what you thought when you read who Betty was.'

'Exactly! And yet, you choose to work for her! Don't pretend that it's of no consequence. We both know that if you truly believed that, you wouldn't have lied to me all this time. I was just a few miles away, Rissa. A few miles! Yet you made me meet you in London. You told me you shared a flat with a friend. You took me there for lunch! I'm at a loss to understand why you would do so many terrible things.'

'I *did* share a flat with a friend for a few months,' Rissa protested. 'I only got the job on the farm eighteen months ago. That wasn't a lie exactly. I just didn't tell you when I moved on, that's all.'

Her father narrowed his eyes and Polly watched, fascinated despite her unease. What on earth was the problem? Why did he resent Rissa working in Rowan

Vale, and at Rowan Farm in particular? And what could he possibly have against Betty, of all people? She was a lovely woman. Salt of the earth.

Polly didn't like the way this man spoke about her at all. She'd like to give him a piece of her mind, being so rude and insulting. No wonder Rissa didn't exactly confide in him, poor girl. Maybe that was why she could be so rude and offish. Her dad hadn't exactly set her a good example, had he?

'But even if that's true, why would you want to work at Rowan Farm? You know what happened there! You know how badly they behaved!'

'Dad, that was bloody decades ago!'

'Don't swear at me, Rissa.'

'Sorry. But come on. Nick and Betty weren't there then. You can't blame them.'

'In the article, it says Betty is the granddaughter of Alfred and Helen Rowland.'

Polly's hand flew to her mouth. Alf and Helen had managed the farm back in her day. What did they have to do with this man? With Rissa?

'So what if she is?' Rissa cried. 'Betty's all right. She's not them.'

'They have men at the farm, don't they? Men masquerading as prisoners of war for entertainment! For the tourists to stare at, as if it's all some big joke.'

Polly knew she couldn't actually be sick, but it sure as heck felt like she was going to be.

'Dad, it's really not like that,' Rissa said with a sigh.

'I've looked at the website,' her father said. His tone was cold, distant. He wasn't looking at his daughter any longer. He stared ahead of him and for a moment, Polly had an awful, sickening feeling that he was staring straight at her.

But of course, he wasn't. Instead, he was gazing into the middle distance, and she had the feeling he was struggling to contain his thoughts, to choose his words carefully.

'When I read the article, I checked my facts before I came here. They have turned what happened here into some sort of entertainment. But we know the truth, Rissa. We know what happened here in those dark days. We know what really happened to those poor men.'

'We *don't* really know,' Rissa protested. 'Grandma was just guessing.'

'My mother cared for my grandfather in his dying days. She saw how distressed he was. I saw it myself! I saw him cry, Rissa! You think we made this up? You think he lied?'

'He was ill, Dad,' she said gently. 'Old and ill. He was rambling. We don't know—'

'Don't make excuses, Rissa, please.' The man slumped and rubbed his forehead wearily. 'This place...' He gazed around him and said softly. 'It is so beautiful, and yet beneath the surface, it is ugly. It has an ugly history. I don't want you working here. I don't want you to live here. I want you to come home with me and look for another job. Get away from this place.'

Rissa gave a bitter laugh and shook her head. 'I like it here.'

'If you won't do it for me,' he pleaded, 'at least do it for him! For his memory!'

'I never met Great-Grandpa,' Rissa pointed out desperately. 'I'm sorry, Dad, but it's true. He's just a name to me, and that's partly why I came here. I know how much he meant to you, and I wanted to be where he spent those years. I don't want him to be just a name. I want to know who the real Gerhard Janssen was and—'

Polly didn't hear the rest of her words. She reeled back, feeling as if she couldn't catch her breath, which was crazy because she hadn't taken a breath in years.

Dazed, she walked slowly to the river and stared across the water, over the fields towards where Rowan Farm lay.

She squeezed her eyes tightly shut, hearing again

her own voice pleading for mercy. The pistol shot. The sudden, excruciating pain. The biting cold that seeped through her body from the hard, frost-bitten ground into her bones. The nauseating, metallic smell of the blood that seeped *out* of her body into the land. The shock and the fear that gave way to a strange calmness and acceptance.

It had been so long, and she'd done such a good job of keeping those memories at bay. But hearing his name again...

And this man was Gerhard Janssen's grandson. Rissa was his great-granddaughter. All this time, she'd been living in the same village as Polly and Polly hadn't known. Hadn't guessed.

She crouched down, her arms wrapping tightly around her knees, and watched a family of ducks swimming further along the river. Tourists were laughing and snapping photos of them on their mobile phones. Some of them held the phones up and took pictures of the mill behind Polly, marvelling at how picturesque the water wheel looked as it turned.

'What a gorgeous place this is,' one of them said. 'Like something from another age.'

It has an ugly history, Gerhard's grandson had said.

Polly couldn't deny that. Her own death was proof of it. But things were never as simple as they seemed...

6

The cinema was across the way from the teashop, tucked into a small cul-de-sac with only a handful of cottages. It wasn't like any other cinema I'd ever seen, and you could almost be forgiven for thinking it was just a large house from the exterior, if not for the sign over the entrance and the movie posters – facsimiles of the originals – attached to the noticeboard by the front steps.

Sir Edward Davenport – Lawrie's father – had decided the village needed a cinema of its own in the early 1950s, and had chosen the location himself, taking the opportunity to convert Briar House into The Magic Lantern when the elderly gentleman who'd resided there for years had moved out.

I only vaguely remembered Sir Edward, who'd died in 1988, but I knew the residents of Rowan Vale had a lot to thank him for.

It had been Edward's grandfather Jeremy's vision that initially transformed the pretty village of Rowan Vale into a living history village. The seeds were sown for the project all the way back in 1910, although the Great War had delayed things somewhat, much to Jeremy's frustration.

In 1923, Jeremy's son Frederick inherited the Estate, and painstakingly restored the mostly derelict, eighteenth-century Ashcroft Mill, turning it into a museum of local life.

Then Edward had taken over when only thirty years old – even younger than Brodie was now. The Harling Estate had been his life, with Rowan Vale his particular passion, and he'd invested heavily in Rowan Farm to enable the Rowlands to continue using 1940s agricultural methods, ensuring that way of farming was preserved.

In the 1960s, he'd extended the living history museum to encompass the railway station at Harling's Halt. The train line between there and a local market town, Much Melton, had been closed thanks to the Beeching recommendations, so Sir Edward purchased that section of railway line along with two steam trains, and turned the whole thing into a heritage line.

Not only that, but he'd created an Edwardian and Great War experience at the station, hiring people to portray soldiers and their sweethearts gathered on the platform, as well as opening a very popular station teashop, with mahogany furniture, polished silver teapots, lace-edged tablecloths, and staff dressed in uniforms not unlike the maids in early episodes of *Downton Abbey*.

Lawrie had inherited the estate in 1988, and had continued his ancestors' work, as committed to the idea of heritage and preservation as they'd been. It was Lawrie who'd opened the garage and started the vintage bus service in the village. All the Davenports had contributed something to this place; they'd enriched Rowan Vale and, by extension, the Harling Estate, with their business flair and their love for their home.

So we'd all kind of held our breath when it had been announced that there was to be a new owner, and the age of the Davenports was ending, even though we'd known it was inevitable, as soon as it became obvious that Brodie couldn't see the ghosts.

He'd been our last hope, after it was revealed that Lawrie's son didn't possess the gift. With two generations of Davenports now without the sight, we knew Lawrie had no choice but to pass the estate to someone who did have it.

Callie had been a bolt from the blue. Aunt Polly said the previous owners had all had some connection or other with this place, but Callie had none. She was originally from East Yorkshire and was living in Leicestershire when she visited Rowan Vale with her daughter as part of a school trip, and Lawrie had discovered that she could see all the ghosts.

Although we'd had to accept that the Davenports' time was over, I'll admit we'd been nervous that Callie wouldn't *get it*. That she wouldn't understand how important Rowan Vale and the Harling Estate were to us all, and how much our history and heritage mattered.

So, as I watched her standing on the stage at The Magic Lantern, enthusiastically telling us of her plans and dreams for the 1940s weekend, I couldn't help thinking how lucky we were, because it was pretty clear to me that it mattered almost as much to her as it did to us.

'Lawrie's been in touch with the vintage car club, and the plan is to line up all the vehicles along Church Lane,' she said, her eyes shining with excitement. She turned her head slightly and grinned. 'I know, I know, but Silas will just have to lump it,' she said, clearly answering a comment by one of the ghosts.

There was a smattering of laughter. We all knew Reverend Alexander by reputation, and that he wouldn't take kindly to a line of old cars outside All Souls, attracting even more visitors.

In the seat next to me, Amelia Davies, the vicar of All Souls and the bane of Silas's afterlife, gave me a wry grin. 'Poor old Silas. Bless him, I can almost feel sorry for him.'

From what I'd heard from Aunt Polly, she was the only person who'd ever said that! Fair-haired and rosy-cheeked, Amelia was an easy-going sort of person, which was probably a very good job. How she coped with living in the vicarage, knowing Silas's ghost was sharing her home with her, was beyond me. I'd have been holding nightly exorcisms, just to be on the safe side.

I glanced around, but there was no sign of Aunt Polly, which surprised me. I'd have thought she'd have been one of the first to arrive, eager to hear Callie's plans. Come to think of it, I hadn't seen her all week. I'd been expecting her at the teashop every day, but she hadn't showed, and when I'd popped upstairs to her flat a few times to open a window, dust round, and run a hoover over the carpets, there'd been no sign of her.

I hoped she was all right, before realising she couldn't really be anything else. I mean, it wasn't like I needed to worry about her being ill, was it? She must have found something new to entertain her.

'So what about our shops?' Mrs Chesterton said. 'Where do the Victorian and Swinging Sixties businesses fit into the scheme of things?'

'Well, what I'm hoping for is that, although I wouldn't expect you to change your stock or do anything different that weekend, you wouldn't mind changing the look of the exterior of the shops.'

As a loud murmuring began, she raised her hands. 'Only slightly! Nothing too drastic, I promise! My idea is for every business in the village to tape their windows, the way they did during the war to protect from potential bomb damage and shattered glass. And if you could perhaps hang some vintage bunting, that would be great. A few posters in the window. You know – dig for victory, careless talk costs lives, that kind of thing.'

'But we'd still be able to sell our usual goods?' Mrs Chesterton asked suspiciously.

'I promise, I wouldn't want to cause you any disruption, and of course I wouldn't expect you to change your stock just for one weekend,' Callie assured her. 'All I'm asking is you enter into the spirit of things by dressing your shop fronts up a bit. It would be business as usual inside, and I'd make that very clear on the programmes for the event.'

'What about us?' asked Mandy, one of the girls from the salon. 'Do you want us to do 1940s hairstyles for the day?'

'Honestly,' Callie said, 'it would be entirely up to you.'

The salon usually offered beehives and back-combing to any tourists who wanted to try the authentic 1960s look for themselves, as well as carrying out their usual modern hairstyling for locals.

'Ooh,' Amelia mused. 'Might treat myself to a Betty Grable do, or a Rita Hayworth. I could dye my hair red. What do you think?'

'Maybe you should cut your hair short and stick a moustache on instead,' I said wryly. 'I don't think there were any women vicars in the forties, were there?'

'Oh heck,' she groaned. 'You're right. I suppose I'll have to remove the dog collar then.'

We turned our attention back to the matter in hand.

'I think it would be fun to do forties hair for a

change,' another hairstylist, Ingrid, was telling Callie, her voice full of enthusiasm. 'Victory rolls and pin curls – that kind of thing. We could look it up on the internet and see how you do it and have a good practise on each other.'

Mandy nodded. 'We could. We might be able to find some old 1940s magazines online to put in the salon instead of the 1960s ones, too.'

'That would be brilliant.' Callie sounded delighted and there was an unmistakable note of gratitude in her voice.

'What about us, Callie?' A young man I didn't recognise who was sitting not far from me had stood up, and as he was wearing ordinary, modern clothing, I wasn't entirely sure if he worked at Rowan Vale at all. 'What's happening at the station? Business as usual, or do you want to transform from First World War to Second?'

Callie glanced at Mia, who'd been sitting quietly by her side. Mia worked at Harling Hall not only as housekeeper, but as an admin assistant. In Lawrie's day, she'd been his Girl Friday. She stood up.

'Didn't you get the email, Matthew? There's a meeting at the Victory Tearooms tomorrow for all station staff to attend.'

Matthew – who I guessed must be one of the 'soldiers' at the station – frowned. 'Sorry, Mia. Must have gone into spam.'

'You never check your emails, you mean,' said a young woman sitting next to him. 'How many times have I told you?'

I recognised her. I think her name was Andie. She sometimes took part in the pub quiz at The Quicken Tree, and I knew she worked on the vintage buses, as a conductress or "clippie". She must be this Matthew's friend or girlfriend.

'Sorry, Mia,' she called. 'We've been away on holiday. First day back at work tomorrow, so we'll be there.'

'There'll be another newsletter going out in a couple of days,' Mia assured us. 'This time, it will be individually tailored, so you'll know exactly what we're hoping you'll be able to do and what your part will be in this event. For most of you, it honestly will be business as usual. For others, it will just mean dressing up your shop fronts. We're not expecting miracles, especially given the short notice. However,' she added, glancing at Callie, 'we do have treats in store.'

Callie smiled. 'Special thanks to Lucy and Sam at the record shop, who have sourced some vinyl albums featuring original recordings of 1940s music and a vintage record player. We're going to be playing music through a series of strategically placed speakers throughout the village, that will really help build the atmosphere. And our lovely vicar, Amelia, has also promised that the church choir will be learning some wartime songs and will entertain us all with live music from the period, so that'll be fun, right?'

'She hasn't heard them sing,' Amelia whispered to me before smiling and nodding at Callie.

'And,' Mia added, 'we're hoping there'll also be a special event to round off the weekend, to which you'll all be invited. More news of that as soon as we can share.'

As we filed out of the cinema into the early-evening sunshine, which had made a welcome return, Amelia nodded over to where Betty and Rissa were walking, deep in discussion.

'There's a surprise,' she said. 'Rissa made it very clear to anyone who'd listen that she wanted nothing to do with the 1940s weekend, yet here she is. Well, hopefully that means she's got over Brodie at last.'

'Hey, did you know her dad was in the village looking for her last week?'

Amelia frowned 'Looking for her? Was she lost or something?'

'I don't know,' I said thoughtfully. 'He said that

he'd read in the papers that she worked at Rowan Farm, which I thought was odd. If she's his daughter, surely he'd know she worked there already? It's not like she's only just moved here, is it?'

'Very strange,' Amelia agreed. 'Maybe they've had a falling out or something. Did he seem angry? Anxious? Upset?'

'I'm not sure.' I couldn't help but grin suddenly. 'He was a bit of a looker, though. Made me go all funny inside.'

Amelia's brown eyes widened, and she threw back her head and laughed. 'Shona Bannerman! Did you fancy him?'

I wrinkled my nose. 'Maybe a smidge,' I admitted. 'He was all tall and broad-shouldered, and he had a beard. Funny really, cos I'm not usually one for facial hair on men.'

'As opposed to facial hair on women?'

I shook my head. 'Very funny. You know what I mean. I never thought I'd fancy a bloke with a beard, but this one was really neat, and it suited him somehow. Oh, I don't know. Just me valiantly trying to stir up my last few flagging hormones I guess.'

'Life in the old dog yet, I'd say.'

'Who are you calling a dog?'

'Now who's being funny? Hey, I think I might have

seen him, you know. There was a man in the church-yard last week, eyeing up the graves. He matched your description.'

'Was he – I'm not sure – Dutch? German? Something like that.'

She raised an eyebrow. 'I've no idea. When he saw me approaching, he scarpered, and I wasn't going to go chasing after him. It was the Rowlands' graves he was standing at. He seemed to be reading the inscriptions on their headstones. I wonder why?'

'No idea. Maybe he's interested in the history of this place? Although he really has no idea...' I laughed, thinking of all the past residents of the village who still wandered its streets.

'You say he's Dutch or German?'

'Or something,' I said. 'He had the faintest trace of an accent. It was quite sexy.'

'My word, Shona! Your hormones really are popping.'

'Don't be daft. Just an observation.'

'So, Rissa's got foreign blood in her veins, eh? Well, judging by her own accent, she grew up in this country, so maybe he's been living here a long time.'

'Unless,' I said slowly, 'her parents are divorced, and she's grown up in England with her mum, and that's why her dad didn't know where she was. Maybe they were estranged, and he wants to rebuild their relationship. Aw...' I sighed. 'That would be lovely. I hope they forgive each other.'

Amelia smirked. 'You've made up a whole backstory for them in your head, haven't you?'

'I just like happy endings,' I admitted. 'Nothing wrong with that, is there?'

'Nothing at all,' she agreed, nodding towards Rissa, who was walking with Betty not far in front of us. 'Maybe if he comes back to visit her again, there might be a happy ending for you, too?'

'Me? What do you mean by that?'

'Well, a highly fanciable man of foreign extraction with a sexy accent. According to you, divorced. Family ties to Rowan Vale. I mean, come on. It practically writes itself. You're young, free, and single—'

'I have no idea if he's divorced! I was just daydreaming. He could be happily married to Rissa's mum and about to celebrate his thirtieth wedding anniversary for all I know. Although,' I added, 'he wasn't wearing a wedding ring.'

'You checked?'

'Not on purpose. I just couldn't help noticing.' I cleared my throat. 'Anyway, I'm far too old for all that stuff. I'm fifty-two!'

'That's not old,' Amelia said with a laugh. 'Stop

putting obstacles in your own path. About time you had a bit of romance in your life after the crappy time you had with Luke Bannerman.'

'What about you and Tully?' I asked mischievously.

'What about us?' She shook her head. 'If you're hinting that we should get married, you're wasting your time. I've told you before, Tully and I are very happy as we are. He's got his life, and I've got mine, and when those two lives collide, it's very lovely and a lot of fun, but he's hardly vicar's husband material, and I'm definitely not milking goats for anyone.'

I laughed. Tully was Amelia's boyfriend, for want of a better word, of eight years. He lived on a small farm on the outskirts of Kingsford Wold, where he kept goats and made cheese and ice cream from their milk. It sold well in the local shops, and he was a busy man, which suited Amelia as she was pretty busy, too.

Their unconventional relationship was one more thing for Silas to complain about and, according to Aunt Polly, he did – frequently and very loudly.

'No.' Amelia gave a contented sigh. 'I love my life just as it is, and I wouldn't change a thing. You, on the other hand...'

'Feel exactly the same,' I said firmly.

'Really? I always got the impression you liked

being married. Don't let Luke Bannerman put you off, Shona. I'd hate for him to rob you of any chance of lasting happiness.'

'It's not that,' I said. 'It's just – well, I'm happy too.'

And I was, finally. After I'd signed the divorce papers, I'd wasted a whole year wallowing in misery and moping around the house we'd bought in Birmingham to be closer to Luke's work, until one day, I suddenly thought, *What the heck am I doing? I've got a crappy job in a not-very-good cafe, the kids' schools are rubbish, and I hate this house.*

I'd nervously called Dad and asked him how he felt about me staying with him while I figured out what to do next and, to my relief, he'd been over the moon. The kids were delighted at the prospect of moving to Rowan Vale and seeing much more of their beloved grandad, so we packed up and headed to the Cotswolds.

Within two weeks, I was back working at the old family teashop. Within three years, I was manageress, when the woman hired to take Mum's place after she'd passed away decided she was ready for retirement. From that point, I'd never looked back.

'I've got my dad and Aunt Polly, and a job I love. Christie's happily married and I have two lovely granddaughters. And Pippa's doing well at the newspaper so...'

'So?'

'So why would I need anything else? Honestly, I'm the happiest I've ever been. There was a time, not long after the divorce, when I panicked a bit about ending up alone forever. But that panic's long gone. I love my life just the way it is. Why rock the boat?'

'As long as you mean that,' she said cautiously. 'Seriously, I'd hate for that man to take anything else from you.'

'He hasn't,' I said. 'He won't. Life's good and I'm going to make sure it stays that way.'

It had been a nice little interlude, feeling that flutter of attraction when Rissa's dad walked into the teashop, but that's all it was. Good to know I was still capable of feeling that way about a man, but I had no interest in taking things any further.

I was just relieved I wasn't poor Rissa, struggling to get over someone who no longer loved her. Been there, done that. Never again.

7

POLLY

Polly was intentionally hiding from Shona – and from Jimmy. She was feeling all mixed up inside and wasn't at all convinced that she'd be able to hide her feelings from her loving family.

That, she knew, would lead to all sorts of questions because they'd be concerned about her, and she really didn't want to worry them. She also didn't want to answer their questions. She wasn't convinced she *could* answer them, because how could she tell them the truth? That had been locked away a long, long time ago. She couldn't change the story now. It was far too late.

Oh! Why did he have to come here? That man. That man with the voice and the accent. That man who, it turned out, was related to Gerhard Janssen. His grandson, no less.

Polly had, after many years and a great deal of angst, managed to lock that part of her past into a box, along with the truth. She'd blocked all the pain and anguish that had come with it and focused on the here and now, because what else was there?

It had been one heck of a shock to find herself continuing after her death – although living in Rowan Vale, there had always been a possibility that she'd become a ghost. All the residents were aware of that chance, after all. Once she'd got her head around the fact that she wasn't going anywhere anytime soon, she'd focused on building an afterlife for herself. She'd determined to find nuggets of happiness anywhere she could. After all, nothing could hurt her now. She'd been through the very worst things and survived, in a fashion.

The trouble was, seeing and hearing Rissa's father last week had changed things. His presence had chipped away at the barrier she'd constructed between herself and the past, and all sorts of feelings were swirling around inside her.

Knowing how sensitive Shona was to her moods, Polly had decided she needed to keep well away until she could get a grip on her emotions and calm down enough to put on a brave face. That meant leaving her home – for now at least.

All those years ago, after Charlie's death, she'd rattled around in their cottage for a few months but had decided she needed a fresh start. Of course, her mum and dad had wanted her to move back to Starling Cottage where they could take care of her, but she'd refused. She wanted somewhere new where she could learn to be herself and come to terms with her new life as a war widow.

The flat above the teashop had been Mum's suggestion. It was in a bit of a state, but Sir Edward had agreed to let her off the rent for a few weeks, while she cleaned and tidied it up. Mum and Dad had mucked in, along with Norman. They'd helped her turn an empty, dusty space into a cosy and welcoming new home, and she'd moved in, hoping for a fresh start.

Since her death, she'd been quite contented there, but it was now proving to be a bit too handy for Shona to pop in. Polly had decided she needed to find somewhere else to hang out, so she'd thrown herself on the mercy of Edwardian station porter, Percy Swain, a kindly soul who lived in a cottage on the edge of the village.

The cottage was rented by a middle-aged couple, the Armstrongs, who worked at the mill museum, and as neither of them were originally from this part of the country, and had no blood ties to any ghosts here, both Percy and Polly were free to come and go as they pleased without any fear of being seen or heard.

Percy confessed that he liked living with the couple a lot better now that their children had grown up and left home. He hadn't been keen on the noise they'd made when they were growing up and couldn't believe the racket that passed for modern music. Also, he was firmly of the belief that youngsters had lost all respect for their elders, and if he'd been able to, he'd have given those kids a clip around the ear on many occasions. Worst of all, there'd been no spare bedroom, so he'd found himself sleeping in the attic, which was hardly becoming for a man of his age.

Polly had asked him why he hadn't looked for alternative accommodation, but he'd explained that he and his wife had lived here back in the day, and he didn't want to leave because this was where all his memories were.

Polly could understand that in a way, but she'd been the opposite with Charlie. She'd wanted to get away from a home that had seemed full of sadness to her. A place which, no matter how much she tried to fill the rooms with flowers and music, always felt drab and empty and way too quiet, now her husband was gone.

She supposed everyone was different.

Anyway, there were now two spare bedrooms at the cottage, and Percy was quite happy for Polly to stay a while until she 'sorted herself out' as he put it.

She liked Percy. He didn't ask awkward questions and never pushed her to explain why she'd left her own perfectly good flat to come here. He amused her, too. He would check his pocket watch every morning, even though it always showed the same time, and leave for 'work', as if he was still a proper member of staff and badly needed. Bless him, he was no use to anyone these days, but the way he carried on, you'd have thought he was running the railway station.

Although, when she thought about it, she supposed he did have one use. He was always on hand to break up the fights between Ronnie and Bill – two young soldiers from the Great War, who'd been fighting nonstop on the station platform for as long as she could remember. Percy considered them a disgrace to their uniform and was forever telling them off.

She supposed it gave them all something to do. Much like her spending so many hours each day in the teashop, where she'd watch Shona or one of the other ladies baking, muttering words of advice or shaking her head if she didn't think they were doing things the way she'd have done them. She often peered closely at the tables after they'd been wiped, checking they were clean enough. And she loved sitting in on the discussions in the kitchen, when new recipes were being tried and new menus worked out.

If she was honest, though, it could get a bit depressing. She didn't like to keep pestering Shona, so mostly kept her kitchen visits to when her great-niece was serving out front. She couldn't communicate with the other staff members, so her suggestions and advice went unheeded. She couldn't run a finger over the tables and counter to check they'd been properly cleaned. And she couldn't play any active role in team meetings or discussions, because it wasn't fair on Shona if only she could hear her, as it would distract her from what everyone else was saying.

Mostly, Polly sat at the tables and eavesdropped on the customers' conversations. Part of her thought it wasn't proper, and she had a good idea what her mum would have had to say about it.

On the other hand, she was discreet. She rarely told Shona and Jimmy what she'd heard, never mentioned anything to Pippa, and wouldn't dream of saying a word to Callie or Lawrie, so she didn't see what harm it could do.

Telling other ghosts was a different matter, obviously, but what difference would that make? They were the souls of discretion. They had no bloody choice.

She liked it best when one of them came into the teashop to see what was going on. It was good to have someone to talk to, and she'd spent many happy hours sitting at a table conversing with Percy, or Walter, or one of the other ghosts.

The one she was fondest of was young Millie, who'd been a waitress here when she was alive back in the 1960s. Sadly, Millie had died when she was seventeen, but she still sometimes popped into the teashop to see how things were going and loved a gossip with Polly when she did.

But even though Millie had seen a lot in the sixty years or so since she'd died, to Polly, she was still a teenager, and not someone she could confide in. Not about her past. Not about the thing that was eating away at her right now.

Sitting on the front lawn of Percy's cottage, she hugged her knees and gave a big sigh. She couldn't settle. And she couldn't hide out here forever. Sooner or later, she was going to have to confront the Big

Scary Thing that was her past. She just wasn't sure where to start.

Without warning, the thought came to her that she knew *exactly* where to start. It was time to return to the farm.

She hadn't been there since before *that* day – the day she'd died. The thought of it made her shudder. That whole area was somewhere she avoided, and yet she knew if there was to be any peace, she had to face up to it.

Maybe it wouldn't be as traumatic as she'd feared. Maybe it would be fine, and she'd wonder what all the fuss had been about.

Her heart couldn't thud. Her pulse couldn't race. And yet, as Polly got to her feet, she would have sworn her body was reacting in exactly that way. It just showed you what your mind could do – conjuring up all these feelings and their accompanying reactions.

'It's not real,' she muttered to herself. 'You're already dead. Nothing can hurt you now.'

Yet she knew that facing the farm again *was* going to hurt her. And as for the woods... She would never go near them. Just the thought of it was almost enough to convince her she was about to be sick.

'Okay,' she said, straightening and jutting out her chin in defiance of her own thoughts and fears.

'Rowan Farm it is. You can do this, girl. And once you've done it, you can go back home, cos there'll be no reason to dodge our Shona. You'll be in control again.'

She headed through the garden gate and marched purposefully down the lane. She'd started her mission now, and nothing was going to stop her. Especially not the ghosts of the past.

She gave a half-smirk. Ghosts of the past. There was irony for you. It would almost be funny.

If it wasn't so bloody terrifying.

8

'So that's one egg and cress sandwich, one ham and tomato sandwich, one cup of tea, and one elderflower cordial,' I said, reading back the order I'd jotted on my pocket notebook and smiling at the young couple who were seated at a corner table. 'Anything else?'

'We'll definitely be treating ourselves to cake later,' the woman said with feeling. 'But that's all for now, thanks.'

I nodded and headed over to the counter where an elderly couple were waiting to pay. It had been a busy morning at the teashop, and it was only going to get busier. Next week, the school summer holidays started, and the village would be heaving. I knew from recent experience that at the busiest times, I'd be having to turn customers away, as I just didn't have the room for them.

Really, I mused, we needed another place to eat in Rowan Vale. The Quicken Tree served tasty pub lunches and evening meals, but we needed somewhere like this, where people could pop in and get snacks and hot drinks or sweet treats.

There were the Victory Tearooms at the station, of course, but not everyone caught the train to the estate, and so missed them entirely. And there was a more formal vibe in that establishment anyway, which wasn't to everyone's liking. I'd have a think about it. Speak to Callie and Brodie. I hated to think that anyone might be put off visiting Rowan Vale because there was a perception they wouldn't be able to get anything to eat.

I took payment from the elderly couple and gave them their receipt, then passed the order to Paige in the kitchen. Returning to the counter, I glanced up as the bell above the door jingled and the smile on my face faltered as my heart skipped rather alarmingly.

What the heck is wrong with you? I guessed my face had gone pink. I could feel my face burning. *Honestly, anyone would think you were sixteen again and George Michael had just walked in.*

'We meet again,' I said brightly as Rissa's dad approached the counter. *Seriously, Shona? Good grief.*

He frowned briefly then nodded. 'Ah yes. You were here when I came in before. Hello again.'

'Hello. I'm Shona.'

I watched myself, in some horror and confusion, hold out my hand for him to shake. In a cafe! Why would he even...

Before I could drop my hand, though, he took it and shook it firmly.

'Max,' he said, not seeming at all surprised by my bizarre behaviour. 'Max Meyer.'

'Shona Bannerman. Or Deakin. Maybe. Well, not yet anyway, but soon, I might be. Not that I'm getting married! Lord, no! I mean, I might be going back to my maiden name because I'm divorced, you see. Not recently divorced. Quite a while now, actually. Did you want to order something?'

Kill me now.

He blinked, clearly not certain what to make of my condensed life story, then cleared his throat. 'I, er, I'm meeting my daughter for lunch. Do you have a table free?'

I glanced around. 'There's one just by the window. You're lucky, because the customers have only just paid and left. I haven't had chance to clean the table yet but if you'd like to sit down, I'll see to that now.'

'I can see you're busy, so I wanted to check that you don't mind me waiting for Rissa. I'm a bit early.'

'Of course not. Would you like to order a drink while you're waiting?'

He hesitated. 'Thank you. Perhaps a pot of tea would be good.'

'Coming right up.'

He headed over to the table by the window and I hurried into the kitchen, grabbed a tray, a cloth and some spray and went over to where he was sitting.

We didn't speak as I piled the dirty crockery and cutlery onto the tray and placed it carefully on a spare chair before wiping down the table, but I was acutely aware that he was watching me, and it's a wonder I didn't knock the chair and send the tray flying or squirt him in the eye with disinfectant spray.

'Very nice touch,' Max said quietly, picking up one of the menus that stood on the table. We'd had them designed to look like ration books as it contributed to the 1940s experience. We had Glenn Miller music playing softly in the background, too, adding to the ambience; judging by the compliments and good reviews we often received from customers, they were welcome touches.

The young women who'd been sitting at the table next to him got up to leave at that moment, so I quickly cleared and cleaned their table, too, just to prove to him how efficient and organised I could actually be.

'Tea won't be a moment,' I told him, picking up the tray and carrying it back into the kitchen with huge relief.

I was literally trembling. It was crazy. What on earth had come over me? Okay, I hadn't exactly had a thrilling love life for the last year or so. Or decade or so. Well, I hadn't had any love life whatsoever, but even so, there was no need for this, was there? I was embarrassing myself. I was a grandma, for goodness' sake! Grandmas didn't behave in this juvenile fashion. Did they?

Paige handed me a tray with the young couple's order on it and frowned at me. 'Are you okay? You look like you're about to throw up. Hey, don't even think about it! I've enough to do without mopping up after you.'

'Cheers for the sympathy,' I said, 'and I'm fine. Just came over a bit hot and bothered, that's all. Could you serve this, please? I've got to take payment from some customers and make a pot of tea for the gentleman by the window.'

'Sure. But are you certain you're okay? If it's a bug, you'll have to go home, you know.'

'It's not a bug,' I promised her. 'And who's in charge here, anyway?'

She grinned and shook her head then took the tray from me. As she delivered the sandwiches and drinks to the couple at the corner table, I collected payment from the two young women, risking a sly glance at Max Meyer as I did so.

He was gazing out of the window and looked deep in thought. I glanced at my watch as I went into the kitchen to make his tea. Ten to twelve. Rissa would probably be here in about fifteen or twenty minutes. He really was early. I wondered how far he'd come to visit her. Well, at least she'd agreed to meet him so whatever was going on in their lives, it seemed they were on talking terms, which was good. Maybe I'd got a bit carried away with my estranged father/daughter theories.

I managed to serve him tea without spilling any of it, and kept my mouth zipped as I did so, merely nodding when he politely thanked me.

It was a relief when the door opened again, and Dad walked in. I hadn't been expecting to see him, so it was a pleasant surprise.

'Grab that table,' I called over to him, indicating

the only spare one remaining. The one next to Max actually, but that was hardly my fault, was it? I didn't want him to wander over to the counter, allowing someone else to walk in and pinch it, leaving him with nowhere to sit. He was my dad, after all.

'What brings you here?' I asked as I wandered over to speak to him, trying very hard to ignore the man sitting so close by. 'Do you want some lunch?'

'I may as well have some while I'm here,' he said, 'but really, I was hoping to see our Polly. She hasn't been near the cottage all week, and I miss her smiling face.'

I frowned. 'Actually, Dad, I haven't seen her either. Odd, isn't it?'

'You haven't? You mean she hasn't been in the teashop? Have you been up to her flat?'

'Of course I have. I've dusted and polished, and opened the windows to air the place, and switched the lamp on at closing and off in the mornings like I always do. No sign of her. It's not like her, is it?'

'It isn't. You've got me worried now.'

I gave him a wry smile. 'Well, I was worried too, at first, but it's not like anything can happen to her, is it? She'll turn up when she's ready, no doubt. In the meantime, what would you like to eat?'

Dad glanced at the menu. 'I'm not that hungry. How about a nice cup of tea?'

'You need to eat,' I said sternly. 'Would you like some soup? We have leek and potato or stilton and broccoli today.'

He liked stilton, and I suspected he wouldn't turn that down. I was right.

'Sounds smashing. Stilton and broccoli, and a nice, crusty bread roll. Ooh, and have you got any of that lemon sponge cake I like for afters?'

I grinned. Sounded like Dad had got over his worries about Aunt Polly already.

'I'll put some aside,' I promised with a wink, and steadfastly refusing to look in Max's direction, I went back to the kitchen.

I'd no sooner served Dad than the lunchtime rush began in earnest, and I was kept busy collecting orders, serving, taking payments and cleaning tables, while Paige worked frantically to keep on top of things in the kitchen, aided, thankfully, by Susie, who'd arrived ten minutes late for her shift, with huge apologies and an excuse we really didn't have the time to listen to. We knew there had to be a good reason, though. Susie was reliable and honest, and I wasn't about to have a go at her for being late on one occasion. We were managing. It was fine.

It was about half-past twelve when I remembered Rissa and realised I hadn't taken any order for her. I glanced over to the table at the window and was amazed to see Dad and Max sitting together, Dad having abandoned his own table and joined Max at his.

Puzzled, I went over to see what was going on, and to enquire if Max would like something to eat.

'Perhaps I will have a coffee,' he said with a sigh.

'Is Rissa running late?' I enquired politely.

'Rissa,' he said heavily, 'is not coming. She sent me a text message to say she has been held up at work and will be eating her lunch on the go at the farm instead of coming into the village. She suggested I make it another day.'

'That's...' I steadied myself, not wanting to take sides in something I knew nothing about, 'a shame.'

'Indeed. Your father and I got chatting and we decided we may as well share a table to free up space for other customers. You've been very busy here.'

'That's very thoughtful of you both. Thank you. Would you like some lunch?' I asked him. 'Rissa might not be coming, but you still need to eat.'

'I'm not very hungry now,' he said briefly. 'Coffee will be fine.'

'What about you, Dad?' I asked, knowing the answer already. 'Ready for that lemon cake?'

'Always, pet,' he told me. He beamed at Max. 'You want to have a slice of that, you know. Never tasted anything like it. My daughter is a fantastic baker, just like her mum. If I were you, I'd grab a slice while there's some left. It will go down a treat with a coffee – although if you ask me, it would go down even better with a nice cup of tea. That's what I'll have, love,' he said, smiling at me. 'Lemon cake and a pot of tea.'

'Perhaps,' Max said slowly, 'I'll have the same. Tea and cake is always welcome, and your father has made it sound irresistible.'

'All right then,' I said, feeling pleased for some stupid reason. 'I'll be right back.'

Susie was in full flow in the kitchen, taking over the cooking and food prep from Paige, who was now working the front of house.

'Why don't you take half an hour for your own lunch?' Paige suggested. 'You might as well sit with your dad while he's here. I'll take my break after you.'

I hesitated. Normally, I'd have happily agreed, but that would mean sitting at a table with not only Dad, but with Max, too. I wasn't sure I could deal with that. I wasn't sure he'd want me to, anyway.

'Don't turn it down,' Paige advised. 'You might not get another chance.'

'Okay.' What was I being so hesitant about anyway? If Max hadn't been here, I'd have jumped at the chance of a natter with Dad. Why should I let a stranger get in the way of that?

Dad beamed at me as I approached the table, carrying a tray with a mug of coffee, two pots of tea, three slices of lemon cake and a plate of cheese sandwiches. Max smiled, too, which annoyingly made my heart flutter again. I'd end up on medication at this rate.

'Your father can't stop singing the praises of this lemon cake,' he informed me, as he helped me unload the tray. 'It looks delicious. And you make this yourself?'

'I'm quite good at cakes,' I said modestly. 'Not quite as good with pastry but we can't be great at everything, can we?' I nodded at the spare chair. 'Do you mind if I join you? It's my lunch break.'

'Course not, love. I've been having a nice chat with Max, here. Do you know he only lives in Chipping Royston? He's a teacher at the academy.'

'You are?' I slid into my seat, grateful that Dad had opened the conversation so there'd be no awkward silence.

Max nodded. 'Yes. I teach German, and I'm also head of the language department.'

'German? So, is that where you're from? Germany?'

I glanced at the framed photograph of Winston Churchill and the propaganda posters that adorned the teashop walls and wondered how he felt about those.

'It is. From a small town near Hannover, actually. But I moved to England in 1997 when my wife got a job at a hospital in London.'

'Oh, really?' Married then. Not that it mattered. Not in the slightest.

'She was a surgeon,' Dad said, sounding impressed. 'Proper power couple, eh?'

'Hardly that,' Max said quietly. 'But she was very good at her job, and I was proud of her.'

Dad nodded sympathetically. 'She passed away six years ago, Shona,' he told me. He gave Max a rueful smile. 'I know how that feels. I still miss Debbie every minute of every day. She was like your Nina – taken far too soon. Life can be very unfair at times.'

It brought me no pleasure to discover that Max was single after all. The sadness in his eyes was enough to make me realise that he still wasn't over his wife's death, and I wouldn't wish that on anyone. I'd seen how much Dad had struggled.

I nibbled my cheese sandwich, realising that if anything had happened to me, Luke would have moved on pretty quickly. I'd hardly been the love of his life.

'I'm sorry for your loss,' I said. 'It must have hit Rissa hard, too. She's still only young, after all.'

He nodded. 'Of course. Although, it must be said, she was always a daddy's girl.' He shook his head sadly. 'Hard to believe now, right? But when she was born, my Nina went straight back to work and I gave up my job to stay home and take care of our daughter. Rissa and I were very close. I was with her every day until she started school. Then I got another job in a local secondary school, and I was there until Nina died.'

I waited for him to continue but he didn't. There was a moment's silence and then, thankfully, someone's phone beeped. I say, someone's, but I knew it wasn't mine as I'd left it in the kitchen, and Dad didn't possess one, so it had to be Max's.

Sure enough, he fished in his jacket pocket and frowned at the screen, while I took a big bite out of my sandwich, realising I was hungry and running out of time.

His face broke into a proper, genuine smile which made him seem ten years younger, and he looked up at us, his eyes suddenly brighter.

'It's Rissa. She's changed her mind. She's coming here for lunch, after all, and she's on her way!'

'Aw, that's...' I stopped, aware that my cheeks were bulging with cheese sandwich. Not a good look.

'That's smashing,' Dad finished for me. 'I'm sure you two can sort out whatever it is needs sorting.'

'I wonder,' Max said, shaking his head. 'We were so close once, but now... I sometimes feel I hardly know her.'

'Dads and daughters, eh? You'll get through it, mate. And, trust me, it will be worth it. There's no finer bond than that between a father and his little girl.' Dad laid his hand over mine and squeezed it.

I swallowed my sandwich and smiled. 'Dad's right,' I said. 'I'm sure you two will patch it up. Whatever *it* is.'

I'm not sure if I'd meant that as a hint for him to tell us the problem, but if I had, it didn't work. Max merely shrugged and said, 'We'll see.'

But there was a look in his eyes I couldn't quite work out. Was it anxiety? Or sadness? Or annoyance? Perhaps all three. Whatever was going on with him and Rissa, it might take more than a quick lunch at the teashop to fix it.

9

POLLY

Polly stood at the farm gate and stared ahead of her at the farmhouse. It was so long since she'd been here but not much had changed. Clearly, it had been spruced up. The paintwork wasn't shabby and peeling as it had been back in her day, and it looked like the windows had been replaced. She was sure they used to have smaller panes of glass in them.

Even so, it was surprising how similar it looked to the farm in her memories. She supposed it was inevitable. After all, this place was run as a 1940s farm, so they'd hardly modernise it, would they?

She got quite a start when she saw Erin striding towards the house, her red hair pinned up in that familiar vintage style, dressed in dungarees and sturdy shoes, and a short-sleeved, white shirt. She was used to seeing the 'land girls' around the village but spotting her out of the blue like that in this environment – it gave her quite a turn and took her back to a time she had such mixed feelings about.

Erin waved to someone and Polly narrowed her eyes. Rissa was sitting on an upturned bucket in the farmyard. Erin stopped to speak to her for a moment, then left her to it, walking into the house while Rissa stayed where she was.

Funny place to sit. What was the girl up to?

Polly went through the motions of taking a deep breath, even though it was an impossible feat. Funny how your reactions stayed the same, she mused. She could swear she had a dodgy tummy right now, but of course she couldn't possibly have. It was just her nerves playing tricks on her.

'Just walk through the gate and up the path,' she muttered. 'It's okay. It's not the same.'

Of course it wasn't. Helen and Alf weren't there, for one thing. The land girls, Cissie, Joan and Kathleen weren't there either, nor Dad and their Norman.

Anselm wasn't there.

Gerhard wasn't there.

The pain swirled through her again and she closed her eyes. She didn't want to remember that night but being here after all this time, she couldn't help herself.

'Please! Please don't shoot!'

Polly wrapped her arms around herself as if to shield her poor body from the bullet. Too late. Far too late. Not that her arms could have saved her. The bullet that had penetrated her body had entered through her back as she ran. She would still have fallen to the floor. She would still have felt the cold, hard ground beneath her. She would still have closed her eyes as she wondered why it had to end like this.

She spun round. She couldn't do it. She couldn't go back to the farm after all. This had been a terrible mistake, and she couldn't imagine what she'd been thinking. Why put herself through it, after all? She'd managed to avoid Rowan Farm for nearly eighty years, and if she had her way, she'd avoid it for another eighty.

'Rissa!'

Polly hesitated at the call. Slowly, she turned round again, seeing Betty heading out of the house and towards Gerhard's granddaughter.

She saw Betty speaking to Rissa, and the girl shaking her head in response. Betty folded her arms and clearly wasn't about to take no for an answer. What were they arguing about?

Curiosity got the better of Polly and, determined not to be such a coward, she marched through the closed gate and down the path towards the farmhouse.

'A packet of crisps?'

That was the phrase she heard first as she approached, and she felt a moment's irritation. Is that what they were arguing about? Really?

'It'll do.'

'Don't be so daft,' Betty said. 'I couldn't believe it when Erin told me. What are you larking at, sitting out here on a bucket with a packet of crisps for your lunch? I thought you were meeting your dad at the teashop?'

'So what if I was? I can change my mind, can't I?'

'Well, a bag of crisps isn't going to keep you going all afternoon, so I'll ask you again, are you going to come inside so I can make you a proper lunch?'

'I told you. I'm not hungry.'

Polly edged her way towards the two of them, forgetting momentarily that they could neither see nor hear her. Rissa looked defiant, but also sad. Betty, meanwhile, wore that mother-hen look of concern that she'd clearly inherited from her grandmother, Helen.

'Look, I'm not being funny, but why don't you just

go and see your dad, eh? Whatever it is that's gone on between the two of you, I'm sure it can be fixed.'

'I wouldn't bet on it,' Rissa muttered.

Polly rolled her eyes. She was a moody little mare, that one. Mind you...

She leaned forward, peering at Rissa more closely. Were those tears in her eyes?

Evidently, Betty had spotted them, too, because she said kindly, 'Don't upset yourself, lovely. Look, I don't understand why you didn't tell your dad that you were working here, or why it had to be such a big secret, but the fact that he came here to see you to try to sort this out must mean he cares about you, right?'

When Rissa didn't reply, Betty eyed her for a moment, then her face straightened and she said hesitantly, 'He's – he's not a *bad* man, is he? I mean, you're not afraid of him or anything? Because you can tell me if he is and me and Nick will see him off, no problem.'

Rissa's head jerked up immediately. 'Of course he's not! My dad's a lovely man! He would never hurt me...'

'Well then.' Betty looked and sounded relieved, as her expression softened once again. 'That's good to hear. But if that's the case—'

'He's not the same!' Rissa burst out. 'You don't understand.'

'Well, try me. I'd like to understand but if you won't explain, how can I?'

Rissa sighed. 'It's complicated. It's just, he's not the same person since Mum died. He used to be fun, you know? And kind and loving. But since then, he's different. Colder. And he never lets me in any more. We used to be so close, but now it's like we're strangers.'

'Ah.' Betty nodded, her eyes warm with sympathy, and Polly felt a pang herself for this young girl who was clearly at a loss to understand her father's change of mood.

'Don't look at me like that,' Rissa said. 'I know what you're thinking: *Well, he's grieving*, and I get that. I do. I'm grieving, too. But it's been six years! We have to move on, right? And the thing is, in Dad, it's turned into something more. An obsession.'

'What sort of obsession?' Betty asked warily, and Polly had a sudden image of Rissa's father becoming a male version of Miss Havisham: forever trapped in the past, sitting alone at the dining table while spiders spun their webs around him and food festered and rotted in front of him.

Rissa shrugged. 'It's complicated. Gran passed away fourteen years before Mum, and Dad had to go back to Germany to sort through her belongings with his sister, my Aunt Gisela. When he came back, he had Gran's diaries with him, and he put them away for safe keeping. They didn't really interest him then, but after Mum died, he read them and that's when he started to change. He got quite bitter and—' She broke off. 'Oh, I shouldn't even be saying all this. He'd hate me telling you, of all people!'

'What do you mean, me "of all people"?' Betty asked, surprised.

'Never mind. Dad's just obsessing about something that he can't change and it's not healthy, and I get why he's doing it. Focusing on the distant past stops him from brooding about Mum. He can't deal with his grief over her death, so he's transferring all his attention to something else.'

'Crikey,' Betty said. 'Get you, Sigmund Freud. Who told you all that?'

'My therapist.'

'You had a therapist?'

'Like I said,' Rissa said heavily, 'I was grieving, too. The people at uni were great. They put me in touch with someone and she helped me come to terms with losing Mum. I just wish Dad would have seen someone, too, but he refused point-blank.'

Polly's eyebrows lifted in surprise. Rissa had gone

to university? Who'd have thought it. She wasn't sure about therapists and the like, though she'd heard that they were the 'in' thing these days. Back in her day, you'd just had to grit your teeth and get on with things.

Although, looking back at the suffering that had gone on, she thought maybe it would have been much better if they'd all had therapy. God knows, even the small amount of help given to the returning soldiers was woefully inadequate...

'Well.' Betty seemed at a loss to know what else to say. She stood, watching Rissa finish the last of her crisps, then reached out a hand to take the empty packet. 'You know, I understand what you're saying about your dad transferring his focus to something else, but it doesn't alter the fact that he's in pain. And maybe you're the one person who can help him through that pain. You said you and he were close, so it strikes me that he needs you now more than ever. And if anyone can get through whatever barrier he's put up to protect himself, it will be you.'

Rissa pushed back her blonde hair but didn't reply. She stared at the ground.

'He's reaching out to you, isn't he? He's here, in the village, right now. And it's the second time he's visited recently, so clearly, you matter a lot to him.'

'Because he found out I worked here, and I'd lied about that!'

'Whatever the reason – and I have to admit, I'm baffled why you'd do that – but whatever the reason, he's here. And even though you pushed him away, he came back. Maybe, in his own way, he's trying to break down that barrier? If you turn your back on him now, lovely, who else has he got?'

Slowly, Rissa lifted her head, and Polly put her hands to her chest in compassion as she saw the tears rolling down the girl's face. Maybe she wasn't such a little madam after all. Maybe she was just carrying a heavy burden she couldn't talk about. Polly understood that feeling all too well.

'There now, wipe them tears away and go and see your dad, eh? If nothing else, you get yourself a proper lunch. And mind, I shall call Shona and check that you've eaten. Can't have you working here this afternoon on an empty stomach.'

Rissa gave a half-laugh. 'He might have gone by now.'

'Only one way to find out, isn't there?'

Rissa sniffed and pulled her mobile phone out of her dungarees pocket. 'I'm only carrying it cos it's my lunch hour,' she said hastily.

'Never mind that now,' Betty assured her. 'Just call your dad and tell him you're on your way.'

Rissa hesitated, then quickly tapped out a message on her phone.

'I hate calling,' she said. 'Makes me nervous.'

'You youngsters.' Betty shook her head. 'Don't know how to have a proper conversation these days. It's all gifs and memes and text speak. Oh yes,' she added as Rissa grinned. 'I know all the lingo! I'm down with the kids, me. No need to look so surprised. I'm only in my early fifties, you know, though the way you and Erin look at me sometimes, I'm sure you think I'm in my nineties.'

Polly saw Rissa jump slightly as her phone beeped.

'It's Dad,' she told Betty. 'He's still at the teashop. He says he'll wait.'

'Well, off you go then,' Betty said, making a shooing motion towards her. 'And remember what I said about getting something to eat.'

'Thanks, Betty,' Rissa said awkwardly.

She turned and headed up the path and Polly hesitated. She looked back at Betty, who stood watching the young girl, shaking her head slightly.

'Funny onion, that one,' Betty murmured. 'Seems like not moving on from a lost love runs in the family.'

Polly nodded, as if Betty could see her. Rissa's dad might be hanging on to his grief for his wife, but Rissa had hung on to her feelings for Brodie just as tightly. Maybe it was time they both let go.

As Betty returned to the farmhouse, Polly made up her mind. Shona would be at the teashop, but it couldn't be helped. Polly wanted to know more about this grandson of Gerhard's and the tricky relationship he had with his own daughter.

There'd been no happy ending to her own story.

She desperately needed there to be one for this.

10

POLLY

As she glanced through the teashop window, Polly was taken aback to discover that not only was Shona sitting at a table eating her lunch with Rissa's father, of all people, but Jimmy was there also. She hadn't been expecting that and hoped they wouldn't make a fuss about where she'd been all week.

Following Rissa into the teashop, she saw Jimmy glance in her direction and felt a pang of guilt as his face lit up in obvious relief. Mindful of Rissa and her dad, he said nothing, but managed a discreet wink in her direction, while Shona nodded slightly in acknowledgement.

Polly knew she shouldn't have avoided them all week. They were her family, and they'd have understood. She just hadn't wanted to inflict her misery upon them, especially when she couldn't explain what was causing her to feel all these unexpected emotions, nor why it was Rissa's father who'd stirred them up after all this time.

Anyway, even if she *had* explained the little she could to them, they might have worried what effect the upcoming 1940s weekend would have on her, and knowing those two, they'd have mentioned it to Callie. The last thing Polly wanted was to heap more stress on that poor girl.

She gave Jimmy and Shona bright smiles to reassure them that all was well and slipped into a spare chair at a neighbouring table, close enough that she could eavesdrop on their conversation.

Rissa's dad, she noticed, got to his feet to greet his daughter, which she thought was very polite and respectable of him.

Rissa smiled awkwardly at him. 'Sorry about the mix-up, Dad.'

'It doesn't matter. You're here now,' he said. He waved a hand around the table. 'I expect you know Jimmy and Shona.'

'Only in passing,' Rissa said, blushing slightly. She looked a bit bewildered that her father was sharing a table with them and Polly felt the same. Why on earth was her Jimmy sitting with this fella? She supposed Shona was there because of her dad, or maybe it was the other way around?

As Rissa took a seat, Shona tactfully announced that she'd better be getting back to work.

'Don't go on my account,' Rissa said, though she didn't sound as if she really wanted Shona to stay.

'Lunch break's over,' Shona said with a forced smile. 'Back to work for me, I'm afraid.'

Jimmy cleared his throat. 'Yes, and I'd better be getting back home. I've had my little wander for the day, and I've treated myself to that lemon sponge cake, so I'll take my leave. Nice to meet you, Max. Rissa.'

'Thank you so much for your company,' Max (so that was his name!) said, shaking Jimmy's hand. 'It's been a pleasure to talk to you.'

'Aw, you're very welcome. Maybe we'll catch up again, eh? I'm at Starling Cottage if you ever fancy a chat.'

'You're very kind,' Max said warmly, although he didn't make any mention of dropping by, Polly noticed.

As Jimmy headed towards the door, he discreetly jerked his head towards the door at Polly, and she followed him out of the teashop.

'Where you bin, Pol?' he asked, after glancing

round to make sure no tourists were watching. There
were a few locals in the vicinity, but he didn't bother
about those. Everyone in Rowan Vale was used to
people chatting to thin air. 'Me and Shona were getting worried about you. Not seen you all week.'

'Worried about me?' Polly hoped her laugh
sounded genuine. 'Why would you worry about me?
I'm fine.'

'So where have you been? Shona says you haven't
been at the flat when she's gone there to clean and air
it either. Not like you, Polly.'

'Between you and me,' she said, 'I've been staying
with old Percy Swain. You know, the station porter?
Bless him, he's fed up with Ronnie's and Bill's antics.
They're getting him down a bit, and he needed
cheering up, so I thought I'd keep him company. It
was nice for me, too. Sort of a holiday, like. Sorry to
worry you, Jimmy. I never thought.'

'Aw, that's okay,' he said, the worried creases in his
forehead smoothing immediately. 'Just glad you're all
right, that's all.'

'Well,' she said with a grin, 'apart from being dead,
I'm absolutely smashing.'

He grinned back. 'Will you be popping round later
then?'

Polly nodded. 'Yes, I'll come and see you and

Shona after tea, how's that? We'll have a proper catch-up, eh?'

'We will. See you soon, Pol.'

'Bye, love.'

She waited a moment as she watched him heading along the river path then she hurried back inside the teashop and slipped into an empty seat between Max and Rissa, just in time to hear Max protest, 'I'm not saying she's a bad person!'

'But that's exactly what you're saying,' Rissa snapped. 'Let me tell you something: if it wasn't for Betty, I wouldn't be sitting here with you right now. It was she who persuaded me to see you. Told me to see things from your point of view and try to fix our relationship. You ought to be thanking her!'

'You needed to be persuaded to see me?' he murmured, the hurt clear in his eyes.

'Well...' She shifted uncomfortably. 'What do you expect, Dad? I knew I'd get nothing but grief about working on the farm, and what's the first thing you start going on about the minute I sit down? Little digs about my crappy job and how I should be doing something better with my life than working for *those people*.'

Max massaged his temples for a moment. 'Rissa, you have a first-class honours degree in history, and here you are working as a fake land girl at some tourist attraction! What happened to you being a teacher? That's what you always wanted, remember? You loved your subject. You wanted to teach it at schools, to instil your passion for the subject into children. Why have you thrown your dreams away for *this*?'

'It's not forever,' she said sullenly. 'But I like it here. It's a beautiful place. Look around you.' She waved a hand at the window, indicating the pretty village that lay beyond. 'It was only supposed to be for six months, but I liked it, so I stayed.'

'And how long will you continue to work here?'

She shrugged. 'Until I don't want to any longer.'

He sighed and shook his head, clearly baffled. Polly couldn't help but feel a bit puzzled, too. Rissa had a first-class honours degree? Nothing wrong with working on a farm, of course. She'd done it herself for years and was very proud of the fact, but it did seem a bit odd that the girl had worked so hard to get a qualification to teach and had then thrown her dreams away for a job that needed no formal qualifications at all.

Paige arrived at the table. 'Would you like to order?' she enquired politely.

Max raised an eyebrow at his daughter. 'Hungry?'

'Just coffee will do,' she replied.

Paige grinned. 'Sorry. We've had a phone call from Betty, and she says we've to make sure you eat a proper lunch or you'll be fit for nothing this afternoon.'

Rissa sighed. 'Oh, all right. I'll have a sandwich then.'

'Cheese? Egg and cress? Ham and tomato? Roast beef and—'

'Cheese will be fine,' Rissa said. 'And don't forget the coffee.'

As Paige nodded, Max cleared his throat and gave Rissa a meaningful stare.

'Er, please,' she added, her cheeks turning pink with embarrassment.

'Just coffee for me, please,' Max said politely.

Paige smiled at him and returned to the kitchen. Polly thought that, whatever else he was, Max Meyer was well-mannered at least, and clearly tried to instil those same manners in his daughter.

After a few moments of silence, he said quietly, 'It's a nice place. The teashop, I mean. The staff are very friendly, and the owner seems to be a nice woman.'

'Owner?' Rissa asked sharply.

'The lady who was sitting here when you arrived.'

Rissa frowned. 'Shona's not the owner. She's the manager. This entire village is owned by – well, some girl who got lucky.'

Polly glared at her. *Some girl who got lucky* indeed! Just because Brodie had fallen for Callie, there was no need for Rissa to be so dismissive of her. And just when she was starting to feel sorry for her!

'Really?' Max asked, clearly surprised. 'Well, the manager then. She has a sense of humour, I think. The toilets,' he added, as Rissa gave him a puzzled look. 'There are squares of newspaper hung up in the cubicles. Thankfully, there is modern toilet roll there, too.'

'Oh, yeah.' Rissa nodded. 'We have little touches like that at the farm.'

At the mention of the farm, Max lowered his gaze. He fiddled awkwardly with a napkin for a moment, as if working out what to say next. 'You think our relationship needs fixing?' he asked at last.

Rissa's eyes widened. 'What?'

'You said, Betty told you to try to fix our relationship. Does it need fixing?'

'Well...' Rissa fiddled with her own napkin, her pink cheeks growing ever darker. 'Don't you?'

'I... It's been a hard few years, *mausi*,' he mumbled. 'We have had a lot to deal with, and we've been busy, too. I took the new job at Chipping Royston, and I moved house, and—'

'Left our family home behind.'

'I couldn't be there any longer, Rissa. I needed a fresh start. Everywhere I looked, there were memories of...' His voice trailed off and he shook his head.

Impulsively, Polly put her hand over his. Of course, he couldn't feel it, but she wanted to offer him sympathy in some small way. She understood all too well that urge to start again, away from all the painful reminders of a lost love. Hadn't she left the marital home after Charlie's death for that very reason? Max must have loved his wife very much.

'I know that, Dad. I'm sorry. I didn't mean...' Rissa sighed and sat up straight, throwing her napkin on the table. 'You're right. We've been busy. Your new job, new house, settling in at Chipping Royston, me graduating from uni, working, moving to London then moving here. It's a lot.'

'You know, you could still go back to university,' he said eagerly. 'You could do your teaching qualification. It's never too late.'

'Maybe I will one day. Or maybe I'll do something else.'

'Something else?'

'Yeah. I don't know what. I'm not sure I'm cut out for teaching.'

'But it's what you always wanted to do!'

'Things don't always work out how we planned, though, do they, Dad? Things change. People change. You just have to go with the flow. And here I am.'

His eyes narrowed and Polly knew he was still struggling to understand what she was doing here in the first place. He wasn't daft enough to jump straight into another argument, though. He was quiet for a few moments, considering his next words. She just hoped he'd pick wisely.

'It was very good of Betty to ring here and tell them to make sure you ate,' he said finally.

Polly gave a sigh of relief. Even Rissa couldn't find fault with that statement! She wondered suddenly why all this mattered to her so much. She felt invested in the happiness of these two people and, when she thought about it, that was just daft. They were strangers to her, after all.

And yet, although they had no idea of it, they were connected to her in a way they couldn't possibly imagine. She wanted – *needed* – them to work things out.

'I told you,' Rissa said cautiously, 'Betty's a good woman. Takes care of me. Takes care of all of us at the farm.'

'You live at the farmhouse?'

'No. I share a cottage on the farm with the others.'

Polly knew which cottage she was talking about. Rowan Cottage was an old farm labourer's dwelling, where Joan, Cissie and Kathleen had lived during the war. She'd been to some riotous parties there, as she recalled. Helen and Alf had been very good at turning a blind eye. In fact, Helen had attended a few of them herself, and they'd all had a proper giggle.

'What others?' Max asked sharply, dragging Polly's attention back to the present.

Rissa seemed to consider her answer, but then she shrugged and said, 'Erin, Bram and Lars.'

'Who are Bram and Lars?'

Polly wrinkled her nose. *Uh-oh.*

'They're the two lads who work on the farm with me. They play the German prisoners of war,' she said heavily.

'I see.' He bit his lip as he digested this information. 'That's a lot to unpack.'

'I don't see why.'

'For one thing, you're sharing a house with two men!'

'Dad, I'm twenty-six,' Rissa said impatiently. 'Even if I was having wild sex with them every night—'

'Larissa!'

'Even if I was,' she continued firmly, 'it would be none of your business. I'm a grown woman. As it happens, we're just mates. We work hard during the day, and we have a laugh in the evening, and it's all good. Okay?'

'Are you seeing one of these men?'

'No! I just told you, we're mates.'

'I see. And are you in a relationship with *anyone*?'

Rissa's gaze dropped to the table, and she muttered, 'Not any more.'

'So you were? Who was he?'

Polly rolled her eyes. *Give the girl a break!*

'It really doesn't matter,' Rissa said dully. 'And that's not what you want to ask, is it?'

'It isn't?'

'No, you want to ask me if Lars and Bram are German. Well, no, they're not, as it happens. They're Dutch. But before you start reading anything into that, I'll just tell you that last year, we had two Belgians masquerading as Italian PoWs, so don't start going on about prejudice again. I've told you, you're on the wrong track. Betty and Nick aren't like that. They have no prejudice towards Germans.'

'So you told them your parents were German?'

Rissa's blush returned. 'Well, no. But only because

it never came up. Why should it? I was born here in the UK, so why would I mention it?'

'Or maybe,' he said darkly, 'deep down, you knew how they would react.'

'You know something, Dad? You're completely insane!' Rissa pushed her chair back and half-stood, just as Paige arrived with their order.

'Sit down, Rissa. Please,' Max begged.

Rissa looked torn, but Polly had the idea that the cheese sandwiches had swayed her. Evidently, that bag of crisps hadn't filled her up, just as Betty had predicted.

Paige looked a bit awkward but, at Max's bidding, she placed the cups, plate and pots of coffee on the table, then left them to it.

'Look,' Rissa said flintily, 'it's not about nationality, okay? It's whoever applies for the job. We get a lot of international students here, keen to get some work experience in the UK for a few months. And, for your information, it's not Nick and Betty who hire them. It's the owner of the estate. If anyone's prejudiced around here, it's you.'

'I am not prejudiced!' Max said indignantly.

'Yes, you are. You're anti-British.'

'How can you say that? I've lived here nearly thirty

years! I've worked here. I've raised my daughter here. I love this country. You know this, Rissa.'

'All right,' she said grudgingly, 'but you're anti-Rowan Vale.'

'I am not anti-Rowan Vale. But you must understand how I feel? Those diaries—'

'Oh!' Rissa flung herself back in her chair. 'Those bloody diaries! I wish you'd never read them. You're obsessed. Look, Dad, you have no proof that your grandad was badly treated here. Just a few entries in your mum's diaries and you've pounced on her words and made something huge out of nothing.'

Polly leaned closer. They were talking about Gerhard and his time in Rowan Vale!

'That's not so. My mother nursed her father in his final years.' Max shook his head sadly. 'He said such awful things about that time. He *cried*, Rissa. He cried when he spoke of Rowan Vale. And it was only in his final few weeks that he mentioned the place at all. He never talked about it at all before then. Don't you think that's strange?'

'No, Dad, I don't. You surely know as well as I do that men who went through the war seldom spoke about it afterwards. It's well documented. A way of coping with the things they saw.'

'But that's just it! My grandfather did speak of it!

He spoke of his capture in Normandy. Of being taken to a prisoner of war camp just a few miles from here. He spoke about his fellow prisoners, and about the camp guards, and what life was like in there. But he never, ever mentioned Rowan Vale. Not until he was dying. Now why do you think that was?'

'Maybe he just forgot about it?'

'Forgot? Don't be ridiculous, Rissa. You said yourself, soldiers did not talk about the things that distressed them because it was too much for them, and silence was their way of coping. What was so bad about Rowan Vale that he could bring himself to tell us about the horrors of Normandy, but could not mention this place? Tell me that.'

Polly covered her face with her hands as Rissa gasped, 'Dad, he was rambling! He was confused. You said so yourself. You went to see him before he died and you said half of what he said didn't make any sense, remember?'

'I should have listened more. I should have paid closer attention. I wish I had.'

'The only reason you're paying any attention now is because you don't want to acknowledge what's really hurting you. Face it, you don't want to think about Mum so you're switching all your emotions to this ridiculous vendetta against Betty and Rowan

Vale. You know, deep down, that there's nothing to it.'

'If that's the case,' he said coldly, 'why did you come here? What were you looking for, eh? It's some coincidence that you find a job here, of all places. I refuse to believe that you're not here for a reason.'

'I'm here because the job was advertised, and I thought it would be interesting. I'll admit I thought it was cool that it was where Great-Grandad was put to work during the war, but that's as far as it goes. You know I love history. I thought working at a living history village would be good experience, and I was right. But it could just as easily have been a job at the mill museum, or here, waiting tables. It didn't have to be the actual farm. I'm not that hung up on the past, unlike you.'

'That may be the case,' Max said, 'but if so, why are you still here? You said yourself that people come for a few months' work experience, and you only intended to be here for six months, yet you've been here a year and a half. Why?'

Polly's gaze slid slowly over to Rissa, and she felt a stab of compassion for the girl who had suddenly gone pale.

'I told you. I like it here,' she muttered.

'I don't believe you. There has to be something more than that,' her father replied.

Polly sighed. Max had a point, but it dawned on her that Rissa was more than likely hanging around for Brodie. She hadn't moved on at all, despite him courting Callie. And there was no way on earth the poor girl was ever going to admit it – especially to the father who was clearly looking for any excuse to hate this place and everyone in it.

Rissa ate a sandwich in silence and Max, after waiting in vain for an answer, half-heartedly sipped his coffee. Finally, the torturous meal was over, and Rissa announced she had to be getting back to work.

'No need to visit again, Dad,' she said, her lower lip trembling slightly as she got to her feet. 'I'll come to yours before the summer holidays are over. Promise. I wouldn't want to put you through the trauma of coming to Rowan Vale again.'

'I'd like it if you visited me,' Max admitted. 'But I still think I'm right about what happened to my grandfather, and I will prove it.'

'And how are you going to do that?' Rissa demanded.

Max hesitated. 'I should like to visit the farm properly. I should like to talk to this Betty and see if she volunteers anything about what happened in her grandparents' day. And then I will visit Jimmy at Starling Cottage as he suggested, and we will talk. I'm sure he'll have some stories to tell me about what really went on at Rowan Farm back then. I know he's not old enough to have been there at the time, but his parents will have been. People talk. Families remember. I'm sure he can be of some use or point me in the direction of someone who will be.'

Polly wasn't sure whether to be angry with Max or sad for him. This fella really was in the grip of an obsession. But the last thing she wanted was him digging around in the past, stirring up things that were best left forgotten. And she definitely didn't want Jimmy involved.

She'd better visit Starling Cottage this evening, as she'd promised, and see how Jimmy really felt about Max Meyer. Had he truly liked him, or was he just being polite when he suggested he pop round?

For the first time in a long time, Polly felt fear. Not remembered fear of the past, but real fear of the present, and for the future. For what this man could stir up. If he didn't let things lie, he could cause more pain than he'd ever imagine.

Well, not on her watch. She sat up straight and

lifted her head defiantly. She wouldn't let it happen. Over her dead body... Ah. Not while she had breath left... Hmm. Well anyway, she'd stop Max Meyer somehow. You just see if she didn't.

11

'I'm ever so sorry, love. I didn't mean to worry you.' Aunt Polly blew me a kiss and slipped into an arm-chair, tucking her feet beneath her and making her-self at home. She smoothed the front of her printed cotton dress and patted her dark hair, as if either of them ever needed adjusting. 'Well anyway, I'm here now. Did your dad tell you about poor old Percy Swain?'

I narrowed my eyes. On the surface, she seemed as bright and bubbly as ever, but there was something different about her this evening. She looked almost shifty.

'Yes,' I said, reaching for a chocolate biscuit from the packet on the coffee table. 'Though I don't get why

Bill and Ronnie's behaviour's suddenly upsetting him. I mean, they've been scrapping since 1915 or thereabouts, haven't they? What's the big deal now?'

'Oh, no big deal,' she said. 'But you know, Shona, just because someone's put up with something for decades, doesn't mean it can't get too much for them now and then. Percy's got every right to feel fed up with their antics sometimes. He might be dead but he's still human.'

She nodded at me and I gave her an awkward smile. 'Sorry. Didn't mean to be insensitive.'

She waved my apology away. 'No need to be sorry. Just bear it in mind in future.'

Well, that was me told!

'Anyway,' she said airily, 'enough about me. What have you been up to?'

Dad came through into the living room, carrying mugs of tea for the two of us. I gave Aunt Polly an uncomfortable look, but she didn't seem to be bothered. Was it just me who felt this mean every time I ate and drank in front of a ghost, I wondered? Then again, it hadn't worried me a moment ago when I'd unthinkingly reached for a choccie biccy, had it? Probably because eating biscuits was something I did without even noticing.

'What are we talking about?' Dad asked cheerfully,

putting the mugs down on the coffee table and set-tling next to me on the sofa.

'Aunt Polly was just asking me what we'd been up to,' I told him. 'Mainly,' I added, turning to her, 'I've been working out a menu for the 1940s weekend. I could have done with your input, actually.'

'Aw, sorry love. Never mind, I'm here now. What ideas have you come up with so far?'

I wrinkled my nose. 'Not many, to be honest. I've had a look at some old recipes online, but I can't imagine the customers queueing up to buy mock ba-nana sandwiches, can you? I mean – what's all that about?'

Aunt Polly laughed. 'Don't knock it till you try it. Although, I have to say I was never keen either. But if you close your eyes and imagine you're eating ba-nanas, you can almost get away with it. Tell you what, when we could get hold of cinnamon, we used to sprinkle a little bit of that on them and it really helped.'

'I hate cinnamon,' Dad said. 'What's a mock ba-nana sandwich anyway?'

'Believe it or not,' I told him, 'you chop and boil up some parsnips and mash them with caster sugar and banana essence, then spread them on bread just like you would bananas.'

Dad looked aghast. 'I've eaten some rubbish in my time, but I wouldn't touch that!'

Aunt Polly pursed her lips. 'You say that, our Jimmy, but back then, it was needs must. Some people today would eat the equivalent of our full week's ration in one evening meal. You don't know you're born.'

I eyed the chocolate biscuits and blushed. She had a point, after all.

'I want to be authentic,' I said, 'but I also have to think about my twenty-first century customers, and I really can't see them going for boiled parsnip sandwiches.'

'Well,' Dad suggested, 'why don't you just serve banana sandwiches and put them on the menu as mock mock banana sandwiches?'

I laughed. 'You know what, that might actually work!'

Aunt Polly rolled her eyes. 'Like I said. You don't know you're born. So what else have you come up with?'

'An eggless chocolate cake,' I said doubtfully. 'No idea how that will taste, but I'll give it a go and see how it turns out.'

'What about a syrup loaf?' she suggested. 'Ooh, me and Mum used to love those, and so did our customers. It's ever so simple. Bit of self-raising flour, some bicarbonate of soda, milk, golden syrup, and a pinch of salt. Mind, it can be a bit dry if memory serves, but if we had enough butter, we'd spread some on each slice. Or you can serve it warm with custard, you know.'

'Well, it sounds more palatable than eggless chocolate cake,' I mused. 'Thanks, I'll give that a go, too. What fillings did you have in sandwiches?'

She tilted her head to the side, remembering. 'Potted beef was popular. Spam, naturally, although I liked spam fritters best. Tinned salmon and cucumber.' She grinned suddenly. 'Beetroot sandwiches. Radish sandwiches.'

'Seriously?' I said.

'Seriously. You don't fancy those then?'

'Not really, and I doubt very much that my customers would either. Tinned salmon and cucumber, I can do. Potted beef, probably. Not sure about spam!'

'Mm, a spam fritter,' she said with a sigh. 'I could eat one of those right now. Mind you, no need for you to bother if you don't want to. Isaac tells me they're going to be serving spam fritters at the pub, along with fish and chips, Lord Woolton's Pie, and Homity Pie.'

'I've heard of those,' I said, nodding. 'Lord Woolton's Pie is full of root vegetables, right? And

Homity Pie, that's got potatoes and leeks in it, and a little bit of cheese.'

She nodded. 'Mum always put an apple in her Homity Pie, too. Added a certain something, she said.' She gave a heavy sigh, and I knew she was remembering the taste of her mum's cooking and missing it. She'd be missing any cooking really. I wished I could feed her up.

'I think I'll stick to just a few vintage recipes for the weekend,' I said, 'to go alongside our usual menu. Some people might want to try them since they'll be here to immerse themselves in the forties, but I'm guessing most won't. Nice to have the option, though.'

'That's what Penny at the pub said,' Aunt Polly told me. 'Isaac reckons they're just replacing three of the main dishes with the pies and the spam fritters. Fish and chips are already on the menu.'

'Funny that fish and chips weren't rationed during the war,' I mused.

'I'd have been queueing every night,' Dad said, laughing.

'Just because they weren't rationed didn't mean they were always available,' Aunt Polly told him with a wry smile. 'And anyway, who could afford to buy fish and chips every night? We weren't made of money! Besides, it wouldn't have been in the spirit of things.

We were all in it together, and queueing at the shops for sausages and butter and the like was all part of that.'

She went quiet for a minute, and I sipped my tea, imagining what life must have been like in Rowan Vale back then, and trying to picture Aunt Polly working in the teashop, meeting up with friends, perhaps going to the cinema in Much Melton. She must have filled her days with as many distractions as she could possibly find in a desperate attempt to get over Uncle Charlie's death. It must have been such a terrible time for her.

'Did I tell you the station's getting transformed too?' she asked suddenly. 'The Great War's going to be put on hold for the weekend, so to speak. They're changing the usual background music to songs from the war – *our* war, I mean – and the staff members are going to wear dresses like mine, and modern uniforms.'

'*Modern* uniforms?' Dad asked, grinning.

'Well, forties uniforms! Shut up, our Jimmy. You know what I mean.' Aunt Polly shook her head, smiling at him. 'So the Victory Tearooms will be in direct competition with you. Mind, they'll not have my syrup loaf recipe on their side.'

'I'm sure we'll both do loads of trade,' I said. 'The

pub, too. Let's face it, we're really lucky here during tourist season. It's the winter months, when it all dies down and the profits drop.'

'At least this weekend's in mid-September, so it will extend the summer season a bit,' Dad pointed out.

'A little bit.' I nodded.

'I don't know why you worry,' Aunt Polly said. 'Mum and me kept the teashop going long before there were all these tourists. We all did well enough.'

'Yes, but the village is a tourist-centred place now,' I pointed out. 'Back then, lots of people worked on the land. Now it's nearly all leisure and tourism.'

'Maybe Silas has a point then,' she said thoughtfully. 'About all the tourists, I mean.'

Dad shook his head. 'It's different now. We can't go back to the old days. I know Rowan Farm is run as a forties farm, but all the other farms round here are modern ones with so much mechanisation that they don't need to employ loads of labourers any longer. Farming's changed. If there weren't any tourists, most people would leave the area to get jobs in cities. You can't put the genie back in the bottle.'

'I suppose you're right.' Aunt Polly shrugged then brightened. 'Anyway, whatever else happens, the forties weekend's going to be fun, right?'

'I think it will be, yes,' I said. 'It's not going to be too much bother for me, Susie and Paige. We already wear vintage dresses and aprons to work, and the teashop's set up in the wartime style. Might change the bunting to union flag bunting instead, but other than that...'

Aunt Polly drew an imaginary doodle on the arm of the chair before slowly asking, 'Do you think Max will come here for the weekend?'

I blushed, wondering why she would ask about him, of all people.

'Well,' Dad said, 'I don't see why not. Rissa works here, after all, and now he's been to the village a couple of times, he might well come back for the event. After all, he only lives in Chipping Royston.'

'Does he?' Aunt Polly asked, clearly surprised. 'So quite local then.'

'Very. He's a teacher at the academy there,' I told her.

She rolled her eyes. 'Academy! What's wrong with school?'

'Nice fella,' Dad said, reaching for a chocolate biscuit. 'Very interesting to chat to. Seemed really keen to know more about the village, but then Shona lumped herself down next to him and that was that. Totally hogged the conversation.'

He chuckled as I gasped in indignation. 'I did no such thing!'

'Yes, you did! Do you think I didn't see you, going all goo-goo eyed over him?' He winked at Aunt Polly. 'Think she fancied him, Pol. What do you think to that?'

Aunt Polly looked shocked. 'Really, Shona? You like that man?'

'Not in that way!' I protested. 'I mean, he seems very nice...'

'And not bad looking, eh?' Dad said, nudging me. 'First time I've seen you blush in the presence of any man since that turnip head you married.'

'Do you mind? Luke's the father of my children!'

'Still a turnip head,' he said comfortably. 'Luckily, the girls take after our side of the family. What do you say, Pol?'

'I don't know *what* to say!' Aunt Polly looked a bit taken aback by the direction of this conversation, and no wonder. 'So, *do* you like him?'

'I told you, not in that way!' I helped myself to yet another chocolate biscuit and avoided her gaze. I hoped Dad was joking, but even if he was, there was more truth to his remarks than he realised, and I had an awful feeling Aunt Polly would be able to pick up on that. How embarrassing!

'He's a good-looking fella,' Dad persisted. 'You could do worse. You *did* do worse! And he's a teacher, and head of department, so he'd be a lot more reliable financially than turnip head.'

'Dad, will you stop calling Luke turnip head!' I was quite relieved that my annoyance was masking my embarrassment now. 'And don't ever let me hear you say anything like that about him in front of Christie or Pippa.'

'Have I ever?' he demanded. 'I'm the soul of discretion, me. Mind, I've heard them girls say worse about him. Just because they don't talk like that in front of you doesn't mean—'

'All right, Dad,' I said heavily. 'I get the picture.'

My daughters had no relationship with their dad these days. Believe me, I would never have stopped either Christie or Pippa from seeing him, and for a short while after the divorce, they did visit him. But the visits became sporadic, and in the end, they'd trickled away to nothing, and neither Luke nor the girls made any move to change that situation. I supposed, after everything that had happened, they felt no real loyalty to him.

'This Max,' Aunt Polly said suddenly, and I suppressed a sigh. Why was she so interested in him all of a sudden? 'You liked him, too, Jimmy?'

'Like I said, he seemed a decent fella,' Dad told her. 'We had quite a good chat. Bless him, he lost his wife six years ago, so we had a bit in common. I think he feels a bit lost without her, you know. I told him, he's always welcome at Starling Cottage if he ever fancies a chat.'

'But you barely know him!' Aunt Polly said.

I looked at her, surprised by the tone of her voice. She sounded as if she really didn't want Dad mixing with Max.

'Well...' Dad was clearly surprised, too. 'We don't know anyone at first, do we, Pol? We have to *get* to know them. That's the point. Like I said, he seems a bit lost, and I thought it would be nice for him to have someone to chat to, who'd been through the same experience.' He frowned suddenly. 'Are you okay?'

'Why wouldn't I be?' Aunt Polly gave a laugh that sounded too brittle, and Dad and I exchanged puzzled glances. 'You know what? I think I'm going to head home and have an early night. Staying at Percy's has worn me out, what him staying up all hours of the night to chat, and the couple he lives with watching late-night films. I'm ready for a bit of peace and quiet, so I'll see you tomorrow, eh?'

'Er, sure. If that's what you want.' Dad got to his feet, but she waved at him to sit down again.

'I'll see myself out. Let me know when you want to have a go at that eggless chocolate cake, Shona. And the syrup loaf, too. I can give you some tips. Night, lovelies.'

With that, she was gone, without even giving me a chance to say goodnight.

'What on earth was that about?' I asked, perplexed. 'Was it my imagination, or did Aunt Polly seem put out that you'd invited Max here?'

Dad rubbed his forehead. 'Well, I asked him in front of her and she never mentioned anything at the time. Mind, she didn't think much of the idea when I joked you fancied him either, did she?'

I heaved an inward sigh of relief. So he *had* been joking? Thank goodness for that. But he was right all the same. Aunt Polly hadn't liked it.

'Dad,' I said hesitantly, 'I hate to say this, but you don't think she's... prejudiced?'

'Polly? She's not like that, girl. You know that.'

'But she died in the 1940s,' I pointed out. 'Britain had been at war with Germany for years, and there'd only been peace for a couple of years when she—'

'Died,' Dad said quickly. He never liked to mention *how* she'd died. It was still too much for him to think about and I didn't blame him. I never liked to think about it either, and I knew even less about what had happened than he did.

'Yes,' I said softly, 'when she died. Germans would still have been seen as the enemy. Maybe seeing Max has brought back memories of that time. All they suffered. Uncle Charlie. I mean, how would you forgive the people who were responsible for killing the love of your life?'

'That was decades ago,' Dad said briskly. 'We were at war. People killed and people died. On both sides. Polly's not daft and she's had a long, long time to move on. Maybe it's just him she didn't like? Maybe something about him rubbed her up the wrong way? We all meet people we instinctively dislike, don't we? Often for no good reason. I'm sure it's nothing, love. Don't worry.'

'I'm not worried,' I said lightly. 'It's nothing to me either way, is it?'

But I *was* a bit worried, because Aunt Polly hadn't seemed like herself at all this evening, and considering she'd been missing for a week prior to today, I couldn't help feeling there was more to all this than we realised.

Was it really something to do with Max? Or did Aunt Polly have something else on her mind that was worrying her?

12

It was a warm evening, and I was longing to go home and have a good long soak in the bath after a busy day at the teashop. Even so, I wasn't about to miss out on the next village meeting at The Magic Lantern. I was far too nosy. I wanted to know what was going on and how things were progressing with the forties weekend.

I slipped into a seat a few rows from the front and settled myself down, wondering idly if Dad would turn up. He'd said he might consider it, but really on a day like this, he'd rather be working in the garden than sitting inside a cinema.

I glanced at my watch. Nearly six-fifteen. They'd

better hurry up and get on with it because tonight's film was due to start at seven-twenty.

Amelia plonked herself into the seat next to mine, making me jump. I hadn't even noticed her arrive.

'Here we are again,' she said cheerfully. 'I just hope Callie doesn't ask us how the choir's getting on. I'd hate to have to lie to her – and me a vicar!'

She laughed and I shook my head. 'I heard you all rehearsing the other day,' I told her. 'You sounded pretty good, so stop pretending you're all rubbish.'

'You heard us?' She lifted an eyebrow in surprise. 'Where were you?'

I wriggled in my seat, realising I'd revealed more than I intended. 'I'd been to lay flowers on Mum's grave,' I admitted. 'It would have been her birthday earlier this week. Anyway, I thought I'd just pop into the church and have a few minutes to think. You were in the middle of "Don't Sit Under the Apple Tree".' I nudged her. 'I really enjoyed it.'

She wrinkled her nose doubtfully. 'Really?'

'I wouldn't say it if I hadn't,' I assured her. 'I think it's going to be great.'

'Mm. It's taken us ages just to agree on which songs we're going to sing. I had to be very firm with old Mrs Langham. She wanted to sing "Lili Marleen" in full-on Marlene Dietrich mode. I don't think anyone really needs to see that, let alone hear it.'

I giggled at the thought of stout Mrs Langham – who must have been eighty if she was a day – doing a sultry Marlene Dietrich impersonation. Knowing her, I had a feeling she'd have given it a bloody good shot.

We snapped to attention as Callie arrived and welcomed us to the meeting. I glanced around, pleased to see Aunt Polly had arrived and was clearly chatting to some unseen companion as she headed for the row of empty seats near the back. She looked relaxed and more like her usual self. Maybe I'd been worrying about nothing.

I noticed Rissa was sitting just a few rows behind me, with Erin and Betty. My thoughts drifted as I wondered if she'd really put aside her feelings for Brodie and had decided to become involved with this 1940s weekend after all, given this was the second meeting she'd attended. I wondered if she was disappointed that Brodie wasn't here tonight.

'So thank you, Robyn and Curtis for that,' Callie said.

I blinked. 'Thank you, Robyn and Curtis, for what?'

Amelia rolled her eyes. 'They've announced the films that will be playing over the weekend.'

'Oh,' I whispered. 'What are they?'

'She's just about to tell us,' she hissed.

'So on the Saturday, there will be showings of *Went the Day Well* and *Brief Encounter*,' Callie said. 'Robyn tells me these are quite emotional stories from 1942 and 1945 respectively. I expect you've heard of *Brief Encounter*, at least. One for the romantics, I guess.' She beamed at us all and I wondered how Rissa was feeling about that.

'On the Sunday,' Callie continued, 'we've got some lighter fare. There will be showings of *Whisky Galore* and *Kind Hearts and Coronets*. Both films were released in 1949, so it will be an appropriate way to end our forties weekend. There'll also be early-afternoon showings of children's films: Saturday's will be *Bedknobs and Broomsticks*, and Sunday's will be *Bambi*. I hope you'll all find time to catch at least one of these films over the weekend. We all want to support The Magic Lantern, after all.'

'I'd support it a bit more often if they provided some decent snacks,' Amelia grumbled. 'I know it's a vintage cinema, but honestly, there's such a thing as catering for the modern audience. At least the cinema in Much Melton knows how to feed us. Have you tasted their nachos and dips?' She gave a longing sigh. 'Heavenly.'

'We've been lucky enough to listen to the vinyl albums Lucy and Sam secured for us,' Callie continued. 'There are some amazing songs on there, and some stirring wartime speeches interspersed with the music. It's going to sound fantastic when we rig up the speakers. Talking of music, how's the choir coming along, Amelia?'

Amelia gave me a grin and got to her feet. 'Well, our first review is in, and the critic apparently really enjoyed it, so maybe it's coming along better than I'd feared.' She addressed the audience. 'We've got about fourteen songs lined up, and we'll be performing each afternoon, with a fifteen-minute break in between each set of seven. Actually, Callie,' she added, 'I was wondering if we'd be allowed to ask for voluntary contributions to the church fund? Nothing too heavy. Just a few buckets dotted around for people to drop a coin or two in as they're listening. What do you think?'

'I don't see why not,' Callie said. 'Sounds like a good idea.'

'Excellent.' Amelia beamed and sat down. Then she jumped up again. 'I forgot to ask you, where are we actually performing? Will it be on the green?'

Callie nodded. 'Yes, we're setting up a temporary waterproof gazebo in case of rain so you won't get wet, and we'll be putting some chairs out for those members of the audience who can't stand for long, and those who want to sit through the entire performance. I'm anticipating that most people will drift over, listen to a couple of songs, then move on to the next thing, but you never know. If you're that good, we might need a lot of chairs!'

'Don't worry,' Amelia said. 'I don't think we'll need that many.' She leaned towards me and whispered, 'If they linger too long, I'll get Mrs Langham to sing "Lili Marleen" after all. That'll shift 'em.'

'By the way,' Callie said suddenly, 'and I'm addressing our non-living residents here: have any of you seen Harmony Hill? The 1940s was her era, after all, and I thought maybe she'd like to be part of the celebrations.'

She glanced around the room expectantly as we living residents watched curiously, wondering what was being said.

'No,' Callie said with a shrug to some invisible audience member, 'I've still not met her. It's such a shame because I'd love to introduce myself to her and get to know her a bit.' She hesitated, then added, 'Of course she does, and I'm the last person to intrude on anyone's privacy, but I just thought...'

I glanced round at Aunt Polly. She was listening to

the conversation, and I thought I'd ask her later who Callie was talking to.

'Yes, I know, but she *did* introduce herself to my daughter on our first day here, so she can't be a total recluse, can she?' Callie sighed. 'Okay, no worries. It was just a thought. But if any of you do happen to bump into her, please let her know she'd be very welcome to attend. And that goes for Quintus Severus and any other of our residents that I've not yet had the pleasure to meet. All welcome in Rowan Vale!'

'Aw,' I said. 'Isn't she lovely?'

Amelia nodded. 'We got very lucky with Callie. You'd think she was born to this job, wouldn't you? I wonder if the other ghosts will show?'

'I can't fathom why they stay away from the village in the first place,' I admitted. 'You'd think they'd want a bit of company. Especially that Quintus fella. Isn't he a Roman soldier? How long has he been stuck here, for goodness' sake? I'd be gagging for a chat with someone by now.'

Amelia shrugged. 'Each to their own, I guess.' She winked. 'Maybe he's heard our church choir re-hearsals.'

'Er...' Callie sounded suddenly rather awkward, as if she wasn't sure what to say next.

'Don't be so mean, Bill Fairfax. No need to put her on the spot like that.'

I turned round, hearing Aunt Polly's voice. She was standing up and addressing her remarks to someone sitting just in front of her by the look of things. 'Take no notice, Callie. None of his business if they're going or not.'

Callie cleared her throat. 'I haven't discussed with Agnes or Aubrey if they'll be attending,' she said firmly. 'However, I can say for certain that young Florrie will be going. She's very much looking forward to it. She'll be with my own daughter, Immi, and I'm sure they'll have a lot of fun.'

She paused, listening to someone, and added, 'Well, that was then and this is now. I think you'll find Florrie's far better behaved these days and – yes, thank you, Walter. I'm sure the lessons you're giving her are largely responsible for her transformation, too.'

'You know what?' I said to Amelia thoughtfully. 'I always envied Callie and Lawrie their ability to see all the ghosts but seeing her trying to wrangle them all today, I'm thinking I've probably got off lightly only seeing one.'

'I can't see any,' Amelia said, 'and I'm thankful for that every day.'

'There is one more thing I'd like to announce,' Callie said loudly, as the hum of conversation grew louder, and it looked as if people were preparing to leave. 'An end of the weekend treat. You'll all get formal invitations in the post, but here and now, I'd like to invite you to Harling Hall for a tea dance on the Sunday evening. It's going to take place in the ballroom, and we'll have a live band and lots of tasty food, and it's going to be fabulous!'

'Ooh,' Amelia said. 'Tasty food! I'm liking the sound of that.'

'Thank you all for coming,' Callie called. 'Newsletters will be going out in the next day or two with further updates. Have a lovely evening.'

'You missed the bit about the dancing and the band, then,' I said, getting to my feet.

Amelia shrugged and hoisted her bag over her shoulder. 'Well, obviously that's important, too. A bit.'

'I knew we were friends for a reason,' I said, laughing. 'Are you going to bring Tully?'

'I'll invite him, but who knows if he'll go? Tully and tea dances don't sound like natural bedfellows. Still, you never know. What about you? Are you going to invite your handsome German friend?' She grinned and nudged me as I blushed.

'Don't be daft! He's not my friend.'

'Ooh, but he *is* handsome? Maybe Rissa will invite him anyway, so you won't have to. That's if she can bring herself to go to an event at Harling Hall, given who lives there.'

'Poor Rissa,' I said automatically, though I had to admit, my thoughts were mainly of her father, and whether he'd be at the dance. Surely, Rissa would invite him? If not, would I dare? I mentally shook my head. Why on earth would I? As if he'd want to come to a tea dance anyway! Honestly...

We shuffled to the end of the row, and I turned to see if Aunt Polly was still here. She was standing at the top of the aisle, watching me. It was as if she was reading my mind, and my face burned with embarrassment. She frowned and headed out of the door, leaving me puzzled and confused. I'd have thought she'd have hung around for me, but it seemed she couldn't wait to get away from me.

All thoughts of Max flew from my mind.

Something was going on with Aunt Polly, and I wanted to know what it was.

13

POLLY

Polly had invited some of the ghosts back to the teashop for a get-together after that evening's meeting. She hadn't actually invited Bill and Ronnie from the station, but they'd taken it upon themselves to join the others and she wasn't mean enough to turn them out, although she did warn them that if they started fighting, she'd give them both a clip round the ear and they'd be on their way.

'I love this place,' Brooke said with a sigh, as she glanced around at the pretty, vintage setting and all the framed posters on the walls. 'I just wish I could eat something.'

There were some mumblings of agreement. Most of the time, they all tried not to think about food at all, adopting an attitude of not dwelling on what they couldn't have. Sometimes, though, it was hard to ignore the cravings, and being in a teashop that was known for its delicious cakes and lunches didn't help. At least, with the place closed for the evening, the food was out of sight and not on display on the counter.

'It's going to be awful at the forties weekend,' Millie grumbled. 'Imagine all the food smells there'll be! And people will be wandering around, stuffing their faces right in front of us.'

'People have forgotten their manners,' Walter Tasker said with a tut. 'Eating in the street indeed. I have never agreed with such practices. Dining should take place at a table, behind closed doors.'

'I wouldn't care where it took place if it would just take place at all,' Danny said gloomily.

'Like sex,' Brooke added, much to some of the older ghosts' evident shock.

Danny looked extremely flustered, and Polly wondered, not for the first time, what the deal was with those two. They were very young – she was pretty sure Brooke had said she was twenty-five and Danny twenty-nine when they became ghosts. Although they were dressed in what she'd learned was the style of some 1980s pop stars, they'd in fact only died in 2004 and were the newest ghosts in the village. She'd assumed at first that they were a couple, but she'd never seen them hug or kiss and they didn't speak to each other like lovers. Maybe they were just colleagues or friends?

'How are we all feeling about this forties weekend?' Isaac Grace asked. He beamed round at them all with his usual jovial expression. Isaac still considered himself the landlord of The Quicken Tree Inn, even though he'd died in 1685, and he seemed to have been 'on duty' ever since, always ready with a smile and a listening ear. Especially the listening ear.

'I think it's a great idea,' Brooke said firmly. 'Anything that breaks the monotony has to be a good thing, right? I mean, don't you all get bored? I don't know what to do with myself most of the time and it's really hard not to get depressed.'

'You should come round to mine,' Millie said brightly. 'We can listen to music in my room. Lucy bought me a fab machine that plays music for hours.'

Brooke eyed her doubtfully. 'By music, I take it you mean the Beatles?'

Millie laughed. 'Well, obviously.'

Brooke sighed. 'I'll pass, thanks. Not a Beatles fan.'

'Not a—?' The indignation and disbelief on Millie's face made Polly decide a change of subject was needed.

'What about Harmony?' she asked, knowing full well that would get everyone's attention.

Isaac frowned. 'What about her?'

'Well, has anyone seen her lately? Callie's got a point, after all. Harmony Hill was a big film star in the 1940s. The weekend might bring back nice memories for her.'

'What, like of the night she fell in the river and drowned?' Ronnie asked with a sly grin. 'Can't say as I'd like to be reminded of that.'

'Of the Golden Age of Hollywood, when her face was on all the cinema posters,' Polly said sharply. 'And I'm watching you, Ronnie Smith. Don't think I'm not.' She looked round at all the familiar faces and sighed. 'One of you must have seen her lately, surely? I mean, where does she go? What does she do?'

'No idea.' Peter, a baker who'd died back in 1790 after having a rock thrown at his head by his not-so-loving wife while he was secured in the village pillory, tilted his head as he considered the matter. 'I find it hard to believe that she's at home all day alone. Maybe she leaves there early in the morning and doesn't return until late at night to avoid us. Where she would go in daylight hours, I have no idea, but she doesn't frequent the village. One of us would have spotted her and I never have. Have you?'

'We could always visit her at home,' Isaac suggested. 'I hate to think of the poor little thing all on her own. Maybe we should make more of an effort with her.'

'Isaac,' Percy said firmly, 'we tried that. We tried it when she first died, and we tried it on several occasions for a year or so afterwards. She made it very, very clear that her home was her private space, and she didn't want uninvited guests.'

'Which is fair enough,' Walter said. 'We all have our boundaries, after all. Since we have no physical barriers to our homes, a mutual agreement was necessary, and we've all abided by that.'

'Except she never invites anyone!' Brooke pointed out. 'I don't know. Maybe we should take matters into our own hands. Look, I've only been dead for twenty years or so and I'm already bored off my nut. And *I've* got Danny, for all the use he is.'

'Thanks,' Danny muttered.

'The point is, she's been around for nearly eighty years, and she doesn't mix with anyone. She must have gone doolally by now. We should stage an intervention. Force her to talk to us.'

'I agree,' Danny said. 'It's the only kind thing to do.'

'And what about Quintus Severus?' Polly asked. She felt sorry for the centurion being so alone all this time. He didn't deserve that. She wished she could help him.

Danny quailed. 'Blimey, I'm not going near him! Have you seen the size of those muscles?'

Brooke rolled her eyes then said, 'Well, I'd be happy to volunteer.'

'I'll bet you would,' Danny said.

'Not sure Quintus Severus is likely to enjoy a 1940s weekend,' Percy said, frowning. 'He very much keeps himself to himself, and a Roman centurion isn't likely to have any nostalgic feelings about the Andrews Sisters and spam sandwiches. Besides, you know how much of a loner he is.'

'And so serious!' Millie added. 'I went for a walk up to the stones with Lucy and Sam the other week, and there he was, watching us. Never cracked a smile the whole time we were there, and I waved and everything.'

'All he ever does is patrol the estate,' Walter mused. 'He seems to spend all his time walking the borders and standing guard over the Wyrd Stones. Why, I can't imagine.'

Brooke smirked. 'Well, whatever the reason, he looks bloody good doing it. He's all manly and hunky. I certainly feel safer knowing he's around to protect me.'

'From what?' Danny asked witheringly.

'Who cares?' she said with a shrug and gave him a sweet smile.

'There aren't just Harmony and Quintus,' Percy pointed out. 'We've all seen others on the fringes of the estate. I reckon a lot of them hang out at The Monastery.'

There were a few shudders at the mention of that house, including from Polly. She'd never liked it, and when she was a kid, she'd refused many a dare to go there at night. It was a badge of honour for some of the local children, but Polly had never been that desperate for a badge of honour, thank you very much.

The Monastery wasn't really a monastery at all. Its official name was Woodstone Manor, and it had been commissioned in the mid-eighteenth century by Cecil Ashcroft, the owner of the Harling Estate at the time (and Agnes's father-in-law, if Polly's local knowledge served her right).

There'd been some puzzlement as to why the man who owned and lived at Harling Hall should build another mansion house, especially one so ugly and downright creepy, and on the far side of the woods on the very edge of the estate. But Polly had discovered, since mixing with people like Isaac Grace and Walter Tasker, who'd been around at the time, that Cecil had been leading a double life.

What he envisioned as a grand house in the Gothic revival style was to be a gift for his lover, and their secret meeting place away from the prying eyes of his wife, Frances, and their son, Cyril.

The so-called mansion had vaulted ceilings, a cloistered courtyard, and stained-glass windows. The locals had watched in bewilderment as it took shape, wondering why anyone would want to live in something that looked as if it had been designed as a place of worship rather than a house.

It turned out that Cecil's lover was a well-off member of the aristocracy, and a man of great religious faith. Not so great that he didn't mind having a good old tumble with some woman's husband, Polly thought wryly, but there you go. That was the upper classes for you. One rule for them and another for everyone else.

Woodstone Manor quickly earned the nickname of The Monastery, but it was never completed. Cecil's lover was shipped off abroad by his family. It was rumoured that they'd heard of his indiscretions and were desperate to get him as far away from Cecil, and the ever-spreading gossip, as possible.

From what Isaac could gather – as he made it his mission to hang around Harling Hall and eavesdrop on Cecil's rather bitter and heated conversations with Frances, who clearly wasn't as stupid as Cecil imagined she was – his lover was put to work for the East India Company and never returned to England.

Woodstone Manor, meanwhile, was still only half-finished, and a disheartened Cecil decided that work should stop. Workmen downed tools and the house was left to rot. When Lawrie took over the estate, he'd considered demolishing the building, but it was discovered that it housed a large colony of horseshoe bats which were protected by law, and so the place remained.

Judging by the expressions on everyone's faces, Polly thought they didn't like the manor any more than she did, and she couldn't imagine anyone wanting to hang out there by choice.

'Well,' Percy said, glancing round at all the doubtful faces, 'where else can these others go? Think about it. We never go near the place, do we? But it's just about the only building we stay away from, so it seems the most likely candidate to me.'

'I doubt Quintus Severus is afraid of a few bats,'

Danny said fervently. 'They might be afraid of him, though.'

Polly decided they were running away with themselves. 'Never mind Quintus and any other ghosts who don't want anything to do with us,' she said firmly. 'The person we're discussing is Harmony Hill. I think we should go and see her to formally invite her to the 1940s weekend. She might really enjoy it. Especially the tea dance.'

'She won't thank you for it,' Percy said, shaking his head.

'One should respect a person's desire for privacy,' Walter agreed. 'Mistress Hill has made it very clear that she doesn't want visitors.'

'Look,' Polly said, after a moment's consideration, 'she can always tell me to hop it if she doesn't like it, can't she? See, me and her, we've got a lot in common. We were around at the same time, remember? We both lived through the war years, and no, I don't mean we were there as ghosts like some of you. I mean, we actually *lived* through them. All right, so I was here in the Cotswolds, and she was over in Hollywood, but even so. And we both died just after the war, so...'

There was a silence. Then Isaac said cheerfully, 'Well, I think Polly's right. She can only say no, can't she? And a bit of a shindig might do her the world of good. Harmony, I mean. Maybe if we can coax her into attending this forties weekend, she might start mixing with us all a bit more. She needs the company. No one should be alone all the time.'

'All in favour?' Percy asked.

There was some hesitation then a lot of hands shot up into the air. Walter looked torn for a moment, but eventually raised his hand, too.

'Right,' Polly said. 'That's settled then. I'll pop by her cottage tomorrow. Wish me luck!'

Now she had two missions.

Because first and foremost, she would be keeping a close eye on the comings and goings at Rowan Farm. If Max really did plan to question Betty and Nick, she needed to be there to find out what they were telling him. She wasn't certain how much, if anything, they actually knew, but there was only one way to find out.

'Blimey,' she murmured to herself in some surprise, 'get me! Plain old Polly Herron is turning into a spy. Who'd have thought it, eh?'

14

POLLY

'It's so very good of you to invite me to dinner,' Max said, offering an uncertain smile to Betty as he took his seat at the dining table.

'And sorry he's brought along an uninvited guest,' Polly said, laughing to herself as she stood at the dining-room door, watching the scene unfold at Rowan Farm. Her visit to Harmony's cottage might not have borne fruit just yet – Harmony was proving elusive as usual – but hanging round the farm had paid off, when she'd heard Rissa on the phone to her dad, inviting him to tea on Betty's behalf.

'You're very welcome,' Betty said, beaming at him. 'We're all friends here, and we're delighted to meet Rissa's father. Fancy you only living out at Chipping

Royston all this time! We had no idea. You should have come to see us sooner.'

Max smiled politely and Polly thought he was trying to work Betty out. He'd got a proper bee in his bonnet about her family and clearly wasn't sure if her welcome was genuine. He probably hadn't expected an invitation, and if Rissa had had her way, he wouldn't have got one. Polly had listened as she'd reluctantly called him to tell him that Betty was very keen to meet him, and would he be free to come for tea on Saturday? Betty had been hovering nearby, nodding eagerly as she'd spoken, clearly wanting to encourage a thawing of relations between Rissa and her dad.

As she surveyed the table, which was groaning with food, Polly suppressed a sigh. High tea, she remembered, had always been a hearty affair at Rowan Farm back in Helen's day, and it seemed Betty was continuing the tradition. There were plates and dishes spread all over the table, holding slices of cold meat, cheeses, sliced hard-boiled eggs, potato salad, coleslaw, salad vegetables and goodness knows what else. She knew that, if it were possible, her mouth would have been watering and her tummy rumbling at the sight. Sometimes, afterlife seemed very unfair.

Polly had assumed it would only be the four of

them at the table, but as Max settled himself in one of the hard-backed, mahogany chairs, Lars, Bram, and Erin arrived. Max looked momentarily uncomfortable but quickly masked his feelings and greeted the new-comers with a smile.

Then Betty's husband, Nick arrived. He shooed their beloved cat, Mitzi, into the kitchen then took his place at the head of the table. Polly liked the look of Nick, who she'd seen a few times around the village. He was an amiable-looking man with sandy-coloured hair and blue eyes that shone out from a weather-beaten face. He had a look of Betty's own grandad, Alf.

She smiled as, after welcoming his guest, Nick began to load up his plate. Evidently, there was nothing formal about this meal, and she sensed that Max felt some relief at that.

For a few moments, she battled with herself, won-dering if it would be too torturous to sit down at the table while everyone was eating all this yummy food, but in the end, she decided that she was being daft. After all, she spent enough time at the teashop, watching as people stuffed their faces with all kinds of tasty treats. She could cope with this.

Besides, she was on a spying mission, and spies didn't have time to think about food.

She slipped into the remaining empty chair at the

table as Betty said kindly to Max, 'Now, you just help yourself. We do things in the traditional way here, which I'm sure is just what you'd expect. High tea in summer is more like a buffet. You eat whatever you fancy and don't stand on ceremony.' Her gaze slid over to where the three farmworkers were, like Nick, already digging in. 'See what I mean?' she said with a wry shake of her head. 'Best get stuck in before this lot eat it all.'

'Thank you. It's a marvellous spread. I shouldn't think,' he said carefully, 'that this is how your family would have eaten during the war.'

Polly pursed her lips. Straight in there, no messing about. Direct the conversation to the war. *Well played, Max.*

Nick laughed. 'You're not wrong there, Mr Meyer.'

'Please, call me Max.'

'Okay, and you must call me Nick. No, there's no doubt rationing would have made sure the table wasn't as full back then as it is now. But I daresay Betty's family had a little bit extra now and then, whatever the rules. More than most of the poor blighters in the city had, at any rate.'

Polly agreed. They'd been lucky, despite the rationing. For one thing, so many people in the cities didn't even have a garden or access to an allotment.

How were they supposed to dig for victory in those circumstances?

'It must be strange,' Max said, rather shyly helping himself to some chicken, salad and coleslaw, 'living in the past the way you do.' He eyed the Dutchmen curiously. 'And you, playing prisoners of war. *German* prisoners of war at that, when Rissa tells me you are Dutch.'

The two men shrugged.

'We like it here,' one said. He had dark hair, grey eyes and a cheerful smile. 'We're only here until September, sadly, but it's been fun, hasn't it, Lars?'

The fair-haired one nodded in agreement. 'Yeah. We'll miss it, but real life calls. Can't stay here forever, can we?'

'No indeed,' Max said, giving Rissa a pointed look.

She put her head down and concentrated on her meal.

'So what are your plans when you leave here?' Max enquired politely.

'I'm going back to Nederland,' Lars told him. 'I have a job waiting for me in my father's business.'

'Really?' Max raised an eyebrow. 'What sort of business is that?'

'He owns a haulage company,' Lars said. 'I shall be helping him run it when I return. I have completed my studies in business management with logistics and I look forward to going home when the summer is over and putting my knowledge to work in a practical way.'

Polly had no idea what any of that involved and she wondered if Max was any wiser.

'I see. I'm sure your father is looking forward to your return,' he said politely.

'For sure,' Lars said with a chuckle. 'But my mother is looking forward to it even more. She has sent me food parcels every week since I left and is crossing off the days on her calendar. One would think I was still a child.'

'Says the man who spends every evening playing *Transformers* video games,' Erin said, laughing.

'Hey! It's a classic,' Lars protested.

'I notice you didn't tell your mother to stop sending you the food parcels,' Bram said.

'Well...' Lars squirmed a little. 'It makes her happy to think she is feeding me. Besides,' he added, an accusatory tone in his voice, 'you ate your fair share of them!'

'Guilty,' Bram admitted.

'And what of you?' Max asked him politely. 'Will you be returning to the Netherlands in September?'

Bram shook his head. 'No. I'll be moving to Scotland. I got my Masters degree, and now I'm aiming for a PhD.'

Max's eyes widened. 'A PhD? Impressive. What are you studying?'

'Scottish History at Edinburgh University,' Bram said briefly.

'*Scottish* History?' Evidently, that had really surprised him. 'Why Scottish?'

'My mother is Scottish,' Bram explained. 'I have dual nationality and spent several years living in Scotland during my teens.'

'Nothing so grand for me,' Erin said cheerfully. She flicked back her red hair then speared some chicken with her fork. 'I'm hanging on here. I like the work. I like the Cotswolds. I grew up in Coventry – a country girl at heart trapped in a big city. This job was a dream come true for me and I'm not about to let it go anytime soon.' She winked at Betty. 'You'll have the oldest land girl in history one day, you wait and see.'

Betty laughed. 'You'll always be welcome here, lovely. We'll just have to keep you out of the sun. My mother always said that was the secret to keeping the wrinkles at bay. Mind, I think you might have chosen the wrong profession. You and me both.'

Polly thought that dying at thirty-seven had done a pretty good job of keeping her own wrinkles at bay, and she supposed it was always better to look on the bright side. Max, meanwhile, had seized on the opportunity to explore Betty's family history a little further.

'I believe,' he said politely, oblivious, Polly noticed, to the tension in Rissa's face at his words, 'that this farm has been in your family for some generations?'

Betty buttered a slice of bread as she considered her answer. 'Not "in the family" if you mean we've always owned it,' she explained. 'The farm belongs to the owner of the Harland Estate. Everything round here does. We're all tenants, you see. But my family has been lucky enough to have the tenancy of Rowan Farm for well over a hundred and twenty years, so it certainly feels like ours.'

'And you were happy to live here, Nick?' Max enquired. 'When you married Betty, I mean?'

Nick chortled. 'Happy? I only married her for the farm!'

Max looked startled for a moment, but his face relaxed as Betty squealed with laughter and he realised the farmer was joking.

'My dad runs a farm about thirty miles from here,' Nick explained. 'Farming's in my blood and I never wanted to do anything else. When I met Betty, I'd have moved to the ends of the earth for her, so thirty miles was nothing. Mind, I'll admit it took some getting used to, having to go back in time as it were to all these old-fashioned agricultural methods. Having said that, I wouldn't have it any other way now. There's something calming about working the land the way they used to. It's a more relaxed way of life, even though it's bloody hard work.'

'And your father doesn't mind? He doesn't expect you to take over his own farm one day?'

'Oh no! I'm the youngest son so it was never on the cards, although my older brother would have happily shared if it came to it. We get on really well, you see. But I'm happy here. We feel very blessed, don't we, Betty?'

'We do indeed. And what about you, Max? Rissa tells us you're a teacher at Chipping Royston Academy. Head of department at that.'

'Indeed. Head of Languages,' he said. 'I myself teach German.'

'Yes, we've only just discovered that you're from Germany,' Nick said comfortably. 'We had no idea Rissa had German ancestry. We're a proper multicultural little family, aren't we?'

'It seems so,' Max agreed. 'I come from Hannover, in Lower Saxony. That's in northwestern Germany.'

'So what brought you to England, Max?' Betty asked him. 'Was it the job?'

'Not *my* job,' Max said. He hesitated and Polly wondered what he was thinking, as he seemed to be struggling for words. Finally, he said, 'It was my wife's work that brought us here. She was a surgeon, and she was offered a very good position at a hospital in London.'

Polly's hand flew to her chest – a gesture she always made when something had moved her. She could hear the grief in Max's voice when he spoke about his wife and had no doubt that everyone else at the table could, too.

'Ah, I see.' Betty's eyes crinkled with sympathy. 'And you were all right with that? It's a lot to ask, uprooting yourself from your own country and presumably a job of your own.'

Max glanced over at Nick. 'Like you, I would have moved to the ends of the earth for my wife.'

Nick's expression softened. 'I understand.'

'I'm so sorry to hear about her death,' Betty said kindly. 'When Rissa told us, I was heartbroken for her. For both of you. Your wife was far too young.'

'Thank you,' Max said briefly.

'What brought you to the Cotswolds then?' Betty asked.

Max and Rissa exchanged glances and Polly shuffled forwards on her chair, listening with curiosity.

'After Mum died,' Rissa said, 'Dad accepted a job at the academy and sold our London house to move here.'

'A fresh start,' Max said.

'Oh, I completely understand,' Betty said sympathetically. 'Sometimes, the only thing you can do is start again somewhere you don't know. A clean page as it were. What do you think to the place then? I know I'm biased, but I don't think there's anywhere more beautiful than the Cotswolds, and our little village is the jewel in its crown if you ask me.'

'It's certainly a stunning area,' Max agreed. 'The countryside is superb, and this village is very pretty. I'd like to get to know it better.'

'Well, you'd be very welcome at any time,' Betty assured him.

'Tell you what, Max,' Nick said eagerly, 'you could join us at the pub quiz at The Quicken Tree one Thursday night.' He grinned round the table at everyone. 'How could we lose with another brainbox on the team? You're sort of connected to the village through Rissa, so I'm sure we can square it with Penny.'

'Never misses a trick, does he?' Betty said fondly.

'As it happens,' Max said, 'my family has another

connection with this village. With Rowan Farm itself, in fact.'

Betty's eyebrows shot up. 'Never! Well, what a co-incidence! You never said, Rissa.'

Rissa said nothing, conveniently chewing a cherry tomato.

Nick sounded eager. 'Well, well. What connection is that then, Max?'

'My grandfather,' Max said coolly. 'He was a prisoner of war here. He was kept at the camp a few miles from this village, and he was put to work on this very farm.'

Polly closed her eyes momentarily as the image of Gerhard Janssen flashed through her mind, bringing with it the inevitable pain and sense of dread.

'He never was!' Nick's mouth fell open. 'Did you hear that, Betty? What a coincidence, eh?'

Betty nodded slowly. 'I did indeed.'

'That's amazing,' Bram said. 'Here we are, playing the roles of German PoWs, and your grandfather was here for real. What was his name?'

Max's gaze went from Nick to Betty. 'Gerhard,' he said firmly. 'Gerhard Janssen.'

'Gerhard Janssen,' Nick said, rubbing his chin. 'I'll bet we have photos of him somewhere, and no doubt some documentation, too. We've got loads of stuff from those days. Well, you'd expect us to, wouldn't you, given our circumstances? We'll be able to dig some of them out for him, won't we, Betty?'

Betty looked suddenly flustered. 'I— I'm sure we will,' she said.

Polly shook her head. Was it her imagination or did she sound odd? How much did Betty know?

'That would be so kind,' Max said, watching his hostess closely. 'We have very few photographs of my grandfather when he was young.'

'So – this Gerhard,' Betty said, pushing her food around on her plate and seeming to be examining it with sudden fascination, 'he went back to Germany, I presume? Got married? Had children?'

'Stands to reason, my love,' Nick said, laughing. 'Max wouldn't be sitting here right now if he hadn't, would he?'

'I suppose not.' Betty ran a hand through her hair then fixed Max with a wide smile that didn't reach her eyes. 'Well, fancy that! Your grandfather probably knew mine. What a coincidence, eh? I'm very glad he was happy and had a family. Of course, mainly we had Italian prisoners here at the farm. The German prisoners arrived later. Almost at the end of the war really.'

She sounded as if she were gabbling, and Max

clearly thought that was very interesting. Polly could see the cogs turning over in his mind. He glanced over at Rissa and saw she was frowning, as if she, too, had noticed her employer was acting rather strangely.

'There's a raspberry trifle for afters,' Betty said brightly. 'Hurry up and finish your meal because I'm ready for my pudding now, and I know Lars will be. Never can resist my trifle, can you?'

As Lars admitted that he was indeed partial to Betty's desserts, Max chewed his chicken thoughtfully.

Oh, Betty, Polly thought in despair. *You've just made things ten times worse!*

Now there was going to be no stopping him.

One way or the other, Max Meyer would be determined to find out the truth.

15

The school summer holidays were in full swing and, after a week of rather dull and occasionally wet weather, the sunshine had returned, meaning the village was absolutely heaving with tourists.

The teashop was busy, particularly from around eleven o'clock when the rush would begin. It only started to wind down at around four, and I was becoming increasingly grateful for closing time at five each day.

I tended to relax at home with Dad most evenings, worn out from work. Occasionally, Christie and her family would come for a visit before the girls' bedtimes. Pippa popped by once or twice and told me she was really looking forward to the 1940s weekend, and that they'd been reminding people about it on a regular basis in *The Courier*.

On the evening of the second Thursday in August, she persuaded me to venture out of the cottage and join her at The Quicken Tree for the weekly pub quiz. I was a not-very-reliable member of the Smart Cookies team, which was made up of staff from both teashops and Blighty's Bakery.

It was a light-hearted evening, and the prizes weren't much to write home about, but it was fun to catch up with friends and neighbours. Besides, it was better than yet another night in front of the television with Dad's light snoring to keep me company.

I was pleased to see some of the usual suspects: Callie and Brodie had turned up and were sitting with Clara and Jack Milsom. Callie had struck up quite a friendship with Clara, as their children attended the same school, and they'd made some sort of arrangement with the school run. Things would change from September, I realised. Callie's daughter, Imogen, and Clara's eldest, Ashton, would be going to Chipping Royston Academy on the school bus. I wondered idly if Max would be teaching them German.

As Jack was a train driver, they were part of The Travelling Boffins quiz team, which was made up of station staff, and drivers and clippies from the buses. I spotted Andie among them. I knew I'd recognised her at the meeting that day in the cinema, and she'd brought Matthew from the station with her.

'Shouldn't Callie and Brodie be neutral in this?' Pippa joked. 'Looks a bit dodgy if the big bosses are part of The Travelling Boffins.'

'I shouldn't worry,' I told her. 'They never win anyway.'

'Fair dos. I'll get us a drink, Mum. You find us a seat.'

I made my way over to where the other members of The Smart Cookies were sitting and looked around for Amelia but there was no sign of her. Maybe she was busy with work. Or maybe she was with Tully, I thought with a sudden wistfulness. Amelia and Tully's relationship might not be conventional, but it worked for them. And, for the first time, I thought it would be nice to have *someone*...

Veronica, who managed the Victory Tearooms, leaned over to me, thankfully derailing that train of thought. 'Have you heard we might be getting some new competition? Callie thinks there's room for an-other cafe in the village. What do you think?'

Callie and I had discussed the need for another venue in Rowan Vale a few days before. She'd told me they'd arranged for some food stalls to be on hand during the 1940s weekend, which should help ease the pressure on Mrs Herron's Teashop, the Victory Tearooms, and The Quicken Tree Inn. Having observed the high volume of customers at the teashop, though, she agreed there was probably room for another cafe or restaurant in the village, even if it only opened during the main tourist season.

'The question being, where? And what sort of vibe do we want it to have?' she'd mused. 'Should we make it fit into one of our existing featured eras? Or should we simply open a modern eatery, as you'd find in any village or small town? And if it's the former, where do we put it? Actually, either way – where do we put it?'

'Maybe it's something the whole village needs to think about,' I'd suggested. 'But probably not until after this forties weekend. We've enough to do for now.'

'Agreed!' Callie had said with a sigh of relief. 'I'd better run it past Penny and Veronica, though. Make sure they understand there won't be any threat to their livelihoods and that they're okay with the idea in principle.'

I'll say one thing for Callie: she didn't hang around. Once she made up her mind to do something, she got on with it. Look at this forties weekend! Now it seemed she was determined to push ahead with a new eating place. Considering she'd only been in charge of the estate for a few months, she was certainly all in.

'I think it's a good thing,' I told Veronica, smiling at Pippa as she joined us at our table and handed me half a pint of fruit cider. 'There's more than enough trade to go around. We're turning customers away some days, and the last thing we want is for them to jump in their cars and head to another village where they'll more easily find somewhere to sit and eat in comfort.'

'I suppose you're right,' Veronica mused. 'It's a bit different for me, being at Harling's Halt. People tend to pop in as they arrive or leave, but for you, they're going to be around for a lot longer, and if they can't get food, it doesn't reflect well on the village. I just hope it's not another vintage teashop. Between the two of us, we've pretty much covered that!'

I laughed. 'I'm sure Callie will come up with something different,' I assured her. 'Oh, talk of the devil.' I raised my glass in greeting as Callie and Clara headed over.

'What are you two doing, fraternising with the enemy?' Pippa teased them as they squeezed into the small gap between me and Veronica.

'The quiz hasn't started yet,' Callie pointed out with a grin.

'Even if it had, we're hardly going to contribute to it,' Clara said, rolling her eyes. 'I don't think I've answered more than two questions the entire time I've been doing these quizzes, and they were about *Peaky Blinders* and Taylor Swift.'

'I think we're safe, Mum,' Pippa said, nudging me.

'You really are,' Clara said. She yawned and I raised an eyebrow.

'Are we keeping you up?'

'Oh, it's my wretched hormones,' she moaned. 'Bloody perimenopause. How long does this go on for?'

'About five years or so, I think,' I said. 'And just think, when that's over, you'll be straight into full menopause. What fun!'

'Bloody hell, who'd be a woman?' she groaned. 'Why don't men suffer with their hormones the way we do? Jack swears he's going through the so-called male menopause, but all that's happened is he's developed a bit of a beer belly and a sudden urge to buy a motorbike. Not fair!'

'Is he getting a motorbike?' Callie asked, interested.

'What do you think? We've got better things to spend our money on. Besides, we might be too busy with other stuff.'

'Ooh, sounds interesting,' I said. 'What other stuff?'

'The model village,' Clara told us. 'We're in discussions with the boss here,' she jerked her thumb in Callie's direction, 'about opening it up to the public.'

'Really?' Pippa and I exchanged delighted glances. We both loved the model village which had been constructed in the 1930s and was a faithful reproduction of the Harling Estate at that time. It even had little models of all the ghosts who'd been around then, which had come in so useful to those of us who couldn't see who we shared our village with.

'We need to work out a way of getting the visitors into the paddock without going through the courtyard at Honeywell House,' Callie explained. 'It will mean rejigging the route to ensure privacy for Clara's family. If we can't work it out, we might have to relocate it somewhere else, but either way, Clara and Jack will be in charge of it.'

'Jack's really keen,' Clara said enthusiastically. 'To be honest, so am I. It will give me something to do now Freddie's at school and I've got my life back. I'd love to get a job and overseeing the model village will be perfect. Jack's considering giving up the trains to work on it, too. He'd be in charge of maintenance, and of building new models.'

'We'd really like to update it,' Callie explained. 'The current model shows the village as it was in the thirties, but we'd like to show it as it is today.'

'To be fair,' I said, 'I shouldn't think there'd be much to change. Rowan Vale's barely altered over the last century or so.'

'It would mainly just be the business names,' Callie acknowledged. 'But we'd also like models of the ghosts who weren't around when the model village was constructed. People like Florrie, and Danny and Brooke, and Harmony Hill – and your Aunt Polly.'

'I'll bet she'd love that,' I said, smiling. 'Sounds brilliant.'

'Jack's more than up for it,' Clara told me. 'You know his great-grandfather was one of the original craftsmen who built the model village, and the one who came up with the idea in the first place. He's keen to carry on the family tradition and he's always thought it should be open to the public. As I say, the sticking point is the crowds traipsing through our courtyard to see it, so if Callie can come up with an alternative suggestion, it would be fantastic.'

'Brodie's working on it as we speak,' Callie assured her. She glanced round to where Brodie was deep in conversation with Jack and shrugged. 'Well, not as we speak, but he's dealing with it, I promise.'

'How are things going with you two?' I asked. 'Are you still love's young dream?'

Callie blushed and tucked a strand of her dark-auburn hair behind her ear, clearly shy about the subject. 'Good,' she mumbled. 'Really good.'

'Really, *really* good,' Clara said, her eyes gleaming with mischief. 'Despite having a lively eleven-year-old, a ghostly ten-year-old, and a very disapproving Regency lady keeping their beady eyes on them, things have moved on very satisfactorily.'

'Clara!' Callie said, now blushing furiously.

Clara laughed. 'Sorry. I'm only jealous. My libido's vanished without trace.'

'I don't see how Agnes can disapprove of you, anyway,' I said. 'Isn't she shacked up with Aubrey? Aunt Polly says Silas Alexander is furious because, obviously, they're living in sin as far as he's concerned.'

'I suppose technically, they are,' Callie mused. 'But honestly, you should see them together. They're adorable. Agnes's bark really is worse than her bite, and Aubrey's a sweetheart. They belong together, married or not.'

Clara took a long sip of her drink. 'Will they be attending the 1940s weekend?' she asked eventually. 'Only, it's common knowledge that they don't come into the village, isn't it?'

'It seems to be a bone of contention among the ghosts,' I agreed. 'Aunt Polly says they haven't been out of the grounds of Harling Hall for well over a decade to the best of her knowledge. She thinks Silas must have upset them more than usual, but who knows? Maybe they're just too good for us.' I shrugged, not particularly bothered either way. I couldn't see or hear any ghost but Aunt Polly, so what did it matter?

'I wish they'd make the effort,' Callie said sadly. 'I'm sure it can't be good for them to be stuck at the Hall all the time. And it would be nice for Florrie to have them with her, since to all intents and purposes, they're her parents now. And, you know, I'm sure Aubrey would jump at the chance if Agnes would consent to it. He's much more sociable than she is. It seems a shame.'

'Maybe you shouldn't blame Agnes,' Clara said, putting her glass on the table. 'Maybe it's Aubrey who's staying out of the way and she's just going along with it?'

Callie laughed then her eyes widened. 'Oh, you're being serious? Why on earth would you think that?'

'Why would you think otherwise?'

I noticed the tension in Clara's voice and frowned. What had rattled her cage suddenly?

As if she'd realised how cross she'd sounded, Clara sighed. 'Sorry. There go my moods again. Just, it annoys me when women get the blame for things with no real proof. I know you like Aubrey, Callie, but that doesn't mean he's perfect. I just don't think we should automatically assume the worst of Agnes.'

Callie looked a bit startled. 'No, of course, you're right. It's just... Oh well, whatever the reason, I hope one day, they get past the problem and venture out of the grounds. I'm sure they'd be happier mixing with the other ghosts and seeing what's going on in the village.'

Clara nodded. 'I'm sure you're right. Well, what will be will be.' She picked up her glass again and said, 'I suppose we'd better be getting back to our table. The quiz is due to start any minute. Oh! Look who's arrived, Callie. If you feel a death ray boring into the back of your head all evening, it's because Rissa's turned up.'

Callie groaned as we all turned to the table in the corner where The Rowan Brainiacs usually sat. That was the team consisting of the staff from Rowan Farm, and Rissa hadn't really bothered to turn up for the quiz for some weeks. Not since Callie and Brodie got together, in fact. I couldn't help but feel sorry for her in the circumstances.

My attention swung from Rissa to the man slipping into the seat next to hers. Max! What was he doing here? He was sitting between Rissa and Nick, and Nick seemed to be chatting quite amiably to him. There was no sign of Betty tonight, I noticed, though Erin, Bram and Lars had all turned up.

'Who's the man sitting next to her?' Clara asked.

'That's her father,' I said. 'Max. He's a German teacher at Chipping Royston Academy. Head of the Language Department, actually. He might be teaching your kids soon.'

She lifted her eyebrows. 'Rissa has a dad? Thought she'd been manufactured in some soulless factory somewhere.'

'That's not very nice,' I told her, shaking my head.

Clara rubbed her forehead. 'I know, I know! I'm sorry. I'm all over the place lately. Honestly, I'm a total bitch one minute and sobbing into a cushion the next. Ignore me.'

Callie put her arm around her shoulders. 'It's okay,' she soothed. 'It's not your fault. But it's not Rissa's either. She can't help it that she still has feelings for Brodie. It must be awful for her.'

'Oh, wow,' Pippa said, shaking her head in disbelief, 'you're way too nice, Callie! She's been bloody horrible about you. And the way she looks at you!'

'How do you know?' Callie asked, which was a fair question given Pippa no longer lived in Rowan Vale.

Pippa cleared her throat and sipped her drink, trying not to look in my direction.

I sighed. 'I may have mentioned a couple of instances... Sorry.'

Callie picked up her glass. 'Well anyway, I'm trying to be understanding in the circumstances. I'm sure Rissa will get over Brodie at some point and then, maybe, we can all be friends.'

'I'm sure,' I said, though I wasn't. Not at all. 'In the meantime, it's good that she has her father visiting her. Maybe he can talk some sense into her. He seems the reasonable sort.'

'You know him?' Clara asked, surprised.

'Oh, she knows him,' Pippa said with a giggle. 'Grandad's been winding her up that she's got a bit of a thing for him. Apparently, he's a very charming man.' She stared over at Max's table as if she'd never heard of discretion. 'I've been wondering what he looked like. Quite nice for a man of his age. Maybe you should give it some thought, Mum.'

'Give it some thought? Oh, don't you start, too,' I said. 'Bad enough with your grandad's jokes. One handsome man arrives in the village and suddenly, I'm madly in love.'

Three heads turned in my direction and three pairs of eyes looked at me knowingly.

'One handsome man, eh?' Pippa asked and I tried to laugh.

'Well, looked at dispassionately, I would say he's attractive, yes. And he seems very polite and well-mannered.'

'Well, you don't want that!' Clara groaned. 'No red-blooded woman wants polite and well-mannered!'

'I thought your libido had vanished without trace?' Callie reminded her.

'I'm living vicariously,' Clara told her. 'If I can't get *my* kicks any longer, I'd like to think other women can. Especially someone like Shona, who's been through this hormonal tornado and come out the other side. It would be encouraging to know that there's light at the end of the tunnel.'

'Don't look to me for confirmation,' I said. 'I've got no interest in relationships.'

'Who said anything about relationships?' she said, looking aghast at the idea. 'I'm talking about—'

'Okay, okay,' I said hastily. 'Can I remind you my daughter's sitting right here?'

Pippa rolled her eyes. 'Yes, and I'm a delicate little flower who must never know that my mother is an actual flesh-and-blood woman with wants and needs of her own.'

'I don't have wants and needs!' I protested, blushing furiously. 'I'd rather have a flapjack than a man.'

Callie laughed. 'Okay, I think we've traumatised poor Shona enough. The quiz is about to start. Isaac's waving at me to take a seat.'

'He'd better not tell you any of the answers,' I said, glad of a change of subject.

'He shouts every one of them at me,' she replied airily, 'but don't worry. I never pass them on.'

'Which is why we usually come last in this bloody quiz,' Clara grumbled.

They got to their feet, glasses in hand, and we all wished each other luck.

'You do realise we've probably got no chance against the Rowan Brainiacs' team,' Pippa said. 'What with two blokes with Masters degrees, and Rissa's dad being Head of Languages at an academy, they must be well ahead of the rest of us.'

'We're counting on you,' I told her with a smile. 'You're the only one on our team with a degree.'

Pippa groaned. 'Blimey, if that's the case, we really are sunk!'

'Don't worry,' Veronica said as we all shuffled

closer, now Callie and Clara had gone. 'The questions in these quizzes aren't aimed at university graduates. It's very much basic general knowledge. You'll probably get more questions about films and sport and celebrity couples than history, geography or science.'

'Celebrity couples?' Pippa brightened considerably. 'In that case, prepare for victory!'

16

It was my half-day at the teashop, and I was on my way home. It was a warm, but breezy, August day, and I was looking forward to an afternoon in the garden. I had a load of washing to put on but that was okay; the clothes would dry beautifully on the line in this weather. Christie and Scott had invited Dad and me to dinner at their house tonight, so I didn't even have to think about cooking.

Dad had decided his bedroom needed redecorating and had caught the bus to Harling's Halt then treated himself to a ride on the steam train to Much Melton. He'd texted me on his ancient Nokia phone at ten that morning to tell me he was having a wander round the shops and would have lunch in a cafe be-fore returning home – hopefully with some wallpaper and paint samples. He told me not to worry; he'd defi-nitely be home by five when Christie had said Scott would be picking us up.

So I basically had the afternoon to myself, which was a rare thing, and at that moment as I crossed the footbridge over the river and headed along Faran Lane towards home, I felt there was no one luckier than me in the entire world.

Passing The Quicken Tree, I smiled to myself, re-membering the pub quiz last Thursday, when our team had come third. It had been won by the Bright Sparks – the staff from the Swinging Sixties street – with the Mill Crew coming in second. To our amaze-ment, and, it had to be said, amusement, the Rowan Brainiacs had come in last. And with three postgrads among them!

As we'd left the pub, laughing and teasing each other, I'd caught Max's eye and had felt myself go all funny when he smiled warmly at me and raised a hand in both a greeting and a farewell.

I'd awkwardly waved back and smiled before I'd been nudged along by the crowd leaving the pub. With Pippa at my side, I hadn't dared hang back to talk to him. I wouldn't want my daughter to get the wrong idea, after all.

Starling Cottage wasn't particularly big, but it always felt huge when Dad wasn't at home. As I put down my bag on the kitchen counter and flicked the kettle on to boil, I tried to imagine it as it had been in Aunt Polly's day, with her mum and dad and two younger brothers living here. It always gave me a warm feeling, knowing this house had once been home to my great-grandparents, my grandad Norman, and great-uncle Ray, as well as Polly, of course.

When my great-grandad, Raymond had passed away, Grandad Norman had taken over the tenancy of Starling Cottage, and then my dad had taken it over from him. I wondered if, one day, I'd take it over from my dad. I supposed it was inevitable. Where else would I want to go?

And after me? I couldn't imagine Christie and Scott moving here. They were happy in Kingsford Wold and the girls were settled there. I wondered if Pippa would one day settle down with someone and have a family. Would she be happy to live in Rowan Vale? If not, it would mean the end of the Deakins at Starling Cottage.

I shook my head, wondering where all these

maudlin thoughts had come from suddenly. I busied myself putting on the wash and made myself a cup of coffee, which I carried into the back garden, along with a book I was halfway through.

It was a rare treat not to have to think about cooking, and I was determined to enjoy my afternoon of leisure in the sunshine.

I'd just pegged the first wash load onto the line and was adding a capsule to the second load when I heard the knock on the door.

Slamming the washing machine door shut, I quickly set the programme and headed into the hallway, wondering if Dad had come home early and forgotten his keys, or if Amelia had decided to pop by as she sometimes did on my afternoon off.

I'm almost sure my mouth dropped open in a deeply unattractive fashion when I saw Max standing on the step, holding, of all things, a bunch of pink roses.

He cleared his throat and handed them to me. 'Good afternoon, Shona. I hope you'll forgive the intrusion, but I thought I'd take Jimmy up on his kind offer and pay him a visit. I really enjoyed our chat at the teashop the other week.'

I looked down at the blush-pink roses and felt my face flushing to match them. 'Er, you'd better come in,' I said, thinking who on earth these days brought roses for someone they barely knew, merely out of politeness? He was like some old-fashioned Regency gentleman, the sort I'd just been reading about in my romance novel.

'I'm sorry,' I told him as I closed the front door behind him and led him into the kitchen, 'I'm afraid Dad's not home. He's gone into Much Melton for some wallpaper and paint samples. He's got it into his head that his bedroom needs decorating. It doesn't,' I added, 'but he gets these fancies now and then.'

Max kindly ignored my flustered ramblings and smiled. 'I see. Ah well. Perhaps another time. I'm sorry to have disturbed you.'

'You haven't disturbed me!' I said quickly, rummaging in the cupboard under the sink for a vase. 'It's my afternoon off and I'm just sitting out in the garden. I was about to make myself another coffee, actually. Would you like one?'

Max hesitated then shrugged. 'Why not? If you're sure it's no trouble?'

'No trouble at all,' I assured him, although my shaking hands as I filled the kettle with water told another story. 'Why don't you sit yourself down outside and I'll bring the coffee out to you.'

'Thank you.'

He headed into the garden, and I puffed out my cheeks, trying to calm myself. As the kettle boiled, I arranged the roses in the vase, thinking how beautiful they were and how lovely he was to have given them to me.

What was it with this man? Why did he have such a peculiar effect on me? Honestly, no man except Luke had made me feel this way, which wasn't reassuring. Look how me and Luke had turned out!

Not that there seemed much danger of me and Max going the same way. There *was* no me and Max for a start, and he'd probably run a mile if he suspected for a moment that part of me really wished there would be one day.

'Your garden is lovely,' he told me as I carried two mugs of coffee outside and set them down on our patio table. 'You're obviously a keen gardener.'

I laughed at that. 'Me? Not at all. It's Dad who looks after the garden. It's his pride and joy. After Mum died, he threw himself into making it beautiful in her memory. I think it helped him, you know? Helped him to cope with her loss somehow, making something so lovely to counteract the sadness within him.' I remembered, too late, about his wife and groaned inwardly. 'I'm sorry. I didn't mean—'

'But you're right,' he assured me. 'It's good that he found a way to deal with his grief.'

'And have you found a way to deal with yours?' I asked him gently, while wondering at the same time why on earth I thought I had the right to question him about something so personal.

He didn't seem offended, though. 'Grief is a very strange thing,' he confessed. 'It comes in waves. Sometimes, it's manageable, like tiny waves lapping on a shore, and one can almost forget the loss one has suffered. Almost. But at other times, it's a savage onslaught. Like a tidal wave, crashing down upon you and wiping out everything else, so all you can think about is how to survive. Sometimes, in the darkest moments of early grief, you wonder if it's worth the struggle.'

I put my hand to my mouth as tears welled up in my eyes. 'I'm so sorry,' I murmured.

'Please.' Max held up his hand. 'There's no need to be sorry. Death is part of life, and we must all find our own way after the loss of loved ones. I have far more days of gentle waves than tidal waves now. Today is a good day and I'm grateful for that.'

I sipped my coffee, not sure what to say to his words without sounding trite. I wondered what he'd say if I told him that this village was full of ghosts, and death wasn't quite as straightforward as he imagined.

'The pub quiz was fun,' he said, breaking our silence, much to my relief.

I grinned, glad to have something else to talk about. 'Even though your team came last?'

He rolled his eyes. 'The humiliation! Although it must be said, the questions weren't what I was expecting. How am I supposed to know how many top ten hits some band has had when I've never even heard of the band?'

'How can you not have heard of Status Quo?' I demanded. 'Everyone knows who they are!'

'Not everyone, clearly,' he said, his hazel eyes twinkling. 'I'm only half-convinced they ever existed. I think maybe the lady doing the quiz made them up to confuse us.'

I laughed. 'Penny, cheat? Never! I can promise you they're a real band, and really good. I have some of their albums somewhere.'

'Hmm. If you say so. Rissa says they are for old people, so maybe I would enjoy them.'

My eyes widened in indignation. 'Do you mind? I'm only fifty-two!'

He held up his hands, laughing. 'They were not my words! They were Rissa's. I am older than you by a couple of years, so believe me, I am not insulting you. Anyway,' he added, dropping his hands and eyeing me thoughtfully, 'you don't look fifty-two. You must stay out of the sunshine.'

I felt quite flustered by his offhand compliment. 'Oh, people always say that. I tell them, it's the fat plumping up the wrinkles.'

Oh no! Why had I said *that*? Fancy drawing attention to my size-eighteen body! Although, it had never bothered me before, so why should I start worrying now? Honestly, this is what men did to you. Made you all self-critical and timid. Luke had a way of doing that – of sapping my self-confidence and making me feel worthless. I wasn't going to let anyone else do that to me, no matter how good-looking he was.

Max looked quite taken aback by my comment and clearly wasn't sure what to say in response. I could almost see him trying to work out how to answer without offending me in some way.

'It's okay,' I said hastily. 'I wasn't hoping you'd tell me I wasn't fat. I'm a bit on the curvy side, I know, but that's just me and I don't care. No false compliments needed.'

'I wasn't going to give you any,' he said with a shrug.

'Oh.' *Charming.* 'Okay.'

'You are who you are, and it suits you,' he said in a matter-of-fact voice. 'There is nothing more attractive than a woman who is comfortable with herself.'

His eyes widened suddenly, and two spots of colour appeared on his cheeks as if he'd suddenly re-alised that he'd given me one heck of a compliment actually, and that it didn't sound in the least bit false.

Bless him, he needed rescuing.

'Have you come to the village especially to see Dad, or did you visit Rissa first?' I enquired, changing the subject.

He visibly slumped with relief. Picking up his cof-fee, he took a small sip to steady his nerves before replying.

'I came to see your father. I popped into the teashop first to see if he was there, but the girl behind the counter told me it was your afternoon off so he would probably be at home.'

'It was kind of you to bring us roses,' I said.

He glanced around the garden. 'Clearly, there was no need. I should have brought you chocolates or wine. You have enough flowers already. Never mind. I think it's the polite thing to do. I always bring a gift to my host. I took flowers to Betty when she invited me to tea with them at Rowan Farm. She was surprised, too.'

'You went to tea at Rowan Farm? That's lovely,' I said enthusiastically. 'It's good that you're seeing more of Rissa.'

'It must be a puzzle to you,' he said slowly. 'My relationship with my daughter.'

'It's none of my business,' I told him firmly, although I'll admit, there was a part of me that was dying to know what was going on between them. Why hadn't he known that Rissa worked here, for a start? 'Unless,' I added hopefully, 'you want to talk about it?'

'I'm sure it would bore you, and you have far better things to do than listen to my worries,' he said.

'Nope. Not a thing,' I assured him, pushing my book further away and leaning forward to signal I was ready and waiting if he wanted to talk.

'The thing is, Rissa and I were always so close,' he said sadly. 'My wife, Nina, was a busy doctor and spent a lot of time at the hospital. I gave up work to care for Rissa when she was born and we really bonded, you know? She was my angel, and I adored her. I returned to work when she started school, but we remained close.' He sighed. 'Nina's job was highly pressured. She was on call a lot and spent so much time away from home. I think she regretted that at the end. I think we both did. We had talked about our future so many times – about taking early retirement and spending our later years together. But that wasn't to be, and we realised far too late that there would be no early retirement. No time to be together.'

He massaged his temples then gave me a wan smile. 'I'm sorry. I've wandered from the subject a little. Well, as I say, I was Rissa's primary caregiver, and we were inseparable at weekends and during the holidays. But then Nina died and – and I let Rissa down quite badly.'

I wasn't sure what to say to that. Any response I thought of sounded so feeble and how was I supposed to know the truth of his words? Maybe he *had* let her down badly?

'I forgot that Rissa was grieving for her mother,' he explained. 'I made it all about me. I was so lost in my grief that I couldn't see that she was lost, too. When I should have been there for her, I was absent. She was amazing. She stayed at university, and she got her degree. I was so proud of her. But the damage was done. We had grown apart and I think there is a part of her that will never forgive me.'

'I'm sure that's not true,' I said gently.

'Why else would she take a job here, of all places, and not tell me?' he asked, the anguish clear in his voice. 'I believed she was living and working with an old schoolfriend in London. She let me believe that. And all the time, she was living and working here, just a few miles from me. I think,' he added sadly, 'that she punished me for selling our house and moving to Chipping Royston. She probably expected me to keep our family home, but I just couldn't. I didn't want to be there any more. Not without Nina. I needed a fresh start. Do you understand?'

'I do understand,' I said. 'And I honestly think you're being too hard on yourself. We can only do the best we're capable of at the time. When grief comes along and knocks us off our feet, it's all we can do to keep our heads above the water. We don't always have the strength to hold up other people, too, even the ones we're responsible for and love more than anything. Believe me, I know.'

He raised an enquiring eyebrow. 'You sound as if you have experienced something like this?'

'I have. Sort of.' I gulped down some coffee. 'I can't claim it's anywhere near what you and Rissa went through, but I did experience a sort of grief, and I did let my girls down just as badly as you believe you let Rissa down.'

'I'm sorry,' he said. 'I had no idea.'

'My husband didn't die,' I said quickly. 'He – well, embarrassingly, he left me for another woman.'

Max frowned. 'That's – I'm sorry. Embarrassing only for him, though. To behave in such a fashion.'

I gave him a wry smile. 'I don't think he was particularly embarrassed about it. He was too busy figuring out how to keep me hanging on for him until he knew if his new girlfriend was in it for keeps or not. I was basically his insurance.'

'I'm sorry?'

'He didn't tell me about her at first,' I explained. 'In fact, he didn't tell me about her at all. He just said he needed space to figure out what he wanted. It went on like that for months – him promising me he was thinking things through, that he still loved me and just needed time. But then they were spotted together by – of all people – our eldest daughter, Christie. She was only fourteen at the time and out shopping with her friends.' I puffed out my cheeks, remembering the chaotic scenes that had ensued. 'She almost got arrested when she flew at him and attacked him in the street, prompting his new girlfriend to call the police.'

Yeah, that's how I'd found out. Not a great day.

'Luckily, the police were very understanding and, despite his girlfriend's protests, Luke refused to press charges. I suppose there was a kernel of goodness in him somewhere. Anyway, it was all a bit messy,' I finished with a shrug.

'That's disgraceful!' Max gasped. 'To behave in such a way towards his wife and daughters! What kind of man is that?'

'Well, not much of one, I guess. But at the time, believe it or not, I was heartbroken. Devastated. And I'm afraid I fell to pieces for a while there. I basically spent all my time crying, listening to sad songs from our dating days, and eating flapjacks. I didn't have the headspace for my children's grief, and they must have been going through it just as much as I was. They'd lost their dad, after all.

'He more or less stepped away from their lives and I didn't help them through that process nearly as much as I should have. It's my biggest regret, and something I can never make up to them. So,' I finished, rather sheepishly, 'I do kind of get how you feel. I failed my daughters spectacularly, I'm afraid. I don't know how they've ever forgiven me but I'm so grateful that they have.'

We both sat in silence for a few moments, then Max shook his head. 'Your husband did not deserve you, or your children. No wonder you struggled. At least I knew, at the end, that Nina had loved me and our daughter. To suffer what you did... I cannot imagine the pain you must have inside you.'

To my horror, tears welled up again at his words.

The kindness and understanding in his voice had unlocked something I thought I'd buried deep within me. I'd worked so hard to keep it hidden away and I couldn't believe it was suddenly right there again, unfurling inside me and threatening to knock me off balance after all this time.

I was over this! I was! Why now?

'Shona?' he asked gently. 'Are you okay?'

I nodded, not daring to speak.

'Would you like another coffee?' he asked, nodding at my empty mug.

'I'll make it,' I managed, jumping to my feet.

'Let me,' he said, half-rising from his chair, but I shook my head furiously.

'Please, I'll do it.'

He sat down again. 'Of course.'

In the kitchen, I banged around, getting clean cups from the cupboard instead of simply rinsing the used ones out, and finding biscuits to offer my guest. I couldn't understand that sudden attack of emotion and felt bitterly ashamed of myself.

'I'm so sorry,' I told him as I returned, carrying a tray with two coffees and a plate of biscuits. 'I can't think what happened there.'

'There's no need to be sorry,' he said kindly.

'But it makes no sense!' I desperately wanted him

to know that I was over Luke. I desperately wanted to remind *myself* that I was over Luke. 'He and I, we ended years ago, and honestly, I'm glad we did. He wasn't right for me. He treated me terribly. He treated our girls terribly. I don't love him. I don't miss him. So I don't understand what those tears were about, I really don't.'

'Maybe,' he said, reaching for a biscuit as he considered the matter, 'you are over your husband, but you haven't yet fully dealt with his betrayal. Maybe you still carry pain and anger at the way he treated you and your daughters, and it's that which made you feel so emotional.'

'Or maybe,' I admitted slowly, 'I'm just as angry at myself as I am at him. I put up with his crap for ages, and I let him walk all over me. And then, when he'd done his worst, I fell to bits as if he mattered! And by doing so, I let my kids down. That's what makes me furious. It's me I'm angry at, not him.

'Well,' I added, 'I *am* angry at him, but to be honest, even the anger's faded now. I just can't be bothered with him at all these days. But you're right, the pain of how he treated me might well still be raw. I've tried so hard to bury it, you see. I just wanted to put our lives back together and make the girls happy, and I could only do that by pushing the sadness deep down inside where it couldn't touch me. Talking about it just now with you, I realised it's still there. I wasn't sure how to deal with it. I'm sorry you had to see that.'

'I think we've both shown our more vulnerable sides today,' he said, waving a biscuit in the air and smiling at me. 'It has been a therapeutic afternoon for us, hasn't it?'

I smiled back. 'I guess it has.'

We sat in amiable peace for a while; the only sound, apart from the humming of insects and the odd chirp from garden birds, was the crunching as we ate our biscuits. I was quite pleased to see he obviously enjoyed a chocolate Hobnob just as much as I did. Luke hadn't approved of chocolate Hobnobs. He hadn't approved of anything that made me smile, really.

'Dad'll be home soon,' I said, glancing at my watch and noticing it was gone four o'clock.

'I'll get out of your way,' Max said, brushing crumbs from his jacket. 'You'll want to prepare your dinner.'

'Not tonight,' I told him cheerfully. 'My son-in-law's picking me and Dad up at five to take us both back to their house in Kingsford Wold. We're having dinner at theirs for once.'

'That's lovely,' he said warmly. 'I hope you have a wonderful time with your family.'

'If I *was* cooking,' I said hesitantly, 'I'd have invited you to stay.'

He glanced down at what remained of his coffee before returning my gaze. 'If you *were* cooking, I would have accepted the invitation.'

We smiled at each other, and I felt a very different emotion take over my body, crushing the sadness and anger I'd experienced earlier into dust.

'I will leave you to it,' Max said, getting to his feet suddenly. 'I must be going home now anyway. I have my own dinner to prepare. Thank you, Shona, for a lovely afternoon.'

'You're very welcome.' I collected the coffee cups, and he picked up the plate, and we headed back inside. 'Maybe you'll come for dinner another evening?'

'That's very kind of you. We shall arrange it one day when your father is home, yes?'

My heart sank. Of course. I'd almost forgotten it was Dad that Max had come to see today, not me.

'Sure. I'll call you and let you know when he's available.'

Like Dad was ever not available! Him being out today was a total fluke. What the heck was I babbling on about?

Max gave me a brief smile and left for home. I closed the door behind him, then leaned against it, shaking my head at my ridiculous behaviour.

It was only when I went back into the kitchen to unload the washing machine that I remembered I didn't have his phone number, and he hadn't asked for mine.

17

POLLY

Polly didn't like going out after dark. As soon as dusk approached, she would make her way back to her flat above the teashop and nothing and no one would persuade her to leave until the following morning.

She knew it made no sense. It wasn't as if anyone could hurt her, was it? But the darkness held terrifying memories for her, and she couldn't help herself. Shona knew and understood, bless her, and made sure a lamp was left on in the living room and landing of the flat every evening so she could always have light if she needed it.

She wasn't sure if Shona knew *why* she was so scared of the dark. They'd never discussed the events of *that* night. She supposed Jimmy must have explained some of it to her, but then he didn't know it all either. She and Norman had agreed on that. It was best kept quiet. Let the past keep its secrets.

Even so, tonight, Polly was doing the unthinkable. She was braving the darkness to go to Appleseed Cottage where Harmony Hill lived with an unknowing Mrs Smithson. It was a big cottage on the outskirts of the village and quite a walk from the teashop. Normally, Polly would have thought nothing of it, but having to cross the footbridge over the river and walk up the long, winding lane towards the cottage in the darkness was something else entirely.

'Bloody Harmony! Why does she have to be so stubborn?' Polly muttered to herself as she walked.

She clutched her chest as she saw something move out of the corner of her eye, then felt weak with relief when she realised it was just a fox. The relief didn't last long, though. She was wary of foxes. She remembered how her mum and dad had hated them, because one had got into the chicken coop and killed the hens.

Ray and Norman had stuck up for them, telling their parents that foxes had to eat, and that didn't make them cold-blooded killers. They were only doing what they had to do to survive, after all.

She recalled how foxhunting had been very popular back in her day. Despite her wariness, she was glad they'd put a stop to that. Yes, foxes killed, but they didn't deserve to be hounded to their deaths, poor things.

Polly faltered as the fox stopped and looked directly at her. Ray had once told her that foxes were guides to the spirit world, and thinking about that now made her shiver.

Even so, she felt quite sorry for it – this lonely, nocturnal creature, living mostly in the woods, treated as vermin by some and branded a killer by many. She couldn't deny it was beautiful, and there was a gentleness in its eyes that Polly found enchanting.

The fox sniffed the air, as if trying to catch her scent. Then it trotted away as if it had realised she wasn't of this world and he shouldn't linger near her. Maybe this solitary creature was more scared of her than she was of him?

Shaking her head, she hurried on. 'This won't get the baby its bonnet, Polly Herron. Just get to Appleseed Cottage. The sooner it's done, the sooner you can go home.'

She felt better hearing her own voice. It grounded her, somehow. Maybe she should sing to herself? It might keep the fear at bay anyway.

She began to sing 'A Nightingale Sang in Berkley

Square' but found it too emotional, so she switched to the more upbeat 'Everything Stops for Tea'. Her dad used to love singing that to her and her mum when they got home from the teashop. Mind, as her mum had often told him, he was no Jack Buchanan.

Remembering her mum and dad made her feel even sadder. Must be the dark. It was bringing all those buried feelings to the surface. Maybe she should stop singing. Then she remembered when Millie used to waitress in the teashop, back in the early sixties, and how they'd all got very sick of hearing one song in particular that she would insist on singing over and over again. How did it go now?

Polly grinned to herself and walked a little faster as she sang 'Love Me Do' at the top of her voice.

'Good heavens, Mistress Herron, why on earth are you caterwauling at this time of the night?'

Polly's hand once more flew to her chest, and she jumped in fright before her mind had time to register that it was friend, not foe, who'd approached her. Or that he'd just insulted her singing. Bloody cheek!

'Walter! Oh my word, you frightened the life out of me.' Realising what she'd said, she gave a nervous laugh. 'Well, you know what I mean.'

'Indeed. What are you doing out and about in the darkness?' he enquired politely. Walter Tasker, former teacher of William Shakespeare no less, was always polite, but she could see he was also deeply suspicious. Everyone knew she didn't venture out at this time of night.

Polly hesitated, aware that Walter hadn't really approved of the ghosts' plan to visit Harmony Hill.

'I'm off to Appleseed Cottage,' she admitted reluctantly.

'At this hour?'

'No bloody choice, Walter. She's never in during the day. I've tried a few times now but she's not home, and there's no way I'm going over to Woodstone Manor to see if she's there. I don't care what anyone says; no one will persuade me to venture to that creepy place.'

Walter shuddered in agreement. 'I don't blame you. What a terrible place it is, and who knows what evil lurks within its depths?'

His eyes widened and he struck a pose, making Polly's heart sink as she realised what was coming.

'"*By the pricking of my thumbs, something wicked this way comes.*"'

'One of yours, Walter?' she asked mischievously, knowing his propensity for claiming that much of his famous former pupil's work was directly copied from his own verbal outpourings.

'Alas, no,' he said. 'But it's quite catchy, don't you think?'

'It doesn't calm my nerves, though, so thanks for that. As if I'm not nervous enough.'

It crossed her mind briefly that it made no sense for either her or Walter to be afraid of ghosts, or anything else for that matter, but common sense went out of the window when darkness fell. At least, in her case. She didn't know what Walter's excuse was.

'Would you like me to accompany you to Appleseed Cottage?' he asked kindly.

'You wouldn't mind?'

'Of course not. I know you aren't comfortable walking abroad at this hour, and I can't sleep anyway, hence my nighttime wander. I should be glad to walk with you if it will ease your discomfort.'

'Oh, Walter, you're a diamond!' she told him gratefully, as she slipped her arm through his and they headed along the lane towards Appleseed Cottage. 'I know you don't really think we should be bothering Harmony.'

'I understand your motivations for doing so,' he assured her. 'You go with a good heart and that's enough for me. Please be aware, however, that she may not be receptive to your pleas. I hope you will respect her right to privacy if that is what she desires.'

'Of course I will, Walter. I just want to make sure she knows about the forties weekend, and that she understands there are no hard feelings. Just because she's shied away from us for most of the time she's been here, we don't bear her any grudges. She needs to know that. After that, she can make her own mind up.'

'Very well then. I see no harm in that,' he said.

They walked along the lane, chatting about the forthcoming event and wondering how busy it would get.

The lane was quiet and the only person they encountered along the way was, of all people, Silas Alexander, taking his evening constitutional.

He glared at the two of them. 'Out walking together at this time of night? Disgraceful!'

Before they could respond, he marched off again, muttering to himself, leaving the two of them staring after him.

'How *does* his mind work?' Polly mused, shaking her head.

'I'm sorry, Mistress Herron. Your reputation has been compromised by walking alone with me in the dark. I should have thought.'

'Don't be daft, Walter. It's him. Always thinks the worst of everyone, doesn't he? Take no notice. Not our fault if he wants to twist a simple act of kindness into something sordid, is it?'

'If you're sure?'

'Quite sure,' she said firmly. 'Now, what were we talking about?'

They resumed their journey, and Walter told her he'd heard there was to be a new teashop opening in the village, which was news to Polly, though he assured her Shona was well aware of the fact and seemed to approve of the idea.

'You know everything, Walter,' she said admiringly. 'It's amazing how much you pick up.'

'I must admit,' he said, sounding rather pleased with himself, 'that since I've started teaching the children at Harling Hall, I have been privy to more information than in previous years. It's quite surprising how much you hear as you wander the corridors of that illustrious house.'

Walter was teaching three of the ghost children at the Hall: Florrie, who was a ten-year-old wartime evacuee who'd been unofficially adopted by Agnes and Aubrey, and her friends, John and Robert, two little ragamuffins aged nine and six, who'd died in 1790. He was assisted in his mission to educate them by Lawrie, as well as Callie's eleven-year-old daughter, Immi, who shared her mother's ability to see all the ghosts.

'I meant to ask you, as a matter of fact,' Walter continued, 'if you'd care to come to the Hall to talk to the children about life during the Second World War. We're doing a project on it at present, and you'd be perfect to chat to them about what what it was like to live through those times.'

'Me? Heck, I don't know about that, Walter! What could *I* tell them? Besides, you were there. You know as much as I do.'

He shook his head. 'No, Mistress Herron. I merely observed those times. You *lived* them. You know what it was like to be afraid for those you loved who were away fighting. You know how it felt to worry about rations, and queue for whatever supplies you could get hold of at the shops. About digging for victory. Making do and mending.'

Polly laughed. 'I think someone's been browsing the old propaganda posters,' she said, giving him a playful nudge. 'All right, Walter, if you think it will help, I'll be glad to. I expect the kiddies are looking forward to this 1940s weekend then?'

'They are extremely excited,' he agreed. 'It will certainly help them to remember what it was like back then. Florence is looking forward to hearing the music,' he confessed. 'John and Robert, on the other hand, can't wait to smell the food.'

'Bless them.' Polly shook her head. 'I must say, sometimes it's hard not to crave some of the dishes our Shona serves up in her teashop. But do you know what I miss most of all, Walter?'

'Pray tell, Mistress Herron,' he said, smiling at her.

'A bloody strong cup of tea! What I wouldn't give. None of this fancy stuff that our Shona doles out. Just a nice brew in a big, heavy mug, with a bit of sugar and a splash of milk.' She sighed. 'Bliss.'

'I confess I've never tasted tea,' Walter told her. 'I have tasted coffee, which I quite enjoyed, but tea – no.'

'Oh, Walter!' Polly exclaimed in sorrow. 'What you've missed! I feel quite sorry for you.'

'There is no need. You cannot miss what you have never had.'

'I suppose...' Polly's voice trailed off as they approached Appleseed Cottage. 'Do you want to come in with me?'

He shook his head. 'I feel this is a conversation best left for you two ladies. However, I will wait outside for you and escort you home.'

'I can't ask you to do that!'

'You didn't ask me,' he pointed out. 'I offered. I

couldn't leave you to walk home in the dark, knowing how you feel about it. Especially when you are only here from kindness.'

'Aw, Walter.' Polly was deeply touched. She leaned over and planted a kiss on the startled man's cheek. 'Good job the Reverend Alexander didn't see that, eh? But I don't care. What a star you really are.'

'A diamond *and* a star. You honour me!' Walter's eyes twinkled. 'I shall not be far away, Mistress Herron. I wish you luck in your endeavours.'

'Fingers crossed she's in,' Polly said, holding up her entwined fingers for luck.

18

POLLY

Polly left Walter at the gate and headed straight through the front door of Appleseed Cottage, finding herself in the hallway. She didn't really consider this a cottage. It was too big in her eyes. One of them grander buildings built for the middle classes, she supposed. She couldn't imagine why old Mrs Smithson still lived here, all on her own. It made no sense since it had four large bedrooms and two bathrooms, of all things! Fancy having two bathrooms to choose from. She'd have been glad of that back when she'd been living at Starling Cottage.

There was an agreement between the ghosts that, since walls and doors were no barrier, they wouldn't visit each other's homes without an invitation, but since you had to actually see someone face to face to invite them, that didn't really work with Harmony. Polly did feel a bit guilty as she checked the downstairs rooms to see if the elusive Hollywood star was anywhere around, but needs must.

'It's for her own good,' she murmured as she headed upstairs. Anyway, she had to admit it was interesting, seeing what Appleseed Cottage looked like these days. No ghost, to her knowledge, had visited here since Harmony had claimed it as her home.

'Harmony? You up there?' she called, feeling it only fair to give the woman some warning.

There was no reply, and for a moment, she wondered if she was on another fruitless mission. Then there she was. Harmony Hill. The Hollywood goddess, standing at the top of the stairs, staring down at her as if she couldn't believe what she was seeing.

It was funny, Polly thought, how she'd gone to the pictures to see Harmony in her films, and had been so excited when she'd learned the movie star was filming just a few miles from Rowan Vale, back in the summer of 1946.

If she'd known Harmony had been in The Quicken Tree that night, she'd definitely have paid a visit to gawp at her. Discreetly, of course. Who knows, maybe she could have got chatting to her? Maybe she could have stopped her getting quite so drunk? Maybe she could have stopped her falling into the River Faran and drowning?

But she hadn't known, so that was the fate that had befallen this young woman who was still only thirty years old, yet had been the darling of the silver screen and the pin-up for many adoring soldiers during the war.

She looked incredibly glamorous, in wide-legged, navy-blue, high-waisted trousers and a smart, short-sleeved print blouse with shoulder pads. Her shoulder-length hair was platinum blonde, worn in the Old Hollywood Waves style favoured by other glamorous film stars like Lauren Bacall and Veronica Lake. She was beautiful, and for a moment, Polly felt completely starstruck before remembering that Harmony was now just like her, and that she was here for a reason.

'I'm so sorry to disturb you, Harmony,' she said, wondering if she should address this icon as Miss Hill.

'Yeah? So why did ya?'

Without waiting for an answer, Harmony headed downstairs, pushed past Polly and vanished into the living room.

Polly shook her head, reminding herself to be patient, and followed her, to Harmony's evident irritation.

'Jeez, can't a girl get some privacy? I thought we all had a deal?'

'I know, and we do in normal circumstances, but we've had a meeting, and I sort of volunteered to visit you and tell you about an event that's coming up soon.'

Harmony sank onto the sofa and eyed Polly warily. 'What kind of event?'

'It's a 1940s weekend,' Polly explained. 'The whole village will be involved. There are going to be food stalls, and the shop fronts will be made to look as they did in the forties, and there'll be music. And films!' she added eagerly.

'Movies?' Harmony sat up straighter. '*My* movies?'

Polly wished she'd thought that through. 'Er no. But good films.'

'Whaddya mean, good films? You saying my movies weren't good?' Harmony sounded outraged, and Polly rolled her eyes, realising she'd have to tread carefully if she was going to get the young woman to listen.

'Your movies were excellent,' she assured Harmony, meaning it. 'I think they probably didn't want to upset you by showing them. I was such a massive fan of yours. I went to the pictures all the time to see them.'

'Oh yeah?' Harmony sounded doubtful. 'Which ones?'

Polly groaned inwardly. It had been such a long time ago and now she was under pressure, her mind had gone blank. 'Er, *One Weekend in Connecticut*,' she said, grasping at the title of Harmony's breakout film gratefully. 'Loved that! So funny, and you were wonderful in it.'

Harmony leaned back on the sofa and closed her eyes for a moment. 'Yeah, I liked that one, too,' she said quietly. She opened her eyes and grinned at Polly. 'You know, Betty Grable wanted the part, but I whooped her ass with my screen test. The kid couldn't catch a break, but what can ya do?'

Polly was tempted to point out that Betty Grable hadn't done so badly for herself in subsequent years. On balance, she thought it best not to. Luckily, Harmony didn't seem to expect an answer.

'1935. I was nineteen years old, and after that movie, I was box-office gold.' She gave a wistful sigh then turned to Polly, her expression curious. 'Say, what's this weekend gotta do with me anyway? What makes you think I care?'

'Well...' Polly hesitantly sat down on the chair opposite and folded her hands in her lap as she tried to explain the ghosts' concern. 'Thing is, we were kind of hoping you'd attend just to have a bit of fun. The truth is, we're all a bit worried about you.'

Harmony's eyes widened. 'About me? Why would you be worried about me?'

'Since you – since that night – you've never really mixed with us. You keep yourself to yourself, and we're worried you're a bit isolated. Well, a lot isolated, actually. We thought a bit of fun would do you some good, and we all want to meet you properly, you know? My mum always said it doesn't do any good to wallow.'

'Wallow?'

'You know.' Polly wasn't certain if Americans had the same word for wallow. 'I mean, just moping around, dwelling on the past. We have to make the most of our afterlives. What's the alternative? I know it must be hard for you, what with you being a big star and so far away from home. Harder than it is for the rest of us, because we know this place and love it, but you've got no connections here, have you? Which is why—'

She broke off, staring in dismay as Harmony faded to black and white. She looked just as she had in her films. It was a trick she seemed to possess that none of the other ghosts did. Whenever someone said anything to upset or annoy her, the colour would drain from her, as if it was her way of trying to disappear from their sight.

'I'm so sorry,' Polly cried. 'I didn't mean to upset you.'

'Who says you upset me?' Harmony demanded, tilting her chin in defiance.

'Well, er...' Polly looked helplessly at the actress's monochrome form.

Harmony followed her gaze and slapped her thigh in exasperation. 'Damnit! What gives with this anyway? I can't control it. Does it happen to you?'

'No,' Polly admitted. 'I don't know that it happens to any other ghost of my acquaintance.'

'I was kinda worried you'd say that.' Harmony sighed, and as she did so, the colour gradually returned to her, easing Polly's mind a little.

'You look just like you do in your films,' Polly reassured her gently. 'As beautiful as ever.'

Harmony smiled. 'You're a nice girl, honey. What did you say your name was again?'

'I didn't,' Polly admitted. 'Sorry, that was rude of me. It's Polly. Polly Herron.'

Harmony's eyes widened and she stared at Polly as if she'd just seen her for the first time.

'Polly Herron?' She tilted her head, eyeing Polly in an unnerving manner. 'So, *you're* Polly, huh? I guess I shoulda known. Your clothes, your hairstyle. Only you and me here from the forties, right?'

'You, me, and a little girl,' Polly corrected her.

Harmony sat forward. 'A little girl? Oh! You mean the bossy kid from Harling Hall, I guess?'

Polly laughed. 'Yes, Florrie. She's sort of been adopted by Agnes and Aubrey.'

'She has, huh? Well...' Harmony studied her beautifully manicured nails for a moment. 'How old is she anyway?'

Polly shrugged. 'Ten, I think. She's an evacuee from London.'

'Ten? You sure?'

'Well...' Polly thought about it. 'Yes, she's definitely ten, because she and Immi were the same age when Callie moved here but then Immi had her eleventh birthday, so yes. Florrie's ten.'

'Right.'

Was it her imagination, or did Harmony sound disappointed?

'Does it matter?' she asked, puzzled.

'Huh? No, no of course it don't matter. Just thinking how sad it is that a kid died so young. I mean, I thought thirty was bad enough, but jeez...' Harmony shrugged. 'It's good to meet you at last, Polly.'

'It is?' Polly felt flustered and ridiculously flattered. 'Actually, we have briefly met before, but we weren't properly introduced. You sort of took off before we could say anything.'

'I did? When was that?'

'Oh, it was not long after I crossed over,' Polly said with a shrug. 'Some of the ghosts took me under their wing and decided to take me on the rounds to meet everyone. You were sitting on a bench outside the church, and you seemed miles away. You didn't notice us approaching you until we were right beside you, and when Isaac tried to tell you who I was, you got up without speaking and walked away.'

Like you couldn't get away fast enough.

'Gee, I'm sorry. I guess the air was blue after I left, huh?' She shook her head. 'I was still pretty new to it all back then, ya know? I was used to people chasing after me for autographs and I still felt the need to get away.'

But what's your excuse now?

'You arrived not long after I...' Harmony bit her lip and closed her eyes briefly. 'After I died,' she said at last.

'I did,' Polly said, surprised that Harmony knew even that much about her. 'You passed in June 1946, and I passed in January 1948.'

'New Year's Day,' she murmured.

Polly stared at her. 'How did you know that?'

Harmony shrugged. 'I don't know. Musta stuck in my mind, you know? I hate that expression, by the way. "Passed". Passed where, for chrissakes? Do not pass go, do not collect two hundred dollars.' She sighed. 'We died, Polly. End of.'

'But it wasn't the end of, was it?' Polly pointed out.

'You think? Well, it hasn't done much for my career, I'll tell you that much.'

Polly burst out laughing. 'Mine neither, love, but I suppose I was never likely to win an Oscar for my apple crumble, was I?'

'I loved apple crumble,' Harmony said in a longing tone.

'Me an' all. And chocolate cake.'

'And pumpkin pie!'

'Never tasted that,' Polly admitted. 'Sounds bloody awful, though.'

Harmony laughed this time, her face transforming instantly. Polly was dumbstruck by how attractive she really was, but there was something else... Something she couldn't quite put her finger on.

'Guess we'll never taste anything good again. Or anything at all,' Harmony said.

'But on the plus side, you'll never get fat,' Polly pointed out, making Harmony laugh again.

'Or old. Sheesh, I've seen Mrs Smithson's newspapers and magazines over the years. Some of my so-called friends in the business aged *badly*. More wrinkled than a walnut! Either that or they look like wax dummies. I nearly died all over again with fright at the state of them!'

Her humour emboldened Polly to reach over and lightly touch the film star's arm. 'Will you come to the 1940s weekend?' she pleaded. 'We'd love to see you, we really would. We're a friendly bunch, honest, and everyone would welcome you with open arms.'

'But maybe,' Harmony said, her smile fading instantly, 'I don't deserve friends.'

'Of course you deserve friends!' Polly gasped. 'Everyone does. Why the heck would you think otherwise?'

'You're a very sweet girl, Polly,' Harmony told her. 'Let me ask you something. Do you think everyone can be forgiven? No matter what they do?'

'Of course! I mean, it's not for us to forgive anyway, is it? That's what the vicar always told us on a Sunday when we went to church. And let's face it, we've all done things we're not proud of.' It felt as if her stomach rolled suddenly, even though that was impossible. 'Things other people wouldn't approve of. Things many would say were wrong.'

'You think forgiveness is for everyone?' Harmony watched her intently. 'Even Hitler?'

Polly wrinkled her nose. 'Like I said, it's not for me to forgive anyone. Not even sure *he* was human, so maybe he doesn't count.'

'And what about the guy who murdered *you*, Polly? Would you forgive *him*?'

Harmony's green eyes seemed to bore through her. Polly had that awful sensation of feeling sick again, even though she knew it was impossible.

'I–I—' She couldn't make herself speak about it. If she started, she might well break down, and then who knew what she might say? Especially with Harmony Hill, one of her all-time idols, looking at her with such sympathy and even understanding. Like – like she *knew*.

Polly mentally shook her head. Of course she didn't know. No one knew. Correction. No one *alive* knew. Except, possibly Betty. She had a funny feeling that Betty had been told the truth, judging by her expression when she learned who Max Meyer was. But apart from Betty, there was no one. But there was the teeniest, tiniest chance that a ghost or two had witnessed what had happened. Well, she knew for a fact that one of them had, but maybe there'd been another one hanging around? Someone who didn't like to mingle with the others in the village. Someone who might have been wandering through the woods alone that night...

'I'll take that as a no,' Harmony said, sounding bleak suddenly. 'And that's what I mean. Some things can't be forgiven, and some of us don't deserve friends, or a happy ever afterlife.'

'But you – you're not a murderer?' Polly asked, bewildered.

'No, I'm not. But if I was...' Harmony smoothed her trousers and got to her feet. 'It was swell of you to call on me, Polly, but I think I'm ready for bed now. Can you show yourself out?'

Polly stood, feeling thoroughly confused. 'Will you think about it?' she begged. As a sudden thought occurred to her, she added, 'You can bring Quintus Severus, too, if you like? Maybe he'd come into the village if you were with him?'

Harmony stared at her. 'The Roman? Now why the heck would you think that?'

Feeling suddenly foolish, Polly said, 'Sorry. We just assumed... I mean, you must go *somewhere* during the day, and no one sees you around the village, so we thought maybe you went to keep him company. He must talk to someone, surely? I hope he does, anyway. We wondered if maybe you were visiting him at wherever it is he lives. Woodstone Manor perhaps?'

Once again, the colour faded from Harmony. 'You make a lot of assumptions, Polly. You think I'd go anywhere near that creepy place? You gotta be kidding me! It's like a set from a horror movie. As for the Roman, he keeps himself to himself. Some of us prefer it that way.'

'I'm sorry,' Polly said, thoroughly embarrassed. 'I didn't mean to offend you.'

'You didn't. Now I'm bushed and ready for my beauty sleep, so like I said...'

'Of course. Goodnight, Harmony.'

'G'night, Polly.'

Walter was waiting patiently for her by the garden gate as she left Appleseed Cottage feeling awkward and not a little confused.

'You were quite some time, Mistress Herron,' he said, taking her arm. 'How did it go with our esteemed neighbour?'

Polly turned to him, her mind whirling. 'To be absolutely honest with you, Walter, I haven't a bloody clue.'

19

It was raining. In fact, it had rained for three days in a row and Callie was already panicking. She'd been into the teashop that morning and stared glumly out of the window, muttering things like, 'I knew the weather would turn,' and, 'Why did I think September would be a good month for an event?' and, 'This is going to be a disaster, isn't it?'

Luckily, calm and sensible Mia was with her, and between us, we'd managed to reassure her a bit, pointing out that there were still three weeks to the 1940s weekend and plenty of time for the weather to change – probably multiple times.

'Besides,' Mia had said, 'we've got the gazebo for

the singers, the sound system will be fine whether it rains or not, so there'll be music whatever the weather, the tea dance is in the Hall so it can pour down for all we'll care, and there are plenty of shops for visitors to dash into to get out of the rain if necessary.'

'And they can grab a bite to eat here,' I'd added. 'If they don't fancy standing outside with food from the stalls.'

'We really should have another cafe or something,' Callie said with a sigh. 'If only the fish and chip shop had capacity for seating. I wonder if we can look at that for the future?'

'Maybe,' Mia agreed, 'but for now, let's just take one day at a time and get this event over and done with, eh? Everything's on track. The costumes for the staff at the station have arrived and Brodie's got someone to fix up the sound system. We've got the stuff for the shop windows, the stalls are booked, and the band's been hired for the tea dance. Everyone knows what they're doing.'

'Never again, though,' Callie said glumly. 'One event is quite enough for me. I must have been mad.'

'I'll remind you of that when you announce your next bonkers idea,' Mia said, laughing. 'Come on, let's go home. I need to go over the catering for the dance and you promised the girls that you'd watch *Wallace and Gromit* with them.'

'So I did.' Callie picked up her bag and prepared to leave. 'Immi's friend from her old school is staying with us for a couple of weeks, which is bad timing really, given the weekend planning, but I did promise,' she explained to me. 'Anyway, she's a nice girl. Of course, Florrie's tagging along with them and she's really looking forward to *Wallace and Gromit*, bless her.' She grinned suddenly. 'By the way, your Aunt Polly's proving very popular with the children. Walter says she's made the lessons very lively, if you know what I mean. The kids adore her.'

'Oh! I didn't realise she was helping Walter,' I said.

'We discussed it a few weeks ago and Walter asked her if she'd be willing, and she said yes. We're thinking of asking some of the other ghosts to take lessons covering different historical eras,' she explained.

'Makes sense,' I agreed. 'Aw, I'm glad it's going well.' Although I couldn't help feeling sad that she hadn't told me about it. Aunt Polly seemed to be very elusive these days, whereas at one point, she'd been there every time I turned around. I supposed she had her own afterlife to lead, and I had to let her get on with it.

'It is. She's got them really looking forward to the 1940s weekend. Oh heck, I've got that back in my mind again now. Right, *Wallace and Gromit* it is. See you later.'

I'd waved them off and cleared away their teacups, noting that the teashop was now empty – something that rarely happened. I glanced out of the window at the angry, swollen sky, and heavy rain spattering on the glass, and thought there wasn't much chance of it getting any busier today.

'Why don't you take your lunch break now?' Paige suggested, as I carried the tray into the kitchen. 'We're hardly run off our feet, and you should have clocked off an hour ago.'

I looked over at the clock on the wall, noticing it was half-past one. I'd completely forgotten about my lunch! That was something else that very rarely happened.

'What about you?' I asked.

She shrugged. 'Already had mine. There wasn't much else to do in here.'

'May as well then,' I said. 'If I sit near the window, any passing tourists might be encouraged to come in and eat. You never know.'

'Passing tourists?' she wrinkled her nose doubt-fully. 'Maybe a family of passing ducks.'

With that, our eyes widened as the bell above the door jangled.

'Here come the ducks,' Paige said, smiling, as I headed back into the teashop to greet my new customers.

Well, a customer – singular, as it turned out. Max. He was busily folding a sopping-wet umbrella and glanced up as I reached the counter.

I gulped as he smiled a greeting at me.

'Shona! I was hoping you'd be here.' He glanced round and shrugged. 'I see there is plenty of space for me to sit down today.'

'Well,' I said, nodding at the window, 'is it any wonder? There's an umbrella stand over there by the coat rack.' I indicated the small area near the door to the toilets. 'Just shove your wet things there and take a seat. Are you eating, or is it just a drink you want?'

'I definitely am eating,' he said. 'I was hoping for a pot of tea and a slice of that divine lemon cake. It was so good, I've been dreaming about it.'

I decided tea and cake seemed like a good enough lunch for me, too.

'I'm on a break,' I said hesitantly. 'I can join you, if you like?'

'I'd like that very much,' he said, and I was pretty sure he meant it, so I grabbed the lemon cake from the counter and rushed into the kitchen, where I prepared a pot of tea for two and cut two *very* generous slices of cake.

'Ooh,' Paige said, noticing the size of the portions as I loaded the tray, 'VIP guests?'

'One of them's for me,' I said sheepishly.

'And the other one?'

I gave her a sweet smile and carried the tray into the teashop, where Max was sitting at the table he'd occupied last time he was here.

'I don't think Dad will be in today,' I told him, setting the tray down and taking a seat. I'd decided it was best to make that clear to him from the off in case he'd been hoping to bump into him here.

'I should think not in this weather,' he said. Having removed his coat, I saw that he was wearing a charcoal sweatshirt and jeans. I'd never seen him dressed so informally before, and I liked it. It made him look younger and more approachable somehow. 'I thought I would visit him at Starling Cottage later, if you think that would be okay?'

'Of course. I'm sure he'd love to see you again,' I said. 'He gets a bit fed up, especially on days like this, when he can't go out in the garden and it's too wet and miserable for a walk.'

'Yes, on days like today, it's hard to stay positive,' he agreed softly, gazing out of the window. Then he turned to me, shaking his head slightly. 'But the weather will change again, I'm sure. In the meantime, we have tea and cake and— oh my word!' His eyes widened. 'Those are *enormous* slices of cake!'

'I was a bit peckish,' I admitted. 'I haven't had lunch today. You don't have to eat it all.'

'I don't think that will be an option,' he said, his eyes twinkling. 'Once I begin, I won't be able to stop until every last crumb is eaten.'

'I'll hold you to that,' I told him, relieved that the chocolate Hobnobs hadn't been a fluke, and he really wasn't some calorie-counting fitness fanatic who would judge me too harshly on my propensity for ginormous slices of cake.

I poured tea and asked him politely if he'd heard from Rissa. He said they'd exchanged a few casual texts.

'She doesn't like talking on the phone,' he said, looking puzzled. 'It's very strange.'

'My girls are just the same,' I told him. 'It's all texts and WhatsApp messages with them. The worst things are the Sunday-morning video calls! God, it's all you need when you're still in bed and your hair's all over the place, and there's your daughter's face staring at you in disapproval because you should have been up hours ago, and you can't end the call because she's got your granddaughter on her knee who "really wants to talk to Grandma". Nightmare!'

As he laughed, it occurred to me that I'd just basically told him I was a lazy sod who looked a mess in bed, which was hardly the picture I'd wanted to plant in his mind.

Then it occurred to me that it shouldn't matter to me what picture I planted in his mind, and he probably couldn't care less how I looked in bed.

Then I realised that was quite depressing, actually.

Then I thought, I wonder what *he* looks like in bed.

Then I decided I was shameless and shouldn't be having thoughts like that at all given my age and my responsibilities as a dutiful grandparent.

All that going on while I somehow managed to gulp down some tea, then shovel a whopping big forkful of cake into my mouth. Who says women can't multitask?

We chatted for a while about our children. He told me about Rissa's love of history and how well she'd done at university. I told him about Christie, Scott,

Autumn and Maddie, and about Pippa's job at *The Cotswolds Courier*, and how she shared a flat in Much Melton with two other young women.

'Rissa shares a cottage with two men,' he said glumly. 'I'm not sure I'm altogether happy about that.'

'Oh, don't worry about it,' I reassured him. 'Lars and Bram are lovely blokes, honestly. Anyway, don't forget Erin's there, too. They're all just friends and colleagues, that's all.'

He sighed. 'I know, I know. Sometimes, I overthink things. And sometimes,' he admitted honestly, 'I forget that she's in her mid-twenties and entitled to do whatever she pleases. She certainly doesn't need my permission any more. Besides, Lars and Bram are leaving soon. They are looking to the future, unlike my daughter.'

'She's planning to stay then?' I asked cautiously. I'd hoped, for her sake, that now Brodie was all loved-up with Callie, Rissa might decide to move on with her life. The land girls and PoWs didn't tend to stay very long at Rowan Farm. Those jobs were always viewed as temporary, and Rissa had been there longer than most.

'It would seem so.' He clearly didn't think much to that, and I wondered again why he hadn't known she was working at the farm. Yes, he'd told me he and

Rissa were no longer close, but even so that was a big thing to keep from him.

'It must have been a heck of a shock,' I said, 'seeing that interview with Betty in *The Courier* and realising Rissa was in Rowan Vale, not London.'

'You could say that.' He picked up his fork and prodded morosely at his cake. 'She says it's just a job, but I wonder. I still think she came here just to punish me for selling our family home. Why else would she work at Rowan Farm?'

'It's not that bad!' I protested. 'It's a nice little job, to be honest, and Betty and Nick are so lovely.' I narrowed my eyes, seeing a shadow pass over him at the mention of Rissa's employers. 'What is it? Am I missing something?'

'No. Nothing.' He broke off a piece of cake then laid down his fork with a sigh. 'It's Rowan Farm. I don't like the place.'

'Why ever not?' I was more than a bit puzzled by his confession. Rowan Farm was a postcard-pretty location. The sort of place that belonged in old Enid Blyton books.

His brow furrowed as he stared at me for a moment, as if debating with himself how much to tell me. Then he leaned back in his chair and said, 'I perhaps haven't been so honest with you.'

'About?'

'About why I don't want Rissa working here. About why I want to talk to your father.'

I put my own fork down, my appetite for cake suddenly vanishing. Instead, I took a calming sip of tea. 'Go on,' I said. If this involved Dad, I wanted to know what was going on.

'Rowan Farm has connections with my family,' he said heavily. 'My grandfather, Gerhard Janssen, was captured in Normandy and sent to the nearest camp to this place in 1944. It was a camp for the prisoners who were considered safest. Those not indoctrinated with the Nazi beliefs. After a while, he was allowed to work on a farm. Rowan Farm.'

'Oh.' I took another sip of tea, thinking. 'So he probably knew Betty's grandparents then?'

'Indeed.'

There was something quite flinty in his tone which surprised me. 'Is there something else? I still don't see—'

He leaned forward, elbows on the table, his clenched fists supporting his chin. 'I believe he was cruelly treated at the farm, and that must mean he was cruelly treated by Betty's grandparents. Or her grandfather, at least.'

'What?' I could hardly believe that. Everything

Aunt Polly had told me about Alf and Helen Rowland had convinced me they were a lovely couple, much like Betty and Nick. 'Why would you think that?'

'I loved my grandfather very much,' he told me. 'He was a good man. Gentle. Kind. I always detected a sadness within him, though. My mother told me sometimes, he would withdraw into himself and then even *her* mother couldn't reach him.'

'I expect that was the war, and Normandy in particular,' I said sadly. 'My Great-Uncle Ray was injured there. He'd seen some terrible things. Awful. He was never the same again. My dad told me that he had what we'd call PTSD now. He was in such a state. The owner of the estate back then, Sir Edward, was so concerned, that he got him a job on a farm in Northumberland. You know, a fresh start.'

I didn't add that hearing the news about Aunt Polly's murder had set my great-uncle back so much that he never came back to Rowan Vale for the rest of his life, bless him.

'We can't begin to imagine what those poor men went through, so it's no wonder if your grandad was still suffering bouts of depression. My dad said most men who came back from the war never talked about it. It was too much for them to deal with. They just pushed it down and tried to pretend it had never happened.'

'I understand that,' he said patiently, 'but my grandfather wasn't one of those men. He *did* talk about it. He talked about the horrors he'd seen. He told my grandmother and my mother about Normandy, and his capture. He even told me about his time in the camp – about the friendships he'd formed there, the guards, the food. You know the only thing he never talked about?'

I had an awful feeling I knew what was coming. 'Rowan Vale?'

'Exactly.' He slapped the table with his hand, as if his point had been proven. 'Doesn't that tell you all you need to know?'

'Not really,' I said doubtfully.

'When he was dying, he began to murmur things about this place,' he continued, as if he hadn't heard me. 'Most of it didn't make sense. But he kept crying about the cold and the blood. Crying, Shona! I had never heard my grandfather cry before. My mother nursed him in his final days and wrote some of the things he said down in her diary. I found those diaries after she died, and I read them a few years ago. I am in no doubt that something traumatic happened here.

Can you imagine how it felt to read that? What did they do to him?'

He snatched up his cup of tea and drained it in one gulp as if it were whisky. I suspected he wished it was.

'Thing is,' I said carefully, not wanting to pour scorn on his theory, which he clearly nursed closely to him, 'people say a lot of things when they're very ill that just aren't true. I don't think you should believe that what he said while in pain, or perhaps highly medicated, is accurate. And even if it was, you've no proof whatsoever that Betty's family was involved.'

To my horror, Max's eyes filled with tears, and he looked fiercely at me, blinking them away. 'He was begging for his life! Now do you understand why I think the Rowlands were not such good people? What went on at that farm? Did they treat other prisoners badly or was it just my grandfather? How many people were involved in this?'

I didn't know what to say. It sounded awful, whatever had gone on. But Aunt Polly had always spoken fondly of the Rowlands and Dad said the family were lovely. His own dad and Uncle Ray, Aunt Polly, and my great-grandparents had, at one time or another, worked on the farm, and our two families had a long history together. I just couldn't imagine they were capable of doing whatever it was Max's granddad's fevered ramblings implied.

'I can see how it looks,' I said eventually, realising he was waiting for me to answer, 'but honestly, there could be a totally innocent explanation for it all. Not least medication. He could have got confused with stuff that happened to him earlier in the war and what happened at Rowan Farm. I mean, he can't even have been there that long, can he? The war ended the following year.'

'But the prisoners were not allowed home!' Max said fiercely. 'It was 1948 before my poor grandfather returned to Germany. The British government kept their prisoners of war long after the conflict ended, so they could put them to work and force them to help rebuild the country. They needed the labourers, you see? As if they weren't needed in Germany!'

I hadn't known that and realised, rather guiltily, that I'd never talked much about the war and its aftermath to Aunt Polly. But then, it was a tricky subject, what with her losing Uncle Charlie and everything. Not to mention her murder.

'I'm sorry,' I said, because what else could I say?

His expression softened suddenly, and he laid his hand over mine. 'No, *I'm* sorry. I didn't mean to get so passionate.'

No, Shona. Now really isn't the time to dissect that remark or let your mind go wandering.

Max removed his hand, to my regret, and stared into his tea. 'It's just, as I say, my grandfather meant a lot to me, as he did to my mother. It must have been very painful for her to hear all this from him. I was very moved when I read her diaries. My sister says we should forget it. That it's over and done with and there's no way of ever knowing the truth. But how can I? Would you forget it if a great injustice had been done to your ancestor?'

Like getting shot in the back? That was pretty much all I knew about Aunt Polly's murder. That, and the fact that it had happened in the early hours of New Year's Day. As 1948 took its first breath, she was taking her last. Had I ever tried to find out what happened? Who'd killed her?

No. The truth was, I'd not really wanted to know. I knew Dad was protective of Aunt Polly, and he said she'd not seen her killer and didn't want to talk about it, so I'd just gone with that. For the first time, I wondered if I should do more. Should I try to get justice for her, since she seemed to have been forgotten? What happened to her had been brushed under the carpet. No one made to pay.

I could hardly explain all that to Max, though, so

instead, I said, 'Have you ever visited Chipping Marsham?'

The small town lay about twenty-five miles away and the prisoner of war camp was just outside it. I'd never visited the camp myself, but I thought it might do him good to go and see where his grandfather had stayed.

'The camp, you mean?' Max nodded. 'When I first moved to the Cotswolds, I visited. There really isn't much to see. Roofless, derelict, brick buildings, which nature has reclaimed. There is moss and ivy creeping up what remains of the walls. Trees grow where men once slept. I didn't sense my grandfather there. It gave me no peace.'

'What do you think *will* give you peace?' I asked gently.

'Answers.' He sighed and rubbed his forehead. 'I know you think I am wrong, but when I spoke to Betty about my grandfather, when I told her his name, she seemed to know who I was talking about. There was a shift in her attitude. I saw it distinctly. I didn't imagine it. Oh, she was perfectly pleasant to me, but something had changed. But if she does know something, she's hardly likely to confide in me, is she?'

'No. I guess not. Although,' I added, picking up my fork and digging into the cake as my stomach growled, reminding me that I'd only eaten one mouthful of cake all day and it couldn't imagine what was going on since this was unheard of, 'I still think there must be another explanation. Look, maybe I could have a word—'

'With Betty?' His eyebrows shot up in surprise. 'You would do that?'

'Well...' I wondered how I got myself into these messes. 'Yes, okay. I mean, me and Betty get on all right, and I'm sure if I explained what you'd just told me and how worried you are, she'd be able to put our minds at rest.'

'She might lie,' he pointed out.

'I'd know. I've known Betty all my life. We went to the same school, although she was two years ahead of me. If she knows something, I'll see it.'

'And you'll tell me?' he asked. 'You promise?'

I covered his hand with mine and said, 'Promise.' As I saw the hope in his eyes, I said impulsively, 'Look, why don't you come with me? Then you'll know I'm not keeping anything from you, and I'll know if Betty's being odd around you.'

He gazed steadily at me for a moment. 'Thank you. That would give me peace of mind.'

'Tomorrow morning? It's my half-day – I don't start until one. The weather forecast is miserable again, so I don't think Betty will be busy with tourists. What do you think?'

'I shall meet you here,' he said, his eyes shining. 'We shall walk to the farm together.'

'Smashing,' I said. 'Shall we say ten o'clock? Right, now that's settled, can we please tuck into this cake before it dries up and I have to get some fresh slices?'

He picked up his fork, smiling. 'Definitely. Suddenly, I have my appetite back.'

20

I met Max, as we'd arranged, outside the teashop at ten o'clock the following morning. It was still raining, so I was all wrapped up in jeans and a Pac-a-Mac, as it was too warm for a coat, but I needed something waterproof with a hood. I didn't have an umbrella. They really annoyed me; they blew inside out on windy days, and having to hold them up inevitably meant that rainwater trickled down my sleeve.

Max clearly had no problem with them, though, as he was carrying his again. He wasn't wearing a coat, and I didn't blame him. It was quite muggy, and I suspected even the bottle-green sweatshirt he was wearing with black jeans might prove too warm for him.

'How is Jimmy?' he asked politely as we headed over the nearest little stone footbridge that crossed the Faran.

'Ummm...' I wasn't entirely sure what to say to that. Max had visited Dad as planned yesterday afternoon after he'd left the teashop, and when I'd got home, I'd half-expected him to still be there, chatting. I'd imagined inviting him to stay for dinner as promised, but he'd gone.

Dad had acted strange when I'd asked him how the visit went. 'All right,' he'd replied cagily. 'We had a couple of biscuits and a cup of tea. He only stayed an hour or so.'

'Really?' That had puzzled me. 'Did he – did he want to talk about anything in particular?'

To my alarm, Dad had almost growled at me. 'If you mean did he want to talk about his grandfather, then yes. And it's the biggest load of rubbish I've ever heard.'

'Okay, Dad,' I'd said, holding up my hands. 'I know you remember Helen and Alf but—'

'I do remember them, yes. And a nice couple they were, too, as were Betty's parents. The idea that they'd have mistreated that man is rubbish, and I told Max so.'

'You said it a bit more tactfully than that, I hope?'

I'd said, dismayed. 'He's just trying to get some answers, Dad. You can't blame him for that.'

'He kept it very quiet, didn't he? Not mentioning who his grandad was or why he was here? Downright sneaky, I call it.'

This was so unlike Dad that I hadn't known what to make of it.

'Well,' I'd said uneasily, 'I've sort of promised him I'll go with him to the farm tomorrow to talk to Betty about it.'

'No "sort of" about it, from what I've heard,' Dad had said. 'You must do as you think fit. But you're wasting your time. The Rowlands wouldn't hurt anyone, which is more than I can say for some.'

And that was as much as I'd been able to get out of him, so I didn't really have an honest answer for Max.

'It's okay,' he said quietly. 'I left your father early yesterday because our conversation took a rather heated turn. I completely understand. Your family is apparently close to the family at the farm. Your father clearly believes the Rowlands were incapable of any wrongdoing. I disagreed, so we agreed it best I leave. I had hoped he would calm down after my departure, but perhaps that was optimistic.'

'It's not like Dad,' I said, feeling even more worried

now. 'He doesn't get angry like that, and he's certainly never rude to people.'

'Perhaps,' Max said, giving me a wary look, 'he knows more than he's letting on.'

'About the Rowlands?' I didn't want to think that was possible. 'He wouldn't cover up for anyone who mistreated another person,' I said firmly. 'I know that for a fact.'

'Well,' Max said heavily, 'I guess today we might take one step closer to finding out what really happened to my grandfather.'

'Let's just hope Betty's available to talk,' I said. I hadn't wanted to call her to ask if it was okay to come over, because she might have asked why, and I'd have had to tell her. I thought it better if we saw her reaction face to face – not because I thought it would catch her out, but because I wanted Max to see for himself that she had nothing to hide.

Sadly, my plan went out of the window as soon as we arrived, because Betty met us at the door, cradling her cat in her arms, and said, 'Well, you'd better come in. Your dad called me, Shona, so I know what this is about. Gerhard Janssen, right?'

Max and I exchanged glances. *Great! Thanks for that, Dad.*

We followed Betty inside the farmhouse and, after

we'd wiped our feet and hung up my wet mac and his wet umbrella in the boot room, she set Mitzi on the floor and invited us to take a seat at the table.

The kitchen was warm and comfortable, and just as you'd imagine a cosy, old farmhouse to be. With the rain lashing down outside and the smell of freshly baked bread in the air, it should have been a pleasant visit, but my stomach was in knots now as I saw the uncomfortable look on Betty's face.

'Tea? Coffee?'

I gave Max an enquiring look, but he said politely, 'No, thank you. I am awash with tea and coffee. I've never drunk so much since I started visiting here.'

He said it with a smile and clearly meant it to be humorous, but Betty gave him a thoroughly disapproving look and, after I'd also declined a drink, she sat down at the table and eyed us both grimly.

'So,' she said to him, 'you came here because you think my grandad treated yours badly. Is that why Rissa came here, too? Is that what *she* thinks about my family?'

Max shook his head. 'Rissa has done nothing but defend you. She came here because she loves history and thought it would be good to see somewhere that involved her own family history. She likes it here very much, and she has never said a bad word about you.

That's probably why she never told me she was working here,' he admitted.

Betty looked highly relieved. 'I'm glad to hear that,' she said. 'I'm fond of Rissa, and the thought that she—' She folded her arms. 'Well anyway, *you* clearly think the worst of my grandparents. How could you sit here eating high tea with us when you believed all that of them? I ask you, Mr Meyer, do you really think my family treated your grandfather badly?'

'It's Max, remember?'

'Yes, I thought it was,' she said heavily. 'Now I think Mr Meyer might be more appropriate. You're wrong, you know. What you're thinking. It's rubbish. My grandad wouldn't harm any man, let alone someone like Gerhard, who was so far from home and who'd been through more than enough already.'

'With respect, Betty, you weren't there,' Max said calmly.

'And with respect, *Mr Meyer*, neither were you.'

'Okay,' I said hastily, 'this really isn't getting us anywhere. Betty, Max just wants to know what happened when his grandfather worked here. Gerhard never spoke about Rowan Farm, even though he talked easily enough about the camp at Chipping Marsham, and even about things that happened to him during the war, so you can see why his family were worried when Gerhard started saying stuff in his last few days and weeks.'

'What kind of stuff exactly?' she asked suspiciously.

'Heartbreaking stuff,' Max told her. 'About blood and darkness and cold. And he—' He visibly swallowed before continuing, 'He begged for his life. *Someone made* him beg for his life. I want to know if it was someone here, and if so, who it was and why they would treat him so badly.'

'He begged for his life?' Betty looked to me as if I could confirm it. I shrugged and she bit her lip. There was a long silence as she evidently tried to work out what she should say in response, and maybe even if she should say anything at all. Finally, she sighed and said, 'I'm not sure I should talk about this. I made a promise to my mum and I've kept it all this time.'

Max sat forward eagerly. 'So, you *do* know something? Please, Mrs—' He hesitated, clearly not sure of her surname.

'Whittaker.'

'Please, Mrs Whittaker. If you know anything that will clear up this mystery and put my mind at rest, I would be forever grateful. My sister and me – our thoughts are running riot. We are imagining all sorts of horrible deeds and it's hard to bear. We loved our grandfather very much.'

'I'm sure you did,' she said, plucking nervously at the tablecloth, 'but there's more people to think about in all this than just you and your sister, with all due respect.'

'But it was so long ago,' Max pleaded. 'Surely, after all this time?'

'It might have been a long time ago, but in places like this, time doesn't always have much meaning.' Betty's gaze slid over to me, and I frowned. What was she getting at?

'Please,' I said, 'if you can tell him anything, it would be appreciated.'

'Are you sure?' she asked me. 'Really sure?'

'Of course,' I said, surprised. 'It's the kindest thing to do, isn't it?'

'All right, but this is between us three and I want your word on it. I don't want this getting round the village, stirring things up again, getting tongues wagging the way they did back then.'

'Of course,' I said.

Max nodded. 'You have my word.'

'Well, Mr Meyer, in that case... Has it ever occurred to you that perhaps your grandfather wasn't the innocent you think him to be? That maybe when you heard him begging for his life, it wasn't something he'd once said, but something someone once said to *him*?'

Max looked stunned and I sat back in my chair, wondering what on earth Betty meant by that remark.

She shook her head impatiently. 'This is bloody hard to say, it really is. You say your grandfather suffered here. Well, maybe he did and maybe he didn't. But shall I tell you who *definitely* suffered here? My grandparents, that's who. Nearly broke them. They considered leaving this village if you must know, and all because of your grandfather.'

Max's mouth fell open. 'I don't understand.'

'No, you really don't. The thing you may not know is, there was a murder in the village back when your grandfather was here.'

Betty didn't look at me, even though she must have sensed my eyes boring into hers as I silently begged the question, *Are you talking about Aunt Polly?*

'A murder?' Max asked, astonished.

'New Year's Day, 1948,' Betty continued, still refusing to look at me. She jerked her thumb in the vague direction of the door and said, 'Out in the woods. Young woman. They never caught her murderer.'

Max was dazed for a moment as he clearly tried to

grasp her meaning. Then slowly, incredulously, he said, 'Are you saying that has something to do with my grandfather?'

'Gerhard Janssen had been welcomed into this family,' Betty said. 'He was put to work on the farm, as was another prisoner, Anselm Bauer. They weren't allowed to fraternise with local families, but even so, they had nothing but kindness shown to them here. Mind,' she added, holding her hand up to silence Max before he could even speak, 'I'm not saying they were so welcome with everyone in the village. There was a lot of bad feeling still, and some people had lost loved ones in the war. And people were suspicious, scared. The idea of having two Nazis in the area—'

'My grandfather was no Nazi!' Max burst out.

'I never said he was,' Betty said. 'If there'd been any inkling of that, my grandad wouldn't have let him near the place. Besides, that camp over at Chipping Marsham was for low-risk prisoners only. But to some people, all German soldiers were the enemy, simple as that. Hard to credit now but that was the mood back then, wasn't it?

'Well, the men would do their work and be returned to the camp, but as time went on and the war ended, things changed a bit. By Christmas 1946, they were allowed to have tea at the farmhouse, go into the village, that kind of thing. Mind, they couldn't go into the shops or the pub or anything like that, but they had a certain amount of freedom, although they had to always wear their prison uniforms so they could be easily identified.'

She paused and tucked her hair behind her ears. 'Eventually, they were allowed to stay at the farmhouse, so they did – with certain restrictions, of course. But by late 1947, almost all those restrictions had been lifted, though many of the PoWs had gone back to Germany by then. Some of them wanted to stay and make a new life here in Britain. I don't know what plans Anselm and Gerhard had made, but I do know feelings towards them in the village had softened by that point, and my grandparents had grown very fond of them.'

My heart was thudding now. Late 1947? We were creeping very close to the time of Aunt Polly's murder. What had Gerhard got to do with that?

'That night – New Year's Eve – the two of them had joined the celebrations in The Quicken Tree. My grandparents didn't go with them. They'd never been ones for drinking or the like and, besides, they were used to early nights.'

She puffed out her cheeks and shook her head. 'Look, I'm telling you now what I've been told by my

mum, who was told by her mum, all right? At two
o'clock in the morning, or thereabouts, my grandparents were woken up by a loud banging on the door.
My grandad told Grandma to stay in bed and he'd
deal with whatever it was. Well, Grandma did as she
was told, but she heard raised voices, and she swore
blind one of them was Sir Edward Davenport's.

'Now, as I say, this is what Grandma told my mum
after Grandad passed away. She reckons that Grandad
never came back to bed that night and there were
doors opening and closing and muttered conversations for ages. But the upshot of it is this: the following
morning, it was all over the village that Polly Herron
had been shot dead in the woods.'

'Polly Herron?' Max asked, frowning. 'Herron as in
the teashop?'

'That's right, although it was Deakin's Teashop
back then. Polly Herron was the manageress.' Betty
gave me a sideways glance and I saw the sympathy in
her expression. 'I'm sorry, lovely.'

Max turned to me, puzzled. 'Why is she saying
sorry to you, Shona?'

'Because Polly Herron is – was – my great-aunt,' I
said after a short pause.

He exhaled slowly. 'I see. How terrible for your
family. I am sorry for your loss. But I still don't see—'

'It didn't take long for accusations to start flying,' Betty continued. 'Polly was a lovely young woman, and very popular in Rowan Vale. No one wished her any harm. So naturally, thoughts turned to the – well, not to put too fine a point on it – enemy within.'

'Meaning the Germans, I guess?' Max said wearily.

She nodded. 'They were different times back then,' she said. 'There was no motive for harming Polly, you see. And the thing was, she'd been shot in the back. The villagers reckoned no British person would be so cowardly as to shoot a woman in the back. Therefore, it had to be a foreigner, right? And there they were, right on the doorstep. Two Germans, no less.'

'But what motive would they have for killing her?' Max demanded.

'Didn't need a motive,' she explained. 'When push came to shove, Gerhard Janssen was an enemy prisoner of war. The war might have been over but all that forgive and forget stuff went straight out of the window when one of our own was killed so brutally.'

'But Gerhard wasn't arrested? And what about the other German?' I asked.

'Anselm? No, he was off the hook. He'd left The Quicken Tree at ten o'clock and gone back to Briar House, as it was then, with a crowd of other merrymakers. There were six local men who swore he was with them all night and didn't even leave the cottage until around four in the morning. And then two of them walked him back to Rowan Cottage.'

'And Gerhard?'

Betty straightened. 'Well, you see that's the thing. Gerhard Janssen left the pub at nine o'clock alone. He'd have been for it, but my grandad gave him an alibi. Said he'd been with him in the kitchen at Rowan Farm from about twenty past nine, and they'd brought the new year in together.'

'So – so my grandfather couldn't have been involved!' Max cried, sounding highly relieved.

'Except my gran knew perfectly well that she'd been sitting in that very kitchen until half-past ten, and the only person who'd been with her was my grandad. And when she went to bed at twenty to eleven, he went with her, only getting up for that knock on the door. My grandad,' she finished heavily, 'lied to the police. He gave Gerhard Janssen a false alibi and my gran knew it.'

'But why?' I said, bewildered. 'Why would he do that?'

Mitzi leapt onto Betty's lap and Betty absently rubbed her between her ears. 'He never discussed it with my gran,' she said. 'Shut the subject down entirely. Like I said, it was only after he died that she felt able to confide in my mum about the business, and it nagged away at my mum for years until she finally told me. We couldn't work it out, but Gran was in no doubt. She was firmly of the opinion that it was Sir Edward's doing. She believes he came to the farmhouse that night – probably with Gerhard Janssen – and put pressure on my grandad to give him an alibi.'

'But why would Sir Edward do that?' I asked. It didn't make sense. If Sir Edward thought Gerhard guilty, why make Alf Rowland swear he'd been with him? Why protect a murderer? Why cover up for the person who'd killed my lovely Aunt Polly?

'We were never able to fathom it out,' she said, shaking her head. 'If Sir Edward was so sure Gerhard was innocent, why didn't *he* give him an alibi? Why didn't Gerhard *have* an alibi, come to that? Where was he when Polly was shot? No.' She shook her head fiercely. 'Something very dodgy about the whole business. But what could Grandad do, eh? My gran never blamed him. Sir Edward owned the farm. Owned their home. Where would they have gone if he'd have said no, and Sir Edward evicted them?'

'But you said they were considering leaving the village?' I remembered. 'Why was that?'

'Because before long, people started saying that

my grandad must be lying. People wanted the murderer caught. They were afraid. They couldn't believe one of their own was responsible and Anselm was definitely in the clear. They wanted to hang it on Gerhard so they could put the whole nasty business to bed and sleep soundly again. But my grandad's insistence that he was with Gerhard that night meant it couldn't be resolved to their satisfaction, so they started muttering that maybe there was something in it for him. Or maybe Gerhard had threatened him. Either way, they didn't believe my grandparents were telling the truth and life became a nightmare for them.'

'Oh.' I understood now why it had been such a sore subject for Betty. I could imagine all too well how people had reacted if they believed the Rowlands had given Gerhard a false alibi.

'Their neighbours and friends turned on them. They were spat at. Called liars and traitors. My gran nearly had a nervous breakdown, and Grandad – well, like I said, he considered leaving Rowan Vale altogether and starting over somewhere new. He was even prepared to take work as a farm labourer to get away. People were making up all sorts. Do you know, they even decided that Hollywood actress, Harmony Hill, had been another victim! It stood to reason, they said.

She'd drowned in 1946 only eighteen months before Polly. And why would she drown in such a shallow river, eh? The fact that everyone knew she'd been drunk as a skunk the night she died was conveniently forgotten. It must have been murder and ten to one the German had been responsible for that, too. By extension, that meant my grandparents were covering for a double murderer, and who knew who'd be his next victim?

'It was only when the rumour started about some vagrant that had been seen in the place that the focus shifted from Gerhard. People swore they'd seen some dodgy character lurking near the woods, and several people said they'd had things stolen from them in the days before the murder. Gradually, the consensus shifted, especially when Sir Edward confirmed that his estate manager had chased the vagrant from the land, and that he'd recently discovered that one of his shotguns was missing and had reported it to the police, that everyone decided this person was the killer and left my grandparents alone.'

'I'm so sorry,' I murmured.

'Not your fault, nor your family's,' she said. 'My family should never have been in that position, but I'll never believe Grandad would have lied to the police if he hadn't been pressured to do so and only Sir Edward had that much clout.'

'But my grandfather...' Max put his head in his hands, clearly unable to articulate his feelings at that moment.

I felt sorry for him, but there was one thing I wanted to know more than anything.

'Did your grandparents believe Polly was murdered by Gerhard?' I asked Betty.

She looked across at Max then back to me. We both waited, and I wondered if his stomach was churning as much as mine.

Betty shrugged. 'Grandad never mentioned it again as far as I'm aware. Gran just wasn't sure. She told my mum that she'd been very fond of Gerhard, but after that business, she couldn't feel the same. She couldn't trust him and never understood why, if he was innocent, he had no real alibi. Gerhard apparently barely spoke a word to anyone after that night, and he was sent home to Germany in the March, which I'm sure came as a relief to everyone. But the so-called vagrant was never caught either.

'Truthfully, I don't think they ever knew for certain, but I do know that they were angry and disappointed with the villagers, and that they never truly felt at home in Rowan Vale after that, even though, after a while, the locals acted as if they'd never had the slightest suspicion about them. My grandparents didn't forget being treated like that. I know that much.'

'No,' I murmured. 'I don't suppose they did.'

'It's just a shame that the one person who should be able to tell us what really happened can't,' Betty said, looking at me with meaning in her eyes. 'If only Polly Herron could speak, eh?'

'But,' I said, shaking my head slightly, 'she was shot in the back so probably didn't see who her killer was.'

'Yes,' Betty sighed, forgetting all about discretion for the moment, 'that's what I'd heard, but I always hoped something would come back to her.'

Luckily for us, Max wasn't even listening. 'There must be some explanation,' he mumbled. 'There has to be.'

Well, obviously there did. But what was it? Had his grandfather really been responsible for the death of my great-aunt? And if so, why had Sir Edward Davenport, of all people, made Betty's grandad cover for him?

21

Max was clearly distressed by the conversation we'd had with Betty and needed time to process what he'd heard. He wasn't the only one. Nothing she'd said really made sense, and instead of getting some answers, it felt as we'd simply been handed a whole lot of questions.

'I never expected any of this to lead back to Aunt Polly,' I said, feeling dazed as we walked back to the teashop. 'Who'd have believed her story would be intertwined with your grandfather's?'

'We don't know it was,' he said quickly. 'There is no evidence of that. Only rumour and gossip from people who nursed their prejudices.'

'I'm not accusing him of anything,' I said. 'But

their stories *are* intertwined because, true or not, my Aunt Polly died, and your grandfather was believed to be guilty of her murder.'

'What do *you* think, Shona?' he asked, giving me a troubled look. 'Honestly. I appreciate this must be difficult for you, with the murder victim being a distant relative of yours.'

Not as distant as you imagine, mate. 'Please don't call her "the murder victim",' I said. 'She has a name.'

'I'm sorry. That was insensitive of me. Polly. Polly Herron.' He glanced up as we reached the teashop and frowned. 'So, this was Deakin's Teashop once? When did the name change?'

I swallowed, suddenly uncomfortable. 'Er, in 1948,' I said. 'Sir Edward Davenport changed the name in memory of Aunt Polly.'

We looked at each other. Max frowned.

'You don't think...'

'No, of course not.' I knew exactly what he'd been going to say. But no, no way! Sir Edward and Aunt Polly? Just no. Surely?

He rubbed his forehead. 'I should go home. I need to think. I came to this village to ask Rissa what she was doing here, and then her insistence that my grandfather's final words were just mad ramblings made me determined to prove that someone had

harmed him. Now I find myself involved in an un-
solved murder case.'

'Why don't we grab a cup of tea?' I asked, nodding
at the teashop.

He shook his head. 'I don't really want to sit in
there today. I don't want people staring at me.'

'For a start, why would they be staring at you?' I
said, half-laughing. 'For another thing, I doubt we
have many customers in this weather.' I glanced up at
the bleak sky as the rain continued to pour down. 'I
mean, look at it.'

'I don't know... It doesn't feel right, going in there
of all places. Not today.'

He sounded so glum that I really didn't want to
leave him like this. Besides, thinking about it, Aunt
Polly might be in there. I definitely didn't want her to
overhear our conversation. 'Well, how about a drink
in The Quicken Tree?'

He considered that for a moment. 'Okay. Maybe a
strong coffee would be my best option at this point.'

We headed quickly into the pub, which was so
cosy and welcoming that it lifted my spirits immediately, despite my confusion over what we'd heard at
Rowan Farm.

After I'd hung up my coat and Max had put his
umbrella in the stand by the door, I found us a table

while he went to the bar and ordered two coffees. He joined me moments later and glanced around him as he took a seat.

'Nice room. I like it in here, now it's quieter.'

'Yes, it's surprisingly rowdy on quiz night,' I agreed. 'Although usually, it's pretty busy in here every day, especially at this time of year. It's just the atrocious weather that's keeping everyone at home.'

He nodded and I thought we were really skirting around the one issue we both wanted to talk about but didn't know how. It was bad enough that his grandfather was implicated in such a serious crime. But the fact that the victim was my lovely Aunt Polly made it all so much more complicated.

One of the young bar staff brought our coffees over and informed us that if we'd like to order food, we should just come to the bar or download their app and order from the table. We thanked him politely, but I'd quite lost my appetite, and I had a feeling food was the last thing on Max's mind.

'Have you never wondered?' he asked suddenly, as I poured milk into my coffee.

I dropped in two sugar lumps and stirred. 'Wondered what?'

'Who killed your great-aunt, of course! Surely it must have been a source of great anguish to your family over the years? Have you never tried to get the case reopened? You must want justice?'

'After all this time? It's hardly likely, is it?'

'But your parents, your grandparents, they didn't push the subject? They didn't demand answers?'

'I don't know about my grandparents,' I said uncomfortably. 'But I think Dad decided it was best to let sleeping dogs lie.'

'And you don't think that strange?'

I thought of Dad's attitude when he'd realised who Max's grandfather was and wondered if he suspected Gerhard's involvement. Did Aunt Polly suspect him too? Had she really seen no one that night or was she lying? And if so, why?

'You don't think, perhaps, that they were *pressured* to keep quiet?' Max mused.

'Pressured? By who?'

'By the one man who had power and influence over their lives, of course. By Sir Edward Davenport.'

I sighed. 'We don't even know that he was involved at all,' I said. 'Helen Rowland only said she *thought* she heard his voice that night.'

'But think about it.' He leaned forward, his arms folded on the table, his voice eager. 'Say it *was* Sir Edward that night at the farm with my grandfather. Say he *did* force Alfred Rowland to provide a false alibi.

Why would he do that? And then he changed the name of Deakin's Teashop to Mrs Herron's Teashop in her honour. And for some reason, your family never pushed for answers. Doesn't that strike you as odd? Unless he was in it up to his neck and they knew if they spoke out, they would be unemployed and homeless, just as Alfred would have been if he'd refused to give Grandfather an alibi.'

'I really don't think it was like that,' I said awkwardly. How could I tell him that my family had Aunt Polly to consider, and it had been her feelings they'd been thinking about when they didn't push for answers? Even so, now that I thought about it logically, *why* didn't she want them to? You'd have thought she'd want to know who killed her. Unless she already suspected the truth, and it was too painful for her? Or perhaps she *was* protecting her family, knowing that if they came close to uncovering Sir Edward's involvement, they'd be turfed out of Rowan Vale?

I massaged my temples, feeling thoroughly confused. Dad had always insisted that I didn't discuss the subject with Aunt Polly, because naturally, she didn't want to think about those dark days. I'd always respected that, but I couldn't help feeling that maybe it was time to push for answers. If nothing else, to clear Gerhard Janssen. Or condemn him.

'You have another theory?' Max asked. He cradled his mug of coffee and looked doubtfully at me. 'I'd love to hear it if so.'

'No,' I admitted. 'I haven't a clue what went on that night. It's all a bit of a mess really.'

'My grandfather was no killer,' Max said firmly.

I wondered how to word what I needed to say. I supposed the best thing was to be blunt about it.

'You don't really know that, though. Think about it,' I said hastily, as he opened his mouth to protest. 'Gerhard had been through a long and bloody war. He'd seen who knows what? *Suffered* who knows what? How many people had he killed in conflict? I'm not blaming him for that,' I added. 'They had no choice, whichever side they were on. It was kill or be killed and I get it, honestly. But that might change someone. Make them immune to the horror of killing. And being kept prisoner for so long, even after the war ended and he should have been sent home, who knows how much resentment was building in him?'

'No,' Max said stubbornly. 'My grandfather would never have killed someone in cold blood like that. Wartime was different. As you say, it was kill or be killed. But to shoot a young woman in the back? No. Never.'

'Even if someone made him do it and then pro-vided an alibi for him?'

The thought had just popped into my head, and I'd spoken it out loud without processing it. But now that it was out there, I couldn't deny it made sense.

Max evidently thought so, too. 'You mean, Sir Edward?'

I nodded, almost reluctantly. 'If Sir Edward wanted Aunt Polly dead, he wouldn't get his hands dirty, that's for sure. He'd have made someone else do the job, and who better than a German PoW? Someone with no real friends or family in the area. Someone who'd be going back to Germany very soon anyway. Someone who would never be believed if he was caught and tried to tell them why he'd done it.'

'So he forced my grandfather to kill her then in-sisted Alfred gave him the false alibi!'

'But why would Sir Edward want Aunt Polly dead?'

'Because,' Max said triumphantly, 'they were having an affair and something went wrong. Maybe she wanted to end things. Maybe she threatened to tell his wife. Who knows? Whatever the reason, he had to get her out of the way, so he forced my grandfa-ther to shoot her.'

'All right, Poirot,' I said. 'Steady on. If Sir Edward wanted her dead, why name the teashop after her?'

He frowned, tilting his head to think. 'To throw people off the scent, of course,' he said at last. 'People would have been thinking how kind he was, and how much he obviously valued his employee to change the name of the teashop in her memory.'

'Or maybe he still loved her, and wished he hadn't had to kill her,' I said.

He grinned. 'All right, Miss Marple. You're beginning to think Sir Edward might be the culprit, aren't you?'

'I don't know,' I said honestly, 'but I'm willing to keep an open mind.'

'At least you haven't pronounced my grandfather guilty,' he said, sounding grateful. 'Given Polly was your family, I thank you for that.'

He reached out and squeezed my hand and my heart thudded. Even with this mystery on our minds, I couldn't deny that part of me was just revelling in spending so much time with him. He was so attractive and something about him pulled me to him. I couldn't explain what it was, but I'd felt it from the moment he'd first entered the teashop.

Max smiled at me, his hazel eyes warm and affectionate, and I smiled back, thinking it was a good job he couldn't tell what was in my mind.

But then his gaze slowly lowered to land on my lips, and the look in his eyes changed subtly, and I felt his grip on my hand tighten as my heart practically bungee jumped in excitement. The air between us felt charged as we moved closer together, as if compelled by a force greater than ourselves.

'Would you like to see today's specials?' The young waiter gave us an embarrassed look as we pulled apart. 'Er, sorry. I can come back—'

'No, no need.' Max's voice was brisk, businesslike. 'We're not stopping for food. Just a quick coffee and then I must be getting home.'

The waiter nodded and left us to it and Max quickly drained his mug.

I could barely hide my disappointment as he scraped back his chair and got to his feet.

'You're going?' I managed.

'I have things to do,' he explained. 'We may have six weeks' holiday officially, but in reality, we have much work to get through before term starts again. Thank you for taking me with you to speak to Betty. You've given me much to consider.'

'Yeah, me too,' I said.

He gave me a brief smile, said goodbye, and left

me with a half-empty mug of coffee. I sighed and sat back in my chair. If that waiter hadn't arrived at the table at that precise moment...

But he had, and he'd brought us both back to earth with a bump. Judging by Max's actions, he was extremely grateful for the interruption. I didn't hold that against him. I knew he still had issues with the loss of his wife, and this was new to him, and had probably been a shock. It had been a shock to me, too. I never in a million years thought he'd almost kiss me.

But he had.

He really had!

So close...

But I had to keep my mind clear of all this right now. I needed to talk to Dad about his aunt's murder and what had happened afterwards. And if I couldn't get any clarity from him, maybe it was finally time to broach the subject with Aunt Polly herself. I just needed to find a way to be gentle, because the last thing I wanted to do was cause her any pain. She'd been through enough already.

22

Talking to Dad had to wait until after my shift at the teashop. By the time I left The Quicken Tree, I barely had time to rush home, get changed, and run a comb through my hair before heading back out, so it was just a brief, 'Hello, Goodbye,' to my dad before I dashed off to work.

That evening, I cooked him his favourite dinner: steak and ale pie with mashed potatoes, broccoli, green beans and gravy. That, I thought, should put him in a good mood and make him more receptive to my gentle questioning.

'Well, love,' he said, laying down his knife and fork after eating the very last mouthful, 'that was fantastic. Thank you very much. I could do with a nap now.'

He grinned at me but taking a nap was the last thing I wanted him to do!

'Go into the living room,' I said, 'and I'll make us both a nice strong cup of tea to wash it all down with. I thought we could watch that film you wanted to see later. You know, the one with Clint Eastwood?' I mentally groaned at the thought of it, but I wanted to keep him in a good mood.

'By, you're spoiling me tonight,' he said, raising an eyebrow in surprise. 'Should I be suspicious?'

'Of course not!'

He watched me in silence for a few minutes as I cleared the table and loaded the dishwasher.

'You never told me how you got on at Rowan Farm,' he said abruptly. 'Judging by the way you're fussing round me tonight, I'm guessing you've got a few things you want to get straight with me.'

With my back to him, I rolled my eyes as it occurred to me that I'd never been able to fool him yet, and clearly that wasn't about to change anytime soon.

Slowly, I turned to face him. 'As a matter of fact, Dad—'

'I knew it,' he said heavily. 'Betty's told you, hasn't she?'

I gave him my most innocent expression. 'Told me what?'

'Don't give me that,' he said. 'Something wasn't right about that alibi her grandad gave the German, and everyone knew it.'

'Did she tell you that?' I asked.

'She didn't. My dad told me what had gone on in the village at the time, with all the suspicion that fell on Alf Rowland. He personally thought it was a disgrace, and said Alf was a good man who would never do such a thing, but then your grandad could be very naive at times. I've always found,' he said darkly, 'that what they say is true. No smoke without fire, an' all that. I liked Alf and Helen and I don't think for a moment that they did anything bad to Gerhard Janssen, like that Max fella was insinuating. But as to the alibi they gave him. Well. I think there's more to that than meets the eye.'

'So can we finally talk about it?' I asked. 'Because for as long as I can remember, our Aunt Polly's murder has been a taboo subject, and that really needs to change if you ask me.'

'Knew it,' he said. 'Steak and ale pie and Clint Eastwood? Bound to be an ulterior motive.'

'Go and sit down, Dad,' I said, 'and I'll bring those cups of tea in.'

He didn't argue but headed into the living room, muttering something under his breath that I couldn't catch. I fervently hoped Aunt Polly wouldn't turn up unannounced, because if we were going to discuss the night of her murder, I definitely didn't want her to walk in on that.

I quickly made the cups of tea then carried them into the living room, where I set them carefully on the coffee table. I sat down and looked at Dad expectantly.

He gave me a sideways glance. 'What do you want me to say?' he asked, a bit snappily.

'I want you to tell me what you know about the night Aunt Polly was killed,' I said firmly. 'We've had Betty's version and don't ask me to tell you anything about that because we promised we wouldn't. But we really need to know what you've got to say about it all.'

'Oh,' Dad said, reaching for his cup, 'it's *we* now, is it? Since when?'

'You were very frosty earlier when you found out I was helping Max,' I said. 'Why? All he wants to do is clear his grandfather's name, and that's not much to ask, is it? And why don't you want to know who killed Aunt Polly? Does she really not know? Did none of you know? There must have been more suspects around at the time than this mythical vagrant.'

'How should I know?' he demanded. 'I wasn't even born then!'

'But you do know something,' I persisted. 'I can see it in your face.'

'Nope. Not like you're thinking anyway. You think I know who killed her, don't you? I don't. But I'll be honest, to my way of thinking, it had to be Gerhard Janssen. I've always thought so and I don't see any reason to change my mind now.'

'But why? What motive would he have?'

'What motive would anyone have?' he demanded. 'You know your Aunt Polly. She's a lovely woman and everyone loved her when she was alive. My dad told me she didn't have an enemy in the world, and I believe him. She was the light in our family, she really was. Her mum and dad adored her. Uncle Ray and Dad worshipped her, and Charlie too. She was liked by the people she worked with on the farm and later at the teashop. She had friends. Charlie's parents loved her. Who would want to kill her?'

'No one, it seems,' I said.

'Exactly! Which makes me think it had to be someone who'd no attachment to her. Someone she barely knew, if at all. What I think,' he said, leaning towards me, his brow furrowed, 'is that she came across that German fella doing something he shouldn't, and he killed her to shut her up.'

'Something he shouldn't? Like what?'

'Who knows? But I'll bet he was up to no good. They should have sent them back to Germany after the war, not kept them prisoner in this country.'

'Dad!'

'What? I mean as much for their sake as ours. They wanted to go home, most of them. Only natural. Why should they have to stay and help rebuild our country when their own was in pieces? It wasn't fair, and there was quite an outcry about it, you know. My dad told me that people lobbied the government, saying it was cruel to keep them here. And illegal, too. Broke some sort of international rule or agreement or something. It was bound to cause resentment among the Germans, wasn't it? If he got fed up and started doing stuff he shouldn't, and then Polly came across him, well, he'd have panicked, wouldn't he? If she'd told anyone, he'd have gone to prison or worse, and then he'd never get home. When Polly tried to run away, he shot her. That's what I reckon anyway.'

I nibbled my thumbnail, thinking. It was possible, of course. I had no idea what Gerhard was like. I only had Max's word that he was a gentle, kind man who wouldn't dream of shooting anyone outside of military combat. But Max hadn't known his grandfather at that age, had he? People mellowed as they grew older.

Maybe Gerhard had been a very different person back in the forties.

'What did your dad tell you?' I asked. 'What happened that night? And afterwards, with the family, I mean. I want to understand what was going on back then.'

He lifted his cup of tea and sighed. 'Does it really matter after all this time?'

'How can you say that? For one thing, Polly never got justice, and that's not fair. For another, Gerhard Janssen might be innocent of this and it's wrong that some people believe he killed her. Mentioning no names,' I added, giving him a hard stare.

'All I know is what my dad told me,' he said. 'But if you're that set on hearing about it, I'll tell you, although I'd rather you didn't mention this to Pol. She doesn't want to hear it. Never has. Traumatised, like your poor Uncle Ray, I reckon. Well, waking up and finding yourself dead would do that to a person, wouldn't it?'

I couldn't promise him that I wouldn't mention anything to Aunt Polly, but luckily, he seemed to take it for granted that I'd agreed to his request.

He took a long sip of tea then settled back on the sofa. 'Polly was last seen alive in the village at about half-past eight that New Year's Eve. She was on her way to lay flowers on her mother-in-law's grave and—'

'At half-past eight at night?' I asked. 'Funny time to be laying flowers, isn't it?'

'Are you going to interrupt me every five minutes?' he demanded. 'I might change my mind and put that Clint Eastwood film on now if you're going to do that.'

'Sorry, Dad. Go on.'

'It was New Year's Eve, remember? Like a lot of war widows, she didn't have a grave for her husband, what with him being killed abroad, but she wanted to wish him a Happy New Year and his mum was the closest person to him. Nothing wrong with that. She'd laid flowers on her grave on Christmas Eve too. That's just the way she was. Is. Good person, see?'

I nodded.

'She bumped into a couple of women from the village who were on their way to The Quicken Tree. They asked her if she was going to join them, but she said she just wanted a quiet night in and was going straight home after she'd visited the grave. They said goodnight and went on their way. That was the last time she was seen alive.' He took a long drink of tea and sighed. 'It was my poor dad that found her.'

'Grandad! I had no idea,' I gasped.

'Yeah. He'd been over in Little Barlham cos he was

courting a young lass there at the time,' Dad said. 'He was on his way back and had cut through the woods, and there she was, lying on the path. Stone dead.'

'What did he do?'

'Well, he admitted he got a bit hysterical like. Who wouldn't? Cradled her in his arms and tried to shake her awake, but it was no use. She'd gone. And then suddenly, there she was in front of him. His sister's ghost. Can you imagine the shock?'

Even though living in Rowan Vale, you got used to the idea that there were ghosts around, it must still be a heck of a disturbance to see someone you've loved suddenly turn up as a spirit. Poor Grandad must have been beside himself.

Bit like Aunt Polly, I thought, before chastising myself for my dark sense of humour.

'Of course, he begged her to tell him who'd done this to her, but she said she didn't know. She'd just been walking along one minute and the next, she'd found herself out of her own body, looking down on that lifeless form with no idea what had gone on. Whoever it was had shot her in the back, so she likely didn't hear or see anyone coming up behind her.' He shook his head. 'In a way, I suppose it was a blessing. She didn't suffer. She swore that to Dad.'

'So what did he do?'

'He didn't know what to do. He was in such a state, but Polly took charge. She told him to run and fetch Sir Edward and he'd sort everything out. He didn't want to leave her, but she insisted, so he went running off to Harling Hall and fetched Sir Edward, and then Sir Edward and his gamekeeper took charge after that and sent Dad home to break the news to his parents.'

'Sir Edward?' I murmured. 'Why did Polly want Grandad to fetch *him*?'

'Well...' Dad shrugged. 'I suppose because he owned the estate, and everyone looked to him to take charge.'

'But why not ask Grandad to call the police?' I said, baffled. 'Why Sir Edward, of all people?'

'She'd just been shot dead, Shona,' he pointed out. 'I shouldn't think either her or your grandad were thinking that clearly. Anyway, like I said, Sir Edward took charge from that point, and he was brilliant, by all accounts. He took care of all the funeral arrangements and paid for it an' all. And he spoke to the police and informed Uncle Ray for them and was basically worth his weight in gold.'

'How did Uncle Ray take it?' I asked, having heard that he'd already been in quite a state when he'd left to live in Northumberland.

'Badly,' Dad said grimly. 'Your Uncle Ray adored

his big sister, as did my dad. They idolised Charlie too, you know. He was like a big brother to him and to your grandad. Ray only enlisted because he wanted to be like him. He was too young, but he added a year to his age, and they didn't question it too closely. Gran was heartbroken. She'd thought he'd be safe because he worked on the farm and didn't have to fight, but he insisted he wanted to do his bit, like Charlie.

'Of course, a year later, Charlie was dead. Ray made it to the end but paid a high price. He needed a fresh start and Sir Edward got him a job on a farm in Northumberland, working for a friend of his. He'd only been there a week when the news came through about Polly and he was devastated. According to his new boss, he only lasted a few weeks in the job and then cleared off somewhere. Said he couldn't cope with it all. He never came home. Another casualty of war most likely. Reckon it's a good thing they never knew what happened to him because my dad says another dead child would have finished Gran off. She was that broken up about Polly, she was never the same again.'

'But Polly was still around,' I pointed out.

'Remember, your great-gran was like our Christie,' he said sadly. 'She couldn't see Polly's ghost. Fair broke her heart.'

'Of course! Oh no...' I couldn't imagine anything
so painful as what Aunt Polly's mum – my great-
grandmother – had been through. To lose Polly and
then not be able to see her spirit when other members
of her family could. Devastating. I sipped my tea,
thinking about what Dad had told me. He'd painted
quite a picture, and I could see why Aunt Polly didn't
like to talk about it.

Even so...

'Dad,' I said hesitantly, 'you don't think Sir Edward
and Polly...?'

He frowned. 'Sir Edward and Polly what?'

I cleared my throat. 'Well, er—'

'Shona Deakin!'

'Bannerman,' I said weakly.

'I don't care who you are, don't you ever dare talk
like that about your Aunt Polly again, do you hear me?
As if she'd carry on with a married man! Who's put
that idea in your head? Oh, let me guess. Max
Janssen.'

'Meyer. His name's Max Meyer. And don't blame
him! He's a lovely man. He's just trying to find out
what happened and what upset his grandfather so
much that he only mentioned Rowan Vale on his
deathbed.'

'That's probably down to guilt,' Dad said crossly. 'And what do you mean, he's a lovely man?'

I gulped. 'Nothing.'

'Don't tell me you really have got a thing for that fella,' Dad said, sounding horrified at the thought of it. 'I was having you on about that. I never thought you really liked him.'

'We're straying from the point here, Dad,' I said. 'Is there any chance that Sir Edward—?'

'I won't hear a word said against that man,' Dad said, banging his cup down on the coffee table. 'He did everything he could to ease things for our family. He created the teashop, he gave your gran and Polly jobs there, he even named it Deakin's! He got your poor old Uncle Ray to Northumberland to start again, he dealt with all the paperwork and official business when Pol died, and he renamed the teashop in her honour. He was a good, kind man, and I don't want you casting no aspersions about him. And you can tell your *friend* that an' all!'

He stood up and I gave him a pleading look. 'Don't get all huffy, Dad. Where are you going?'

Dad straightened. 'To my room,' he said, with dignity. 'I shall watch that Clint Eastwood DVD from the comfort of my own bed, thank you very much.'

23

POLLY

Polly was sitting on the bench near the teashop, watching with interest as a group of men worked to install the sound system. Two of them were up ladders, fixing brackets to the old-fashioned lamppost; the other two were deep in conversation as they faffed around with cables and a toolbox.

There was another group of men also working in the village doing the exact same thing. She'd stood watching them for a few minutes as they'd fitted speakers to the lamppost on the green and had seen a few of the older residents of Rowan Vale shaking their heads at the folly of it all. Millie had wandered over and admired one of the electricians who, she said, had a distinct look of George Harrison.

Then Brooke and Danny had joined them, and they and Millie had moaned about the fact that it was 1940s music that was going to be played and that they wished Callie would treat them to some modern sounds – modern, in Millie's eyes, being anything from 1964.

Polly had left them to it and headed to the mill complex to sit in the sunshine on the bench. Even though she couldn't feel the sun on her skin, the sight of it shining in a clear, blue sky cheered her up no end. The awful weather had finally ended and the dying days of August were lovely and no doubt warm, judging by the clothes people were wearing. The rain had been a bit depressing, but it had probably done the flowers and trees the world of good, she thought. Always a bright side.

She tried to pay attention to what the electricians were doing, but when she heard them calling something about 'amplifiers' and 'power source' to each other, she zoned out again. She wasn't interested in *how* the music was going to be played during the 1940s weekend. She just wanted to hear it!

She'd popped into the church the previous day to listen to the choir practising their wartime sets. It had been lovely to hear all those old songs again. She'd sat quite near the front and closed her eyes, letting happy memories wash over her.

Of course, she'd had to battle to keep out the bad ones. The day she heard Charlie had been killed, for one. All that grief and anger. All those nights of sobbing herself to sleep, trying to put on a brave face during the day when she went back to work, forcing herself to go out with her friends because she knew it would make them and her mum happier if they thought she was getting over it.

Getting over it. Funny expression, that. What did it even mean? She remembered the resentment she'd felt when one of her friends had assured her that time would heal, and she'd move on with her life. She hadn't wanted time to heal. She hadn't wanted to move on. And more than anything, she hadn't wanted to get over Charlie. She'd loved him! What didn't people understand about that?

Every day that passed after his death felt like another day further away from him. She was leaving him in the past and she didn't want to. Each New Year's Eve, she would howl at the injustice of it all. Leaving Charlie behind in 1941, while on her wall, new calendars came and went, reminding her of how far away he was from her.

She hadn't thought she'd ever love again. She

hadn't wanted to. Charlie had been the love of her life, and she'd rather spend the rest of it alone than with someone who could never live up to him.

But she *had* found love again. And in the most unexpected place, with the most unexpected man. A kind man. A man very different to Charlie. And no one had known because no one must ever know.

She gazed at the teashop. Mrs Herron's Teashop. Sir Edward had named it after her. She remembered the day the sign was changed from Deakin's. People had thought it a lovely gesture, but only she knew the real reason he'd done it. For her.

There'd been no need, but it had been a lovely thing to do. Sir Edward had been a good man, and it was a shame he and Lawrie had never got on. That was all to do with Lawrie's mum and how she'd carried on, and how Lawrie had blamed his dad for neglecting her. Well, she supposed that was partly true, because Sir Edward had been devoted to this village and the wider estate, but for her own part, she wouldn't hear a bad word said about him.

'Good morning, Polly.'

She looked up, surprised to see Isaac, the former landlord of The Quicken Tree, standing beside her. She hadn't noticed him approaching.

'Morning, Isaac. Lovely day.'

'It is that.' He sat beside her on the bench and folded his arms, surveying the electricians as they fitted the speakers to the lamppost. 'All over the village, they are,' he said. 'Them contraptions on the posts, I mean, not the workers. Although I've seen a few of them an' all. Ah, it's going to be a smashing event, this. I'm proper looking forward to it, aren't you?'

'I am. Reckon it will bring lots of folks to Rowan Vale who haven't been here before,' she said. 'Our Shona's bound to make a killing.'

'Talking of killing...'

Polly's eyes narrowed as she saw him shift awkwardly on the bench.

'What's up, Isaac?' she asked, seeing the way he was looking at her, with an almost guilty expression on his face.

'Now, Polly, you know me. I don't like to gossip and I'm not one for eavesdropping,' he said, which made Polly almost laugh out loud, knowing how untrue that statement was. 'But the fact is, I heard something the other day in The Quicken Tree, and it fair knocked the wind out of my sails, I won't lie.'

'Oh? Well, you don't want to believe everything you hear,' she said.

'I know that, and I know some folks will blether any old rubbish,' he agreed. 'But not your Shona. She's not the type, is she? And when she's talking, I tend to believe her.'

Polly frowned. 'Our Shona? You were eavesdropping on her? Shame on you!'

'Now, now, no need for that. She was sitting with that young fella with the funny accent, so I was bound to be curious, wasn't I?'

'Young fella?' Polly nodded. 'Ah! You mean Max, Rissa's dad?'

'That's him.'

She supposed that, after hundreds of years stuck in Rowan Vale, Isaac probably considered a man in his fifties a young fella. But what was Max doing in a pub with Shona? Was Isaac about to tell her the two of them were getting all romantic, because she honestly didn't want to hear it. It was way too complicated. Or was it even worse than that?

'It seems the two of them have been doing a bit of investigating. I won't say into what. I'm sure you can imagine.'

Polly groaned. So, Max had kept his word to find out what happened to Gerhard all those years ago. And he'd roped Shona in to help him!

'This is about Gerhard Janssen, isn't it?' she said.

'Well,' he said slowly, 'it was a bit. But mostly, it was about you.'

Polly's nails dug into her palms. 'Me?'

'You. And – well, I hardly like to say this, but I think you have a right to know – Sir Edward Davenport.'

Polly stared at him, fear coursing through her at the unexpected mention of Sir Edward. 'What were they saying about him?'

Isaac's mouth tightened and he looked at her, clearly wary of repeating anything else he might have heard, given her reaction.

'Isaac, this is important! What were they saying about him?'

'All right, all right. They seem to be under the impression that – well – that he wasn't a very nice man, shall we say?'

'Well of all the flaming cheek!' Polly glared at him, as if it was all his fault that Shona and Max had been saying such things. 'Our Shona said that? Why? What would make her say something so horrible?'

'Calm down, lovely,' Isaac said, patting her shoulder gently. 'But I should warn you, they seem to be on a mission to solve a particular crime, if you know what I mean.'

Polly's jaw clenched. 'I know what you mean,' she said.

'I wouldn't have told you, but what they were saying was odd, to say the least. They seem to think Sir Edward and you were carrying on, and that he was the person who killed you.'

Polly put her head in her hands as the fear increased its grip. 'I knew this would happen! Why do they have to go meddling in things that don't concern them? Why bring this up after all these years? Some things should be left alone, shouldn't they?'

'That they should,' he agreed. 'Although,' he admitted sheepishly, 'there are a few of us who did wonder.'

She glared at him. 'Wonder what?'

He held up his hands in defence. 'About who killed you, my lovely. That's all.' He leaned a little closer to her. 'Do you really not know?'

'You haven't told anyone else about this, have you?'

'Of course not,' he said indignantly. 'Nobody else's business, is it?'

'Make sure it stays that way. I mean it!'

'Whatever you want, Polly.'

Polly jumped to her feet. 'I need to see our Jimmy,' she said. 'He needs to put a stop to all this nonsense, right now!'

Her nephew *had* to make his daughter see sense.
Shona had no idea what damage she could do if she
kept digging.

24

I'd honestly never seen Dad look so scared.

We'd snuggled down for the evening, looking forward to a cosy night in watching a new drama that we'd been waiting for with great anticipation. I'd bought us a big bag of crisps each, and made us both a mug of hot chocolate, and we were settled in our respective armchairs, eyes glued to the television screen.

Then in she stormed. Aunt Polly.

She'd never struck me as scary before, despite being a ghost. Tonight, though, she looked different. Her mouth was set in an angry line, and her eyebrows knitted together in clear fury.

Dad just managed to save his bag of crisps from

spilling onto the carpet as he jumped to his feet in alarm.

'Pol! What the heck's the matter?'

Aunt Polly was shaking, and I placed my hot chocolate and crisps on the coffee table and turned the television off. We could catch up with the drama later. It looked like we had enough of our own to be going on with.

More than enough, judging by the way she glared at me suddenly.

'What do you think you're playing at?' she demanded.

Dad and I exchanged nervous glances.

'I'm sorry?'

'So you bloody well should be! What gives you the right to go meddling, eh? What gives you and that man you're suddenly so cosy with the right to interfere in my business?'

Dad groaned. 'What have you done, Shona?'

'Nothing,' I said indignantly. 'Well, nothing much.'

'Casting aspersions!' Aunt Polly cried, turning to Dad. 'That's what she's been doing, Jimmy. Blaming Sir Edward, of all people!'

'Ah,' Dad said heavily. 'Well, yes. I know—'

'And you just let her get on with it, did you?' she demanded. 'You didn't put a stop to it?'

'Put a stop to it?' Dad asked. 'Be reasonable, Pol. She's not a kid any more.'

'You should keep her in line,' she said coldly.

'Hang on,' I said, my own anger stirring. 'What do you mean, "keep her in line"? I'm a grown woman!'

She didn't even seem to hear me. She was pacing up and down now, shaking her head.

'You've got it all wrong. You couldn't be more wrong if you'd tried. And what business is it of yours, anyway? It was *my* life and my death!'

'I thought you'd want to know who...' I hesitated, not wanting to say the word, but plunged on as my anger and indignation soared, 'murdered you!'

I heard Dad gasp, but my blood was up now. 'Why *don't* you, anyway? Any normal person would want to know, but you—'

'Normal person?' She came to a standstill in front of me, shaking her head in anger. 'So I'm *not* a normal person? That's it, is it? That's the way it is? Well, thanks very much. I'm so sorry if my reaction to being shot dead isn't the correct one. I must have mislaid the rule book. Silly me.'

'She didn't mean anything by it, Pol,' Dad began, but I didn't need him to speak up for me.

'You know perfectly well I didn't mean that,' I said.

'What's got into you anyway? And who told you what we said about Sir Edward?'

One look at Dad's ashen face told me it hadn't been him, so who? Only Max and I knew about our conversation. Unless...

'Isaac told me, if you must know,' she said.

'Isaac? The landlord from The Quicken Tree? You mean he was spying on us?' I could hardly believe the cheek of him. 'Well, of all the—!'

'Don't be blaming Isaac. This isn't about him, any-way. It's about you. You and that man. You're getting too close to him, if you ask me. Were you canoodling with him?'

'*Excuse me?*'

Dad looked horrified. 'You weren't, were you?'

'Why doesn't she ask Isaac?' I suggested bitterly. 'I'm sure he'll tell her every word of our conversation and she can report back.'

'Don't be cheeky to your Aunt Pol,' he said.

'Don't be cheeky to your father,' Aunt Polly said at the same time.

I dropped back into my armchair. 'Wow. All we're trying to do is find out what happened to Max's grandad, and how he's mixed up with your murder. I honestly thought you'd want to know who killed you. I thought I owed it to you to find out.

That we'd let you down somehow by not pushing for justice.'

Aunt Polly sagged suddenly. She rubbed her face and sighed. 'Well, you haven't. And I don't *want* to know, do you understand? It was a horrible time for me, and I don't want to have to think about it again. Just drop it, Shona. Please.'

'But are you sure Sir Edward—?'

She glared at me again. 'Get this through your head, Shona Deakin, or Bannerman, or whatever the hell you want to call yourself. Sir Edward Davenport was a good man. The best. And he did so much for our family that we could never repay him for. But the one thing I can do for him now is to tell you to back off and stop blackening his name. I won't have it, do you hear?'

'We hear you, Pol,' Dad said heavily. 'Don't we?' he added, giving me a ferocious look that dared me to disagree.

I tilted my head, staring at Aunt Polly in confusion. 'So,' I said slowly, 'you and he weren't—?'

'Say that out loud,' she cried. 'I dare you! Have you heard this, Jimmy? What's her mind like? She didn't used to be like this, did she? This is all since that Max Meyer arrived, poking around in things that don't concern him.'

'But Gerhard was his grandad,' I pointed out.

'For God's sake, Shona, will you just drop it?' Dad said wearily. 'Can't you see how upset your auntie is? She's still traumatised and doesn't want to know who killed her, and that's that. Have some respect for her wishes, will you?'

I had to admit, Aunt Polly looked really shaken, and I hated seeing her so upset. Shame overwhelmed me. This must be really hard for her if she was behaving so out of character. What had I done?

'All right,' I said quietly. 'I'm sorry, okay? I didn't mean to hurt you, Aunt Polly. I'll stop digging.'

'You promise?' she asked, her green eyes fixed on mine. 'Swear it?'

'I swear it,' I said reluctantly.

'Well, good,' she said at last, after studying me for what felt like forever to assess whether I was telling the truth or not. 'Because the thing is, Shona, if you don't let this go, I'll never speak to you or your dad ever again.'

'You don't mean that, Pol!' Dad protested, shocked.

Aunt Polly's chin jutted in defiance as she faced him. 'Oh, but I do, Jimmy,' she told him. 'Just you try me.'

'Shona...' He gave me a pleading look.

'Like I said, I'll stop digging.' I didn't have much

choice, did I? I couldn't cause Dad and Aunt Polly to fall out. It would break both their hearts. Whatever she said, Aunt Polly needed us. We were her family, after all. I couldn't put her through any more trauma. 'And I'm sorry,' I added. 'Truly.'

She wrapped her arms around herself and closed her eyes for a moment. Then she opened them again and nodded.

'Thank you. We'll say no more about it, then. As long as you keep your promise, we're fine. But Shona, stay away from that man. No good can come from it, you know.'

With that, she turned and left as suddenly as she'd arrived.

Dad almost fell into his chair, looking dazed by the whole thing, as if he could barely believe what had just happened.

He wasn't the only one. I'd had a gagging order put on me by my aunt, and there was no choice now but to let sleeping dogs lie. How was I going to explain that to Max? But even though I'd sworn to stop digging into the mystery of her death, I'd made no such promise about not seeing Max again. I just hoped he'd still want to see *me* when he knew I could be of no further use to him.

25

So here I was in Much Melton, about to knock on Max Meyer's front door.

It had been over a week after our almost-kiss at the pub that he'd got in touch with me. I still hadn't given him my mobile number, but he'd had a brain-wave. He'd looked up the teashop online and emailed us at the address given, asking if the manageress could get in touch with him as a matter of urgency.

Luckily, it had been me checking the emails that day, and I'd replied immediately, saying that if this wasn't teashop business, it might be better for him to contact me personally. I'd given him my number so he could do so.

He'd rung me within fifteen minutes, which was a relief. I couldn't believe he'd actually done that, given the way he'd shot out of the pub after our close encounter.

'Hello, Shona.'

'Hi, Max.' I'd deliberately kept my voice bright and cheery, because I'd been determined not to scare him off. I hadn't wanted him to think I'd been sitting around thinking about him nonstop for a week, after all. He'd definitely have been put off by that.

Instead, I'd aimed for a carefree tone that suggested I'd been really busy so had barely given him a thought since we'd last met, while at the same time making it obvious that I was delighted to hear from him. 'What can I do for you?'

There'd been a long pause, and I was just about to ask him if he was still there when he'd said, 'I think we should talk. Would you like to come to dinner at my house tonight?'

Okay, so what did we need to talk about? Because if it was the whole Aunt Polly/his grandfather thing, I had bad news for him on that score.

On the other hand, if he wanted to tell me how that almost-kiss had been a huge mistake, or worse, pretend it had never happened...

Either way, it wasn't going to be an easy conversation.

'Great,' I'd said. 'What's the address?'

I'd opened a note on my phone, and he'd reeled off the address, which I'd typed in as quickly as I could, repeating it back to him to make absolutely certain I'd got it right.

And now I was at his home, my stomach churning with nerves as I glanced down at my jeans and tunic top and wondered if I should have dressed more formally. But, to be honest, I'd had other things to think about. Not least my dad's attitude when he heard I was visiting Max.

'You remember what we said,' he'd told me, his eyes flashing a warning. 'You promised.'

'I know that, Dad,' I'd said with a sigh. 'I won't let you down.'

His eyes had softened. 'This isn't about me. You know that. Do it for our Polly.'

I'd nodded and left the cottage, wondering how I was going to explain all this to Max. I owed him *some* sort of explanation, but it wasn't going to be easy.

But the truth was, I owed Aunt Polly more. I couldn't let *her* down.

Max's house was nothing like I'd expected it to be. I'd imagined a gorgeous, large cottage built of honey-coloured Cotswold stone, with gables, and roses round the door. In fact, it was a semi-detached, brick new build on a small estate, with nothing remarkable about it at all that I could see. It had a small, lawned front garden and an adjoining garage, and looked exactly like every other house in the neighbourhood. I couldn't deny it was a bit of a disappointment.

I knocked on the door and waited, smoothing my top and hoisting the strap of my bag higher on my shoulder.

After what seemed like an eternity, the door opened and there was Max. To my relief, he was wearing jeans, too, teamed with an open-necked cream shirt. He smiled but I could see a trace of nerves in his eyes, which I wasn't sure was a good or bad sign. It was good that I wasn't the only one feeling nervous, but it could be a bad thing if he was worried about hurting my feelings in some way.

'Shona, come in. You look very nice.'

I supposed 'very nice' was better than nothing. I smiled. 'So do you.'

I stepped into a hallway with wooden flooring and white walls. Very clean. Very tidy. Not a bit of character anywhere in sight.

'Come through,' he said, ushering me into a living room and another world. Talk about a vivid contrast!

It should have been lovely and bright in the early-evening sunshine, with its white walls, and French doors opening out onto a patio and small garden, but quite frankly... I mean, how can I put this politely? It was so full of *stuff* that it was a tip.

There were two large, dark-green sofas and two armchairs squashed into a room that simply wasn't big enough for them. One wall was entirely taken up by bookcases, where so many books fought for space on the shelves, it made me twitch. Where was the organisation? There were books of all shapes and sizes stacked together in a higgledy-piggledy fashion. As someone whose own – admittedly much smaller – bookshelf had books neatly stacked in alphabetical and size order, I could hardly bring myself to look at this chaos.

A chunky, oak coffee table stood in the centre of the room on a dark-green rug that covered most of the wooden flooring. There was another shelving unit squashed into a corner that contained stacks of DVDs. I caught a few of the titles and sighed inwardly. Very arty, highbrow films. Not my cup of tea at all.

'Please take a seat and I'll be with you in a moment,' Max said, heading back into the hall, presumably to the kitchen.

'Do you need any help?' I asked.

'No, not at all. It's all in hand,' he assured me.

I squeezed past the enormous coffee table, settled myself on one of the sofas, and gazed around me, trying not to be too nosy. A huge, flat-screen television dominated the wall opposite the bookshelves. With all those books to read and DVDs to watch, it was a wonder Max had time to go to work.

'No fireplace,' I murmured. It didn't feel right. I'd never lived anywhere without one and, even though we had central heating at Starling Cottage, I still liked the look of a fireplace in a living room. There were plenty of photographs, though...

I peered through the open door to see if there was any sign of Max returning, then cautiously crept over to examine the framed photographs that hung on the wall opposite the French doors. The largest one was of a blonde woman, perhaps in her early forties. She was smiling at the photographer, whoever that was, and looked relaxed and happy. From what I could see in the background, it looked like she was on a beach somewhere.

Was this Max's wife, Nina? She wasn't as glamorous as I'd expected, though I don't know why I'd thought she would be. She'd been a surgeon, not a model. But although there was a surprising ordinariness about her, she looked nice. Friendly. Fun. The sort of woman I could probably have been friends with if I'd known her.

My gaze ranged over the other photos and I swallowed as I realised they were mostly family photos of Max, Rissa, and the same woman. One, in particular, caught my eye. Rissa must have been about twelve. The three of them were sitting on a lawn, Rissa in the middle. She had her arms around her parents' necks, pulling them closer to her, and they were all laughing. A happy family.

I blinked away tears, feeling a pang of sympathy for Max and Rissa for their loss, and wishing things could have been different for them.

Suddenly, I regretted coming here. What was the point? Max was clearly still in love with Nina, and maybe that almost-kiss never happened. Maybe it was all in my mind? Wishful thinking. What was I even doing here?

I dropped onto the sofa, wondering if I should make some excuse and leave. This felt all wrong. Awkward. I wanted to go home.

'Dinner's ready,' Max said.

I looked up and saw him standing in the doorway, smiling. His face fell and he said, 'Are you all right?'

It was on the tip of my tongue to say that Dad had just called, and I had to get home. But knowing him, he'd insist on running me back and he'd want to know that Dad was okay, and it would all get even more complicated, so I simply smiled and said, 'Of course.'

'Okay. Good.' He looked a bit puzzled but said, 'Well, would you like to come through?'

I hardly dared think what horrors the kitchen held, but I followed him into what turned out to be a large kitchen/diner, and yet another complete surprise. Honestly, it could have been a different house. There were French doors in here, too, which made it a lovely, light room, though I thought a bit of colour wouldn't go amiss. White walls, pale flooring, white kitchen units... Even a white table and chairs. I felt as if I was in the *Imagine* video. All it needed was a piano and Yoko Ono faffing with the curtains.

I couldn't get my head around it all.

I took a seat as requested and waited for Max to serve. Something smelled really good, and my stomach growled in anticipation.

'It's nothing fancy,' he told me, sounding anxious. 'Don't expect anything too grand.'

'Well, whatever it is, it smells lovely,' I told him. 'What is it?'

'Just chicken and pasta with some roasted vegetables,' he said with a shrug. 'Courgette, pepper, cherry tomatoes, garlic. There are some chilli flakes in there, too. Hope that's okay.'

All I heard was garlic. For shameful reasons.

'Lovely,' I said brightly. I hadn't expected a repeat of that almost-kiss anyway, and clearly, he wasn't planning on it.

'Would you like some wine?' he asked. 'Or would you prefer a soft drink or tea?'

'Whatever you're having,' I told him, feeling unaccountably shy as he set two plates of utterly scrummy-looking food down on the table.

'I'll be driving you home, so I'm having non-alcoholic sparkling wine,' he told me.

'Oh no! I came on the bus and I can get one back.'

'I wouldn't hear of it,' he said.

'Well, in that case, I'll have the same as you,' I decided.

'You don't have to.'

'Honestly, I like the non-alcoholic stuff,' I said. 'And at least I won't have a headache tomorrow.'

'Well, that's fair enough.' He smiled and poured us both a glass of sparkling not-wine then sat down opposite me. 'Please, eat,' he said, waving a hand at the plate in front of me.

I picked up my fork and hesitantly took a mouthful

of food, hoping it wouldn't be too bad because the last thing I wanted to do was offend him, and when it comes to food, I'm not that good an actress.

My eyes widened in delight. 'Oh my word!' I hastily covered my mouth with my hand. 'Sorry, but this is yummy!'

He looked thrilled. 'Really? I've never made it before, but I found the recipe online and thought it looked fairly simple, even for me.'

'Great job,' I said. 'You're a man of many talents.'

He gave an embarrassed laugh and took a gulp from his glass.

We tucked into our food and, although it really was delicious, there was no denying it was an awkward meal. The only conversation we made was general stuff about recipes and cooking techniques. It was friendly enough, but not really the sort of chat you want to have over an intimate dinner for two with a man who almost kissed you.

But then I remembered the photos of Nina in the other room and thought, maybe this was as good as it was going to get. And I really didn't blame him. It was fine. We could be friends. It was probably better that way. In fact, when I told him what I'd promised Dad, I'd be lucky to even have friendship.

'You must let me wash up,' I told him as he cleared away the plates.

He looked shocked. 'Certainly not! Anyway, we have dessert now.'

'Dessert?' Unexpected bonus. 'Ooh, fab.'

'I hope you enjoy it,' he said, 'It's a *käsekuchen*. I'm afraid I fell back on an old favourite as I spent all day clearing the living room for your arrival.'

Clearing the living room! Bloody hell, what had it been like before? Was he some sort of hoarder or something? I'd seen documentaries about people who couldn't throw anything away and could barely get inside their houses. I wasn't so sure about him any longer...

Then he placed a plate bearing a yummy-looking baked cheesecake in front of me, and all my doubts flew out of the French doors.

'Well,' I joked, 'that's me sorted. What are *you* having?'

He laughed. 'I hope you like it,' he said, and brought two shallow bowls over. We cut large slices of cheesecake and tucked in.

'This is absolutely gorgeous,' I told him, meaning it. 'How have you managed not to crack it on the top? I've made baked cheesecakes before, and they've ended up looking as if they needed grouting.'

'The secret to a good *käsekuchen* is to let it cool in the oven,' he explained. 'It can take a couple of hours but it's the only way I've found to ensure it doesn't crack much. And you should always serve it at room temperature, never straight from the fridge.'

I decided I was in love. I mean, not only could this man make the most heavenly cheesecake, but he didn't bat an eyelid when I requested seconds. He even joined me. Why weren't all men this much of a catch?

I remembered Luke's disapproval when he caught me eating. Not particularly desserts and chocolate or anything like that. I mean when he caught me eating, full stop. It was if he believed women over a size ten should starve themselves as punishment.

Well, I hadn't been a size ten since I'd got pregnant with Christie, and to be totally honest, I'd only been a size ten before that because I was so besotted with Luke, I could barely eat. Once Christie arrived and he showed his true colours, food seemed like a whole lot more fun than he did, and when he left me "to get some space", flapjack became the new love of my life. Without Luke to police my eating habits, I'd gone a little crazy for a while.

But Max didn't seem to mind what I ate. I remembered what he'd said about there being nothing more attractive than a woman who was confident in herself. *I must stay confident*, I thought, and stop thinking about Nina and how she really didn't look like the sort of woman who'd eat two portions of baked cheese-cake after scoffing a big bowl of pasta.

'It's so light and airy,' I said, sighing with pleasure. 'And it has such a fresh, tangy taste, and the pastry is divine.'

'We make the filling with Quark rather than cream cheese,' he explained. 'The pastry is *mürbeteig*. A shortcrust pastry. I'm so glad you like it.'

'Fancy you being able to bake,' I said, wide-eyed. 'I never would have believed it.'

'It was when Rissa was a little girl and I was at home with her all day,' he explained. 'I wanted to use the time to learn a new skill, and baking was something I'd enjoyed when I was a boy and visited *Oma* – my grandmother. As Rissa got a bit older, it became something we did together.'

'Is *Oma* your grandmother's name then? It's very pretty,' I said.

He grinned. 'No. *Oma* is an informal word for grandmother. Her name was Bettina.'

'Lovely,' I said, then realised Bettina may have been Gerhard's wife and I really didn't want to get Max onto that subject. 'So can you bake other cakes then, or is this the only thing you're good at and you're deliberately misleading me into thinking you're a talented baker?'

'I'm not bad,' he said with a modest shrug. 'The trouble is, I love to bake but I also love to eat. I give a lot of my cakes away now or I'd be enormous. I have some very happy neighbours and work colleagues.'

'I'll bet you do,' I said with a sigh, as I spooned up another creamy mouthful from the bowl.

'Would you like another slice?' Max asked eventually.

Wouldn't I just! I shook my head. 'No, thanks. I couldn't eat another thing,' I lied. I wondered if he'd send me home with some so it wouldn't go to waste.

He put the remaining cheesecake in the fridge and set to stacking the dishwasher. He wouldn't let me help no matter how much I insisted it was only fair.

'Pour us both another glass of that stuff,' he said, nodding at the bottle, 'and we'll go through to the living room.'

To be honest, I'd have been more comfortable in the kitchen, despite it looking more sterile than a dental surgery. At least there were no photographs in here. The thought of sitting on that sofa, trying to hold a decent conversation with Nina's husband while she stared down at us was disconcerting, to say the least.

I carried two glasses of not-wine into the living room, wondering as I did so if Nina's ghost was around. That would be sooo awkward! But then I remembered she hadn't died in this house. They'd been living in London at the time of her death.

I sat down and stared across at the photo. She beamed back at me.

'Sorry,' I muttered. 'He didn't kiss me, honestly he didn't.'

But he might have done, if not for that waiter.

Was that my voice in my head, or hers?

I sighed and took a long, long drink of not-wine as Max entered the room.

'Wow,' he said, 'good job I brought another bottle.'

I'd drained my glass! I blushed fiercely. 'Sorry. I was thirsty.'

'It's no problem. Would you like some water?'

'No, no. I'm fine with this stuff,' I insisted, nodding at the bottle.

He topped up my glass and we sat side by side on the sofa in amiable silence for a few moments.

I thought about Aunt Polly and Dad, and I knew I had to tell him something. Something he wasn't going to like.

'Max,' I said hesitantly.

'Yes?'

Oh heck, I couldn't. I just couldn't.

'I like your house,' I said feebly. 'It's very, er, modern.'

He glanced around the living room and shrugged. 'I bought it new about five and a half years ago. Our old house was Victorian and very different. Very large.' He grinned. 'As you can probably tell from the size and quantity of the furniture that's squashed in here.'

Oh, thank goodness! At least he recognised the fact and wasn't totally oblivious to it. Maybe there was hope after all.

'I thought that was what I wanted,' he explained. 'The complete opposite to what I'd had before. A fresh start. When it came to it, though, I couldn't bring myself to part with our belongings. Leaving the house was hard enough. As you can see, that presented me with a bit of a problem. You should see upstairs.'

We both blushed as we realised what he'd said.

'Er, the kitchen's not like this, though,' I said hastily.

'The kitchen isn't only where I do my baking. It's where I do my best thinking. I can't be surrounded by clutter in there. Besides, you have no idea how long it takes me to dust in here. I can't deal with that in the kitchen, too. Hygiene! *Oma* would have a fit.'

He gave a low chuckle at the thought, and I tried to imagine him as a little boy, learning to bake alongside the grandmother he'd clearly been very close to.

The thought of it made me put down my glass and squeeze his hand. Don't ask me why. I couldn't even blame alcohol since I was drinking not-wine.

He looked down at my hand on his and said, 'Shona, I think we need to talk.'

'So you said on the phone,' I told him, immediately removing my hand in case I'd overstepped the mark. 'If it's about your grandfather, I—'

'No. No.' He shook his head slowly. 'Not tonight. I think we have other things to discuss, don't you?'

'We do?' I gulped. 'Like what?'

'I think that things have taken an unexpected turn between us,' he said, almost shyly. 'Something I could never have predicted when I arrived in Rowan Vale. Last week, in The Quicken Tree, you and I—'

He broke off and I stared at him, hardly able to believe he was actually going there. And with Nina looking down on us, too!

'I didn't imagine it, did I?' he asked at last, sounding thoroughly confused by the situation. 'You do know what I'm talking about?'

'We nearly kissed,' I said.

He looked relieved. 'We did. Yes.'

'But that waiter interrupted us,' I added. 'Bloody nuisance.'

Max's eyes crinkled with amusement. 'You think?'

'Who cared about the day's specials? Couldn't he see we were busy?'

Sorry, Nina. I always use humour in awkward situations.

He took my hand in his. 'I'm not sure how to feel about all this,' he admitted. 'This is not what I expected. I don't know what to do, to be honest.'

'It's okay,' I said lightly. 'I get it. You're not ready. It was just a moment and that's all right. I'm not asking for anything more.'

'Nina meant the world to me,' he said. 'You know that.'

'Of course I do.' I stared over at the photograph, and he followed my gaze.

'Yes,' he said, in answer to my unspoken question. 'That's her.'

'She looks lovely,' I said truthfully. 'Kind.'

'She was. I was truly lucky to have such a wonderful wife.'

'Mm.' What was I supposed to say to that?

'But we're not here to talk about Nina, are we?' he

asked suddenly. He turned to face me, and I saw his eyes were shining with tears. 'I'm very confused, Shona,' he confessed. 'My feelings for you have come out of nowhere. I didn't ask for this, and I didn't want it. But I can't stop thinking about you.'

'Well, you're not the only one who's confused,' I told him. 'After what Luke did, I swore I'd never get involved with any man ever again. Yet I can't stop thinking about you either.'

He smiled. 'Really?'

'I don't almost-kiss just any bloke, you know.'

'And I certainly don't almost-kiss just any woman.'

'Well then. It must mean something, mustn't it?'

'It must. But what?'

'What would you like it to mean?' I asked.

I held my breath as he thought about it.

'There is a part of me that feels nothing but guilt,' he admitted. 'But there is another part of me that feels hope, for the first time in so many years.'

'I get that,' I said. 'It's so hard to get over the loss of someone you loved, whether that person died or walked away from you. I'm not saying my grief was as great as yours, nor that it's Luke I was grieving for, but I think I *was* grieving for what I'd imagined my future would be. I thought Luke and I would grow old to-gether, you know? I thought we'd watch our children grow up, and that, one day, we'd be doting grandparents. I imagined holidays and Christmases, one big happy family. And he shattered that dream. He walked away and left it in ruins. Left *me* in ruins. And it's taken so, so long to get back to feeling normal again, and not like there was a part of me missing.'

'Yes,' Max said eagerly. 'That's it! As if there is a part of me missing. I come home from work, and I want to tell Nina about my day, the way we used to tell each other. I want to moan to her about the paperwork and the red tape, and the terrible behaviour of some of the children, and how rude some of the parents can be, and how tiring it is trying to teach German to kids who would rather be playing games on their mobile phones.' He sighed. 'But there is no one there to tell. Just an empty kitchen.'

I nodded, understanding.

'Christmas morning is pointless,' he said heavily. 'Even with Rissa here, it feels wrong. I wait for Nina to sit beside me by the Christmas tree, because how can I open my presents without her? Every birthday, I am aware that I am growing older, and she will be forever in her forties.'

'I'm so sorry,' I said. 'It must be really hard for you.'

'It's been more painful than I could ever have

imagined,' he admitted. 'I never thought there would be light in the darkness again, but you, Shona, you have made me see the possibilities again. You have made me look to the future and, for the first time, not face it with total dread. As I said, I have hope. Hope that life is worth living again, and maybe I can find happiness with someone new.'

He raised my hand to his lips and kissed it gently.

'Do you think,' he said slowly, 'that you could be patient with me? I know it's a lot to ask of you, and maybe I have no right to do so. But this feels so strange to me, you know? I have been feeling numb for such a long time and these new emotions are difficult for me. But,' he added, 'I am glad of them. I am glad not to be numb any longer. I just have to allow myself to love again, I know that. *Can* you, Shona? Can you give me some time?'

I leaned forward and softly kissed his lips. 'As much time as you need,' I told him.

His eyes searched mine, as if he was checking that I really meant what I'd said. Then he cupped my face in his hands and returned the kiss. It was hesitant and shy at first, but then it seemed that frozen heart of his thawed just a little bit more as he allowed himself to experience the flow of emotion and excitement between us. The kiss grew stronger, and as we finally pulled apart, he gave a little gasp, as if he couldn't quite believe what had just happened.

But he was smiling, and there was a look in his eyes that made me go all warm and tingly, and convinced me – if I needed any convincing – that I'd wait for him for as long as he needed.

Against all the odds, Max and I had found each other. It was worth waiting for.

26

The next week saw me walking a fragile line to keep the peace. There were things I couldn't tell Max about the conversation I'd had with Dad, and there were things I definitely couldn't tell Dad about the conversation I'd had with Max, so I found myself crossing my fingers with alarming frequency that the subject of Gerhard Janssen wouldn't come up with either of them.

I'd visited Max at his home again on my next afternoon off, and this time, I'd cooked him lunch in his immaculate kitchen as a thank you for the meal he'd made me. School term was about to start, and it was going to be trickier to meet up once he was back at work, so we tried to see each other as much as we could.

We went to the cinema one evening to see the latest must-see film, and both of us agreed it was highly overrated and one heck of a disappointment, but that the nachos and dips had made the trip worthwhile. I'd dreaded him suggesting some arty film that would go completely over my head, but it turned out that those DVDs had been Nina's, and went over his head, too. I was relieved to hear it, and tried not to dwell on the fact that he hadn't even got rid of her old DVDs.

On Saturday, we had a wander around Cheltenham and ate a picnic in Pittville Park. And on Sunday, we drove to Stratford-upon-Avon and visited Shakespeare's Birthplace. Max was fascinated by it, but all I could think about was Walter Tasker, who Aunt Polly had mentioned lots of times with much laughter and fondness, telling me how he'd once taught William Shakespeare and gave himself credit for just about everything the Bard had ever written.

I almost mentioned that fact to Max as we wandered through the rooms of the ancient building, listening to the friendly and knowledgeable tour guides, but remembered just in time that he had no idea about the ghosts of Rowan Vale, and now definitely wasn't an appropriate moment to tell him.

It was a lovely week, and a wonderful break away from real life for a little while. But I knew that things wouldn't remain like that for long. Max was going back to work. If we were to continue to see each other, Rissa would have to know, and how would she react to her father dating someone else? Christie and Pippa would have to know, too. And, hardest of all, Dad and Aunt Polly would have to be told.

How did I explain to them that I was seeing the grandson of a man who, as far as they knew, might have killed Aunt Polly, and who stirred such strong emotions in them both? I tried not to think about it then, because I just wanted to hang on to this new, exciting relationship that was blossoming between Max and me.

When the new term started, we agreed we'd only be able to see each other once or twice a week. It was okay. We'd both accepted that we needed to take things slowly and had only packed in so many outings the previous week because it was our only chance to spend quality time together for goodness knows how long. August had given way to September, and summer had waved farewell as autumn arrived to take its place. Who knew what the new season would bring?

Well, first of all, it was going to bring the 1940s weekend, which was so close now as to be in touching distance.

The village was a hive of activity, with costumes tried on and altered as appropriate, music selected, the speaker system tested, and the gazebo erected on the village green for the choir. Union flag bunting replaced the usual pretty bunting strung across the front of Mrs Herron's Teashop and other buildings, and shop windows were taped with gummed brown paper.

Lots of the villagers – Dad included – wanted to be part of the fun, so taped their cottage windows, too, although they used masking tape instead of the more authentic gummed paper tape.

Propaganda and recruitment posters started appearing in windows and on noticeboards, and every now and then, we'd be treated to a blast of Vera Lynn through the speakers, as Brodie was paranoid that something would go wrong with the sound system at the last minute.

Everyone was getting very excited, including Paige and Susie at the teashop. I'd followed Aunt Polly's instructions and managed to master the syrup loaf, although I can't say it was the best thing I'd ever tasted. Mind you, we all agreed it was better than the eggless chocolate cake.

We'd tried Spam sandwiches and had all been surprised that they weren't as bad as we'd expected. We'd also tested potted beef sandwiches, and they were okay, too. I'd definitely decided against the mock banana sandwiches, but I did add mock mock banana sandwiches to the menu with a jokey note that they were actual banana sandwiches, but I'd be willing to mash up some parsnips if anyone wanted to sample the real thing! I just hoped no one took me up on the offer.

Best of all, Max had agreed to provide some cakes for the teashop. Although many of the ingredients wouldn't have been available back in the forties, I'd thought it would be a nice touch to include German cakes for the weekend, and after some initial doubts, Max had quite warmed to the idea – and then some!

'I shall bake a *marmorküchen*,' he told me. 'It's a marble cake and always looks so good. And perhaps a buckwheat gateau with fruit and whipped cream and chocolate shavings.'

'Smashing,' I said. 'I think—'

'Ooh,' he said, his eyes shining, 'and *buchteln*!

That's a sweet yeast dough roll, filled with jam or lemon curd.'

'That all sounds lovely,' I'd assured him, but he hadn't finished.

'Of course, I must also make *bienenstich*,' he said firmly. 'Ah, Shona, you haven't lived until you've tried a bee sting cake.'

'Bee sting cake?' I eyed him doubtfully. 'Really?'

'They are made of sweet yeast dough, filled with vanilla custard or whipped cream, or even butter-cream, and they have a baked-on topping of caramelised almonds. They must be tasted to be believed.'

'Great,' I said. 'Okay so that's—'

'I suppose I should bake a *Schwarzwälder kirschtorte*,' he said thoughtfully. 'That is probably the most familiar German cake, right? A Black Forest gateau. Everyone will expect it, and I shan't disappoint them. I'll make *Oma's* version. It's so good and you'll love it.'

I didn't like to point out that, at this rate, I'd have no room to stock anything else, and it was so sweet to see him that enthusiastic that I went along with it. So Mrs Herron's Teashop would be providing at least as many German cakes as English ones by the look of it.

Aunt Polly had popped into the teashop a few

times to see how we were getting on. It had been a bit
awkward the first time, but she seemed determined
that our relationship wasn't going to suffer because of
what had gone on recently and acted as if nothing had
happened.

I was glad we were still friends, but the row she'd
had with Dad and me hung over me. I had to talk to
Max at some point, but while he was staying off the
subject of his grandfather, I followed his lead and
stayed quiet. I didn't want to rock the boat while
things were going so well.

I couldn't help feeling guilty that I was keeping
things from him already, though, and I felt equally
terrible that Dad and Aunt Polly didn't know I was
dating Max. What a mess, especially since I was using
a completely oblivious Amelia as an alibi!

One Saturday afternoon, I was whipping up some
butterfly buns in the kitchen when Paige came
through and said, 'That bloke you fancy's here again.'

Flustered, I said, 'I have no idea who you mean.'

Paige laughed. 'Of course you don't. Shall I give
you a clue? Tall, well-mannered, even his beard's ul-
tra-polite. No? German, Rissa's dad...'

'All right, all right,' I said. 'I *do* know who you
mean.'

'Yeah, and you *do* fancy him,' she said, her eyes twinkling as she took the bowl from me. 'Go and see what he wants, and I'll finish these.'

'Are you sure?' I asked, knowing we had a few customers in at that moment.

'Everyone's been served but him,' she assured me. 'Go and do your job. Me and Susie are fine here.'

Susie smirked, and, blushing, I hurried through to the teashop where I saw Max sitting at the table closest to the toilets. Not the preferred table by any means but we were pretty busy. Having said that, there were a couple of empty tables which I thought he'd have chosen.

As soon as he saw me approaching, his face lit up, which made my heart lift.

'What are you doing over here?' I asked, slipping into the chair next to him. 'There's a table free there.'

'I thought it best we didn't draw attention to ourselves,' he explained quietly. 'Rissa...'

'Ah. Well,' I said, frowning, 'she's seen us talking together before. Most people have. I know you haven't said anything to her about seeing me yet, but you don't have to pretend you don't know me!'

'Everything feels very uncomfortable around here,' he admitted, glancing round the teashop as if there were spies everywhere. 'I don't want her to find out from anyone else. And besides, there are other people to think about.'

Didn't I know it! 'But we're allowed to talk, Max,' I said. 'They don't have to know we've been going out on dates.'

'I suppose so.' He didn't sound very sure, though.

'We're just two people chatting,' I told him. 'And we've done nothing wrong! Even if they find out about us seeing each other, it's not as if we've behaved inappropriately, is it? We've gone to the cinema, the park and a museum. Hardly outrageous!'

Plus, we'd only had a few gentle kisses. It wasn't as if we were jumping into bed with each other every five minutes. Far from it.

'No. Not outrageous at all.' He gave me a guilty smile and I squeezed his hand reassuringly, knowing he was still worried about the slow pace of our relationship.

'It's fine,' I told him. 'How was work anyway?'

He sighed. 'It's like the holidays never happened.'

'Have you heard from Rissa?'

He rolled his eyes. 'Oh yes. I have had quite the lecture from her. She and Betty had a long talk, apparently, and Rissa took it upon herself to apologise on my behalf for my unacceptable behaviour.'

'Your unacceptable behaviour? But you only asked—'

'I know, I know! Rissa was embarrassed apparently and wanted to assure Betty that she didn't come to Rowan Vale to cause any trouble or dig around in the past. You know, I wanted so much to tell her that she should be more worried about the fact that her great-grandfather is a suspect in a murder case for the simple reason that he was German!'

'But you didn't?' I said worriedly.

'Not yet.' His mouth tightened and his brow furrowed. 'Maybe it's time I did, though. She should know what's really been going on here. What people believe about him. Maybe then she'll think differently, and she'll want to get to the truth as much as I do.'

'I – I wouldn't do that, Max,' I said faintly. 'Tell Rissa, I mean. Maybe – maybe it's time to let it go?'

His eyebrows lifted in surprise. 'Let it go?'

'It was such a long time ago. Nearly eighty years. Is it really worth going over it all now? Isn't it sometimes better to let sleeping dogs lie?'

He leaned back in his chair, staring at me in clear amazement. 'You don't want to know who killed your great-aunt? You don't want to know if Sir Edward was really involved?'

I lowered my gaze, realising how bewildering my

change of mind must seem to him. 'I just think – well, nothing can come of it all now. Whoever killed Aunt Polly, they're long gone. They can't be punished. And we should be looking to the future, not the past.'

'I don't understand.' He shook his head. 'Is this Jimmy? Is your father telling you to say all this?'

'Dad just feels that it's not worth causing any upset now. Not after all this time.'

'So, it's okay for my grandfather to take the blame for something he didn't do?' he demanded incredulously.

'But he's not, is he? Not really! Only Betty and Dad have their doubts about Gerhard. No one else knows. It was so long ago and there are very few people left in this village who were around in the forties, and even fewer who'll remember anything about that case. It's not like he was ever arrested or charged, is it?'

Noticing a couple of people waiting to pay by the counter, I got to my feet, telling him I'd be back in a minute.

I ended up taking payment from three people and placing an order with the kitchen staff for another table before I could return to Max. There was no preamble from him as I took my seat.

'You say no one knows. *I* know. *You* know. Something very unsavoury happened that night in this village, Shona. Your great-aunt was shot dead, and the landowner insisted a farmer give my grandfather a false alibi. We both know that if he'd believed my grandfather to be guilty, he would have called the police. If my grandfather did shoot your Aunt Polly, it was at the orders of Sir Edward, and we can't let him get away with that.'

'Even if that's true,' I said wearily, 'he already has. Don't you see? They're all gone, Max. Long gone. It wouldn't do any good now to dig the past up again. Let it lie. Please.'

I could see the muscle in his jaw twitching as he watched me. I knew he was trying to fathom where this change of heart had come from suddenly, and how could I blame him? We'd been Poirot and Marple at one point. Now I just wanted to forget the whole thing. Of course he was confused. And probably very hurt.

'No,' he said suddenly. He leaned forward again and said, 'I don't buy this. There's a reason you're behaving like this, and I want to know what it is. Do you know something? Has your father confessed that he knows the truth? What's going on, Shona? Really?'

Well, the ghost of my Aunt Polly has told Dad and me

that she doesn't want us digging into her murder, and if we continue, she'll never speak to either of us again.

Yeah, great. Tell him that, Shona.

But even as I poured scorn on the idea, it occurred to me that maybe now was as good a time as any to tell him the truth about Rowan Vale. Everyone who lived here knew about the ghosts. Maybe even Rissa knew? If Max was going to be part of my life, then he needed to know, too. After all, there were no official rules about it. It was left to our discretion and common sense.

'Just a minute,' I said.

I hurried through to the kitchen and gave a startled Paige and Susie a pleading look. 'Do you think one of you can cover the front for me for fifteen minutes?' I begged. 'I really need to do something, and I promise I'll be back as quickly as I can.'

They exchanged knowing glances.

'Oh yes? Sneaking off somewhere with Herr Meyer, are you?' Paige said, waggling her eyebrows as Susie gave me a wide smile.

'Take no notice of her, love,' she said, patting me on the shoulder. 'I'll cover the front. You go and do whatever it is you need to do.'

'Thanks, Susie,' I said gratefully and shot back into the teashop.

Max got to his feet as I motioned to him to follow me, and we headed outside to the bench. I pushed him down onto it and said, 'Right, look, this isn't easy to say but there's something you need to know. Prepare to suspend disbelief, okay?'

27

Max looked deeply worried by now. I sat next to him and turned to face him.

'This,' I told him, 'is going to sound completely bonkers, but I want you to just listen to me, okay?'

He nodded.

I closed my eyes for a moment then exhaled sharply. 'Okay. Right. Here goes. The reason I don't want to dig any deeper into Aunt Polly's murder is...' I swallowed. 'Aunt Polly has asked me not to.'

He blinked.

'Actually,' I admitted, 'she's practically ordered me not to.'

Max didn't speak. He just stared.

'And Dad's in total agreement with her. Not,' I

added glumly, 'that he'd ever be anything else. He adores Aunt Polly. Well, everyone did, didn't they? Even Betty said how much she was liked in the village. And dying hasn't changed her personality or made her any less likeable. She really is lovely, but for some reason, she's got a real bee in her bonnet about this, and although I thought she'd want to know who killed her, it turns out she really, really doesn't.'

Max shuffled away from me. 'Are you saying you had a seance or something? Because I'll tell you, here and now, that I don't believe in such things. And if you're trying to—'

'Not a seance,' I said quickly. 'There's no need for those things in Rowan Vale, believe me.'

'Shona,' he said nervously, 'are you quite well?'

'Look, Max, I know this sounds mad, I really do, but you have to believe me. There's something about Rowan Vale. About the Harling Estate. Some people think it's something to do with the Wyrd Stones – you know those ancient stones in the woodland? There's a burial place there. A barrow, you know. They found human remains there years ago, from the stone age. And there's a stone circle—'

'I know what the Wyrd Stones are. What do they have to do with anything?'

'Well, that's just it. We don't know. Did the stones

and the barrow cause this to happen? Or were the stones and the barrow put there to mark the fact that this happened? Or was it something to do with the ley lines?'

'What on earth are you talking about?' he said, exasperated. 'What's this nonsense you're throwing at me? Stones and barrows and ley lines. This is what fairy tales are made of.'

'No,' I said firmly. 'When you live round here, you realise, "there are more things in heaven and earth, Horatio, than are dreamt of in your philosophy."'

'Shakespeare?' he said, his brow furrowing.

'Possibly,' I said. 'Or possibly Walter Tasker.'

'Who?'

'Oh! This is so hard to explain. Okay, here's the deal. There are ghosts in Rowan Vale, Max. Ghosts of people who used to live here, going back to the Roman days, in fact. And my Aunt Polly is one of them.'

He let out a splutter of nervous laughter. 'Is this a joke?'

'No. It really isn't. Some of us have ancestors here and we can see those ancestors, but we can't see the other ghosts. But Callie can see all of them. She's the owner of the estate, and the reason she's the owner is because Sir Lawrence Davenport sold it to her as cheap as chips because the owner must be able to see *all* the ghosts, and his son and grandson can't.'

Max slowly stood up. 'I don't know what you're trying to do here,' he said. 'If all this is some attempt to persuade me to give up on clearing my grandfather's name then all I can say is, I'm disappointed in you. I thought better of you than that.'

'I would never do that,' I promised him. 'And I'm not lying, I swear it! It's all true. There are ghosts in Rowan Vale and my Aunt Polly is one of those ghosts. She lives above the teashop as a matter of fact, in that flat up there.'

I pointed to the window that I'd opened just that morning to air the place.

'She moved there after her husband died in the war, and she still lives there now. She comes to Starling Cottage a lot, though, to visit Dad and me. One of my daughters can see her, too, and one of my granddaughters. The baby. Oh, don't look at me like that, Max! It's all true.'

'And your Aunt Polly has told you she doesn't want you to find out who killed her,' he said flatly.

'That's right! She came to see me and Dad a couple of days after you and I had that discussion in The Quicken Tree. You know, after we'd seen Betty? It turns out that we weren't alone in the pub after all.' I pursed my lips, still cross that Isaac had been eaves-dropping on our conversation. If only I could talk to him, I'd give him a piece of my mind!

'What are you talking about now?' he asked wearily.

'The former landlord of the pub, Isaac Grace – he was around in the seventeenth century – he was listening to our conversation, and he told Aunt Polly what we'd been talking about.'

'Well, how very rude of him.'

'I know! I was *furious*... Oh. You're being sarcastic.'

He sat down again and pinched the bridge of his nose. 'I can't decide if you're having a mental breakdown or if you're playing a joke. Or perhaps you're just being cruel for some reason I can't yet fathom.'

'Can't you just at least try to believe me?' I begged. 'Isaac told Aunt Polly what we'd said about Sir Edward and her being closer than they ought to be, and our theory that he'd forced Gerhard to kill her and made Alf Rowland give him a false alibi.'

'And she didn't approve?'

'No, she didn't! She was fuming, actually.'

As succinctly as I could, I told Max about the conversation Dad, Aunt Polly and I had had that night.

'And she said Dad needed to keep me in line, or else. To be honest,' I said, frowning, 'I was quite annoyed about that. Not like Aunt Polly at all. Fancy talking as if Dad had control of me! I'm a grown woman of fifty-two, for goodness' sake. I'm older than her! Well, unless you count the birthdays she's had since she died.'

'I think,' Max said, 'that you're either quite insane, or you're mocking me. I can't decide which would be worse.'

'You're not going to listen, are you?' I said sadly. Max was the first outsider I'd ever told the truth about Rowan Vale to, and this was the response. No wonder Dad, Aunt Polly, and even Luke had warned me to be very careful about sharing the secret.

'I *have* listened, Shona, and I am at a loss to know what your purpose for saying such things is.'

'I wouldn't have told you,' I said, 'but for two reasons. One, Dad begged me to drop it for Aunt Polly's sake, and I don't want to fall out with him or her. I love them both too much for that, and there has to be a reason she's behaving in this way. I have to respect her wishes. It was her murder, after all.'

'I see,' he said. 'And the second reason?'

'Well... If you and I are going to have any sort of relationship, then you needed to know the truth about where I live. About what this place is. I needed to be honest with you.'

'And this is you being honest with me?'

My eyes filled with tears. 'I'm not a liar. I *am* being honest here. Every word I've said is the truth. Ask anyone who lives in Rowan Vale. They'll tell you about the ghosts.'

'The people in Rowan Vale can't always be trusted, can they? My grandfather would have told me that if only he could. Sadly, he couldn't, because we don't have ghosts in Hannover.'

'For all you know,' I told him. 'Just because you can't see them—'

'That's enough!' He jumped up. 'There are no such things as ghosts. When people die, they're gone. They're gone for good. They don't hang around having conversations with their relatives and living in flats above teashops. I've never heard anything so ridiculous. I don't know what you hoped to achieve by this little joke, but if it was to drive me away, you've succeeded. Congratulations. Now, I'm going home.'

I grabbed his hand. 'Please listen to me, I'm not lying. And I'm sorry!' I realised, too late, that this talk of ghosts had made him think of Nina, and it was too much for him to bear. 'Not all people who die become ghosts,' I added desperately. 'Most go on somewhere. It's just that the percentage in Rowan Vale is far higher than anywhere else.'

He deftly removed my hand from his. 'I'm going home,' he repeated. 'Goodbye, Shona.'

I couldn't exactly physically restrain him, so I simply slumped on the bench, watching in despair as he marched away from me as quickly as he could without actually breaking into a run.

I wanted to say goodbye, because I knew we were over. Finished. Yet somehow, I couldn't even manage to get the words out. I massaged my temples, knowing I had to go back to the teashop, put a smile on my face, and just get on with things. What else could I do?

I got to my feet and jumped as a flash of russet startled me. A fox was slinking slowly round the side of Blighty's Bakery.

A fox in broad daylight? What was it even doing here at this time of day?

It stopped as if it sensed me watching, and turned to stare at me, sniffing the air.

'You're after scraps from the bakery, aren't you?' I murmured. 'Are you really that hungry? Bet there are plenty of pickings in the woods.'

We rarely saw foxes in the village itself, so this was quite a treat. Dad would have loved it. He was very fond of 'Old Reynard', as foxes were also known.

Reynard blinked and I smiled hesitantly at him. He sniffed again then slowly stalked away in that peculiar way foxes have – half-canine, half-feline. There was something quite unearthly about them, really. Maybe it was because they were usually nocturnal creatures and seemed so solitary.

I wondered if Max liked foxes, or if he considered them vermin as some people did. Then I realised I'd probably never get the chance to ask him and rubbed my eyes as tears threatened once again.

But no matter what, I knew I'd done the right thing. I'd told him the truth. It was all up to him now.

28

POLLY

'Well, I have to say, I really like this music!'

Polly turned to see Brooke and Danny doing their best to dance to Glenn Miller's 'In the Mood' as it blasted out through the speaker system.

She couldn't help laughing. Brooke's huge hair (which always reminded Polly of the straw hair on a scarecrow that used to stand in the Rowlands' field) was adorned by a floppy, red bow. She was wearing trousers that were too short for her, and big, heavy boots and red braces like a man's.

Danny, meanwhile, was dressed in flamboyant clothing with some sort of military-style jacket, looking like a cross between a soldier and a Jane

Austen hero, except that he had make-up on his face, of all things!

They looked so ridiculous that the sight of them trying to jitterbug to the popular wartime music was hilarious. Then again, Polly recalled, 'In the Mood' had never been the easiest piece to dance to anyway, so these two stood no chance. She and her friends had usually sat that one out, much as they'd loved the tune.

The 1940s weekend had kicked off at last, and Rowan Vale was already filling up with tourists. Many of them had dressed for the occasion, and it was a strange, though uplifting, experience to see the village filled with people wearing the sort of clothes she'd seen every day during her life.

'Polly!' She turned as Millie came rushing up to her, her eyes shining with excitement. 'Come and see what they're doing at the salon. It's so wild!'

Polly smiled fondly at her and followed her to Churchside, where she found the shop fronts of the Swinging Sixties street had been transformed. Every window had the gummed, brown-paper tape criss-crossing the glass, and each window display had been changed to reflect the 1940s, even though inside the shops were the usual 1960s goods.

The toyshop had removed its bright and cheerful

games and toys from the 1960s and replaced them with the starker, more basic 1940s toys for its window display. Callie had managed to secure several items on loan from local museums for the weekend. She, Brodie and Mia had worked so hard on this, and Polly was amazed by how much they'd achieved in such a short space of time.

She peered through the glass, feeling a pang of nostalgia at the cardboard tanks, paper dolls, rag dolls, cardboard aircraft, bags of marbles and jacks, and packs of playing cards. She smirked at the dartboard with Hitler's face on it. She'd bet lots of families had fun with one of those!

The newsagent, meanwhile, had stuck copies of 1940s front pages all over his window, and Polly dawdled for a while, scanning the headlines and remembering how people had lived for the daily newspaper and the next wireless broadcast so they could find out what was going on "over there". A headline could make your day or break your heart. It had been the most unsettling and disturbing time people of her age had ever known, though sadly many of the older villagers had been through it all before, and not so long ago either.

'Polly!' Millie called impatiently.

'Won't be a minute,' she replied automatically,

steadying herself against the assault from so many bittersweet memories.

Passing the boutique, where the display of miniskirts and hotpants had been replaced with dresses, suits, hats and coats far more familiar to her, she followed the teenager into the salon, where she found Ingrid, Marie and Mandy hard at work giving giggling tourists vintage hairstyles similar to the ones they were now sporting themselves. Gone were the beehives. Now they were wearing styles very much like Polly's own, although Ingrid had gone for something a bit more sophisticated, similar to Harmony's.

There were posters on the wall of Betty Grable and Veronica Lake, and she noticed the magazines were ones she used to read herself. She stared at the covers of *Woman's Weekly* and *Woman's Realm*, *Woman and Home*, and *Home Companion*, remembering the endless knitting and sewing patterns, recipes that helped you make the most of your weekly rations, short, romantic stories that let you escape from the harsh realities of life for a little while, and the beauty tips for women who owed it to the nation to make the most of themselves and not let standards drop!

The strains of 'Boogie Woogie Bugle Boy' drifted into the salon and Polly closed her eyes, allowing her thoughts to drift away.

Images floated through her mind: moving into The Brambles with Charlie, their first proper home together; going to work each morning and spending the day with Mum, Eileen and Rosie as they made Deakin's Teashop a success; testing new recipes, chatting with the customers, laughing and joking in the kitchen; the growing tensions as the likelihood of war increased; 11.15 am on Sunday 3 September, when Neville Chamberlain had announced Britain was at war with Germany; the day Charlie told her he was enlisting, and how she'd pleaded with him not to because he was an agricultural worker and exempt, and she couldn't bear to think of him in danger; waving him off the day he left the village, her mum hugging her and telling her to be brave and not let him see how upset she was; the fear all over again when Ray joined up; Charlie's death; rebuilding her life one painful piece at a time...

She stopped there. She always stopped there. Everything that came later was too much for her to bear. Anything good had been damaged beyond repair. The pain wiped out all the happiness. The fear wiped out all the love. It was why Max Meyer's arrival in Rowan Vale had changed everything for Polly, and she didn't know how to deal with it.

'Isn't it fab?' Millie sighed. She twirled a strand

from her heavily backcombed, blonde hair around her forefinger. 'Wish they could do my hair for me. Just temporarily. I'd love to try something new for once.'

Polly shrugged her sadness away and put her arm around the young girl. 'You look lovely just as you are,' she told her.

'I'll never have a boyfriend, though, will I?' Millie said sadly. 'I'll never get married or have children.'

'I never had children either,' Polly said softly. 'But we have to make the best of things, love. We're luckier than some of the ghosts, aren't we? I've got Jimmy and Shona and my family, and you've got Lucy and Sam. One day, Lucy might have children, and then you'll have babies living with you and I'll bet you anything you like you'll be wishing you could go back to the days when you had peace and quiet.'

Millie laughed. 'They'd better not touch my bedroom! Thanks, Polly. It's just hard sometimes, you know?'

'I know, love,' Polly told her. 'I know.'

She left Millie sitting on a chair watching in fascination as the stylists gave customers pin curls and victory rolls and headed back into the street. Her nose twitched as the smell of fish and chips drifted towards her, and she shook her head at the size of the queue outside the shop. Some things never changed!

She turned off Churchside and wandered down Mill Lane but didn't go back to the mill complex where the teashop was. Instead, she turned down Victoria Walk which led to the village green.

This was where the Victorian shops and house were situated, overlooking the green with its ancient wishing well. She'd heard the photography studio had switched to photographing customers in their 1940s clothing for the day, instead of hiring out their usual Victorian costumes, and thought it might be fun to watch that for a while.

Before she reached the green, though, she felt a tug on her arm and spun round in surprise.

Her surprise increased when she saw Harmony Hill standing before her.

'What the heck? Harmony, you came!'

Her surprise gave way to delight, and she had to stop herself from physically hugging the actress. She didn't want to scare her away, after all.

'It ain't so bad, ya know?' Harmony shrugged. 'I just spent way too long standing by a stall selling baked potatoes. The smell was to die for! Man, what I wouldn't give...' She sighed. 'Ah well, here we are. I've been looking for you. You and me need to talk.'

'We do?' Polly couldn't believe her luck. Here was her Hollywood idol, not only tolerating her, but actively seeking her out. 'What about?'

'Come with me,' Harmony said, and led Polly away from the green and along the footpath by the river. Skirting the mill complex, they continued on their way into the open countryside, passing the odd cottage and a few tourists who'd entered the estate from the north side and were making their way to the centre of the village for the event, judging by their clothing.

Polly was beginning to wonder where Harmony was taking her when the young woman finally came to a riverside bench and sat down, indicating that Polly should do the same.

'Are you feeling all peopled-out already?' Polly asked her, feeling some sympathy. It had probably been a lot to ask of Harmony, attending a busy event like the 1940s weekend when she'd shunned company for so long.

'It's not so much people as all the noise,' Harmony admitted. 'I live a quiet afterlife these days. I used to love music and dancing and all that stuff. Now – not so much.'

'I think it would get easier in time,' Polly said gently. 'Once you get used to it all again.'

'Maybe. But that's not what I want to talk to you about, anyway. I had a visit the other night.'

Polly's eyebrows shot up in surprise. 'Who from?'

She thought they'd all agreed. No bothering Harmony Hill. Polly had done what she promised and invited her to the event, and then it was up to her. Who'd taken it upon themselves to visit her?

'That big guy with the booming voice. Jeez, that guy can talk! Mrs Smithson was sound asleep, but he was so loud, I thought he'd wake the living!' She laughed and Polly realised she wasn't as annoyed about the visit as she might have been, which was a relief.

'Big guy with the booming voice?' she mused. 'I'm guessing you mean Isaac. Isaac Grace. He was the landlord of The Quicken Tree back in the seventeenth century.'

'Yeah, that's the guy,' Harmony said. She shuddered. 'Dang, I wish I'd never gone in The Quicken Tree that night. Then again, if it hadn't been there, it would have been somewhere else...' She shook her head and turned to Polly. 'Do you know there are rumours among the ghosts that I was murdered?'

Polly's eyes widened. 'Murdered? No! You weren't, were you?'

Harmony gave a brittle laugh. 'No way. What happened to me was entirely my own fault. I was on a mission to self-destruct and boy did I ever succeed.'

Polly watched as the actress faded once more to black and white. 'You've done it again,' she remarked gently.

Harmony held out her arm and snorted with impatience. 'This is real unfair, you know? I'm an actress! I should be able to hide my true emotions, but this is giving me away every single time. Gee, being a ghost sucks.'

Polly said nothing. Sometimes, she thought the afterlife was a lot of fun. At other times, she agreed with Harmony. It really did suck. No eating or drinking. No hugging your living relatives. No reuniting with the ones that had passed over. No knowing how long you were going to be stuck like this. Forever was a long, long time...

'So anyway,' Harmony said, 'what they're saying is that you and I were murdered by the same person. Which is crazy because the only person who killed me is me, and I sure as hell didn't kill you.'

Polly couldn't understand any of this. 'Why are they all talking about this now? It's nearly eighty years ago! And most of them were around at the time and must have known how we died and that it wasn't connected.'

'It seems,' Harmony told her, 'that this guy, Isaac, overheard some conversation in the bar about you. You have a niece, right?'

'A great-niece,' Polly corrected her. 'Shona. Is this about her conversation with Max?'

Harmony waved a hand dismissively. 'I have no clue who she was talking to, but she was talking to someone, and they seemed to believe that you were murdered by Sir Edward Davenport – you know, the guy who used to own this place?'

Polly's jaw tightened. 'I know who Sir Edward was.'

'Yeah, well, I don't know what it is, but the ghosts have really got excited about this conversation. Strike that, I know *exactly* what it is. They're bored, and this is something new to talk about, right? So now they're coming up with theories of their own. They've got some kind of bet on, and Isaac came to me for inside information. Like, was I absolutely sure I hadn't been pushed into the river – that kind of thing.'

'He never did!' Polly gasped.

'Oh, he did, honey. I guess you can't blame him, or any of them.'

'I bloody can!' Polly was furious. 'They have no right, stirring all this up again after so many years. Don't they have any idea how painful it is, thinking about that time? It's not some detective serial on the wireless. It was my *life*.' She lowered her head. 'It was my death.'

Harmony picked at some imaginary loose thread on her trousers. 'You know what else Isaac told me?' she asked, giving Polly a sideways glance. 'He told me that your niece and this guy she was with almost kissed. And they would have done if the bartender hadn't interrupted them.'

Polly didn't know how to respond to that. 'Are – are you sure?' she said at last.

Harmony shrugged. 'That's what Isaac reckons, and he was sure close enough to see it all.' She rolled her eyes. 'He was sitting right there at the table with them. So rude! I'd have socked him one if he'd tried that with me. Then again, I guess we have to get our kicks where we can these days.'

'Shona and Max!'

Her great-niece – Norman's granddaughter – and Gerhard's grandson...

'Ya know, Isaac says he's been trailing the two of them, trying to pick up clues, and he's pretty convinced they're in some kind of relationship. But it might be all over already.'

Polly mentally shook her head and switched her

attention back to Harmony. 'Over? What do you mean?'

'She told him about us. About the ghosts. Told him she couldn't help him find out what happened to you because it would upset you too much and she didn't want to hurt you. How lucky are you? You've got living family right here in the village, and they love you so much, they'd sacrifice their relationships for you. Some of us ain't so fortunate.'

'She told him that?' If Shona had revealed the truth to Max about this village and about Polly, in particular, she must care about him a lot. And Polly had been so hard on her, telling her to cut contact with him because it was too uncomfortable for her!

But I wasn't being selfish. This isn't just about me.

'Polly, can I ask you something?'

Polly blinked and turned to Harmony, vaguely noticing that she'd returned to full colour again. 'Of course.'

'Remember when you came to see me, and I asked you if you could forgive the person who killed you?'

Polly nodded, her throat feeling tight at the memory.

'You didn't reply. D'ya think you can answer that question now?'

Polly's eyes filled with tears she could never shed

as she stared at the actress who was watching her with surprising compassion. 'Why does it matter to you so much?'

Harmony seemed to slump. 'I guess – I guess I'm hoping that if even a murderer can be forgiven, there might be hope for me.'

'But what on earth did you do that was so terrible?' Polly asked, aghast.

Predictably, Harmony's colour drained again, but Polly felt it best not to mention it.

'Something real bad,' Harmony said. 'Something I've regretted ever since. You know, I figured I'd been punished enough for it. Twice over, in fact. But it don't make no difference. I still can't get past it. I just need some folks to forgive me. I mean, they ain't around or nothing, but even so... So, can you?'

'Forgive him?' she whispered.

'Is it too much?' Harmony asked gently. 'I totally get it if it is. I was just wondering...'

'I forgave him a long, long time ago,' Polly managed, her voice thick with emotion. 'How could I not? I *loved* him.'

Harmony squeezed her hand. 'Wow. Really? And love cancels out what he did?' She gazed ahead of her for a long moment, then turned back to Polly. 'Aw, honey, you've had such a tough time of it. All these years when you've had to carry your secrets, not even able to tell your loved ones. But maybe it's time you trusted them with the truth, huh? Time to face up to what happened and let it all go. For their sake as much as yours.'

Polly gave her a stricken look. She could feel the panic rising in her as memories tumbled through her mind. She never went there! But the mental block she'd placed on them seemed to be breaking down, and she didn't know how to stop it.

She was dimly aware of Harmony's arm going around her shoulders.

'That's it, honey. Have a good cry. Well, the best you can in the circumstances. You know, I'll bet it doesn't feel that way right now, but this could be the best thing that ever happens to you. It's time to face up to the past, Polly, and you know what? If you do that, I promise you things are going to get a whole lot brighter for you. I swear it!'

'You don't understand. You don't *know*!' Polly sobbed.

'Aw, sweetie.' Harmony lifted Polly's chin with her little finger and faced her, her own eyes shining with unshed tears. 'I do know. I know it all.'

So Harmony *had* been in the woods that night! She'd seen everything!

'You – you didn't tell Isaac?' she whispered.

'No way! This is between you and your family. Let the others think what they like. But, Polly, have courage now. Go and tell them what really happened. Trust them.'

'What if they hate me?'

Harmony laughed. 'They won't hate you! Jeez...' She broke off and shook her head. 'Tell them, Polly. Then just watch when things start to get better all round.'

Deep down, Polly knew she was right. Shona had put her first and possibly lost the chance of a new love because of it. Jimmy and Shona's relationship had been damaged, which would have been unthinkable just days ago. And Polly was tired of keeping so many secrets from the people she loved. Tired of carrying the burden on her own.

Harmony had a point. Polly needed to trust them. Trust that they'd understand. Trust that they'd forgive.

It was time to be brave.

29

It had been one heck of a day. The teashop had been packed from early morning to close of business at five o'clock. Even with various street vendors, the fish and chip shop, the Victory Tea Rooms, and The Quicken Tree serving food all day, it didn't seem to have lessened demand for tea and cake at Mrs Herron's Teashop.

To my surprise, the spam sandwiches had proved popular, as had the mock mock banana sandwiches. One bright spark had taken the challenge to try an actual mock banana sandwich, which had been a bit annoying, but since I'd said on the menu that it was an option, I could hardly complain. Paige evidently had more foresight than I had, because she'd peeled, chopped, and boiled some parsnips early that morning just in case, which saved a lot of time. Needless to say, the mashed parsnip, sugar, and banana essence didn't exactly thrill the customer, or have him queueing up for seconds!

Most popular of all, though, by some margin, were the cakes that Max had provided. They'd been delivered by a courier which seemed typical of him. He might not have wanted to see me – well, there was clearly no 'might' about it – but he was a man of his word.

The cakes were delicious. Obviously, I'd had to taste everything before I could serve it to my customers. Ahem. He was right about the *bienenstich*. Those bee sting cakes were heaven on earth. And his Black Forest gateau was a sight to behold. It seemed almost criminal to cut into it.

His baking was a triumph. But of Max himself, there was no sign.

I was tired out by the time I headed home. I'd hardly had any chance at all to wander round the village and see what was going on for myself. I hadn't even made it to the green to watch the church choir singing and was determined I'd find the time tomorrow. At least we'd had music drifting in through the open door and windows from the speaker system, though it was a bit unnerving when the likes of Vera Lynn and the Andrews Sisters were interrupted by the sound of air raid sirens, or one of Winston Churchill's speeches.

I hadn't seen Aunt Polly all day and wondered how she was coping with all this. Dad hadn't been into the teashop either, although one of the locals who popped in for a pot of tea and a cheese scone informed me that she'd seen him out and about in the village, and he'd seemed to be enjoying himself, so that was something.

Christie and Scott turned up with Maddie and Autumn. Christie had pulled out all the stops, dressing in a very similar fashion to Aunt Polly, even though she'd never seen her in person. We did have some old photos of her, and I guessed she'd used those as inspiration. They were all very excited about the event, and Christie said she'd had a hard time dragging Scott away from the long line of vintage cars that were lined up in front of the church and were apparently attracting a great deal of admiration.

Pippa was in the village somewhere, too, interviewing visitors and locals alike and soaking up the atmosphere to report back to *The Cotswolds Courier*. She was coming back to Starling Cottage for dinner and staying the night, since she'd be reporting on day two of the weekend and it made no sense for her to go home in the meantime.

As I walked up the path to the cottage, I reflected that I hadn't seen Rissa around either. I wondered if Max had told her about us. Probably not. There was no 'us' any more clearly, so what would be the point? It was true that I'd half-expected he wouldn't attend the event, given what had happened the last time we'd met, but that didn't stop the disappointment and sadness seeping through me as I realised I might never see him again.

Now that I'd told him I couldn't help him in his mission to clear Gerhard's name, he had no further use for me. Besides, he thought I was either a lunatic or an exceptionally cruel person. Either way, why would he want anything to do with me now?

My spirits lifted a little when I found Pippa in the kitchen when I got home. They lifted even higher when I saw she was unwrapping fish and chips, and that the kettle was already boiling for tea.

'I thought I'd treat us all,' she announced, smiling as she saw me standing by the door, looking happier than I'd been all day, no doubt. 'I couldn't be bothered to cook, and I don't see why you should after the busy day you've had.'

'Oh, thanks so much, lovely,' I told her, grateful

that I had nothing to do but dive into the delicious smelling fish and chips without so much as having to reach for a pan.

'Go and sit down, Mum,' she said. 'I'll bring it all through as soon as I've dished it out.'

I found Dad sitting on the sofa, a tray on his lap in readiness, and a wide smile on his face. He looked more relaxed than he had all week.

'She's a good girl, our Pippa,' he told me, as if the awkwardness between us had never happened. 'What a treat! I'm looking forward to this, aren't you?'

'Did you have a nice day?' I asked him stiffly, trying not to feel a twinge of resentment at his high praise for my daughter when all she'd done was bring in fish and chips. I mean, I was grateful to her, too, but I cooked for him every single night, and he seemed to take that for granted!

It had never bothered me before. I loved looking after Dad, normally. Maybe, I thought sadly, I was just struggling to get over the way my feelings had been steamrollered by him and Aunt Polly, as if they didn't matter at all. Trying to do what was best for the two of them had probably cost me my relationship with Max, and even though it had been my choice in the end, I couldn't help feeling a little anger that I'd ever had to make it.

'I did,' Dad replied. 'They've done a great job, haven't they? I'm looking forward to tomorrow.' He cleared his throat, suddenly looking uncomfortable. 'I was going to pop into the teashop earlier, but it looked really busy, so I didn't want to get in the way.'

It might have been the truth. Then again, he might be just saying that because he felt bad about not coming in. Either way, I didn't have a reply for him, so I sat down and stared at whatever it was on the television without absorbing a word of what was being said in the programme.

Pippa came in carrying Dad's fish and chips and a mug of tea, which she carefully put on his lap tray.

'Do you need a hand, love?' I asked her, but she shook her head.

'Stay there. I'll be back in a minute.'

She was, too, carrying a lap tray for me with my fish and chips, bread and butter, and a mug of tea. A third trip with her own meal meant she could finally sit down, and we could begin eating.

She'd even put the salt and vinegar on mine and hers and added the obligatory ketchup to Dad's. It was bliss, and I felt my mood lifting a little as we ate in companionable silence.

'Ooh, they smell good!'

We all looked up to see Aunt Polly standing there.

She sniffed the air and said, 'You can't beat a chippy tea!'

'Oh, Aunt Polly,' Pippa said sorrowfully, 'I'm so sorry. Do you want us to put these away until later? We can warm them up and—'

'You bloody well won't!' she said, sitting on the sofa next to Dad. 'To be honest with you, I'm not even hungry. If I could eat, I'd probably say no. I've got – well,' she shrugged, 'other fish to fry, as you might say.'

'You okay, Pol?' Dad asked her, his eyes crinkling in concern.

She did look a bit on edge, despite her cheerful attempts at conversation. I wondered if she'd come to lecture me again and pointedly shovelled some chips into my mouth, determined not to let her spoil this evening. I'd had a rough day, and I just wanted to eat my dinner, have a nice hot shower, and an early night.

'As it happens, Jimmy, no I'm not. Not really,' Aunt Polly confessed. Her voice sounded weird, nervous, and I glanced up at her despite my annoyance.

Dad gave me an accusing look. 'You haven't done anything...' He broke off, remembering Pippa was sitting there.

Aunt Polly squeezed his knee. 'Now, Jimmy, don't be having a go at our Shona. She's done nothing wrong. Absolutely nothing. If anything, we should be apologising to her.'

Well, that was unexpected! I frowned as Dad said, 'Apologising to her?'

'Yes. And Shona, love, I *am* sorry. I really am. I should never have given you that ultimatum. It was cruel and unnecessary, and I'm sorry it's cost you so much.'

I gulped. 'Who told you?'

Which one of the ghosts had been spying on us this time? Because clearly, someone had informed Aunt Polly that Max and I had... Well, could I say broken up when we'd never really got together in the first place?

'Harmony Hill,' she admitted. 'But it was Isaac who told her.'

'Bloody Isaac,' I said crossly, before looking at her in surprise as her words sank in. 'Harmony Hill? She's been speaking to you?' We all knew that the Hollywood actress was reclusive and didn't mix with the other ghosts, so this was a real breakthrough. I almost felt honoured that my boring little life had given her so much interest that she'd deigned to speak to my aunt about it.

'Me and Harmony, we're like that,' she said, entwining her fingers and laughing. 'No, there's still a way to go before she integrates with us all, but she's doing better than she was. Maybe one day... Anyway, that's not why I'm here. Well, I suppose it is in a way. Oh, just finish your fish and chips and we'll talk about it then.'

'Oh no,' Dad said firmly. 'You tell us what this is about now. We can eat and listen, you know.'

Aunt Polly seemed to be pleating the hem of her dress, and I could feel how nervous she was from where I was sitting. Any last bit of annoyance I felt faded away to be replaced with concern for her. Something was obviously bothering her a lot and I didn't want to make things any tougher for her. Besides, she'd apologised, and I wasn't one to hold grudges.

'What is it, Aunt Polly?' I asked gently. 'Whatever it is, we're here to listen.'

'Aw, Shona. And after everything I said to you!'

'What's this about?' Pippa asked, clearly baffled. 'What have I missed?'

We all looked at each other.

'I – I was helping Rissa's dad,' I admitted eventually. 'He's the grandson of a German PoW, and when his grandfather was dying, he said some things. Things that made Max believe he'd been badly treated at Rowan Farm while he was working there after the war.'

Pippa frowned. 'Okay. And?'

'And we went to talk to Betty at the farm about it all, and it ended up turning into something else entirely,' I admitted, giving my aunt an apologetic look.

'Like what?'

I could see Pippa's interest was piqued, and mindful of the fact that she worked for a newspaper, I said quickly, 'It's private, love. Not something for the public to know about.'

She gave me an indignant look. 'Well, obviously. I'm asking as your daughter, not as a reporter.'

I glanced at Dad and Aunt Polly, not sure how much they'd want me to tell her.

'It turned into an investigation,' Aunt Polly told her quietly, 'of my murder.'

Pippa gasped, and to be honest, so did Dad and I. We'd never heard her say that word out loud before and hearing it from her own lips was quite chilling. Poor Aunt Polly. Whatever else had gone on, I had to remember that she was the victim in all this. Her feelings counted way more than mine.

'I – right,' Pippa said, obviously stunned. 'Okay.'

'The thing is,' Aunt Polly rushed on, 'although I understand that you were trying to help Max, you've both got it all wrong. You shouldn't blame Sir Edward. He did everything he could to help.'

'Sir Edward?' Pippa looked from me to Dad. 'You thought Sir Edward Davenport killed her?'

'You may as well tell her,' Aunt Polly said. 'She's just going to keep interrupting if you don't.'

Carefully, I told Pippa about the conversation we'd had with Betty, and about our theories regarding Sir Edward, making sure not to mention anything that might give away the fact that Max and I had grown much closer as a result of our detective work.

'Well,' she said when I'd finished, 'that's some theory! And I can see why it would work, too. But you're certain that it wasn't Sir Edward, Aunt Polly? You've always said you didn't see who killed you, so how can you be sure?'

Aunt Polly looked thoroughly miserable. 'Because,' she said softly, 'I was lying. I know exactly who killed me. Truth is, I've always known.'

30

I think it was Dad who spoke first.

'You *know*?' He placed his lap tray on the coffee table, switched off the television, and turned to face her. 'Polly, are you serious?'

'Aw, Jimmy, don't let your dinner go cold,' she said.

'Sod the dinner,' he told her. 'Pol, this is important. Are you saying you knew who your murderer was, right from the moment it happened? Well, who? Who was it? And why the hell did you cover up for him?'

'It's not as simple as all that,' she explained. 'I had my reasons, believe me. And when I tell you the truth, you'll know why I couldn't say anything. Please, just try to keep an open mind and don't judge, okay? This is really hard for me, and it's only because of our Shona and Max that I'm doing this.'

'No, Aunt Polly,' I said, my heart going out to her as I saw the anguish in her face, 'don't do it for us. If it's too much for you then you don't have to tell us anything.'

'Doesn't she?' Dad demanded. 'I reckon you're hoping she'll change her mind, so she doesn't drop that Max's grandad in it. You're a bit too close to him for my liking.'

'What?' Pippa's mug of tea wobbled precariously in her hand. 'You and Max?'

'It's over,' I said desperately. 'Not that it really started. Just a few dates and some very innocent kisses, that's it.'

'Mum! Why didn't you tell us?'

'Because I wasn't sure how everyone would react,' I admitted. 'Given the circumstances.'

'She means me,' Aunt Polly said sadly. 'I put pressure on her not to carry on with the investigation, and she told Max she couldn't help him. She told him about me. About the ghosts of Rowan Vale. Needless to say, he didn't believe her.'

'Oh, Mum, I'm so sorry,' Pippa said.

'Aren't we getting away from the point?' Dad asked. 'Who was it, Polly? Was it that Gerhard Janssen? Because if it was, I think his grandson should be told, so he knows what kind of man his grandfather was.'

'I think he knows *exactly* what kind of man his grandfather was,' Aunt Polly said, suddenly sounding a lot stronger as she lifted her chin and faced her nephew. 'A kind, sweet, wonderful man. A man of integrity. A man I loved.'

There was a stunned silence.

'Pol!'

'Aunt Polly, really?'

She got to her feet and stood in front of the fireplace, facing us as we all stared expectantly at her.

'Gerhard Janssen,' she said, 'was a lovely man. And – and we planned to marry.'

'No.' Dad shook his head, dazed. 'No, that can't be right. You loved Uncle Charlie!'

'Of course I did!' Aunt Polly cried. 'I loved him heart and soul, and if he'd still been around, I would never have looked twice at any other man, I swear it.'

'Of course you wouldn't,' I said, giving Dad a fierce look. 'But you'd been alone for a long time, hadn't you?'

'A war widow,' she said, smiling gratefully at me. 'It's a horrible title, and not one I'd ever have wished for. But I had to make the best of it, didn't I? I had to carry on with my life, and I did. I went back to work. I went to the pictures with friends. I put a smile on my face and just got on with it, because that's what everyone did. We all had to. What choice was there? I never expected to love anyone else, but Gerhard...'

'But he was a German, Polly,' Dad murmured.

'Meaning?' I said coldly.

'I've nothing against Germans, Shona,' he said firmly. 'Don't you ever think that about me. But this was wartime, remember? He was an enemy soldier. A prisoner. Can you imagine what people would have said if they'd known about it?' He faced Aunt Polly again. '*Did* anyone know?'

She wrapped her arms tightly around herself, as if for protection, and it was then that I noticed something. Something I should have noticed years ago.

'Aunt Polly,' I said slowly, 'where's your coat?'

Dad's brow furrowed. 'What are you on about?'

Aunt Polly, though, was simply looking at me as if she'd been waiting for someone to ask her that for decades.

'She went out to lay flowers on a grave that evening,' I said. 'She was never seen alive again. But it was New Year's Eve. It would have been dark and freezing cold. Why wasn't she wearing a coat?'

Pippa let out a long, 'Ohhhh!'

Dad rubbed his forehead, clearly confused.

'Well...' Having no answer, he simply stared at his aunt, a question in his eyes.

'I should start at the beginning,' she said. 'There's no point otherwise. It's important that you know it all, so you can understand. It was 1944 when Gerhard was sent to Chipping Marsham Camp and started working at Rowan Farm, along with another prisoner, Anselm. I used to go to the farm for eggs and milk and the like, and I was friends with Helen, so I bumped into them a few times. They were always very polite, but we didn't make conversation. Back then, they were under close supervision, and the rules were very strict, but gradually, things began to get more relaxed. The war had ended, but the Germans were still held in this country.'

'Why?' Pippa asked. 'Why weren't they sent home?'

'Because the British government needed labourers,' I said briefly. 'The country was in ruins and prisoners were needed to repair it. Roads needed fixing, houses needed building, farmland needed working.'

Aunt Polly nodded. 'By then, the prisoners were allowed to socialise a bit with the locals. And by the end of 1946, they were able to do almost anything. Gerhard and Anselm were billeted on Rowan Farm instead of being stuck at the camp.

'They came into the teashop one day, and we got talking. It was just a friendly chat, that's all, but I liked Gerhard straightaway. He was sweet, you know? And so polite and gentlemanly. He treated me with respect, he really did.'

I thought wistfully that it seemed as if Max had taken after his grandfather, then.

'We started bumping into each other a lot. It's a small village and by then, most people had accepted them and liked them. Not everyone, but most. We saw each other at the farm, and at the pub sometimes, and he started coming into the teashop just to chat. He couldn't buy much – they were only paid pocket money. A shilling a day, I think it was. I used to slip him the odd treat. A slice of cake here. A sandwich there. You know.'

Dad was staring at her as if he couldn't believe what he was hearing, but I could see Pippa was as entranced as I was.

'So when did this new friendship turn to love?' I asked.

She hesitated. 'It was the summer of 1947,' she said. 'You must remember, I'd been a widow for six long years by then. It's not like I was carrying on with just anyone! Gerhard was special, and yes, I'll admit it, I was in love with him. He was very handsome, and that voice...' She gave me a wry smile. 'You know what I mean, Shona.'

I nodded. I knew all too well.

'Anyway, I won't go into any details, especially with our Jimmy sitting here,' she said. 'I can tell this is making him uncomfortable.'

'I don't begrudge you a bit of happiness, Pol,' he told her. 'You'd lost Uncle Charlie a long time before that, and I know he'd have wanted you to be happy. But you were taking a risk, even in 1947.'

'I know,' she said. 'We both knew. There was a woman in a nearby village who'd been courting a German prisoner, and they made her life hell. She was spat at and even slapped. The names they called her! It didn't stop them, though. They got married as soon as it was allowed, although it meant she had to give up her British citizenship, if you can believe that.'

'And even knowing that, you still planned to marry this fella?' Dad asked incredulously.

'I loved him, Jimmy,' she said simply. 'We'd have been happy. I know that.'

'So – so Gerhard didn't kill you?'

'Do you really have to ask that, Shona?' she said.

'No. I just wanted to hear you say it. So I can tell Max. Put his mind at rest once and for all, even though he never believed his grandfather capable of such a thing anyway.'

'And he's right about that,' she assured me. 'He was the sweetest man.'

Dad ran a hand through what was left of his hair and gave a heavy sigh. 'All right then, so Gerhard Janssen didn't kill you. But, Polly, who did?'

'Now, Jimmy,' she said, holding up her hands, 'I want you to be open-minded about this. You're not going to like it and it's going to hurt. Are you sure you want to know?'

'Of course I want to know! Who killed you, Pol?'

We all waited anxiously as she closed her eyes for a moment.

Then she faced us all with as much calmness as she could muster and said, 'Ray. It was your Uncle Ray. My brother.'

'No way!' Dad cried. 'It can't have been! Pol, you've got this all wrong. Ray wasn't even in Rowan Vale when you died. He was in Northumberland, remember? Working for that pal of Sir Edward's with the big estate.'

Aunt Polly took a seat next to him on the sofa. 'I'm sorry, love. I know it's hard for you to believe, but I promise, it's true. It was Ray all right.'

'No.' Now Dad got to his feet and began to pace up

and down, rubbing the back of his neck as he tried to work it all out. 'It must have been the shock made you see things. Ray was in Northumberland. Dad told me.'

'He was supposed to be in Northumberland,' Polly agreed. 'He never went there.'

'What was he supposed to be doing in Northumberland again?' Pippa asked. 'I'm a bit hazy on the details.'

Aunt Polly turned to her. 'When your Uncle Ray got back from the war, he was a changed man. What they called shellshocked in the Great War. PTSD, your mum says it's called now.'

Pippa nodded. 'Yes, I remember that. Normandy, right?'

'Normandy was the final straw, maybe, but he'd seen a lot of terrible things even before that. Then he was wounded, quite badly, and sent to a hospital ship before being returned to Britain. He was in hospital down south for quite a while, and while he was there, he got the news that Linda – she was his girl – had married someone else and left Rowan Vale.'

'I never knew that!' I said. 'Poor Uncle Ray.' Then I remembered he'd murdered Aunt Polly and wondered if I was supposed to feel sorry for him at all.

It was as if she'd read my mind, because she said, 'Yes exactly. Poor Ray. He was a broken man by the time he came home. Him and Linda had been to-gether since they were kids, like me and Charlie, but it was all over. He'd almost lost a leg and was left with a limp, and had scarring on his face that made him feel ugly, and like no one would ever want him again.

'But it was even worse than all that. The night-mares. The flashbacks. The mood swings. Mum and Dad really struggled to understand, and to make it better for him. He was living with them, you see, in Starling Cottage. He was so angry all the time, Mum was a bit scared of him. But she wouldn't turn her back on him, of course. She adored him.' She bit her lip. 'We all did.'

'So, when did he decide to move to Northum-berland?'

Aunt Polly hesitated. 'It was Sir Edward's idea,' she said at last. 'Norman had gone to him and told him how much Ray was struggling and how hard it was for Mum and Dad to cope. Ray had refused to work at Rowan Farm, even though Helen and Alf had wel-comed him back with open arms. He wouldn't work with Anselm and Gerhard, you see. The war was over, but as far as Ray was concerned, they were still the enemy who'd caused him so much pain and loss. He blamed them for everything. For Charlie's death. For Linda running off with another man. For his leg. For the scars. For all the terrible things he'd been through. It didn't matter that they'd suffered, too. That they'd lived through the horrors of Normandy. That they'd lost friends and family. He hated them. He hated them with an intensity that scared the life out of us all.'

'It must have been hell for all of you,' Pippa said with feeling.

'It was. In the end, like I said, Norman went to Sir Edward and told him what was going on, and asked if he could help. Ray needed a job. A fresh start. Rowan Vale just reminded him of Linda, and he hated seeing the pity on our neighbours' faces. He wanted to be where people hadn't known him as he was before. Sir Edward arranged with a good friend of his who owned an estate up in Northumberland for him to work there. We all thought it was for the best. Even Ray seemed to agree. He left for Northumberland the day after Boxing Day, 1947. At least, that's what we all believed.'

'He pretended to leave?' Pippa asked.

'Did he know about you and Gerhard then?' I asked. 'Is that why he did it?'

'Gerhard and I planned to marry and stay in England,' Aunt Polly explained. 'Mum and Dad didn't know about us yet. No one did except our Norman.'

Dad's head jerked up in shock. 'My dad knew?'

'He did. I trusted him, and he never meant to give us away. I know that. We'd told Norman and Alf, because we wanted them to be our witnesses when we got married. We planned to tell Mum and Dad when it was done, because then there'd be no trying to talk us out of it. They weren't unreasonable people, and they weren't prejudiced either, but they were my parents, and they loved me. I knew they'd worry themselves sick if they knew about it, so I thought it best to just get it over with and tell them afterwards.'

'Dad knew. I can't believe it. He never said a word,' Dad murmured.

'Don't blame him for that, Jimmy,' Aunt Polly said. 'He did what he thought was for the best. We all did.'

'And Alf knew too! Not Helen?'

She shook her head. 'Helen was lovely, and I adored her, but we all knew she couldn't keep a secret like that for long. It was Alf who told us not to mention it.'

'But Grandad gave you away?' I asked.

'He let slip something about me and Gerhard one day in front of Ray,' she explained. 'He was terrified, but Ray didn't seem to pick up on it. He was packing for Northumberland at the time, and Norman said he thought he hadn't heard him but felt he should warn us just in case. Then Ray came to say goodbye to me and told me he loved me and would miss me, so I thought Norman must be right, and Ray hadn't heard him.

'Norman and Mum and Dad saw him off on the bus and he promised he'd write soon and let them know how he was getting on and – to be honest – we all heaved a sigh of relief, even though we were still worried about him. We really thought that a new job and home would help him. But he never went. I don't know how far he got but at some point, he made his way back to Rowan Vale. Only he didn't let anyone know.'

Dad had gone pale. 'You mean, he *planned* to kill you? He came back deliberately?' His voice was little more than a whisper and I felt terribly sorry for him. This had clearly been a heck of a shock. It was enough of a shock to me, but Dad had grown up hearing all about his heroic uncle and couldn't believe that he was a cold-blooded murderer.

'Gerhard and me – we decided to get a licence to marry in the new year,' Aunt Polly continued, her voice heavy with sadness. 'That night, I went to lay flowers on Charlie's mum's grave. I know it sounds daft, but I wanted to tell her the news so she could tell him for me. I wanted to explain. I wanted him to know that, even though I'd met someone else, I would always love and remember him. I didn't want him to think I'd forgotten him.'

'Oh, Aunt Polly,' I said, my eyes filling with tears. 'I'm sure he never would have thought that.'

'I wanted to make sure,' she said. 'Anyway, after I'd done that, I... I headed for the woods.'

'The woods? But you hate them!' Pippa said. 'Oh. Sorry. Of course, you only hate them because of what happened there. But why did you go there?'

'To meet Gerhard,' I said. 'That's right, isn't it? He left The Quicken Tree at nine. He was going to meet you, wasn't he?'

'We thought it would be the safest place. It was New Year's Eve. The streets were busy. People were going from their homes to The Quicken Tree, and to each other's cottages. And can you imagine if they saw us together when they'd had a few drinks inside them? But we wanted to see each other to wish each other a Happy New Year. It didn't seem like much to ask for. Evidently, it was.'

'Ray followed you?'

She shrugged helplessly. 'Must have done. Either that or he was trailing Gerhard. Anyway, we met up and stayed together about fifteen minutes.' She gazed into the fireplace, completely desolate for a moment.

'We talked about how 1948 was going to be our year. We were so excited to be getting married. We were going to make a new life, have children. I so wanted a family...'

She swallowed and I wished with all my heart that I could put my arms around her and hug her tightly.

'Then I said goodnight to him, and we kissed, and I headed back to the flat. But I'd only been home a few minutes when our Norman came flying in telling me I had to come quick because Ray had got Gerhard and he was going to kill him.

'Well,' she gave me a wry smile, 'I didn't even stop to grab my coat. I just ran after Norman. He'd been cutting through the woods on his way home from seeing his girl in Little Barlham, and he'd heard men's voices, so he'd crept through the trees to see who it was. He couldn't believe it when he saw Ray pointing a shotgun at Gerhard.'

Dad moaned. 'This is just... That my dad experienced all this and never said. He told me he'd found your body on the way home through the woods, not his brother waving a shotgun at Gerhard Janssen.'

'He was begging for his life,' I murmured. 'That's what Max told me. When Gerhard was dying and reliving the past, he was begging for his life.'

Polly put her head in her hands. 'That's how we

found him. Begging Ray to let him go. He told him we loved each other, and I'd already lost one man I loved. He pleaded with Ray not to take another from me. But that only made Ray angrier. He told Gerhard never to speak about Charlie, and how dare he compare himself to that man in any way? He said some terrible things. Awful things. But Gerhard kept trying to calm him down, to make him see reason.'

She lowered her hands. 'But I knew. I knew Ray was way beyond reason. And I knew what was coming. So I ran. I didn't even think about it. I just ran, and as I ran, I begged Ray for mercy. But he pulled the trigger and I...'

She couldn't go on, but she didn't need to.

'You ran in front of the gun,' I said. 'You were trying to protect Gerhard.'

'And I did, didn't I?' she whispered. 'If I achieved nothing else in my life, I achieved that. But I couldn't save them both.'

'Both?' Pippa asked.

Dad looked as if he was going to be sick. 'Ray?'

She nodded. 'It all went dark, Jimmy. I just remember Gerhard screaming my name, and the ground. The cold, cold ground. It was *so* cold. *I* was so cold. And I thought, what a way for it to end. And then it was dark. Then – I don't know how long it was

– I was standing there, looking down on myself. And Gerhard was cradling my body and crying. And Norman... Norman was on his knees, sobbing over the body of our Ray.'

'Dad...?'

'No! No, Jimmy love. It was Ray. He never meant to kill me. He wouldn't have hurt me for the world, you know that. He couldn't stand it. He had to end it, so he did.'

'He shot himself?' I murmured. 'Oh, my God!'

'Better that than the hangman,' Dad said. 'They didn't have much understanding of trauma in them days. Even if they'd believed him, he might have ended up locked away in an asylum for the rest of his life. Best way out.'

'Dad!'

'I'm being realistic, Shona,' he said, tears rolling down his cheeks. 'What else is there to say?'

'But how come no one knew about Ray?' I asked. 'And how did Sir Edward get involved?'

'I told our Norman to fetch him,' Aunt Polly explained. 'He could see me. It was weird. It was like I was still alive in some ways. I was so calm. So sure of what had to be done. Sir Edward had looked after our family, and he'd been good to Ray. I couldn't think of anyone else who'd know what to do, and the last thing

I wanted was for Mum and Dad to find out. I remember sitting next to Gerhard, trying to reassure him that I was okay. I so wanted him to know I was there, but I just couldn't make him hear me. He had no idea about Rowan Vale. It wouldn't have occurred to him that I was still around. Norman brought Sir Edward to the woods, and it turned out it was his gun that Ray had stolen from the Hall. He was amazing. He knew just what to do. He told Norman to stick with Gerhard and make sure he didn't do anything stupid and that he'd be back very soon. Well, when he came back, he had company. Quintus Severus.'

'The Roman centurion?'

'Yes. I could barely take it in. I'd never met him face to face before, and it was all a bit much. I think the shock of it all finally sank in, and I just went to pieces. I couldn't help Gerhard, because he had no idea I was there, and he was inconsolable. Norman was in a state of panic by then, and there was our Ray lying on the ground just feet away from my body. Oh! I couldn't even look at him.

'Sir Edward told Quintus Severus to take me to Harling Hall as fast as he could and hand me over to the Wyndhams, but that neither of us was to tell them who'd killed me. He made me swear it and told me to think of my parents. Of course I agreed. I didn't have the energy to argue. The Roman took me to the Hall and Agnes and Aubrey took care of me. Well, Aubrey did. Agnes was in hysterics at the thought of there being a murderer on the loose. The little girl, Florrie, she was agog. They kept telling her to go to bed, but she wasn't having that. In the end, she stayed and helped Aubrey look after me, and it was Agnes who went to bed.'

For the first time, a smile passed her lips as she remembered the scene at Harling Hall that night.

'But what about the bodies? What was happening in the woods?' Pippa asked.

'You mean, me and Ray?' Polly asked her wryly.

Pippa blushed. 'Sorry, Aunt Polly. I didn't mean—'

'It's all right, love. I know you what you meant. I believe my body was left where it was until the police took it away. But as for our Ray... I don't know, and that's the honest truth. I never knew. Sir Edward got Norman to go home and tell Mum and Dad what had happened to me, but not to mention Ray. He went back to the Hall and made a few calls, including to the police. After that, he sorted it all. It was days before I started to think straight again, and by then, it was all taken care of.'

'Sir Edward took Gerhard to the farm and asked

Alf to give him an alibi,' I said. 'And now I understand why.'

'Asked being the operative word,' Aunt Polly said firmly. 'There was no forcing, contrary to your theory. If Alf had said no, Sir Edward would have come up with an alibi for him, believe me. He just thought it more plausible that Gerhard would have been at the farm. And Alf was happy to go along with it, once everything had been explained.'

'So Alf knew the truth?' I asked.

'He did, but he swore he'd never tell a soul, and it seems he kept his word, despite all the abuse he got from some of the villagers.'

'And your mum and dad died believing you'd been murdered by some unknown assailant?'

'They did. And that Ray was alive and well somewhere. Norman couldn't bear the thought of them knowing the truth. It would have broken them. I'm grateful every day to your dad, Jimmy, for the way he hid that from them. Sir Edward and his estate manager put a story about that a vagrant had been seen in the area, and that one of the shotguns had been stolen from the Hall. It didn't take long for the stories to be embellished by locals, who were all too keen to claim they'd seen the vagrant, too. In the end, people stopped accusing Gerhard and Alf, and the case was eventually closed.'

'But some things don't add up,' Pippa said. 'What happened to Uncle Ray's body? And why did everyone in the family believe Ray had taken your death badly and moved on from Northumberland?'

'Because that's what his new employer told them. He was a good friend of Sir Edward's. When my murder was discovered, the police wanted to interview everyone who was close to me. They sent local police from the village in Northumberland to talk to Ray. Only it wasn't Ray. It was someone Sir Edward's friend knew, who had Ray's identity documents because Sir Edward gave them to him.

'The local police reported back that Ray had been on the Northumbrian estate on New Year's Eve, and that was that. They weren't interested in checking that out. Why would they be? Everyone in the village had seen him leave on the bus, and they all knew Sir Edward had got him a new job. Besides, Ray adored me. They all knew that. *I* knew that.

'Sir Edward felt it better that my parents believed Ray had wandered off somewhere, searching for another job, than that they learned the horrible truth. They'd never have got over it if they'd known he'd killed me, then shot himself.'

'But his body?' I asked. 'Where did they bury him?'

'I honestly don't know,' she said. 'Sir Edward said it was better that I didn't know. He told me to trust him, and that he'd been respectful. And I wasn't in any fit state to question that. To be honest, I was just grateful he'd dealt with it all.'

'This is...' I had no words. My main concern was Dad, who looked completely drained. I was also worried about Aunt Polly, who'd finally told us the truth. It must have taken it out of her.

'Why now, Aunt Polly?' I asked her. 'Why have you told us what really happened after all this time?'

She took what felt like forever to answer.

'Someone asked me today if I could ever forgive the man who'd killed me,' she said at last. 'And I told her what was in my heart. I forgave him almost immediately. I forgave him because I knew he was sick. He wasn't in his right mind. The Ray I knew before he went to war would never have behaved that way. Ray loved me. And I loved him. Nothing changed that. And then I realised that it was the first time I'd properly let myself think about Ray for decades. Ever since it happened, I'd been blocking out the memories. The fear of that night was too much for me to deal with, so I didn't think about it. I didn't think about Ray. And I didn't think about Gerhard.'

She hugged herself tightly. 'When Max arrived in the village and I heard his voice... Oh, it was so much like Gerhard's, Shona. It began to stir things inside me that frightened me. I couldn't risk feeling those emotions again, so I shut down. And I tried to shut you down, too, and I'm so sorry for that. I was trying to protect Ray's memory, but I was also trying to protect myself. That's the truth of it. I didn't want to have to remember. It was too painful.

'But when Harmony asked me if I'd forgiven him, and I said yes, I realised suddenly that not only had I forgiven him but that I missed him, too. I missed him so much, and I missed Gerhard. I *wanted* to think about them. I wanted to remember them and grieve for them so I could get past all that pain and reach the happy memories again. To do that, I had to face up to the past and bring it out into the open. Mum and Dad aren't here to be hurt by this any longer. I needed to share it with you all so you can know the truth about our family, and remember them as they really were, with love.'

She looked round at us all. 'Because that's the thing. For too long, this has been a story of murder and hatred and secrets and lies. I want it to end. The truth is, it's always been a story of love. My love for Gerhard. Ray's love for me and Charlie. Norman's love for us all. War took so much from us. It took my husband. It took Ray's mind. It can't take anything else. That's why I've told you.'

'I wish, more than anything in this world, that I could give you a cuddle,' Dad told her.

'Me, too,' I said, and Pippa nodded in agreement.

'Well,' Aunt Polly said smiling, 'just give each other one big hug, and I'll be right in the middle of you.'

'Group hug!' Pippa called.

And yes, Aunt Polly *was* right in the middle of us, at the heart of our family, where she'd always belonged.

31

POLLY

It was Sunday, and the final day of the 1940s weekend. Shona had managed to wangle an hour off work, which was only fair as Paige and Susie had taken the time off the previous day. Polly was accompanying her as she wandered round the village, pausing for a while to chat to locals, and then making her way to the green where Amelia and the choir were in full flow.

'Oh! I love this song,' Polly told her, as the singers began their next number, 'Moonlight Serenade'. 'It's so romantic.' She began to sway in time to the music, her eyes closed as she softly sang along with the choir.

'Are you okay, Aunt Polly?' Shona asked anxiously. 'This isn't too much for you, is it?'

Polly opened her eyes. 'I'm more worried about you, lovely,' she said. 'You keep smiling, but there's a sadness behind your eyes that I know all too well. It's Max, isn't it?'

'I'm fine,' Shona told her. 'I just need to let him know that Gerhard is innocent, but I don't know how I can prove it. I mean, I can tell him my ghostly Aunt Polly told me what happened, but he'll probably think I've gone crazy again or I'm messing with his head. He seems to believe that already.'

'I expect it's a lot to take in if you're not from around here,' Polly admitted. 'It's different for us. We were brought up here, and we've known about ghosts since we were younger than our Maddie is now. But for outsiders – well, it must seem ridiculous.'

'Exactly. And how can I convince him? I can't show him any ghosts, can I? And even if I got Callie to tell him the truth, he'd just think she was covering for me. If someone doesn't want to believe, they won't. Simple as that.'

'I suppose you're right,' Polly said sadly. 'I'm so sorry. This is all my fault.'

'Of course it's not,' Shona consoled her. 'And don't you worry about me, Aunt Polly. I'm just glad to see you looking so much brighter today. At least, you were until you started fretting.'

It was true that Polly had woken up that morning feeling brighter and happier. Now that she'd allowed the memories through, the terrible events of that night had stopped being so scary. They were still terrible, of course, but she could see past them. It was like they'd been a huge boulder blocking the road, obstructing her view of Gerhard and Ray who were standing behind it. But the boulder had moved a bit, and now she could peer round the side and see them. She couldn't quite get to them yet, but they were there waiting for her, and she knew it wouldn't be long before she could fully embrace her memories of the happy times she'd shared with each of them.

She was full of gratitude that Shona, Pippa and Jimmy had been able to forgive Ray, too. The fear that they'd turn on him had scared her for years, so knowing their image of him had changed somewhat but hadn't been tarnished made her happier than she could say.

The only thing spoiling her happiness was Shona's sadness. If only she could fix things between her and Max. But Shona was right. If someone didn't want to believe, they wouldn't. Nothing anyone said or did would make a difference, and there was no way to show him that ghosts existed. That Polly really was around.

Maybe Max didn't care enough about Shona to even try?

Polly sighed and glanced around, wondering if Pippa was anywhere close by. Maybe she could spend a bit of time with her mum. Cheer her up.

Then she straightened, her eyes widening as she saw Max standing near the wishing well. He wasn't looking at the choir who were standing under the gazebo. His gaze was fixed on Shona, and the sadness in his face matched the look in Shona's eyes.

'Maybe,' Polly murmured to herself, 'he does care enough after all. But he needs to push past that fear and doubt, just like I had to.' She raised her eyes to the heavens. 'Oh, Gerhard, my love, if you can hear me, you need to do something. Give him the courage to believe the impossible. Let them have the happiness that was taken away from us.'

As she watched, Max squared his shoulders and walked away, leaving Polly feeling frustrated and wretched.

'Won't be long, love,' she whispered to Shona. 'Just going to have a chat with some of the ghosts.'

'Are you sure? Do you want me to come with you?' Shona asked.

Polly laughed. 'And what would be the use of that? You can't see or hear anyone but me! No, I'll be fine.

I'll pop into the teashop later and see how it's going. You enjoy your friend's choir for a bit.'

Shona nodded and Polly hurried off before she could change her mind. Max was just ahead of her, walking slowly along the path, his hands in his pockets and his head down. He wasn't going towards the farm. Surely he wasn't leaving already?

'Dad!'

Both Polly and Max spun round to see Rissa running towards them. She flew straight through Polly before Polly could move out of the way, which was a bit disconcerting.

'You're not going home, are you?' Rissa asked.

Max seemed surprised to see her. 'I thought you said you'd be busy on the farm?' he asked.

'Well,' Rissa said, kicking awkwardly at the grass, 'we are. But Betty's given me an hour off to come and find you. I did shout to you when I saw you leaving the green, but you didn't hear me. Or did you?'

'Of course I didn't. I would have waited for you. Surely you know that?'

'I – I wasn't sure. I'm sorry, Dad, I know I've been horrible lately, and I should never have lied to you about where I was. You should hate me.'

Max put his arms around her and held her tightly. 'I could never hate you, *mausi*. You're my child, and I love you always. I'm only sorry that you doubt that. I know I let you down—'

'No, Dad, you didn't,' Rissa said. She stepped back from his embrace and looked up at him. 'You were grieving, and I didn't make enough allowances for that. I wanted you to look after me, but I never thought I should have been looking after you, too. I know how much you loved Mum. I was so angry when you sold the house, and I couldn't understand why you'd want to leave such precious memories behind. But I think I understand now.'

'You do?'

Rissa led him to the bench in front of the church and Polly followed them. She thought vaguely that she really ought to give them their privacy and imagined her mum tutting in disgust that she was eavesdropping, but they were Gerhard's family. She desperately wanted them to be happy.

'Those cars are proving quite the draw,' Max said, nodding at the long line of vintage vehicles that took up most of Church Lane.

Polly followed his gaze and admired the gleaming motors that were surrounded by eager enthusiasts. She was astonished to see Silas Alexander among them. He was walking from car to car, doing his best to stroke them, and had a look of childlike excitement on his face that she'd never have believed if she hadn't seen it for herself.

Who'd have thought it?

Her attention was dragged back to the Meyers suddenly as Rissa said, 'Dad, I'm leaving Rowan Vale.'

'You are?' Polly gasped.

'You are?' Max said, clearly surprised. 'When did you decide this?'

'I've been thinking about it for months,' she admitted. 'I just didn't want you to know because... well, I hated that you were right, and I was wrong.'

'Wrong about what?' he asked.

'About wasting my life. About hanging around here hoping for something that will never happen.'

Max frowned. 'What's wrong, *süsse*? Is there something you haven't told me?'

Rissa nudged him. 'Is there something *you* haven't told *me*?'

Polly watched as two spots of colour appeared on his cheeks. 'Like what?'

'Like you and Shona. Betty seems to think there's something between you. She wasn't gossiping,' she added quickly. 'She assumed I knew. This is a small village, and people have been talking, you know.'

'I'm sorry,' he said quietly, so quietly that Polly had to strain her ears to hear him.

'Why?' Rissa asked. 'So, you *are* seeing Shona?'

'We went on a few outings together,' he told her. 'But I don't think it will lead anywhere.'

'Why? Don't you like her?'

Polly waited. If she'd been able to breathe, she'd have held her breath. Instead, she fixed him with a piercing gaze and willed him to admit that he did.

'I like her very much,' Max said finally. 'But it's complicated.'

'Dad, if this is about Mum, you can't let it stop you,' Rissa urged him. 'She wouldn't want you to be alone for the rest of your life. You know that, deep down. She'd be happy for you. Shona's never going to take Mum's place in your heart, but that doesn't mean she can't have her own place in it. You've got so much love to give. Plenty to go round for us all, I reckon.'

Polly's hands flew to her chest, and she sighed. What a lovely thing to say.

Max grinned and ruffled his daughter's hair. 'Listen to you, being all wise.'

Rissa tutted and smoothed her blonde locks. 'Not that wise, Dad. I've been a bit of an idiot, to be honest.'

'What is it, Rissa? You changed the subject quite masterfully, but I suspect there's something you want to say.'

'I'm going to Germany,' she told him. 'I'm going to stay with Aunt Gisela and Uncle Louis for a bit.'

'You are? When was this arranged?'

'Just a few days ago. I asked them not to tell you. I wanted to break it to you myself.'

'But why? And for how long?'

'I'm not sure how long. I can stay for up to ninety days without a visa, but if I want to stay longer, I could apply for a residence permit. I could even apply to study or work there, I guess. My German's excellent, thanks to you and Mum making sure I grew up bilingual. I'm going to see how it goes. I'd like to see something of Germany. I know we went there a couple of times when I was a kid, but I didn't really take much of it in back then. I'm ready to embrace my German heritage now.'

'I'm very glad to hear that,' Max said slowly, 'but I can't help thinking there's more to this than you're telling me.'

Rissa was very quiet for a few moments, then she looked up at him. 'Remember when you asked me if I was seeing someone, and I told you I had been, but it was over?'

He nodded. 'I do. I've been wondering who it was ever since.'

She smiled. 'Sorry, I shouldn't have been so enigmatic about it all, but I was ashamed.'

'Ashamed? Of what?'

'Ashamed because he didn't love me, Dad. I don't think he ever did. When I started to get too serious, he broke it off with me.'

'Oh, he did? Well, tell me who he is, and I'll have words with him.'

Rissa laughed. 'No, you won't! He didn't do anything wrong. He just didn't feel for me the way I felt about him. Not his fault. He didn't promise me anything, and when he realised how much I loved him, he broke up with me as gently and as kindly as he could. He's with someone else now and I think it's the real deal. I didn't want to face up to that but there comes a point when you have to, doesn't there? You can't lie to yourself forever. And the truth is, I'm sick of it all. Sick of being Poor Rissa, who everyone knows is still pining for Brodie Davenport.'

'Davenport?' Max asked sharply. 'Is he related to Sir Edward Davenport?'

'I think he was Brodie's great-grandad,' she mused. 'Used to own this estate. Anyway, the point is, it's over, and it's time for me to move on. And that's why I understand why you had to leave our old house behind. You can't cling to the past forever. You have to move forward. A fresh start. I was scared to do that, but then I realised if *you* could do it, after all the heartbreak you'd suffered, then I could do it too.'

He put his arm around her shoulders. 'I am very proud of you, Rissa. Have I ever told you that?'

'Not so much lately,' she admitted. 'But then, I haven't really given you cause to, have I?'

'I am always proud of you,' he promised her. 'I love you so much. Never forget that.'

'I won't, Dad. So, are we good?'

'Always,' he said.

'And what about you and Shona? Are you going to make a go of it with her?'

'Do you like Shona?' he asked, his eyes narrowing.

'Yes, I do. She's always been decent to me, even when I haven't been that polite to her. And, like you, she makes some cracking cakes,' she added, laughing. 'Between the two of you, I reckon you'll gain twenty stone by the end of the year.'

'I don't know. There are things I don't understand about her,' he admitted.

'So, spend some time working them out.'

'But it's not that simple. Her past and my past, they're entwined in ways I can't fathom. And she said something about—' He broke off, shaking his head. 'It doesn't matter. It sounds insane.'

'Ghosts?' Rissa suggested.

Max sat up straight and stared at her. 'Why would you say that?'

'It's this place,' she said, gazing around with a puzzled expression on her face. 'I've been here over eighteen months, and I've heard whispers. Rumours. I get the feeling there's something strange about Rowan Vale.'

'But there are no such things as ghosts,' Max said.

'Keep telling yourself that, love,' Polly said, rolling her eyes.

Rissa raised an eyebrow. '"There are more things in heaven and earth, Horatio..."'

'Walter Tasker?'

It was his daughter's turn to stare. 'Where did you hear that name?'

'Something Shona mentioned,' he said. 'Like many other things, it made no sense.'

'I've heard Brodie mention him,' Rissa admitted. 'You know, some of the things he told me made no sense either. He was a bit cagey about a lot of things when I think about it, but he definitely mentioned Walter Tasker. Said he'd died in Rowan Vale centuries ago. Apparently, he was one of William Shakespeare's teachers.'

'Didn't it bother you, when Brodie said strange things?' Max asked, curious.

Rissa shrugged. 'Not really. I loved him.'

'But didn't you think he was perhaps having a joke with you?'

'No, definitely not. Brodie was a decent man. He wouldn't play mind games. I didn't understand everything I heard him talking about, but there was no agenda. I couldn't make him love me, but I knew I could trust him.'

'Yes,' Max murmured. 'I see.'

And so did Polly. It might not work, but she'd had a sudden brainwave about how she could convince Max that ghosts did exist, and it was so simple, she couldn't imagine how she hadn't thought of it before. All she had to do was relay this conversation to Shona, and when Shona repeated it to Max, he'd realise she wasn't lying after all. Bingo!

Polly leapt to her feet. Time to fix this mess once and for all.

32

'I just don't see why you won't do it,' Aunt Polly grumbled. 'Personally, I think it's a brilliant idea. One of my very best, and I've had some smashing ones in my time.'

'It's not that I won't do it,' I explained patiently. 'I'll probably have to, because how else am I going to explain to Max that I know for a fact his grandad was innocent? What I'm saying is, I'm not happy about it.'

'But why ever not? This could solve everything. He'll finally believe that ghosts exist. He'll have no choice.'

'Yes, and he'll know that my great-aunt was sitting on the bench next to him and his daughter, eavesdropping on their private conversation. He's going to be paranoid! What with you and Isaac, how is he ever going to dare say anything ever again in this village?'

I sighed heavily, realising that may not be an issue much longer. Now Rissa was leaving Rowan Vale, and the mystery of Max's grandfather was solved, he would have no reason to return.

There was, I thought, no point in dwelling on all that. I would go to his house one evening this week and tell him what he needed to know. Then I'd leave and that would be that.

Anyway, for tonight, I was determined to put it all behind me. Here I was in the ballroom at Harling Hall, surrounded by friends and neighbours, and re-solved to have a bloody good time if it killed me.

Callie and Brodie had hired a seven-piece swing band for the evening, and all the villagers had been invited. They'd extended the invitation to Christie and Scott, and to Pippa, naturally, as a thank you for her support in *The Cotswolds Courier*.

Most of us had got dressed up for the occasion, though few were in 1940s costumes. I think maybe we were all costumed out. After all, we spent most of our working lives dressed as people from other eras, and it was good to cast all that off and just be our contempo-rary selves again.

Callie looked lovely in a dove-grey dress, and

Brodie was handsome in a dinner suit. It was nice to see Lawrie there, too. He hadn't been into the village much in recent months, as his mobility wasn't so good, but Aunt Polly had told me he was enjoying a new lease of life, helping Walter Tasker teach the ghost children.

'That girl can sing,' Christie said, as she and Pippa came over to join us. She nodded at the temporary stage that had been erected at one end of the ball-room. The swing band were performing the first of their two sixty-minute sets, and the vocalist was belting out 'Taking a Chance on Love'.

The dance floor was already busy, although the buffet table was seeing its fair share of the action, too. It was the first time I could remember when I didn't feel any interest in exploring the food options.

'This is such fun,' Pippa said, sipping a cocktail. 'What a shame Grandad didn't come.'

'I think your grandad's had a trying few days,' I told her. 'He needs a bit of time to get his head around everything.'

'But he will, won't he?' Aunt Polly asked, her green eyes troubled. 'You do think he'll be okay?'

'He'll be right as rain,' I promised her. 'In a way, he's relieved it's all out in the open. I think it's been at the back of his mind all these years, wanting to know the truth but not wanting to push you for answers. The truth might not have been what he wanted to hear but it was what he *needed* to hear, and now he can begin to process it all.'

'And he understands? About Ray, I mean. He wasn't a bad man. I want you all to know that. He was just so confused. He thought he was protecting me. He thought Gerhard had forced me to be with him. He didn't understand that I loved him.'

'I know,' I reassured her. 'We all know. If you can forgive him, so can we. He was ill. We get it.' I gave Christie an apologetic look. 'Sorry, love. I know it must be frustrating for you when we talk to Aunt Polly.'

'It's okay. I'm just glad everything's sorted out now. I wish I could tell Aunt Polly how much I love her, even though I can't see her.'

I glanced at my aunt, who smiled and nodded at me.

'You just did, love,' I told Christie.

'And I love her too,' Aunt Polly added.

'Aunt Polly says she couldn't care less and to go away and stop pestering her,' Pippa told her sister.

Christie burst out laughing. 'So, she loves me too, right?'

'Damn, there's no winding you up these days,' Pippa complained.

Polly laughed. 'These girls of yours are a tonic,' she told me. 'I'm glad they came tonight.' She gazed around the ballroom. 'Tell you what, it's proving a popular event with the ghosts. Loads of them are here.'

'Any sign of Agnes and Aubrey?' I asked.

She craned her neck to get a better look but eventually admitted that she couldn't see them anywhere.

'Florrie's here, though,' she said, smiling. 'She's dancing with Imogen. They're having a whale of a time.'

'Any sign of Harmony Hill?' Pippa asked eagerly. 'What I wouldn't give to interview her! But even if I did that through you, Aunt Polly, no one would ever believe it. I'd probably be sued for libel or something.'

'She's not here anyway,' Aunt Polly told us. 'I didn't really expect her to be. She's been pushed out of her comfort zone quite a lot lately, and I think she probably needs to recharge her batteries as you youngsters say. She'll come back to us when she's ready. I think there's hope for her yet. Ooh, there's Isaac. Now, I want another word with him about his eavesdropping on private conversations. Bloody cheek.'

She hurried off and I shook my head, realising

that she didn't see the irony of that at all, even after all the nosying around she'd done lately!

Callie and Clara came over, both looking flushed and excited.

'Having a good time?' Callie asked.

'Fantastic,' I said automatically. 'You've done a great job, Callie. The whole weekend's been brilliant.'

'So much better than I expected,' Callie said. 'I've just been speaking to Robyn from The Magic Lantern. She says they've had a sell-out weekend! She's over the moon with the takings. Hey, and get this! She asked me what I thought about them offering more contemporary snacks at the cinema in future. Apparently, some of the visitors were disappointed with the squash and ice cream options.'

'Get away,' I said, laughing. 'Who'd have thought it?'

Amelia wandered over at that point, just in time to hear the good news. She looked delighted.

'Wonderful,' she said. 'I might even visit myself if they get something decent to eat. At the very least they could offer popcorn. That was definitely around in the 1940s. I know. I checked.'

'I went to see *Brief Encounter*,' Clara admitted. 'I just wanted an hour or so's peace from the kids and Jack. Worst mistake ever.'

'Was it boring?' Christie asked, wrinkling her nose. 'I've never fancied it myself.'

'Boring? I blubbed my way through the entire thing. I was a wreck when I left that cinema. Honestly, and this is me who didn't even shed a tear during *that* scene in *Titanic*. I was hoping Jack would push Rose off the door and climb on it himself.'

'Oh my God,' I gasped. 'You're a monster!'

'I know, right? Yet there I was blubbing over some posh couple in a train station. Pathetic.'

'Er, Mum?'

I turned to Pippa. 'Yes, love?'

'Be prepared for a shock,' she murmured, and slowly turned me round to face the door.

Max had just walked in.

'Ooh,' Amelia said. 'Your handsome friend is here.'

'Handsome friend?' Clara asked. 'What have I missed?'

'Mum and Max have been, er, walking out,' Pippa said, showing a remarkable lack of discretion.

'You have?' Callie squeezed my shoulder. 'That's fabulous news.'

I was still staring at Max, who was standing alone, looking quite lost and uncertain. What was he doing here? There was no sign of Rissa.

'They've had a bit of a falling out,' Christie whispered to an enthralled Callie and Clara.

I didn't even know Christie knew about me and Max! Pippa must have told her. Honestly, I'd have to speak to my daughters about family loyalty and how to keep it zipped unless otherwise instructed.

'Well, he's here now,' Amelia pointed out.

'But not for me,' I said.

'Who else then?' Pippa asked.

At that moment, Max spotted me. He gave me the sweetest, shyest smile, and a hesitant wave.

'Aw,' Clara said, sounding suspiciously tearful, 'who needs *Brief Encounter*?'

'Go and talk to him, Mum,' Christie urged. 'You know you want to.'

She was right. I did. But I was scared. What if it all went wrong again? What if we started arguing? What if...

Then I thought about Aunt Polly and Gerhard. Aunt Polly and Uncle Charlie. She'd had her chances of happiness ripped away from her twice by circumstances she couldn't control. The only person standing in the way of my chance at happiness was me.

'Wish me luck,' I muttered, and forced myself to walk to where Max was standing.

His eyes widened as I approached, and he anxiously ran a finger around his collar before greeting me.

'Shona,' he said. 'You look wonderful.'

Well, that was a huge improvement on 'nice', I thought. And he looked absolutely gorgeous to my undeniably biased eyes, in a smart charcoal suit, white shirt and tie.

'I wasn't expecting to see you,' I said. 'Is Rissa with you?'

'No. It would have been difficult for her, in the circumstances.'

I knew exactly what he meant, given that Aunt Polly had briefed me on his conversation with Rissa. Max knew all about Brodie now.

'But you still came,' I said.

'I had to come. You did invite me, after all, and I accepted. It would have been rude not to turn up.'

'Oh, I see.' Polite and well-mannered as ever then. 'Well, I hope you have a good time.'

I half-turned, not entirely sure what else I could say, but he caught my hand.

'Shona, don't go, please. I have something I want to say to you.'

I closed my eyes briefly, knowing I had something to say to him, too, and really it would be better if I just got it over with. He might not appreciate the fact that a ghost had been spying on him, and who could blame him for that? But at least he'd know the truth about his grandfather, and that would mean the world to him. I turned round. 'I have something—'

He shook his head. 'Please. Me first.'

I was surprised. I'd have thought he'd have insisted on allowing me to speak first, so he must have something very important to say.

'I want to apologise for the way I spoke to you that day,' he said. 'I was unforgivably rude. I was so surprised by what you told me that I didn't know how to react. It's not every day someone tells you they speak to ghosts, is it?'

'No,' I said. 'It isn't. And I really do appreciate how hard it was for you to take it all in. We're so used to it around here that we don't give it a second thought, but for someone like you, it must seem crazy.'

'It does,' he admitted. 'And I still don't fully believe it, although Rissa tells me she thinks there might be something in it. She's been here longer than I have. She's heard things. Anyway, that's not really the point. The thing is, whether ghosts are real or not, what I've come to accept is that my feelings for you *are* real.'

'Max,' I said, 'I think—'

'Please let me say this,' he begged. 'My nerve might fail if I don't.'

I nodded. 'Okay. Go ahead.'

He took hold of my hands. 'I will always love Nina. You know that. But I know there is room for you in my heart, too. It was Rissa who made me realise that. She made me see that it's okay to move on, and that I shouldn't feel guilty about it. Nina would want me to be happy, and I think you can make me happy. And, after everything you went through with your ex-husband, I want to make you happy, too. I never want to cause you pain the way he did. Will you give us the chance to make each other happy, Shona?'

There was a pleading look in his eyes that made me crumble.

I threw my arms around his neck and kissed him, because frankly, that's all I'd wanted to do since the moment I'd seen him standing by the door, looking all nervous and irresistibly handsome.

He laughed. 'Can I take that as a yes?'

'You certainly can,' I told him, and kissed him again, just to make sure he knew that I meant it.

'Shona, you have made me so happy,' he told me, his eyes shining as he held me to him.

'Oh, Herr Meyer,' I said softly. 'I haven't even got started yet!'

33

POLLY

Polly was thrilled to see Shona and Max stepping through the French doors onto the terrace at the side of the Hall. She'd watched in delight as the two of them had kissed and made up, and realised Shona was about to tell him the truth about his grandfather. For that, they needed privacy.

Even so, she didn't think Shona would mind if she was hanging around nearby. After all, her niece might need some support if Max still struggled to accept the reality of ghosts.

She moved forward but was surprised to hear a voice say, 'Oh no you don't, Aunt Polly!'

Pippa moved to her side and shook her head, a look of amusement in her eyes.

'I don't know what you mean,' Polly said in-dignantly.

'I think you do. You were going to follow Mum and Max and do a bit of eavesdropping, weren't you?'

'I was not! I was simply going to offer your mother my support if Max proved difficult.'

Pippa laughed. 'It's me you're talking to! We're too much alike, Aunt Polly. Incurably nosy. Why do you think I became a reporter?'

Polly hesitated, then she started to laugh. 'All right, you have a point. I'll leave them to it. It's looking very promising though, isn't it?'

Pippa nodded. 'It really is. Fingers crossed, eh?'

Polly held up her hand, showing her fingers tightly entwined. But in the next moment, her hand dropped, and she murmured, 'I don't believe it!'

She heard Pippa ask, 'What is it, Aunt Pol?' but didn't reply.

She looked around, wondering if the other ghosts had noticed anything and saw some of them certainly had, as there was a great deal of staring and muttering going on.

Then Callie and Lawrie moved closer to the door, stunned expressions on their faces, and the other ghosts, including Polly, followed them.

Quintus Severus!

The big, burly, Roman centurion was standing on the threshold of the room, as serious and official-looking as always.

'Quintus, my dear fellow,' Lawrie cried. 'How marvellous to see you here!'

'I'm so pleased to meet you,' Callie said, a wide smile on her face. 'I'm Callie Chase. I'm the new owner of the Harling Estate.'

Quintus gave her a stiff bow. 'An honour to meet you,' he told her.

Polly couldn't take her eyes off him. It had been a long, long time since she'd been this close to him, and she hadn't been in any fit state to really take in any details. He was a big, burly man of North African origin, and there was something incredibly magnetic about him. She wanted to hug him. To thank him for all he'd done that night. But she was too nervous, and besides, there were all these people around.

Callie evidently shared her admiration, though. 'You look magnificent,' she told him. 'You really do. So, they let you keep the uniform? The armour, I mean. Whatever you call it.'

Quintus looked puzzled. 'Let me keep it? I don't understand your meaning.'

'The bosses. You know, whoever was in charge of

you when you were in the Roman army. They let you keep all that gear when you retired?'

Quintus gazed down at his white tunic, brown sandals, and heavy body armour. He carried a shield and a spear and had a sword strapped to his side. His helmet covered the sides of his face as well as the top of his head, and he had a brown scarf wrapped around his neck and tucked under his breastplate. Impressive wasn't an adequate word for him really.

'I had not yet retired,' he said briefly.

Callie glanced at Lawrie, who shrugged.

'But Lawrie said—'

'No.'

'Okay. But you lived in Gloucester, right? Glevum, I mean.'

Quintus blinked. 'No.'

Lawrie cleared his throat. 'Well, maybe I got a little mixed up. It was an awfully long time ago that he and I talked.'

'Evidently,' Callie said. 'Well, it's lovely to meet you at last. I can't believe you've come to the tea dance. Please, come in and make yourself comfortable.'

The Roman shook his head. To Polly's horror, he pointed directly at her.

'I've come to fetch *her*.'

Everyone turned to look at her.

'Polly?' Lawrie asked. 'What do you want with her, old chap?'

Quintus didn't reply. 'You must come with me,' he told Polly firmly.

Polly didn't like the sound of that. She stepped back, feeling a growing fear. Quintus Severus might have helped Sir Edward back in the day, but he was a soldier when all was said and done, and everyone knew how brutal the Romans could be. What the heck could he want with her? It didn't make sense.

'I'd rather not, if it's all the same to you,' she said.

'Harmony said so,' he told her.

Polly felt a little easier at that, although she was still wary. 'Harmony sent you to fetch me?'

'Will you come?' he asked.

She still wasn't sure. Callie gave her a sympathetic smile and turned to Quintus.

'Would it be okay if I went with Polly? I think she's a bit nervous, you see, and a familiar face might make her feel a bit easier.'

Quintus frowned. 'Why are you nervous? I have been polite, have I not?'

'Well, yes...' Polly said.

He gave her a brief nod. 'Good.' He turned to Callie. 'Very well. You may come with us as you are the owner of the Harling Estate. All others remain here.'

It wasn't a request, and looking at the faces of the other ghosts, Polly didn't think any of them were likely to test him on it. Even Brooke, who was clearly enchanted with the handsome soldier, was looking a bit scared. She'd half-hidden behind Danny, which was almost laughable, given how petrified he looked.

'Let Brodie know, will you?' Callie murmured to Lawrie.

He nodded. 'Don't worry, Callie. He's a good chap. He won't hurt you.'

'Says the man who seems to have got every fact about Quintus Severus wrong so far,' Polly muttered.

They left Harling Hall and began to walk in the direction of the church. A couple of people waved at Callie, completely unaware that she was with two ghosts.

'Lovely weekend,' they called. 'I hope you're going to do it again next year.'

Callie smiled and waved back, but Polly could tell she was distracted, and no wonder. It was hard to keep up with Quintus, as he had long strides and covered the ground far faster than they did.

'Where are we going?' Polly whispered to Callie as they passed the church, crossed the road, headed along the riverbank opposite the green, crossed a stone bridge and headed up the lane before turning off towards the woods.

Polly shrank back. 'We're not – are we?'

'Going into the woods? Looks like it.' Callie eyed her curiously. 'I'm sorry, Polly. Are you afraid of them?'

Polly nodded. 'It's where I – where it happened.'

'Where what happened?' she asked, puzzled. 'Oh! Do you mean you died there?'

'I – I was murdered there,' Polly told her.

'Murdered!' Callie's hand flew to her mouth. 'I had no idea! I'm so sorry. Did they ever catch the person who killed you?'

'No. It's a long story, and not as simple as you'd think. I can tell you about it, if you like. I've kept this to myself for so long, but now I realise that talking about it helps me to manage it all. Silence made it so much worse.' As they walked, Polly briefly filled Callie in on what had happened, and by the time she'd finished explaining, she realised they were already in the woods and Quintus Severus was still marching onwards, not even bothering to check they were behind him. Evidently, he was used to his orders being obeyed, and it hadn't occurred to him that they wouldn't be.

'That's such a terrible story,' Callie said sadly. 'I'm

so sorry for you all. I think you're amazing, the way you've forgiven Ray like that. Poor man. He needed help, and it seems it was sadly lacking after the war. And fancy Rissa being descended from Gerhard! How did you feel about that?'

'About Rissa?'

'About Gerhard having married someone else and had a family. It must have hurt.'

Polly allowed herself a smile. 'Do you know, that was the one thing that *didn't* hurt. I was so happy for him. He was such a beautiful man, inside and out. He deserved a wife and family. I'm so glad he made a new life for himself when he finally got home.'

'You're right,' Callie said. 'It's lovely that he...' She frowned suddenly. 'Are we nearing the Wyrd Stones?'

Polly glanced around and shivered. 'We are. That's the Penitent King over there. Oh, it's getting dark, too. I really don't like it out here at the best of times, but at this time of night...'

It had been decades since she'd last seen the Wyrd Stones or the neolithic barrow. The King's Court was a circle of fourteen stones, with three more stones huddled together in the centre of the circle. The Penitent King was a single, large stone that stood all by itself in a field. The Wyrd Stones and the barrow formed an

almost perfect triangle in the landscape and were surrounded by rowan trees.

'It's been fenced off,' Polly said in surprise, noting
the iron fence that surrounded the Penitent King.

'Sir Edward did that,' Callie explained. 'Over the
years, bits of the stone had been chipped away by vandals, leaving it a bit scarred and misshapen, so he decided it needed protecting.'

'Wait here,' Quintus said suddenly. He marched
into the woods on the other side of the monument,
leaving Polly and Callie standing alone. Callie
shivered.

'Is it cold?' Polly asked.

'It's chilly,' Callie replied, 'but I'm shivering because it's a bit creepy really.'

'You can say that again. What are we even doing
here?'

'I've no idea.' Callie gave her a cheerful grin. 'Still,
it's an adventure, right?'

'Thanks for coming with me,' Polly said gratefully.
'You didn't have to do that. It's lovely of you.'

'No worries. It's nice to get to know you a bit better. I'd like to get to know all you ghosts better, but
some of you are proving pretty elusive.'

Without thinking, she grabbed for Polly's arm.
Polly couldn't feel it, but she saw the amazement on

Callie's face and turned to see what she was looking at. A young, attractive, blonde film star walking beside a huge Roman centurion. Not something you saw every day, even in Rowan Vale.

'Is that – is that Harmony Hill?' Callie gasped.

Polly nodded. 'It is. I *knew* she was a friend of Quintus,' she hissed. 'Why did she deny it?'

'Hey, Polly,' Harmony said. She glanced at Callie. 'And you are?'

Callie looked beside herself with joy. 'I'm Callie Chase, the new owner of the Harling Estate.'

Harmony arched one of her beautifully shaped eyebrows. 'You are, huh? Well, it's good to meet you at last.' She turned to Polly. 'Look, honey, I'm sorry for all this cloak and dagger stuff, but I didn't know how else to get you here. No one argues with Quintus, right?'

'You said you didn't know him. Why did you lie?' Polly asked, rather hurt.

'I didn't *lie*,' Harmony insisted. 'I was *acting*. There's a difference.'

'Not from where I'm standing,' Polly said bluntly. 'And why have you brought us here anyway? It's not exactly the cosiest place to meet. You could have invited me to Appleseed Cottage if you wanted a chat.'

'Appleseed Cottage?' Callie squealed. 'Is that where you're living?'

'Gee, thanks for that, Polly,' Harmony said sarcastically.

'I wouldn't get too excited,' Polly told Callie. 'She's never in anyway.'

Quintus was standing a few feet away, between them and the trees. He was watching them intently and Polly wondered what he thought of all this, and why he'd been so willing to act as Harmony's messenger boy, given that he never went near the village normally.

'Did you do it?' Harmony asked her suddenly. 'Did you tell your family?'

Polly nodded. 'I did.'

'That's swell, honey. I knew you could do it! How did they take it?'

Despite her annoyance, Polly couldn't help but smile at Harmony's sweet face. She looked so hopeful, and Polly was glad to be able to give her good news.

'They were great. Really understanding. They didn't judge me or Ray, which is better than I could ever have hoped for.'

'So, he's not the bad guy then, huh?'

Polly shook her head. 'Far from it. We all know he was ill. It wasn't his fault. He didn't know what he was doing.'

Harmony patted her on the shoulder then turned round.

'You hear that?' she called. 'Told you. Come on, come and say hello.'

'Now who's she talking to?' Polly asked, completely flummoxed by the events of the evening. She stepped back suddenly as a shadowy figure emerged from the trees. A man stepped slowly forward, his gait unsteady and hesitant.

Quintus nodded at him as he passed him, and Harmony reached for Polly's hand.

'It's okay. He's more scared than you are. It's gonna be all right, Polly.'

But Polly couldn't speak as she stared in dumbfounded silence into the face of her brother, Ray.

34

POLLY

If Polly had still had a functioning body, she was convinced she would have fainted clear away. As it was, she couldn't move. She stared at her brother, hardly able to believe he was really there.

'I know this is a shock to you,' Harmony said quietly, 'but it's not easy for Ray either. Remember that.'

'Ray?' Callie gasped. 'This is your brother? The one who...'

'Ray,' Polly murmured. 'Is it really you?'

'Pol.'

That was Ray's voice, but the voice she remembered from before the war. Before the pain. When Ray had been her beloved little brother, and he'd laughed and worked and joked and hugged. Not scarred any more. Not broken. Whole.

'Ray!'

In that moment, Polly forgot all about the terrible events that had overtaken them both. She only knew that the brother she had loved and missed so much was standing there before her, and without a second thought, she threw her arms around him and hugged him tightly.

He squeezed her tentatively then she stepped back, gripping his shoulders and examining him, drinking in all those much-missed features that she'd once known as well as her own. He looked tired and nervous, but he was her little brother again, not that angry man. She could see it in his dark eyes. Her beautiful brother!

'I've missed you so much,' she told him, pulling him close again.

'How can you say that?' he mumbled into her hair. 'After everything I did?'

'It wasn't your fault, darling. I knew that. I always knew that. You were ill! Oh, Ray, have you been here all this time? Why didn't you come and find me? Why did you hide away?'

'I think we should leave them to it,' Callie said

tactfully. 'Would you two like to come and look at the King's Court with me?'

'Sure,' Harmony said. She turned to Quintus. 'Coming?'

'I'll wait here,' he told her firmly. 'I'm on guard duty, remember?'

'You don't have to guard my brother,' Polly told him. 'I'm not going to hurt him. I'm just so pleased to see him.'

'I'm here to ensure you feel safe,' Quintus informed her. 'You are a woman alone with a man who treated you brutally. I will wait with you.'

'But there's no need,' Polly protested. 'Ray wouldn't—'

'It's all right, Pol,' Ray said gently. 'He doesn't mean anything by it. It's just his way. He's a good man.'

'You know him?' Polly was confused. 'Where have you been, Ray? All this time!'

As Callie and Harmony wandered away, Quintus took up position a little further back nearer the trees, and Polly and Ray linked arms and walked closer to the Penitent King.

'Pol, first thing's first. I've got to say how sorry I am. I can't believe what I did. I don't know why it happened, I swear I don't. It's all a fog, but I do remember stepping out of my body and seeing what I'd done and realising *what* had happened, even though I couldn't tell you why.'

'Because you weren't yourself,' she told him. 'You were ill. After everything you'd been through, your mind was damaged. You couldn't help it.'

'I would never have hurt you if I'd been myself. You do know that?'

'Of course I do! And I don't think you'd have hurt Gerhard either, would you? Leastways, the Ray I knew before the war wouldn't have waved a shotgun at some defenceless man.'

'I *never* would have,' Ray said fervently. 'I don't even remember most of it. I can't remember most of the war, to be honest, though I suppose that's a blessing. And then, after I left my body behind, it was like the fog just cleared, and I could see it all, and I was so ashamed. So bitterly ashamed. I can still see you lying there on the ground, all cold and bloody. And yet, you were also sitting there next to that German fella, and he was sobbing his heart out, and you were trying to comfort him. He couldn't hear you. You couldn't let him know you were there. It broke my heart.'

'I didn't see you,' Polly told him. 'I didn't know you were like me. I thought you'd passed over, Ray. If I'd known, I'd have gone looking for you so I could tell you it was okay.'

He shook his head. 'I didn't want you to know. I didn't want any of you to know. I couldn't face you, or Norman, or Mum and Dad. It was too much. I didn't know what to do. I just stumbled into the woods and sat on the ground, crying and shaking.' He nodded towards Quintus Severus. 'And then he came and rescued me.'

'Quintus did?' Polly asked incredulously.

'Yeah. He took me to that place everyone was scared of when we were kids. You remember, Pol? The big old house in the woods.'

'Not The Monastery?' Polly shuddered. 'Please tell me you've not been living there!'

'I have, but it's not like you think. I wasn't on my own. There are others there. People who want to stay away from the village for reasons of their own. They let me find my own way. They didn't ask questions or push me for answers. They just left me to deal with the shock in my own time. If I wanted to talk, they'd listen. If I wanted to be alone, they left me in peace.'

'Does Quintus live there, too?' she asked.

'No.' Ray cast a look at the Roman and gave her a slight smile. 'He's a one off, that fella. I have no idea where he sleeps, but I'll bet it's not very comfortable.'

'And Harmony? You know her?'

His eyes brightened. 'She's amazing! Fancy me knowing a famous film star, eh? She comes to The Monastery every day. She calls it "entertaining the troops".' He grinned. 'Sings, dances, puts on little plays for those of us who want to get involved. She says it's therapy. I mean, I'm not one for all that palaver, and at first, I stayed well away, but after a bit, I started to join in. It's something to do, isn't it? And it turned out to be fun. She's done a lot of us a power of good, Pol, she really has.'

Polly couldn't believe it. 'We knew she went somewhere during the day, but we had no idea what she was up to. Fancy that! She hardly ever comes into the village to mix with us, you know.'

'No, well.' Ray sighed. 'We've all got our secrets and our burdens, haven't we, Pol?'

'I suppose so.' Polly's smile returned and she cupped his face in her hands. 'Oh, Ray! It's so bloody good to see you. I never thought I'd feel this happy again, but I've got my little brother back! Wait till you meet our Norman's lad, Jimmy. And there's Shona – she's Jimmy's daughter. And she's got two daughters of her own and—'

He shook his head. 'They might not want to know me, Pol, and it's okay. I get it. It's enough that you've forgiven me. More than I ever dreamed or hoped for. I can't tell you what it means to me. But when they find out—'

'Ray, you daft ha'porth,' she told him, dropping a kiss on his forehead. 'They already know. And it's okay. They understand, too. You're family. They'll be over the moon if they can see you, especially our Jimmy. He's grown up hearing all about his wonderful Uncle Ray from his dad. Oh, I hope they *can* see you!'

Ray blinked. 'Our Norman told him that? Even after everything...'

'What don't you get, lovely?' Polly said, her eyes blurry with tears. 'We all love you. You're back with your family now. You can come home.'

Ray gave a muffled sob and threw his arms around his sister, who hugged him so tightly in return that even if he'd been able to breathe, she'd have stopped him anyway.

It had been a long, lonely road for Polly and Ray. But now they'd found their way back to each other. It was all going to be okay.

* * *

'Why here?' Callie asked. 'Why did we have to meet at the Wyrd Stones, of all places?'

She and Harmony had joined Ray and Polly by

The Penitent King and now that the two of them were obviously reconciled, Callie had questions.

Polly didn't really care. She had her arm through Ray's and had made up her mind that she was never going to let him go again. She kept looking up at him, hardly able to believe he was there. Oh, Jimmy was going to be ecstatic!

But Ray was looking at Quintus, and Quintus was looking back at him, and his eyes held an enquiry.

'You can tell them,' Ray said at last. 'They have a right to know.'

Quintus nodded. 'This is where he lies,' he said bluntly. 'This is where Sir Edward and the man, Carstairs, put him.'

'Where who lies?' Polly's eyes widened suddenly as understanding dawned. 'Our Ray?' She gazed up at her brother in horror. 'They put you under there?'

All eyes turned to The Penitent King and the ground around it.

'Does Lawrie know about this?' Callie asked.

'No. No one knows. Only Sir Edward and Carstairs.'

'Who's Carstairs?' Harmony asked.

'He was Sir Edward's estate manager,' Polly remembered. 'He was in on it, too then.'

'So many people putting themselves at risk to save

our family, Pol,' Ray said shakily. 'Covering up what I did so Mum and Dad wouldn't suffer. So people wouldn't know I was a murderer.'

'It wasn't murder,' Polly said gently. 'Not really. You weren't of sound mind. And besides, I think they were also trying to keep it quiet that I was about to marry a German. Can you imagine if that had got out?'

'It would have given Ray a motive,' Quintus said simply. 'Everyone knew he refused to work with the Germans, and if they had discovered you were going to marry one, they would have begun to ask if that was why you'd been killed. They might have looked more closely at Ray's alibi. Sir Edward explained it all to me. He put it all together like a puzzle.'

'And he buried me here, in the shade of the stone,' Ray said, staring down at the ground.

It must have been a strange feeling. Polly always felt weird when she passed the churchyard, knowing her body was lying there. But at least it was a proper grave with a headstone and everything. This...

'At first, they put him in the tomb,' Quintus said. His tone was expressionless. He was simply relaying facts and seemed to have no opinion on the subject either way. 'The ground was too hard. It would have been obvious that someone had been digging. No one was looking for a body, but even so. Sir Edward decided the tomb was the safest place.'

'You mean the barrow?' Callie asked. She shivered. 'And how long was he there?'

Quintus shrugged. 'Until the rains came. When the ground was soft and churned up, they brought him here. They put the fence around the stone and said it was to protect it from thieves and vandals. Then Sir Edward told me to guard the stone and make sure no one got too close. I was to tell him at once if there was any danger of discovery.'

Callie's expression softened. 'Oh, Quintus! That's why you're always patrolling the boundaries and watching the stones. You were put on guard by Sir Edward.'

'But Sir Edward's dead,' Polly said, feeling nothing but compassion for this noble Roman soldier. 'He died years ago.'

'No one relieved me of my duty,' Quintus said simply. 'Until I am given new orders, I will continue to guard the stones.'

Callie's eyes filled with tears. 'But there's no need! Not now! Quintus, I'm the owner of the estate, and I hereby relieve you of your duty.'

Quintus looked staggered. 'But – but what shall I do?'

'Maybe get yourself a decent afterlife,' Harmony suggested. 'You've certainly earned it after all this time.'

'What do we do about Ray's body?' Polly asked. 'We can't leave it here. He should be in a churchyard. This isn't decent.'

'But if we exhume the body, there's a risk people will find out,' Callie pointed out. 'And then Lawrie and Brodie will be questioned as to how much they knew from Sir Edward, and the whole sorry case will be dragged up again. None of us wants that, do we?'

They all agreed they didn't.

'Besides,' Callie added, 'if we bring the body to the churchyard, Amelia will have to know, and that wouldn't be fair on her. It would put her in an awful position. We couldn't ask her to allow a secret burial. Morally, it would be indefensible.'

'But we can't just leave him in unconsecrated ground,' Polly said tearfully.

'To be fair, Pol, I don't think it's made any difference, do you?' Ray asked reasonably.

'I don't care! You deserve better than that!' she said fiercely.

Callie nodded. 'Okay, I have an idea. Just leave it with me, okay? In the meantime, I need to get back to

Harling Hall to thank everyone for coming to the tea dance. You're all very welcome to join me.'

'Not me, honey, but thanks,' Harmony said. 'I'm going home. Too much excitement for one day.'

'Me and Ray are going back to the flat,' Polly told them all. 'I know all the family will want to know what's going on and they'll want to meet him, naturally, but for tonight, we just want to be together, to catch up and talk. Right, Ray?'

'Are you sure you're all right with me being in the flat with you alone?' he asked, sounding troubled. 'You're not – you're not scared of me?'

'Don't be daft,' Polly said. She squeezed his arm. 'You're yourself again now. We both know that. Anyway, there's a spare bedroom in the flat if you want it. It's up to you. No pressure but the offer's there. It would be good to have company of an evening again.'

He looked down at the ground. 'Give me a bit of time, eh, Pol? This is all overwhelming. I need to meet the rest of the family first. See how the land lies. I know you said they were okay, but I want to see it for myself. And then... Well, maybe then I'll move into the flat. Is that all right?'

'Whatever you want, lovey. Whatever you want.'

They began to move off, but Callie stopped suddenly and called, 'You go on ahead. I want a word with Quintus.'

'Gee, I hope she persuades him to give up this patrolling the boundaries business,' Harmony said as they made their way back through the woods. 'Poor guy. Can you believe he's been on guard duty all this time?'

'He's one in a million,' Ray said. 'I dread to think what would have happened to me if he hadn't been there to pick me up. Literally. I couldn't even walk, I was that shocked. He actually slung me over his shoulder and carried me to The Monastery. Can you believe that?'

Harmony laughed. 'Nothing would surprise me about him.'

'Bless him,' Polly said. 'Our family owes him a lot. I hope one day, we can repay him.'

35

POLLY

It was a surprisingly cheerful group of people that stood around The Penitent King one evening in late September.

Present and correct were Ray, Polly, Jimmy, Shona, Max, Pippa, Christie, Scott, Lawrie, Brodie, Callie, Harmony, Betty, Nick and Quintus Severus.

Also present – to most people's amazement – was the Reverend Silas Alexander, who had agreed to bless the grave.

Although it must have been very strange to those who couldn't see most of the ghosts, or indeed any of them, nevertheless, everyone was glad to be there, and honoured to have been invited.

'I still can't believe what happened,' Betty admitted as they finally left The Penitent King behind and began to walk back to the village. She gave Max an apologetic look. 'I'm sorry I was so horrible to you. And I'm sorry I doubted your grandfather's innocence.'

'I'm sorry that I believed your grandfather had hurt mine,' Max told her. 'I still struggle to accept that he carried such a huge secret within him until the very end. To witness what he did, to lose the woman he'd loved in such a fashion, and to say nothing. If only I'd known.'

'He gave his word,' Shona said. 'He knew Polly wouldn't have wanted her parents to suffer, and he promised Sir Edward he'd never tell a living soul. And he didn't. He must have been a remarkable man.'

'I think his grandson is pretty remarkable, too,' Ray told her. 'Knowing that I tried to kill Gerhard, he still came here today for this blessing. That's very forgiving of him. I'm glad you've found him, Shona. He's a good man.'

Shona smiled. 'Thanks, Uncle Ray. I'll pass that on.'

Polly had one of those moments where, just then, everything in the world seemed perfect. Shona and Max were back on track, Max having learned the truth about his grandfather, and finally accepting that Rowan Vale really did have its own special secret.

As she'd expected, Jimmy and Shona had been thrilled to finally meet their Uncle Ray after all these years, as had Pippa. Christie was frustrated as always that she couldn't see him, but Maddie certainly could, and Ray was clearly smitten with her from the moment the toddler gave him a beaming smile, showing off her brand-new bottom teeth.

Ray had moved into the flat above the teashop, and to Polly, it felt like the old days. She was in her element, fussing over him and making sure he was comfortable, and Shona, bless her, had been as good as gold, finding them films and programmes that Ray would enjoy and popping upstairs between breaks to change channels on the TV for them and check they had everything they needed.

The ghost community had finally learned the truth about Polly's relationship with Gerhard, and what it had led to, and those with living relatives who could see and hear them had been sworn to secrecy by Callie and Lawrie. Since they'd had Quintus Severus standing behind them, Callie said she was certain no one would dare break that promise. As it turned out, the ghosts were a forgiving bunch and made Ray very welcome in the community.

Quintus, meanwhile, had a new job. Callie told him that things had changed a lot in Rowan Vale since his day, what with all the tourists coming and going.

'I'd really appreciate it if you'd become a sort of policeman for the village,' she told him. 'You know, patrol the streets, keep the peace between the ghosts, let me know if they have any problems or issues, make sure there's no bad behaviour among the day trippers and holidaymakers, that sort of thing.'

She'd given Polly a sly wink as he considered her proposal. Polly had begged her to help the Roman soldier, after everything he'd done for her family, and Callie had agreed he deserved some sort of reward. He was a very loyal and obedient soldier who'd been given his orders and had carried them out in full. They both wanted him to have a better afterlife than the one he'd been leading.

To their relief, Quintus seemed honoured to be given his new role and had sworn to uphold the law and keep the peace in Rowan Vale to the best of his ability.

He'd also agreed to move into Appleseed Cottage after Callie had told him she was worried about Harmony.

'I don't like her being all alone, Quintus. She's too reclusive. And she's far too young to hide herself away from the world. If she doesn't want to mix with the rest of us, I think she'd benefit from having you to talk to. Would you consider moving into her home to keep an eye on her?'

To Harmony, she'd said, 'I'm worried about Quintus. He's not used to mixing with people, and although he's happy to do the job I've given him, I don't think he'll talk to anybody. He's been alone far too long, Harmony. Would you consider letting him live at Appleseed Cottage, just so you can keep an eye on him?'

Quintus had said he would be happy to do his duty by Harmony, and Harmony had rolled her eyes and said, 'I guess. I mean, at least he don't jabber on all the time, and I can't deny he's eye candy.'

So that was that sorted, and Polly had to concede that Callie was a genius. It amazed her that she'd managed to persuade Silas Alexander, of all people, to give a blessing at Ray's grave, but Callie said he'd been surprisingly willing to do so.

'It turns out he remembers a lot of soldiers with shellshock coming back from the Great War,' she said. 'He understood the situation at once. No judgement. And between you and me, I think he was quite chuffed that I'd asked *him* to do the service and not

Amelia. Made him feel useful again. Maybe his bark's worse than his bite.'

Polly wasn't so sure about that, but she was grateful to Silas for performing the ceremony. Whoever would have guessed she would have cause to thank that old buzzard? Wonders would never cease.

'Shona, look!'

She heard Max's voice behind her, low and urgent, and turned to see what he was looking at.

The entire group slowed and stared at the space between trees where a fox stood, watching them.

'Old Reynard,' Shona murmured, and Polly squeezed Ray's hand, remembering how much he'd always loved foxes.

'Isn't he beautiful?' Max whispered. 'I've never seen one so close before.'

A killer, thought Polly. But a misunderstood killer. Not vermin at all. Not a creature who deserved to be hunted or hated. She knew she'd never be wary of foxes again.

'Look!' Shona gasped and Polly saw another fox come to stand by the first one's side. They greeted each other with open mouths and flattened ears, then the second one shook its head and ran into the woods. Old Reynard gave them all one last look, then followed his mate into the trees.

He'd never been alone after all.

36

'I've got a strange feeling of déjà vu.' I rolled my eyes and offered Max a sweet. 'Brace yourself, because last time Callie called an impromptu meeting here, we were plunged into transforming Rowan Vale into a 1940s village.'

'Well,' he said, winking at me, 'that turned out quite well, didn't it?'

'Hmm,' I agreed. 'I can't deny that it did.'

He leaned over and kissed me, and I cradled his face as I kissed him back, excitement fizzing through me as I wondered how I'd ever got so lucky as to find this amazing man.

We were still officially taking it slowly. There was no staying over at his place or anything like that. I wasn't sure he was ready for that, and I wasn't entirely sure I was either. But when he kissed me like that, I realised that whenever it happened, the prospect of it wasn't nearly so scary as it had once seemed.

Rissa had left for Germany, and I knew he missed her, but was happy that she'd broken away from Brodie and was trying to move on with her life.

It was, after all, what everyone had to do at some point. Bad things happened. Life was like a huge wave that swept you off your feet, and just when you thought you were managing the current, the tide would change direction and carry you further from the shore. The trick was never to try to swim against the tide. Let the wave carry you along and you might well end up on a far nicer beach than the one you'd originally headed for.

Like Max. I'd have clung to Luke forever if I'd had my way, but the wave had knocked me off my feet, dragging me away from him and the future I'd visualised for myself. But it had carried me to Max, and I wouldn't have it any other way.

'Ugh, put him down, you don't know where he's been!'

Amelia plonked herself down in the seat next to me and held out her hand to Max.

'Amelia Davies. Vicar of All Souls Church.'

'The vicar?' Max looked stunned as he shook her hand, and Amelia frowned.

'Yes. Got something against female vicars?'

'I think he's just astounded that a vicar would say something like, "Ugh, put him down, you don't know where he's been",' I pointed out.

'Ah!' She dipped her hand into my bag of sweets and unwrapped a fruit sherbet. 'Fair point. So here we are again then. Another of Callie's meetings.'

Callie had announced the meeting just yesterday. Emails had gone to those who were registered for the village newsletter, and paper versions had been hastily pushed through the doors of those who weren't. Meanwhile, Aunt Polly had laughingly told me that Quintus Severus had gone round Rowan Vale to tell every ghost that their attendance was required at The Magic Lantern Cinema, and no excuses would be accepted for any absences. He was certainly taking his new responsibilities seriously.

I looked around, pleased to see Aunt Polly and Uncle Ray sitting a few rows behind us. They'd come to say hello to us as they arrived, before joining Isaac, Peter the baker, and Percy Swain, who'd apparently reserved them some seats. It warmed my heart to see Uncle Ray accepted into the community, and Aunt Polly looking happier than I'd ever seen her.

'What do you think this is about then?' Amelia pondered aloud. 'Are we taking bets?'

'Maybe Callie just wants to tell us how much money the 1940s event raised,' I suggested.

'Or maybe she wants to thank you all for your hard work,' Max said.

'Do either of you really believe that?' Amelia asked.

We looked at each other and grinned. 'No!'

'Thought not. Ah well, we're about to find out,' Amelia said, as Callie and Brodie took to the stage.

Callie gave us all nervous smiles. 'Thanks so much for coming,' she said. 'I really appreciate it. I want to thank you for all your hard work at the 1940s weekend. Brodie has been working out the accounts, and we'll be letting you know the official amount raised in the next few days.'

'It was a lot of fun,' Ingrid called. 'We had a right laugh in the salon. We should do it again next year.'

'Oh,' Callie said, sounding delighted, 'we will! On an even bigger and better scale, hopefully. In the meantime...' She glanced at Brodie, who smiled and nodded encouragingly. 'Listen up, guys. I've had a great idea.'

'Uh-oh,' I said. 'Here we go again.'

Callie beamed at us all. 'I know this is short notice,

but how do you feel about something truly special for Christmas? I'm thinking Victoriana. I'm thinking Dickens. I'm thinking ghosts.'

'What did I tell you?' Amelia said.

I glanced at Max. Christmas was still nearly three months away and we hadn't made any plans. Would he be in Germany by then? Perhaps he'd like to spend the holidays with Gisela and Louis, and with Rissa of course. It was only natural. We weren't living together after all, or anything close. It was early days. I couldn't expect...

'Victoriana. Dickens. Ghosts.' He sounded thoughtful. 'I wonder... How would you feel if I made some German Christmas biscuits for the teashop? *Lebkuchen*, of course, because what is Christmas without gingerbread? Perhaps some *pfefferneusse*? I will make a marzipan stollen, too. We always have one over Christmas.'

'I thought you'd be in Germany,' I said hesitantly.

'I shall visit my family in the new year,' he told me. 'Perhaps – perhaps you might even like to come with me? I'd like you to see my country. Only if you want to, of course,' he added hastily. 'And you don't have to decide now.'

He wanted me to visit Germany with him? He wanted me to meet his family?

'So, you'll be here for Christmas?' I had to double-check, just to make sure it was really true.

He took my hand and raised it to his lips, his eyes shining with happiness.

'Christmas in Rowan Vale with you, *liebling*? I wouldn't miss it for the world.'

* * *

MORE FROM SHARON BOOTH

Another book from Sharon Booth, *Kindred Spirits at Harling Hall*, is available to order now here:
https://mybook.to/KindredSpiritsBackAd

ACKNOWLEDGEMENTS

Thank you so much for reading *Loving Spirits at the Vintage Teashop*. I really hope you enjoyed visiting Rowan Vale, whether you're new to my books or you've followed me from the start. I appreciate your support so much, because it allows me to do the job I love – creating fictional worlds and characters. Now, more than ever, authors need the support of their readers, so we can continue to bring you stories that reflect our shared humanity.

I loved writing this book and delving into the history of German prisoners of war. My own grandad – who this book is dedicated to – was a prisoner of war for four long years, and I often wonder what that experience was like for him. Sadly, he died when I was seven, and I never really got to know him. The first time he met my mum – his eldest daughter – she was four or five years old and had no idea who he was. She never knew the man he'd been before the war, and I always think how terribly sad that is.

He was a man of few words, and I don't remember ever getting any affection from him, but I wish I'd had the chance to know him when I was an adult. Even if he'd refused to tell me about his experiences in the prisoner of war camp, maybe I'd have understood him a little better, in light of what he must have gone through.

I used the story of when he first met my mum in *Kindred Spirits at Harling Hall*, but I thought it would be interesting to tell the story of a German prisoner of war in this book, and for that, I had to research what life was like for them in British camps in the 1940s. It was certainly an eye-opener. I'd had no idea that the prisoners were kept in this country after the war had ended so they could help rebuild Britain.

It was also surprising, and rather moving, to learn how many German men and British women fell in love. Their relationships certainly weren't easy, but it was heartwarming to read about marriages that lasted decades, and how, despite the difficulties they'd faced, most of the couples had no regrets.

I was glad to see that, eventually, their relationships were accepted, and the German men became welcome members of British families and communities. I wondered how easy it was for returning British soldiers to accept them, though, and how old enemies had felt as they tried to move forward together in a new post-war world.

I wondered about men like Ray, who'd lost so much during the war and had returned home broken. And I thought about the lack of treatment and help there'd been back then, when so little was understood about the condition we now call PTSD.

Left to struggle on alone, what might happen to an affected returning soldier, faced with the knowledge that a man who belonged to the ranks of those he'd been trained to kill and hate was now working in his old job, living in his village, and had fallen in love with his own sister? It was a story I couldn't resist, and I really hope I told it respectfully.

But I also wanted this story to be about love, community, and laughter. The 1940s weekend was inspired when I was on holiday in Somerset last year and unexpectedly stumbled across a similar event in a nearby village. It was such fun, and my husband and I spent a very happy afternoon gazing at propaganda posters in shop windows, admiring the fleet of vintage vehicles, and listening to a choir singing a brilliant repertoire of wartime songs! I thought it would be the perfect event for Rowan Vale, and I had a lovely time listening to the likes of Vera Lynn, Glenn Miller and the Andrews Sisters as I planned my own version!

And now for the thank yous. I must thank Team Boldwood, first and foremost, because without them, none of this would be possible. I'm still pinching myself that I'm published by this incredible team, and I'm so grateful to be working with such amazingly talented people. Special thanks to my lovely editor, Francesca Best, for her hard work and cheery emails (and the lovely cake at Betty's!). Thanks also to Debra Newhouse, who did such a grand job of the copyedits, Emily Reader for the proofreading, my marketing contact Jenna, head of marketing Claire, production executive Ben, and everyone else who has helped me in any way. You're all brilliant!

A special thank you to Rachel Lawston for another stunning cover. I feel really lucky to have such a talented artist and designer working on my Rowan Vale books, and I couldn't love the cover for this one more.

I must say thank you to Astrid Bennett Claas, who very kindly gave me some advice about German terms of endearment and proved, once and for all, that googling might be one solution, but if you can ask a real person who knows what they're talking about, it's always the wiser decision. Thanks so much, Astrid!

Thank you to my wonderful, supportive author friends, especially my brilliant bestie, Jessica Redland for just being Jessica, and the truly lovely Eliza J Scott for the long chats, and for giving us the excuse to eat cheese scones! To Cass Grafton, Val Wood, Lynnda Worsnopp, Alex Weston, Jeevani Charika, Jenni Fletcher, Linda Acaster, Sylvia Broady, Kate Kenzie, Karen Drury, Catherine Coles, and the other members of our local writers' group who make the monthly meetings so much fun, and so interesting and informative, and to the Write Romantics, my writing tribe, for being with me through thick and thin for more than a decade.

Finally, as always, huge hugs and a million thanks to my husband. I just couldn't do it without him, and I wouldn't want to.

Recently, he put his arm around me and hugged me while I cried over fictional characters.

What more could any woman ask?

ABOUT THE AUTHOR

Sharon Booth is the author of feel-good stories set in charming, quirky locations, and now writes cosy romances with a magical twist for Boldwood. She lives with her husband in East Yorkshire, England.

Sign up to Sharon Booth's mailing list for news, competitions and updates on future books.

Visit Sharon's website: www.sharonboothwriter.com

Follow Sharon on social media:

facebook.com/sharonboothwriter

instagram.com/sharonboothwriter

youtube.com/@sharonboothwriter

bookbub.com/authors/sharon-booth

pinterest.com/sharonboothwriter

ALSO BY SHARON BOOTH

Ghosts of Rowan Vale

Kindred Spirits at Harling Hall

Loving Spirits at the Vintage Teashop

Boldwood

Boldwood Books is an award-winning fiction publishing company seeking out the best stories from around the world.

Find out more at www.boldwoodbooks.com

Join our reader community for brilliant books, competitions and offers!

Follow us
@BoldwoodBooks
@TheBoldBookClub

Sign up to our weekly deals newsletter

https://bit.ly/BoldwoodBNewsletter

www.ingramcontent.com/pod-product-compliance
Lightning Source LLC
Chambersburg PA
CBHW010656100726
47900CB00010B/2687